Justicar Jhee
and the
Cursed Abbey

-The Justicar Jhee Mysteries Book 1-

by Trevol Swift

To my grandmother who taught my family to love reading.
To my Cousin Snoopy who helped make me the nerd I am today.
Rest in power.

Join the Swiftnesse Community

Join the Swiftnesse Readers' Club to get a free copy of
Justicar Jhee and the Spectral Armada, receive special offers,
and hear about future books!
http://swiftnesse.com/spectral/

1
———

THE YACHT

~

Accommodations

"Taking vows at Tranquility Bridge Abbey may be hazardous to one's health. At least if you are male."

A constituent had sent the message to Jhee's official justicar account via the anonymous crime reporting system. Jhee had queried the area's death records some time ago. While she awaited the results, her junior husband, Kanto, practiced his lute behind her in the stateroom. The Storm Shield's interference left her no other way to address the report mid-voyage.

Lightning drew Jhee's gaze away from the message on her digital conch and to the large, squared portholes of her stateroom. The ensuing crack drowned out Kanto's notes. Beyond the polymer glass of the portholes, stormy skies beckoned. The yacht Jhee and her household had chartered to the capital heaved along the storm-riled seas. Jhee forced her attention away from the storm and the message. Her focus should have been spending time with her second husband, who had just ended another tune.

"Thank you for your patience," Jhee said.

"If your mind was going to be elsewhere the whole time, then you aren't really here with me, are you?" Kanto said.

I

Jhee pushed her seat back from the desk to face the oh-so-very-young Kanto. "Please, play for me. You'll have my complete attention."

Kanto plucked a note on the strings and played beautifully as he always did. It lifted her spirits. Lighter and happier of mood now, she found her foot tapping along as his bright notes filled the stateroom. His expression slipped from smiling to pure absorption in the music. She imagined this is how she looked when she worked on legal decisions or arcana.

The luminosity of his golden eyes intensified, adding a vibrant glow to his deep-brown skin. Kanto's music resonated throughout the room. The extra slick look of his build and blue-black cast to his body hair and braids commanded the eye. No doubt the result of his meticulous grooming and exercise routine. If only their relationship were not so new and awkward. Inland, he would be the toast of the Imperial Isles. There he would find a more suitable household than hers—both him and Mirrei.

Despite her promise, Jhee's thoughts drifted to Mirrei. She played with the edge of a parchment. Both so young. Too young for her. She pinched the bridge of her nose.

Before Jhee could apologize to Kanto for getting distracted again, her conch chimed. A flashing notice announced the data analysis of the death records around the abbey had completed. The lure of the potential case and the arcane-infused storm vied with her youthful husband for her interest. The unsigned message had arrived just before Jhee and her marriage cohort's departure. She skimmed through several results that the analysis had flagged. Most seemed routine. She hovered her thumb over disable search.

The date on the latest deaths caught her eye. Three deaths in rapid succession, less than a long-moon or extended lunar month apart?

Kanto's lute playing intensified as he segued into another selection. Prior to her additional marriages and her reassignment to the capital, Jhee would not have hesitated to follow-up. She closed the search results.

Did Jhee dare work on another design or healing derivation? Soon, Kanto would conclude the musical piece he practiced. With the music's end, Jhee lost another means to politely deflect his romantic overtures. She tidied the digital, seaweed skin parchments then jotted down the last bit of a healing derivation she had previously begun.

In the capital, Jhee would have no time to run down cryptic complaints about crime from unknown folk in the Outer Reaches. Jurisprudence and teaching would replace investigation and legal proceedings. A wave pitched the yacht enough for the seaweed-and-polymer parchments on her desk to slide. She steadied herself then, tucked her hands into her robe sleeves to hide her white knuckles. Assuming the First Makers allowed them to arrive at the capital intact.

The music swelled as Kanto reached the tricky crescendo sequence. Jhee triple-checked her part designs for her Mechanist's ritual objects, then sneaked a peek at the music box schematics.

The yacht lurched. Jhee's parchments scattered along with the tallies from her fishing lanes and the massive ledger of legal findings. Kanto missed a few notes. She gathered her fallen work, then glanced at the clock. That would be all. She had already spent more time working than she said she would.

The musical composition ended. As per their unspoken understanding, Jhee set her work aside once he finished practicing. She stacked the derivations, music box plans, and part designs for her orrery together neatly with the tallies before using them to mark her place in the ledger.

He joined her at the desk and handed her a parchment. "Missed one."

Jhee snatched up the sheet, worried it might be the music box schematics. She wanted that to be a surprise. It turned out to be healing sequences. The handwriting did not match hers, yet the work was excellent. The penmanship on the derivations showed a notable decline the further down the page she read. It brought to mind heavy thoughts of Mirrei resting in the next stateroom under Shep's care. Kanto's time, she admonished. She hastily tucked the sheet into the ledger with the others.

"Arcana?" Kanto asked. "Don't worry. I will shield my poor delicate male eyes."

"Not for these. Healing sequences."

The golden light of his eyes dimmed. He laid his hand with its impeccably manicured and lacquered nail claws on Jhee's shoulder. "How far along are you? Did you need a few more minutes?"

"I think I have some promising avenues. I need to take some time to think about them, though."

"Talk me through them?"

"Which would no doubt bore you to brackishness. This is your time, of which I have already stolen too much for others."

"*Our* time."

Her conch chirped. Jhee winced. Kanto sighed and motioned for her to address it. She made an apologetic gesture to him and picked her conch up. A notice indicated her last attempt to upload to the judicial archives had failed. Miserable weather and interference from the storm zone had made her transfers slow when they worked at all. She checked her conch's holding capacity. It was running low. She restarted the transfer. She brandished and silenced the conch for him to see, then set it aside. He inclined his head in approval.

Kanto laid his lute across his knees. "We should retire."

Jhee's stomach sank at the prospect. She became all too aware of the pitching and yawing of the yacht. "No. Your playing was helping."

"I think that's enough for now."

"If that is your wish, this is your night."

"*Our* night."

As Kanto packed up his lute, Jhee's gaze fell upon the robe he had laid out on the bed when he arrived. He rushed over with a smile. He held it up proudly for her to see.

"Try it on. Mirrei and I finished the last bit of tailoring. I want to ensure the extra pockets didn't ruin the lines."

Jhee undid her sash.

"Let me," he said in a silky voice. He stepped closer and switched the robes Jhee wore. She and Kanto caught each other's gaze. "Perfect fit."

His eyes sparkled and took on a deep golden hue. A smoldering shade she hoped hers matched. They touched their foreheads together. A tingle corruscated through her as he gently brushed his *esca*, the illuminated golden star in the center of his forehead, against hers. He caressed the small of her back. A moan escaped her. He bent in, and she pulled his mouth against hers.

A knock sounded at the stateroom door. Kanto's posture sagged. His eyes pleaded with her, "No."

Jhee, however, refastened her sash with the new robes. Such a smooth, handsome face. Many older women in her position took husbands much more disparate in age. She wanted to make him as happy as he tried to make her. That would be enough to make this arrangement work until the capital. She stepped away from him and affected her most official stance.

"Enter."

~

The Dispute

The first mate stepped in and doffed her cap to Jhee.

"Sorry to disturb, Justicar. We've had a dispute arise amongst the crew."

"Details." Jhee snatched her conch from the desk. The transfer to the archives had failed again. She found and deleted some non-critical files from the spare and sparse, then set it up to record the trial. She still got a critical space warning.

Kanto plopped down on the bed and folded his arms. "More work. Lovely."

She faced him. "I ask your indulgence, husband."

"Go."

"I'll hear their case here. First mate?"

"Yes, Justicar?"

"Have the disputants bring any evidence they wish to present here in fifteen minutes, and I will do my best to render them justice in the Grand Empress and Emperor's name."

The first mate excused herself.

"I'll go next door with Mirrei and Shep."

"Yet, I require your assistance as witness and scribe."

His ears perked up. "You want my help with a case?"

"Unless you don't feel you are up to the task?"

"No, no. What do I need to do?"

The spotty connection did not allow them to do a proper set up of the judicial code base on Kanto's conch. Instead, they painstakingly copied over and adjusted access rights from Jhee's. By the time the follow-up knock came, they had cobbled something together that would work.

"Now, fetch me my stones and tabard from that case over there."

The first mate brought in two crew women. They doffed their caps and seated themselves respectably like two fine and stalwart women. Their extended time above decks had given them denser body hair and flattened noses, which had shifted their appearance towards otters. The rain had caused everyone to take on sleeker aspects gradually enough one might forget. They looked sheepishly at Jhee but stared daggers at each other.

"Now, state your names and what seems to be the nature of your dispute."

Both talked over each other.

"Enough. One at a time. You"—Jhee gestured at one—"go first."

Apparently, the plaintiff had purchased an ice chest full of oysters, clams, and cockles from the defendant. The plaintiff claimed the delivery was light and wanted a refund. Jhee took possession of the evidence they brought with them, namely the chest of sea meat and the payment. She pulled a luggage scale from her arcana toolbox. The defendant turned her cap round via the brim, and the plaintiff appeared smug while Jhee weighed the chest and its contents. Kanto tapped his sketch pencil against the bag of shell coins in dispute. The plaintiff shifted her weight back and forth, coughed, straightened the objects on the table.

Not content to stop there, Jhee called for a mug and a bowl. She doled out portions until she emptied the ice chest. As she did so, the defendant wrung her hat in her hands.

The defendant let out a breath and smiled. "You see, just as I said. One full container of sea meat. She just wants to get out of paying."

"I counted how many mug fulls. I know how many eight quarts of sea meat is and that won't enough," the plaintiff said.

Jhee picked up the empty chest. Too heavy. She placed her hand in the carton and noticed it ended two finger joints higher than the table. More than Jhee could account for with the thickness of the insulation. After motioning for Kanto to stop tapping, she shook the chest. A rattle came from the presumably empty container, and the heft shifted from side to side.

"But wait, what's this?"

Jhee popped open a false bottom containing rocks and sand. The defendant went bug-eyed.

"I knew it! You're a cheat."

The crew members had a brief scuffle over the sack of shell currency.

"Enough," Jhee said, using her siren module to enhance the command.

They stopped fighting immediately. Jhee seized the currency purse and dropped it on the table. She paused. Kanto also perked up. He had heard it too. Too flat.

Jhee dropped the purse on the table again. She hefted the bag a few times. A quick appraisal with cypher-enhanced senses proved some shells gilded fakes. Jhee curtailed a second altercation.

"I'm ready to render my judgment. Are you ready to accept it?"

"Yes, Justicar," they both said.

"I find, in this matter of the first crew woman against the second crew woman, against the defendant. I sentence you to issue a partial refund equivalent to one-quarter the agreed payment. In the countersuit, I further find that the plaintiff was also in breach, and she is to return approximately one-quarter of the sea meat, the amount she shorted her payment. Given that these appear to be what you have already done, I judge the matter settled. Should either of you wish an appeal and review of this finding, you can file with the royal archives for one at your expense."

The disputants left.

A Lesson

Kanto took the kettle and poured them each a cup of tea.

"A chance to see you work up close. You sounded so official and commanding." Kanto handed her pencil sketches along with his notes. "I hope you don't mind. The conch was doing most of the work, so I made these."

"Multi-talented. You shall overwhelm them at the capital."

"Your praise honors me. I enjoyed watching you work, *denbe*."

"I was afraid you'd found it terribly boring."

"Not at all. It gives me insight into how your mind works."

Jhee played with the teacup. "I enjoy the citrus flavor of this tea we're drinking. Tell me about this blend."

"Orange blossom and passionflower from off the Ylush Archipelago's southernmost tip. In the latest dispatches from the capital, all the influencers are drinking it. It's renowned for its properties as an aphrodisiac and fertility aid."

Jhee swallowed the tea hard. She reminded herself she agreed to this marriage and its terms. The dispute, while a fortuitous diversion, had also diffused their romantic momentum. Shep's advice fluttered through her mind.

"He doesn't know you. Don't expect him to yet. If anything he does pleases you, from romance to gifts, don't make him guess."

"I never thanked you for my lovely robe. Thank you."

"I'm glad it pleased you."

"It's subtle how you worked in the house colors via the coral and turtle shell motifs."

"Precisely. I'm glad you noticed."

"I may not always behave like it, but I notice."

"Not as impressive as cyphering equations, but to each their talents." Jhee fiddled with her saucer. Kanto took another sip of his tea. "Did you mean what you said at dinner about getting me arcana training?"

"With the bans lifted, Tihalmec Imperial Academy at the capital has been accepting and teaching male students, even in the cyphering program. I think you would take to it quite well."

"Teach me yourself like you do with Mirrei. Or you could align me so I could be a subject like Shep."

Jhee winced at that characterization of Shep. She steered the conversation away from crosstalk. "I might teach you element drawing. For cyphering, though, the latest research shows the process is different enough for males to warrant special instruction."

"How?"

"Well, I'm glad you asked that question." Jhee gushed about data and articles she had read. Kanto smiled and nodded. She lapsed into a professorial tone. She went silent once his brow had developed a permanent furrow. "Listen to me drone on. You asked for a lesson, not a lecture."

"If anyone can figure it out, you can. It's a puzzle then. A puzzle I could help you unravel. We can start now."

"I'll get you training at the capital."

"Isn't tonight the night you humor my whims?"

Jhee fidgeted. "I want to give you the best. I don't want to limit your potential."

"You will make an excellent instructor, both with me and in your new position. Do you think you'll miss being a Justicar?"

"I'll still be a Justicar, an academic one."

"Teach me then. It will be great practice for both of us."

"Meditation first. Though the situation may make it difficult. Like this." She shook out her arms and planted her feet wide on the deck. The yacht rose and fell again with the rough seas. She curled her toenail claws into the deck boards. She pressed the bridge of her nose. "Clear and center," she said.

Once Kanto matched her stance, she talked him through a visualization of the celestial clockworks of the universe. With it fixed in their mind's eye, they moved hands and body to mimic its celestial motions. Rains driven by the perpetual storm system lashed against the glass in gusts too irregular to match its timing.

The giant mass of supernatural power imbued in the storm outside pressed against her inner essence. She braced herself and deep-breathed.

"The storm's not outside," he said. "It's within."

"Exercise care. Don't let it draw you in. Use the porthole as a buffer. In its current state, it's a muddle where the arcane finds little purchase. Too many have cut, heated, bent, and performed any other innumerable manufacturing processes to shape it into what it is now. Those same traces should buffer us."

The yacht sailed on through the rolling seas. In calmer times, she might have found it anchoring. Now, her stomach roiled. She indicated they kneel. She stilled herself until her stomach settled.

"What next?"

"Unfortunately, it gets much more boring from here. Formulations and schematics."

She awakened her conch to find more notifications. She hesitated on the death irregularities again.

"What was it?"

"Mm?"

"The message on your conch that troubled you."

"Some curious deaths at a cloister of celibates."

"A cloister of celibates. No doubt they killed themselves from being denied one of the Makers' greatest gifts?"

She took the humor as well-meaning, talismanic, and chose not to admonish him for it. "No doubt. This must be so distressing for you. Tell me about the latest fashion trends from the capital."

He folded his hands and looked at her sideways. "Do you really want to know about fashion? I thought we would be poring over charts."

"Tonight is about doing what you enjoy."

"Tonight is about doing what we both enjoy, denbe. It should not be one-sided."

"We do what I want on most other nights. I wish to be more considerate and take an interest in your interests, especially with how neglectful and rude I've been this evening."

"We're still finding common ground. It won't always go smoothly. What bothers me most is how you don't relax with me and let all your other worries go, if only for a few moments."

She touched his hand and gave him an exaggerated once over with her gaze. He pecked her on the nose. Then another tentative one. He gained confidence for a firmer kiss. She squeezed his hand for encouragement. He ended the kiss with a wide grin.

Thunder crashed overhead. Jhee stepped back. "Not exactly the pleasure cruise I promised you. I'm sorry we've had to travel so near the storm zone. The major routes are congested and in disarray. Hopefully, the course the captain has plotted near the edge of the buffer zone will save us time. Don't worry. We'll rejoin high society for festival season."

"I'm not worried. If you say we will be there in time, we will." Kanto indicated Jhee sit. Once she had, he massaged her shoulders. "I want us to attend all the shows when we reach the capital. You can show me off to all the blue-skinned elites."

"We will see."

Few pursuits disinterested her more. Perhaps Kanto's age did not concern her so much, but that they were so ill-matched.

"Those death notices aren't the only matters which have you preoccupied."

"The pirate attacks in the outlands are getting more frequent."

"The location of some of your most lucrative seabeds. Your investments in sustainable aquaculture almost went under because of the shield. Yours was among the few farms to survive."

"Um," Jhee acknowledged, surprised he knew that much about her investments. "I'm hiring extra security, displaced locals. Hopefully, it will be enough to keep them from turning pirate."

"Be mindful of them aiding the pirates from the inside."

She quirked her mouth at him. "What a thoughtful observation."

"I'll try not to feel insulted."

"You gave me a gift. It's only fair I give you one."

Jhee rose and rummaged through the bottom drawer of the dresser. First, she pulled out an unadorned, cracked music box wrapped in a cloth bundle. She rethought and chose the top drawer. She set a jeweled candy dish wrought of smoky polymer glass on the tea table. The amethyst and citrine stones matched the tones of Kanto's robes.

"In my preferred color palette, no less. I think my excellent fashion sense is rubbing off on you." He lifted the lid. "Wait! Are those?"

"Lace root melon taffies."

"My favorites. How did you know?"

"It's what I do. I learn things."

"Grandmamere gave me these when I told her something new about her guests. Sometimes I even received little cherry, citrus cakes."

"Lady Kaydence. This weather has its upsides."

"That she can't contact you regularly."

They grinned. Kanto bristled up his body hair and snuggled against her. It made a noticeable difference with his wiry, slim frame. Jhee enjoyed a nice and full build to wrap her arms around. Her young, virile husband was impressionable and eager to please. Had Jhee done him a disservice by bedding him when she intended not to make him a permanent part of her household? As soon as they reached the capital, if not before, she meant to seek new arrangements for Kanto and Mirrei. Then it would be her and Shep again.

Jhee let her fingers play in his fluffed body hair. "You're quite the cuddler and the least fitful sleeper."

Kanto touched the small of her back like he had earlier. She molded against him. Her mouth set in a thin line when it sunk in the only way he could have known where to touch her to get that response.

Shep. The questions about arcane techniques and historical trivia she knew he cared nothing for. She saw, now, the orchestrated appeals to her vanity. Shep must have coached him. With their night underway and she had already flouted its rules several times, she dared not call Kanto on it.

He cast his gaze down, then looked back up at her. "Don't be mad. Mirrei and I must take our clues from *denme*, senior spouse, on how best to serve our denbe."

"Serve not service."

Kanto had planned on not being called to account. While the premeditation irked Jhee, she had been in the wrong. She mustered the graciousness not to withdraw from him. He continued to stroke the small of her back, and she stroked his ears. The tension and the awkwardness seeped away. All forgiven.

Their travel yacht lurched to a sudden stop. They tumbled into a heap.

2

ARRIVAL

~

Tiles and Tunes

In the stateroom next door to Jhee's, Shep and Mirrei played tiles. Shep fingered his eye scar while he planned how to defend his matriarch tile against Mirrei's onslaught. He had considered getting the facial scar removed, but he wanted the reminder.

The yacht lurched. The tiles scattered in all directions. Shep checked Mirrei, who nodded to show she was fine. He paused to listen.

Yelling came down from above deck. Crew members barreled by their door. Something banged against the door. Mirrei jumped. The doorknob rattled, then turned. Shep flung it open, ready. Jhee and Kanto stood there.

"You can't seriously be going out there?" Kanto was saying.

"They may need an artificer," Jhee answered. "Stay with Shep and Mirrei until I return."

Shep harried them in from the passageway. "Wife?"

"Everyone here fine?" Jhee asked.

Shep gave a quick nod.

"How is Mirrei doing?"

"About the same. What's happened?"

Bax, Jhee's head servant, poked his head in a moment later. "Sorry to disturb you, Justicar."

Bax led Dari, their family's shark dog, on a leash. The hound perked her ears up and whined at the sight of Shep. He and Jhee petted her.

"There, there, old girl. Bax, assessment?" Jhee asked. Bax and Dari were as much a part of their family as anyone in the stateroom.

"Forgiveness, Justicar, the wild wave drove the ship into a reef. The crew's working to free us."

Jhee took the leash. "See what you can do to help. I'll be up there soon."

Bax's wizened face creased with concern. "Aye."

Jhee led Dari into their stateroom. Kanto took the hound from her. "At least change your robes."

Jhee gathered a warm outer robe and deck shoes from her stateroom before she returned to the passageway.

Shep met her, frowning. "*Denye* is right. The world can turn without you for one crisis."

Jhee lowered her voice, "It is nothing to trouble yourself about, dear one. Stay here. I'll assess the situation. Keep everyone reassured."

"As you wish, dear wife."

"Wait, your robes," Kanto said as Jhee headed above deck.

Shep regarded his two *dendes*, junior spouses, and affected a smile. He retrieved the tiles and set up the board again.

"Who wants to play?" Shep asked. Neither responded. He tried again, addressing them by their gaming names to keep the mood light. "Tunes? Sprite?"

"Pass," Kanto said and went to the porthole to sulk. Shep and Mirrei resumed their places at the tile board.

"Will denbe be fine?" Mirrei asked.

"She always returns safe and sound." Shep mixed the tiles and made the first play. "Try that, Sprite."

"You're lucky our last game got interrupted, Pup." Mirrei smiled and countered. Her laughter was interspersed with coughing fits. Kanto gave her his usual sidelong glance then took up his lute. "Could it be pirates?"

Kanto made a musical flourish and switched to a more somber selection. "My thoughts exactly."

Mirrei's eyes went wide, and she leaned forward. Kanto now played a harrowing tune with a sense of urgency.

Shep hoped Kanto caught the rebuke in his expression. Pirates would have found the primary routes as inconvenient as they. They may have made the same calculation their captain did to brave the storm zone instead. "Doubtful. They're finding it far more lucrative to loot sunken homes."

The last thing Shep needed was Kanto's wild stories and drama frightening Mirrei. Although, the youthful woman appeared more intrigued than scared.

"'Don't be another crisis she has to manage,'" Kanto said. He bowed his head and played something light. "We shall take our cues from you on how to respond."

"While you're watching out for us, who's watching out for her?" Mirrei asked.

A question Shep had grown tired of asking. Hopefully, increased familial duties might succeed where he had failed.

◠〜

The Reef

On deck, rain pelted Jhee's face, and the wind howled as if the Wave Witch herself hailed them. Her sleeves snapped in the maelstrom like pennants. What did it say about her she preferred a deadly storm to more time alone in her stateroom with Kanto?

Sailors equipped with long, hooked poles crowded the left side of the deck. The entire crew, like those earlier, also resembled otters more than when their journey had started.

"Careful, ladies. Steady. This is a protected reef," the captain yelled.

Jhee ran to the side. She breathed deep then glanced over. Water, deep blue-black, darker even than the high imperials' skin, gave away nothing. Her throat tightened. She braced, like always expecting to see something slither beneath the surface or catch glimpse of an enormous, scaly, glowing eye. When she saw nothing of the sort, she exhaled. Followed up as always by cursing herself for foolish fancies. She faced away from the sea to address the crew. "Spotlight."

To draw the sea. Almost as daunting a prospect as testing the storm. Jhee rolled up her sleeves and cleared her mind. She engaged the gears of transmutation within herself. The liquid essence of the waves and the fiery source of the spotlight's incandescence became clockworks in her mind. Within her, the Divine Mechanism used her as a conduit to bridge the two. Her esca tingled. The tingling grew as did the spotlight's glow. The deepest blue water lightened as if the water itself illuminated. Not bad for a Water tertiary. She doubted a Water dominant drawer could have done better.

The famed and magnificent sapphire and ruby coral of Bibsbebe's Reef had hooked itself to one railing on the yacht. What an inauspicious omen. She would not conclude their journey and arrive for her new duties at the capital as one who had destroyed the thousand-year-old reef.

Jhee paused. Unless the crew were shipwrights, they should not draw the yacht. It had to be the reef. The contradiction coral was, both flesh and bone. Earth drawer work: the element she had the least expertise with. She looked at the all-female crew. That meant they were less likely to expert Earth drawers.

"Do you have Earth drawers?" Jhee yelled.

A sailor hesitated a moment then at a signal from the captain joined Jhee. "I can do both aspects but as subsidiaries."

"Good enough."

Jhee communicated with hand gestures how she wanted the sailor to manipulate the coral. She steeled herself to look over the side again. She reached out through the universal mechanisms to the water, winding and guiding it away from the reefs so as not to dampen the sailor's watch work.

"You." The captain gestured to another sailor. "Put your hook there. If we get under it, we might dislodge from the reef without damaging it."

The captain looked over and nodded. She waved for the sailors to do as Jhee suggested.

The sailors wedged their billhooks in. With a mighty crack, the yacht shuddered and drifted away from the reef. Sapphire and ruby-colored fragments floated away and sank beneath sight. Nowhere near as disastrous as it could have been. The tingling in her esca ceased as she stopped her concentration on her spell sequence and water drawing. She leaned heavily against the yacht's side, careful not to look back at the water. The winds died down, and the seas calmed, but the rain continued strong as ever. The Storm Child had not done having its fun with them.

Bax came over.

"Assessment," she said.

"We've cleared the reef, Justicar. It damaged the ship. We're taking on water. We must put aground to affect repairs."

"Makers' whim, if it's not one problem, it's another with this journey."

"Aye, Justicar. The pumps should keep us afloat until the squall passes."

"Where precisely are we?"

"Northern edge of District Sixteen."

Jhee stroked her nose. "What's that glow over there in the distance? There's an abbey around here, isn't there? Could that be it?"

"Aye, the storm light from the Drakists on Torilsisle. They have a bay and a dry dock large enough for a yacht such as this."

The death record irregularity searches. "Ask the captain to contact them. Have the monks and nuns dispatch tow skiffs once it's safe. Use my official title if necessary."

"At once, Justicar. Now, please, get below."

The lightning lured her attention again. The storm, the beautiful Storm Shield, had its own slight glow. Thermals and winds and lightning made to behave as mortals willed. Truly, it was the marvel of all marvels. Those who created the storm system used the same methods as she did in her daily works. The scale and sheer number of artificers and elementalists made for a fascinating complexity. One an artificer could be forgiven for wanting to test herself against.

When might it be clear enough for a rescue? The Storm Child had cost her family much in the past. Not today. She thrust her divine-granted will beyond the yacht into the forces of the storm.

The storm yanked at her. Despite her earlier warning to Kanto, she had no buffer to dull the onslaught. She lowered herself into her stance and seized a piece of the storm. She fought to impose an order on it, to reveal its workings like any other device. Residuals of the hundred and thousands of elementalists who had shaped the perpetual storm system bombarded her. Snatches of sound and fury shattered the visualization of the clockworks. She released the storm and let it keep its secrets for now.

Her sleeves no longer whipped back and forth with as much ferocity as before. She heard Bax's voice much clearer now.

"You've done enough, Justicar. Let's get you back inside, or Mr. Shep will have my pouch."

Bax saw her safely below decks. Jhee blanked her expression and counted in her head, both to shed the features she gained via weather adaptation and to present a composed demeanor. She knocked on her cohort's stateroom door, and Shep swept her inside. Mirrei and Kanto sat beside the porthole. She embroidered while he brushed her hair and hummed.

Jhee shook herself off. Shep took a towel and brusquely wiped the moisture from the hair she had developed as her body adapted to the rain. "Let's get you out of these wet things."

"You forgot to change your robes," Kanto said.

She glanced at the pile of clothing, and the new robe was mixed amongst her wet things. Kanto made an exasperated sound. She rubbed the bridge of her nose. Her headache had reasserted itself now the excitement had passed. A sneeze rocked her balance and made her sinuses feel as if they would explode. "I think I may have caught cold."

"Serves you right."

She placed her hands upon his shoulders. Steady voice. Without panic. Without worry. His shoulders relaxed under her grasp. "I know, I know."

Mirrei stifled a cough. Jhee turned her attention to her. Kanto gave up his seat for Jhee.

"Have you no admonishment for me, *dende*?" Jhee asked.

Mirrei hid a weak smile behind her hand. "None that has not already been given, denbe."

"You'll be happy to know we'll be leaving these dreadful waves and cramped cabins for a brief stay on land."

"Where?"

"An abbey nearby."

Kanto narrowed his eyes. "One with a cloister of celibates?"

"Um, yes."

"For how long?"

"Not long. There are some minor repairs we need to do."

"Us too." Kanto held up her robe and shook his head. Jhee jerked her head at Mirrei. He took a position next to Mirrei and squeezed her shoulder. "We'll be in time for festival season. Once we reach the capital, we'll see the Grand Court in all its finery. Catch the biggest shows. Shop in all the finest shops. Won't that be fun? We might even meet the Grand Regents themselves or glimpse the Wave Wanderers. Jhee promised."

Mirrei nodded then was overtaken by a coughing fit. Shep laid a towel on Jhee's shoulders. Everyone exchanged worried glances over Mirrei's head.

～

The Landing

Four deaths not three in half as many moons, Jhee thought.

The Storm Child had returned to hir mischief though with not as much vigor by the time their yacht came within sight of the abbey at Tranquility Bridge. The imposing structure loomed on a large outcropping of rock set apart from the nearby isle. Its storm light swept around in a circle from the highest shell spire with the elongated-conic shape. Three additional spires, each shaped like a different gastropod shell, spiraled up into the sky silhouetted against the ever-present glow of the Storm Shield.

The yacht's crew proved to expert water drawers and had not needed Jhee's arcane skills. Jhee had not spent the time idle as their damaged craft limped towards the aforementioned abbey. With their visit to the abbey inevitable, she had instead trained her faculties on the matter of the abbey's high death toll. A closer inspection of its death notices had revealed the previous abbess had also died unexpectedly.

A cement slab big enough to host a ferryboat projected from the mountainside surrounded by smaller, natural rocks. The skiffs towed the yacht into position where lay brothers and sisters caught their mooring ropes then looped them around mooring posts. A few smaller boats for emergencies and supply runs bobbed upon the waves. Those working the lines paid no attention to crashing waves or sea spray. Within the sleeves of her robes, Jhee dug her nails into her palms every time a storm-driven surge struck the slab or strained the ropes. Her mind filled with the image of them overwhelmed and swept away. What would be worse? Screams or silence.

The dock workers' hails brought Jhee back to the present. Mirrei and Kanto huddled against Jhee as they approached the slab. Shep's reassuring hand on her shoulder blade gave her the support she needed.

Stalwart, Jhee forced her attention to the abbey itself. A different question needed answering. The incongruity of the abbey's deaths dragged Jhee's thoughts further away from images she'd rather forget. Four deaths at the abbey in such a brief span would have been more understandable if they all had happened at once or under similar circumstances.

Antenna arrays mounted to the central spire wobbled in the high winds. Lightning flashed off the sun arrays on its roofs and those in the fields beside it. The brightness gave glimpses of the newly built, glass-domed hothouse modules. Full-sized, life-like figures made of brilliant coral lined the eaves and facade. Preservatives and arcane protections stopped the statues and famed, blood-ruby red walls and emerald green roof from bleaching over the years in the onslaught of sun and rain. Constructions hewed from similar coral to that which had scuttled their yacht. She could not help but think the First Makers wanted her here.

"What a ghastly place," Mirrei said.

"Certainly not what I'd call tranquil. Precisely the sort of austere place I'd expect of ascetics," Kanto said.

Jhee swallowed hard, her stomach churning, as they sailed past the breakers. "This place boasts empire-renowned mineral springs. Very good for the health."

"Is it truly made of coral, denbe?"

"No doubt some form of mineral encrustation subject to rapid fossilization, thus keeping its color. It becomes its own natural coral rag or coral concrete."

Shep moved his hands to Jhee's shoulders. "I think I rather preferred the yacht."

Jhee raised an eyebrow. Had she been alone, she might have kissed the solid ground once they disembarked.

A stern-faced woman about Jhee's age met them at the dock entrance. They exchanged formal gestures of greeting. "Greetings, my Lady Justicar. Welcome to Tranquility Bridge's Redoubt of the Drakists. I am the prioress. I see to the grounds and provisions. Please, pardon our delayed response. We had a tremor here. The second in as many long-months."

Servants, laypeople, and a spattering of shabbier laborers bustled by them with produce and fresh-caught sea meat.

Jhee used her siren module to make herself heard over the din, "Thank you. I must admit to wanting to visit for some time. I corresponded with your abbess, Saheli, about acquiring some of your famous nectar wine. Is she around so I might pay my respects?"

"Saheli passed into the Makers' sphere some months ago."

While Jhee's query had not flagged Abbess Saheli's death, the minimal details and maximal allegory had aroused her curiosity nonetheless. "My deepest regrets. Who may I ask is in charge now?"

"Pyrmo is our current abbess."

"You seem beset by tragedies lately," Jhee intimated, offering her a chance to elaborate.

The prioress frowned at all the baggage Jhee's servants unloaded. "You took all this on a pleasure cruise and in a storm no less."

"I've been reassigned to the capital. I thought we might make an excursion of it. A tremor explains the wild wave that disabled our ship and the collapse I heard about here. The Shell Drake and the Storm Child must be restless."

The prioress grunted. Lay brothers and sisters poured out the gate on the aperture that opened out from the bottom of the crag. They helped Jhee's servants unload their belongings, including a litter for her marriage cohort. Fishing vessels and fisherfolk continued about their daily business with no great urgency. Few spared their entourage a glance. Not all seemed as practiced at their work. Even more lay brothers and sisters transported bundles of kelp and lettuces, sacks of grain, and crates of shore meat-producing animals such as chickens and pigs.

The milled symbol above the gate, a sword piercing a bridge, creaked and groaned in the powerful winds. While Jhee waited until everyone in her charge passed beneath it to safety, she studied the significant number of idle people with lean, hungry looks who watched their entourage pass. The gate swung closed behind her with a definitive rattle, sealing them inside. Or the world outside.

What circumstance caused an abbey named Tranquility Bridge to have a sword as its symbol? The spotty connection only allowed her to do minimal background research beyond what she already knew about the place. When her interest in healing picked up because of Mirrei's condition, she learned of their honey nectar wine. She had always meant to attend their seminars or visit their reliquary, yet she never found the time. Since it was in her district, she always delayed it until later. Later had arrived. The First Makers' Design be done.

"If I may, I'd like to pay my respects to your current abbess."

"This way."

The prioress led her to stone steps while the litter with her cohort disappeared through a passage under it. Jhee motioned for Bax to shadow her and the prioress. The moment she saw the precipitous height of the abbey, she had feared for Mirrei. She insisted all three use the litter because she did not want to single her out. "Is it your order's normal custom to see husbands and wives parted during their stay?"

"This route is far too precarious for a litter. You'll be reunited with them in the dormitory level after your audience with the abbess. She can explain to you more fully the rules by which we ask guests to abide."

The prioress led the way up an interminable number of stairs with a bioluminescent glowtorch. How Jhee wished she had joined her cohort in the litter. She wheezed. "Such a wealth of stairs. They may do me in before that."

"Aside from the mechanical lifts and cranes for moving cargo, we don't use most modern conveniences. Anything other would be a drain on our limited resources. Most non-essential devices have been shut down to conserve power until the storm passes."

"I saw your sun arrays."

"They are our sole means of power."

"I noticed you also possess an antenna array. I can't seem to access anything with my conch beyond the local area. Might I be able to use your communications to contact the Central Authority to inform them of my delayed arrival and the damaged reef?"

"Reception follows the weather's whims. We almost missed your captain's distress call while dealing with the quake aftermath. The broadcast transmitter's power requirements, though, are prohibitive with the overcast skies."

"The limited power and communication must make it difficult to seek aid in a crisis."

"We are a self-sufficient order. The transmitter's usage is reserved for the direst of emergencies."

"Fortunate, you've had none of those lately."

Jhee waited for the prioress to take the opening she offered.

The prioress frowned. "Indeed. You may, however, petition the abbess to use the transmitter."

Jhee sighed. "Please, lead the way."

3

ECHOES

～

Reception with the Abbess

The prioress knocked upon the door to the abbess's quarters. Jhee took a moment to compose herself and catch her breath while Bax hung back. The abbess welcomed Jhee by touching their *escae* as if they were old friends. She gave off an odor of smudging sticks and sacral wine. If she were not so winded, Jhee might have been scandalized by such familiarity.

"I am Pyrmo, the Mother of Rites for Tranquility Bridge's."

"Thank you for your hospitality, Abbess."

Jhee noted the dual nature of the chambers. A cat dish despite vanishing evidence of a cat. The sounding bowl, striker, and meditation rugs she expected of such a pious individual. A low altar for burning incenses. In fact, the room emanated smudge as heavily as the occupant. A hutch desk and simple glow lamp full of parchments. Half-painted easels which had not seen use in months. Shelves of seeds and elixirs gathering dust. It bore the earmarks of the previous owner as much as the current. Pyrmo must not have felt comfortable in her position yet.

"You are most welcome, my Lady Justicar. Please, call me Pyrmo."

"Please, I prefer simply Justicar."

Jhee brushed at the cat hairs on her robes and sniffed a few times. She already felt her eyes watering and nose itching. Did she put her allergy medication in the items they brought from the yacht?

"Is something wrong, Justicar?"

"I wondered if there was a cat about? Mild allergy."

"Cat? Ah, not anymore. Saheli's cat meant very much to her. She used to feed it from her plate and let it drink from her bowl. She painted it and rendered it in many sculptures and reliefs. It died shortly after her. They say it refused to eat out of grief. She was a true artist with a heart as much of an aesthete as an ascetic."

"Very interesting. Died of grief, did you say?"

"Ah, very tragic as many of us loved that cat almost as much as we loved Saheli. Losing them both so closely thoroughly demoralized us. We have endeavored to carry on, though. It pained me to have taken on the position of abbess as she was so respected, and I had enormous shoes to fill."

"I'm sure the Chief Abbess would not have assigned you if she didn't think you were ready."

Pyrmo adjusted her sash of office. "My assignment was a bit of a shock, but I did my best to make the most of it. Ah, you know you are not our only Imperial official and noble hosted here. The imperial vizier, Bathsheba of Toho and Wilobeia, retired to our abbey a few years ago."

"Bathsheba of Toho. Oh, yes." Pyrmo clearly expected Jhee to know who that was. Jhee touched her chin to give herself a moment to wrack her brain. When she came up empty, she improvised, "She was the…"

"The respected sage and former Imperial music tutor."

"Yes, yes. I know someone who may be so delighted to hear that. I must admit having wanted to visit here for some time. Between your seminars and empire-renowned reliquary and wines."

"The vizier works closely with our Mistress of Relics."

"Splendid. I may have corresponded with them regarding access to your archives. I was most saddened to hear of the passing of Saheli, not the only tragedy you have had of late."

Pyrmo frowned and tucked her hands inside her robes. "Yes, it has been unfortunate times. However, today you have arrived on an auspicious day. It's the hundredth anniversary of our residence here long after its sack by barbarian hordes. The abbey is celebrating our founding with a feast."

"The feast explains the commotion I've seen. I'd hate to have thought you went through such trouble for me."

"It's always our honor to welcome a noble servant of the Empire. Would that the weather was better."

"Once the storm zone stabilizes, many issues are liable to address themselves. They say peace will return to the Blessed Isles once more. We will have nothing to fear from the barbarians."

"As the Makers will, so shall it be."

"I've heard you've had communications problems due to the storms."

Pyrmo adjusted her sash of office again. "Low power communications are effectively nullified by the weather."

"That must explain why our initial hails were ignored."

"Ignored? The Justicar's pardon for the discourtesy. Must have been one of our more inexperienced operators. The rest of us were dealing with the aftermath of the second tremor."

"I hoped to use your transmitter to establish communication with the Central Authority. The prioress told me it requires a lot of power."

"Power? Just so. Under the current conditions, we minimize its use, and even then, not until the twin suns are at their maximum height in the skies. Unless you have a pressing need, your best chance of getting a message out is to wait for a storm break."

Jhee thought of her conch full of case files. They kept this long. They could keep longer. Despite her reasoning to the prioress, she had no urgency in telling Central Authority about the damage her vessel did to an imperial treasure. "No pressing need as of yet. Mostly routine work."

"The tremors knocked a few of our systems off-line and misaligned some solar sheets. I'll inquire with the power management and facilities teams to see where we are with power storage and repairs. Perhaps we have enough to power it for a few minutes at full-sun."

"Thank you, Abbess."

"My honor, Justicar."

"As our most gracious host, please pardon my ignorance of what I and my household must do to be most gracious guests."

"We are a chaste order and ask guests to refrain from fraternization with the Prospectives and the Professed. We reserve land meat for the sick or others with heavy protein requirements."

"Shore meat shall suffice. My household avoids raw land meat. Trace amounts are fine if cooked."

"Philosophical or health-related?"

"Both. No need to enact protocols, though."

"Our kitchen complies with Pascoe protocols and Blue Waters guidelines already. We prohibit a few areas to males, namely the mineral springs nearest the temple sanctuary and sections of the archives."

"No doubt to protect them from arcane knowledge."

"We are not only a chaste order. Many of us eschew all arcana."

Did Jhee detect a sneer? A religious order founded by former combatants like Drakist Adepts to her mind would have been more accepting of cyphering or at least the healing arts. "Your restrictions on arcana surprise me. I thought the magnificent preservation of your coral edifice must result from arcane arts. How do you maintain its brilliant appearance without it?"

"A secret, lost art of those who originally built the abbey. We bring in workers now and then to maintain it. More recently, the refugees have been doing the work in exchange for food."

"I did notice many idle people on your docks."

Pyrmo frowned. "Refugees."

"A question about the stricture against the use of arcana here at Tranquility Bridge's, if I may? I have been instructing my youngest consort in its use. As I am unsure of how long we will be here, I wanted to know if there were provisions I could make to continue her instruction."

The abbess looked thoughtful. "There are several fields on the bluff."

"My consort's health is not the best. An arduous trek to the bluffs may be too much. I also worry about such an open location."

"Ah, yes, I see your point and worry about the same within the walls. It is a vow. Many, especially the veterans, employed it in our secular life. We have dedicated ourselves to a life without it, which is sometimes easier in an environment without its constant use. It lessens the temptation. If you need privacy, there is a courtyard on the beach side. We control access. Only one gate and walls are high enough with sharp spikes to discourage idle curiosity. Inform me of your practice times in advance. I'll make additional arrangements to keep the area clear."

"Thank you, Abbess, that would be most ideal. A whole courtyard. I am honored."

"The honor is mine. We are doing some renovations, and it goes largely unused except for a guest who exercises his bull hound there. We'll be starting the feast soon. You and your household simply must attend. You shall be hosted at my table. Then you can have an opportunity to speak to Lady Bathsheba and the Mistress of Relics about access to the archives in person."

A headache pounded fierce behind Jhee's eyes. Her knees screamed in agony. She craved nothing more than to soak her aching muscles in a warm, mineral spring. "Again, your hospitality overwhelms me. As you wish."

Jhee forced a smile and clasped forearms with Pyrmo. Pyrmo flinched.

She held up her hands, which had severe burn scars. She applied a bitter-smelling salve from a tin on her desk. "My apologies, Justicar. I sometimes forget."

"I have some small experience with healing. May I take a look?"

"No need. You must be tired from your travels, and the last thing I should do is put you to work before you have rested and enjoyed our hospitality. You should rest before the feast. I'll have you taken to your quarters so you may refresh yourself."

Jhee nodded politely and left. The prioress led her and Bax to another corridor. Her knees and muscles felt sore.

"Does your abbey have mineral springs underneath it?"

"Unfortunately, they are under the stars and exposed to the elements. Underneath us are only crypts."

"What of baths?"

"Only communal showers."

Jhee sighed. "Whelm."

"I can have a purification and rehab tub brought to you and your cohort's room."

"Splendid. Room singular?"

"Interest in taking holy orders is on the rise. Many have also been stranded here by the beastly storms, among them a troupe of itinerant performers. In fact, they shall be performing at the feast tonight. We've housed you in the dormitories instead of the hostelry with the more common guests."

"What a delight. Although a whole marriage cohort in one room. I shall not have a moment to myself to think, let alone meditate." Both the prioress and Abbess Pyrmo barely acknowledged the young men's deaths. Jhee decided to put this separation from her cohort to another use and seek elsewhere for the message sender and further details. "Best to show me to your shrine immediately," Jhee said.

"This way."

"A moment, please. I want to send my servant ahead." Jhee pulled Bax aside. "Begin making inquiries. Discretely."

"Yes, Justicar."

⌒‿

The Curious Courtyard Shrine

The prioress brought Jhee down a spiral tower to the courtyard. They emerged from the aperture door onto an exposed rain-soaked grotto. Broad First Makers architraves stood in the center without a bit of shelter for anyone who might use the pillars and basins under them for offerings. Though, the perpetual flame and water feature were protected from the Wind Witch, who howled with as much ferocity as her Sea Sister. The rest of the grotto housed many and numerous representations of the Makers and Lesser Makers. At one point, everyone claimed every ancestor or nature spirit to be a Maker.

One death flagged as unusual by Jhee's query mentioned an accident in a courtyard. Might it be this one?

"This way," the prioress yelled. "Here we are, the shrine. Please, take as much time here as you need."

"I will. Thank you."

The prioress directed her to a small, covered shrine off the main courtyard. This shrine did not contain quite so many effigies. Four nooks separated by columns housed a basin and a pedestal. Being Drakists, one held a physical carving of the Double Shell Drakes wound about the Blessed Isles consuming the other's tails. The sky pillar and basin on the left had an everburning candle. It provided the only light to the shrine; light which danced and leaped in partnership with the shadows it cast. The alcove on the right had a water feature on top of the earth pillar. A thin layer of gray-green algae lined the basin. Moss had been allowed to grow on the water feature itself.

A pitcher of water, a striker, and incense were already present in the alcove. Rather than use those, Jhee gave of herself. She knelt before the shrine then breathed on the ever-burning candle. Breath and warmth. She pricked her finger and let one drop of blood fall into the water-filled basin. She also used a nail file on the tip of one of her claws over the bowl. Flesh and blood. The last hollow, dark and full of stricken out totems, venerated the Unknown Maker. She said a few quick prayers and touched her esca to the ground in supplication. Best not to draw too much attention from that one.

While Jhee sought out alcoves for the Lesser Makers whose favor she did court, she took her time, scanning the courtyard for anything amiss. Rain veiled most of the yard from notice. She came upon a crumbling niche housing a rusted Mechanist wheel and axle. The basic device which represented complexity from simplicity required some effort on Jhee's part to turn.

Not much call for Mechanist devotions here it would seem despite the overlap with the abbey's asceticism.

At an early age, Jhee had declared herself a follower of Mechanism. However, her duties as Justicar rarely left her time enough to perform even the minimal devotions required of an avowed Mechanist such as the construction of the devotional items. Her preferred method to honor the First Makers was through applying the force of her faculties to imbalances of justice.

Jhee looked at the message on her conch again. Her work, also, seemed never to leave her sufficient time to manage a family which had practically doubled overnight. With her new position in the capital, though, time would no longer be a problem. First of all, she must find some accommodation with Kanto. The situation as is could not stand. This move to the capital had everything strained to the breaking, least of all her tenuous relationship with Kanto. She jingled a few geld coins before the drum-beating effigy of Futou, Maker of music and freshwater, then bounced a few off his signature drumhead.

At the back of the grotto was a defaced wall carving of Toril, the War Maker. The Toril which lent this isle its name. Most of the body had gone with only the implements left to identify it. Scourge, quoit, dented shield, broken sword. Not all the Makers were equally loved.

Jhee hoped the nectar of Tranquility Bridge's and the time off the boat would do Mirrei some good. That would be at least one pressure taken off her. She prayed to her ancestors and the spirit of Miramar, Mirrei's mother. She placed her hand over the inner pocket where she kept her letter. So many remembrances: the last sight as Miramar and her daughter sailed away after their semi-reconciliation; Mirrei's tale of her standing defiantly on the beach with their sinking home behind her; the final message Mirrei delivered to Jhee. *"Protect and honor my daughter."*

"I will, old friend. I will."

Jhee thought of poor Mirrei so ill and tired all the time. Hopefully, some time on land and the abbey's miraculous nectar would do the trick. The doctors had initially diagnosed her condition as Fresh Lung Sickness. This, however, did not seem to be typical Fresh Lung Disease. Fresh Lung occurred when those from the saltier Outer Reaches moved to water with less salinity. Most recovered from it relatively quickly like Jhee and the rest of her household. Mirrei seemed to get worse the longer they sailed, though. Jhee performed the last of her devotions to Pascoe and Lashae for Mirrei's health.

Jhee performed a few abeyances to other Lesser Makers then turned back to the main grotto. So many eyes upon her. She must make them proud. Once she made a determination about the recent deaths here, she intended to focus on arcane teaching and research. This matter may well be her last field case. Perhaps her efforts were best spent inside where it was warm and dry. Meanwhile, she might also uncover whoever sent her the message.

The prioress led her towards a different aperture to exit the courtyard.

A powerful gust of wind tore the door from Jhee's grasp before she could close it after her. Jhee held onto her cloak and reached for the door. Just then, a lightning strike flashed. A silhouette wearing an elaborate mask embraced a naked, one-armed man from behind. Jhee pulled the door closed. She thought better of what she had seen and opened it again. Jhee raised an eyebrow. So much for the celibate life. She always assumed such a vow was much easier said than done.

"Allow me." The prioress tugged the door from Jhee's grasp before she could object.

"The abbess informed me of your rules against fraternization. They apply amongst the clergy, yes?"

"We are a celibate order."

"Do you impose a penalty for breaking that vow?"

The prioress eyed Jhee and stepped back. "The vow is to the Makers and one's self. One who breaks the vow has already shamed themselves. Who are we to impose additional sanction? The only distinctions we make are fraternization and seduction. One who induces another to break their vows or one who uses their position of authority to tempt the laity. These carry harsh penalty. I do hope the Justicar is not worried for the virtue of herself or her cohort."

"When I was closing the door, I thought perhaps I saw lovers at play. A naked man and another figure locked in an embrace."

"The Justicar is tired."

Jhee went back out into the courtyard and examined where she had seen the figures. The wall appeared solid except for a carving of the sword and bridge. She hurried back to where the prioress waited.

"The building across the way is a storeroom with a blind wall. You must have seen the cloister ghosts."

"Ghosts? Nonsense."

"You would not be the first."

"I prefer your original assessment. I am overtired and a little ill."

"As you have it."

"Please, have the tub for a mineral bath brought to my room as soon as possible."

Jhee needed to clear her head. She had inquiries to perform, and she had no time for nonsense, such as ghosts. "I hope our use of the Zodiac Courtyard won't cause too much disruption. Does that courtyard have the same layout as this?"

The prioress stumbled. "That courtyard has been off-limits as of late. Why do you ask?"

"The abbess said my cohort and I could use it for meditation and arcane study because it was under renovation."

"I see. If you have no truck with ghosts, I should think that would be the last place you'd dally with arcane forces."

"Because a young novice fell to his death there?"

"The young novice died there during the first tremor. Even before that, there have been reports of strange voices, tiny footsteps, the laughter of children, music and whispering in the walls. No one goes there anymore except Mr. Anshu, the animal handler."

They emerged on a residential hallway more warmly lit with glow globes than anything Jhee had seen in this place thus far.

"This is yours. We gave you the biggest, most comfortable rooms we could manage in the circumstances. No insult to your station."

"No insult taken."

4

THE FEAST I

~

The Two Deaconesses

Jhee collapsed in a chair, favoring the bridge of her nose. Her sinuses had now become stopped up. Ghosts. Stuff and nonsense. Shep removed her shoes and massaged her feet while Kanto brushed her hair. The rooms, though plain, had an antechamber and a tea nook with tea service. She eyed it, wishing for nothing more than a hot cup and her conch. She had nearly drifted to sleep when the mineral bath arrived.

Dari whined from a small bed by the bookcase and writing desk, as Jhee lowered herself into the tub. She reached over and gave her a reassuring pat. A little lamp and communication device supplemented the bare overhead glow lights. Kanto and Mirrei had already set up stools near the small window to work on their crafts. The bed, while a decent size, would not be comfortable for four.

Jhee yawned. "This many people in a bed. It's simply uncivilized."

She opened her eyes at the silence. Her spouses had fixed her with expressions fit to kill. She remembered the conditions they had to sleep under on the yacht. She hunkered down in the tub.

"I'll take the floor," Shep said. "You all thrash about too much, anyway."

He dug out their nightclothes and a bedroll.

Jhee shook her head and yawned. "Evening robes, if you will. We've been invited to a hundred-year-feast in the main hall."

Kanto set down his lute and pushed Shep aside. "Let me. Why didn't you tell us sooner? We could have been preparing."

"In the confusion, it slipped my mind. I must attend. The rest of you are free to refuse if you are not up to it. Bring me something more formal."

"Formal wear for ascetics?"

"This cloister boasts Lady Bathsheba as a court official in residence."

"An Imperial tutor?" Kanto touched his hand to his chin in thought. "No. No. No. Our most formal attire is with the rest of our things on the way to the capital. Our more formal attire buried in the luggage."

Kanto whipped out the robe he and Mirrei had made. "Yes, yes. Dry enough. This will have to do. I'll patch and clean it as best I can. We'll do that. A former member of the court, attire should still be simpler. As befits a humble official, such as yourself in a setting such as this. Your breaking it in the other night will only serve to make them seem more modest and humbler."

Jhee offered no input and let him and Mirrei work while she soaked as best she could in the tiny tub. Soon after, Kanto and Mirrei splashed each other with water, depriving her of the blessed silence she craved. She pinched the bridge of her nose.

"I made this sweet-smelling mint poultice to clear your head, denbe. I swear by it."

Mirrei knelt and presented her the poultice.

"A fair sight she'd be meeting the vizier with that on her head, denye," Kanto said.

"Scrape barnacles."

"Lick glass."

"Enough. Both of you," Jhee said. She regretted her sharp tone when Mirrei looked away abashed. Kanto gave Mirrei an accusing glance.

"Put it under a head wrap," Shep said. "No one will even notice."

Jhee took the poultice and let her hand linger on Mirrei's, who smiled. Mirrei faced Kanto self-satisfied. He proceeded to do up Jhee's head wrap and robe unbothered. He punctuated the finishing touches with a smug expression of his own. The feast felt more inviting all the time.

The poultice did, indeed, make Jhee's head feel clearer. She reflected on what she had seen earlier. She slipped away to summon Bax via conch. Outside the rooms, she confided what she had seen.

"One arm, but no blood, Justicar? Distressing indeed."

"It would not be a fresh injury. I've seen few enough monks here. A man missing an arm should not be too difficult to notice."

"Is your ladyship sure it's not ghosts? The servants and the laity say evil forces are at work here."

"Likely of a much more mundane cause. Investigate the storeroom then contact me after the banquet."

Jhee joined Pyrmo and the senior clergy at the high table above the other clerics in the banquet hall. In accordance with sacred geometry, six hallways radiated off the principal, vaulted room. Two exits featured barred doors. The lesser clergy ate separated by gender at long tables and benches surrounding a central stage. A Professed read scripture aloud from the pulpit. Gallery boxes flanked the main eating floor. All save for one was empty. Two men in merchant dress, one younger, one older with a goatee, watched the performance unaccompanied.

No sign of her household, whom Jhee had left to quibble over what to wear and whether to attend. She intended only to stay long enough to meet the vizier and put her mind at ease about the recent deaths.

"Justicar, I hope you had time to reflect and refresh yourself," Pyrmo said.

"Again, Abbess, I must thank you for your hospitality. My household is a bit unsettled and may make their way here shortly. We've had a trying journey." A quick glance at the table revealed nothing but clerics. The Lost Makers' place at the table had a setting but no chair. Abbesses sometimes invited anyone who called the abbey home from the highest deaconess to the lowliest servant to fill the seat and to share the abbey's inner workings with them. A custom households such as her family also followed when she was younger. "Will the vizier be dining with us tonight?"

"She sends her regards. She has chosen to spend the evening convalescing from injuries received in the quake. She asks that I pass along an invitation for tea in her quarters after the banquet."

"I would be most honored." As lovely as tea sounded, the invitation doused Jhee's notions of a short evening. "I chanced a visit to your most impressive courtyard and shrine. Would that I could have seen it in the full light of the sources."

"Bah, this weather," Sister Serra, the traditional figured cleric to Jhee's left, said. She drained the contents of her mg then thumped the cup on the table. "It stunts the plants. If we don't get enough dry time and strong light soon, the Tranquility Blossoms won't produce enough nectar for this season's demand, let alone next."

A Prospective put a fresh pitcher of wine in a central location. Sister Serra reached for the pitcher only to have the gaunt cleric to Pyrmo's right, Sister Elkanah, remove it.

"Then perhaps you should partake less of it," said Sister Elkanah. "Seminar attendance is down too. With all this disruption, we are also not making enough from cafeteria and visitors' fees to pay the upkeep on the reliquary."

"Or the greens houses," Sister Serra added.

The abbess took command of the pitcher and placed it in front of her, sloshing some on the table. Jhee considered the pinkish tinged elixir. Tranquility Bridge's healing nectar wine: one reason she had been so keen to visit.

"May I?"

Jhee pointed her cup at the pitcher. The abbess filled Jhee's cup herself. "Be my guest."

As wine connoisseurs past had instructed her, Jhee held the cup in front of her nose and swirled it to allow the bouquet to tease the palate before she drank. She tipped the cup to her lips. Delightfully sweet and flowery with the slightest peach tang. She made a satisfied sound. "The famed Golden Tranquility wine. I read of its refreshing and curative properties during my study of healing draughts. The descriptions do not do it justice."

The abbess winced. "And now the wine argument."

"Our Select blend," Sister Serra said with pride. "Named after the golden span connecting this structure to the main isle."

"To give such flattery is almost as much of a sin, as to receive it," Sister Elkanah said.

"Netherwise, the Justicar is most welcome," the abbess said.

Jhee imagined her face bore a similar expression when the dispute over the poultice broke out.

The fare they ate was a good deal more elaborate than Jhee would have expected of a cloistered order. A circumstance owed either to the occasion or Sister Serra's evident joy and delight as an epicure. Rosemary mutton with roasted vegetables met everyone's approval, save Sister Elkanah. She eschewed more sumptuous dishes opting instead for boiled potatoes, scrod, and a bowl of thin leek soup.

From what Jhee gathered, Sister Serra ran the farming operations. A horticulturist with a traditional figure, reddened cheeks, and bloodshot eyes, she laughed easily and frequently. While, the slimmer, more severe Sister Elkanah presided over the archives and reliquary. If the prioress's look was one of permanent dissatisfaction, hers was its complement, somewhere between disinterest and disgust. Fresh scratches graced her wrists. She pulled down her sleeves at Jhee's notice.

"I question the need for this banquet anyway and its taste. Our founding coming as it does so near the anniversary of the massacre…. No wonder the spirits are roiled," Sister Elkanah said.

"I should rather think it's the Mist World in retrograde. The current trines of the moons with the fourth planet. The last time they were in this position was on the eve of the massacre. We know this configuration unleashes malevolent energies upon the worlds. More than enough to account for our recent tragedies," Sister Serra said.

"Speaking of tragedy… Abbess, about the arrangements for my pupil and me, might we change them to another courtyard? I heard a Prospective died in the courtyard you've been so gracious to lend us. His ghost may not be the only one that haunts this place."

"Someone's already been telling you tales of our infamous cloister ghosts, have they?"

"The prioress mentioned it after I saw a strange sight in the courtyard. I thought perhaps it might be a residual or echo. The spirits perhaps of the more recently dead. You've had more than your fair share of suffering, both distant and not. I'm not the superstitious sort myself, but it may do well not to chance the whirlpool of fate by cyphering there."

"I'll see what we can do."

A small choir took the pulpit to perform a religious hymn. After which, Sister Elkanah read a selection from Dallighere's Descent to the Trench. The lower clergy and Professed alike sat fish-eyed and gape-mouthed from its elaborate depictions of the torments of the wicked on their way to the Irreparable Place.

"Are you, also, a practitioner of the healing arts, Justicar?" Sister Serra asked.

Jhee's marriage cohort made their entrance dressed modestly. A Prospective showed them to gallery boxes nearest the high table without separating men from women; a courtesy of the abbess no doubt. They seated Mirrei first, who curtsied then finger waved at Jhee. Kanto and Shep gave polite bows to the high table. Shep's bow was perfunctory and straightforward. Kanto's had an extra demure flourish. Their box faced that of the merchants.

"A dabbler. It's become an obsession of late. My wife has the real talent for it."

"Then we must give you a cask of Tranquility Gold for your journey, so you can have a proper sample to study."

"Much obliged, Sister Serra. I couldn't accept such a gift, especially if, as you say, you may not have enough to meet demand."

"I insist."

Jhee licked her lips. If the fruits of her investigations or future study of the wine did not yield harvest, this made the stay worth it. Healing properties or no, sips of this guaranteed a more pleasant remainder to their journey. "Very well, then. Allow me to offer a gift in exchange. Consider my skills in jurisprudence and investigation at your disposal for the length of our stay. We'll also pay the standard rental and materials fees along with a donation equivalent to the market value of say two casks to your repair fund."

The abbess's eyes brightened, while the prioress and Sister Elkanah leaned in. It reminded her of feeding time at the aquarium.

"Your patronage will be greatly appreciated. Saheli's generous heart outmatched the abbey's resources. She had instituted increased alms for the refugees. Unfortunately, we don't have the resources to continue it."

"Thank you, Abbess."

"Nonsense," Sister Serra said. "Have it with our compliments."

The prioress frowned. Jhee decided not to argue the point further here. She began a mental tally anyway and would check the market value of the casks later.

"Don't be daft, Sister Serra. As if Saheli's misplaced kindness hadn't already imperiled us. And save your 'generosity.' Justicar ethics prohibits her from accepting such a valuable gift. She's humoring you," Sister Elkanah said.

Jhee turned to the mistress of relics. "I corresponded with your previous abbess not only about the nectar but about access to your archives. We discussed a donation and archival fees."

The abbess dipped her head, which Jhee took as affirmation she had tacked correctly.

Sister Elkanah sniffed. "Your name does seem familiar. I may recall her passing those along. Our greatest religious texts in their earliest, most fragile forms are there. Their access is usually reserved for the most devout and dedicated of scholars. Your requests were very professional and thought out. I had yet to make my decision. I'll discuss the matter with Pyrmo and our librarian."

Jhee had sent those requests months, if not more ago. If the Sister were inclined to grant them, she might have done so by now. Abbess Pyrmo took the pulpit to talk about the abbey's founding and history of the island.

The feast's tone shifted more toward somber. Jhee only found intermittent enjoyment in the meal, company, or entertainment, anyway. Throughout, her thoughts lingered on the sight from the grotto and the recent deaths. An array of smells bombarded her from incense censers and licorices to spike leaf ointment and other peculiar sharp tangs in the air. Death stalked this abbey. Had she seen a new tragedy or an old as the prioress would have her believe?

"Quite the blood-soaked history Torilsisle has."

"How many Makers do you subscribe to, Justicar?" Sister Elkanah asked.

"Mechanism posits a reasonable case for as many as five, three plus a Prime Maker and an Unknown Maker, with possibly an innumerable number of Lesser Makers."

"What case do you posit? There comes the point when the worship of the various Lesser Makers becomes akin to paganism. Everyone's up-jumped ancestor can't be a Maker."

Sister Serra dipped her finger in her wine cup and then tasted her fingertip. "Mm, I'd argue by definition everyone's ancestor is a Maker, or else none of us would be here."

"Obscene. You mock too much, Sister Serra."

"Idolater."

It would seem Jhee had traded one bickering pair for another. A group including Sister Serra livened attitudes up with dancing and a few bawdy songs.

Jhee swept her cup at the cramped benches. "Quite the full house."

"Supplicants used to be rare. Now we turn them away," the prioress said.

"Ah, yes, the refugees. Many come at our doors to beg. Can you imagine?" Sister Elkanah said.

"More come each day like an enormous unwashed wave, a tsunami that can't be stopped," Pyrmo replied.

"Which is why you sought to turn my messenger away," Jhee stated.

"The Justicar's pardon, again, for the misunderstanding between your messenger and the gate staff," the prioress said.

"Not very hospitable," a woman in noble dress said. "Yes, the gall to ask charity at an abbey."

The carob-brown woman stumbled to the high table. Jhee estimated her too young to be the vizier. The woman supported herself with the table while sloshing various discarded cups to see if they were empty.

"They likely fancied you more beggars or refugees. How long did you leave the esteemed Justicar and her vessel stranded?"

"Rescuing overburdened ships in ill weather can be quite dangerous."

Jhee sipped her wine. After the woman flung aside one last cup, she flailed for a nearby chair. Once she had hold to the chair, she dragged it to the Lost Makers' place with a drawn-out, ear-piercing scrape. Everyone winced. It appears she had found a topic upon which the clerics agreed.

$\sim$

A Recitation

A female announcer came out and spoke. "My gracious hosts, I present you the spinner stylings of Mr. Zane."

A young man took the stage with a series of sticks and staffs and hoops. After a few masterful displays of staff spinning and tricks with the small hoops and the sticks, he switched to larger body hoops. He swirled and undulated his body to rotate the circles about his torso, hips, and at one point, a single shoulder.

The performer's outfit matched neither that of the figure in the mask nor the one missing an arm. Nonetheless, Jhee admired Mr. Zane's skill.

"Mr. Zane is in exquisite form tonight," Sister Serra said. "His *talent* truly is a treat for deprived eyes."

Sister Elkanah replied, "The Sister would do best to at least pretend some restraint."

"Chaste doesn't equal dead. What is the design intent to put such beauties and pleasures in the world if not to enjoy them?"

"Temptation away from the true path. It is a terrible distraction to have so many unmarried men about."

"Terrible for you, maybe. Chastity is a Drakist tenet. Hard to have one without the other."

"Precisely my point. Men should not be here."

"What do you think, Justicar?"

Jhee ruminated on her experience in the grotto, the couple, the effigies. "Does this order not believe any of the Makers males?"

"We do."

"The Design teaches us one of the many joys on the route to release is the marrying and fostering of children. Without household aid, how do they hope to gain their place in the Prime Maker's showcase? Their spirits shall be doomed to wander. Celibacy and paganism negate a societal need. No wonder your cloister is said to be haunted by ghosts. The widowed life mates of these unfortunate men and women."

"Well said," Sister Serra declared. "Then I'd say we have the contradiction backward. I'd argued such for years."

Sister Elkanah's icy stare made Jhee realize she had blundered again.

"The Justicar must then have scores of children. Or else one has to wonder what compliance with the Makers' Design marriage bestowed in lieu of chastity."

From their segregation by gender to their veneration of astrological superstition, Jhee felt as if she had stepped back in time an age. "We may never know anything else of the First Makers' Design. What we do know is they gave us intellect, sensation, and curiosity; tools with which we can know the world and ultimately the Design. Why would they not want us to use them?"

"Do you smell mint?" Sister Serra asked.

Abbess Pyrmo reddened.

Sister Elkanah snorted. "Further proof of the Unraveler's presence."

"Mint?" Serra asked.

"They say curious smells are one of the signs Unmakers are present."

"I thought it was ozone. Everything is a sign of the Unmakers according to you."

"The Unmakers' portents are many and varied."

"Like the Makers.'"

"With as much smudge and incense as you douse yourself with, it's no wonder you can't detect foul beings."

"Going back to the matter of the courtyard," Jhee started.

"What true philosophers I dine with," Pyrmo interrupted. "This light occasion is not the proper time for such heavy topics. A later time, yes?"

Finding out which one of them had contacted Jhee might also waiter for a later time, too. Mr. Zane's act concluded to much applause. Jhee chose strategic silence. She adjusted her mint poultice and wrap once their conversation turned to lighter subjects. Finding out which one of them had contacted Jhee might also wait for a later time, too.

The announcer returned. "In honor of our gracious hosts, we present a reenactment of Freytag's and Ziza's duel before the Last Redoubt of the Shell Knights. As performed by Mr. Anshu and Ms. Hethyr."

"Hethyr. A barbarian name," Jhee said.

"Ah, you are right," the abbess said.

Another man came to the stage in elaborate war gear, including two unlit fire fans. His body fur bore no trace of barbarian stipples or dapples. The mask he wore prevented a proper view of his esca. An assistant lit the tips of the fans then crouched at the foot of the stage with a bucket of water. Beside them, the announcer waited with a large blanket. The hall went silent save for the crackling of the flames as he swirled them in arcs and figure drakes.

A female figure in battle dress joined the first, this one bearing two fiery orbs on leashes. The woman's fur also was a proper, solid brown with no trace of barbarian striping. Jhee sat up straighter. The armor, though, reminded her of what she had seen in the courtyard. Both figures were in full possession of their limbs.

The two battled with their fire props. Their flickering lights swept over and around the faces of the crowd trailing wisps of smoke. Even from the high table, Jhee felt the ambient heat ebb and flow, a tide made of warmth as if the breathing of a deep drake. The pace of the scene picked up. The two darted their flaming weapons at each other. One of the fire orbs clipped Mr. Anshu's headdress in a manner Jhee was not entirely sure was planned. A gasp came from the seclusion boxes. The younger merchant had moved right up against the low wall. His two hands gripped the rail. From then on out, he flinched with each close call. The announcer and assistant's faces remained concerned until the two broke apart and went to opposite ends of the stage; Mr. Anshu nearer the seclusion boxes.

The announcer gestured excitedly at the assistant, who quickly doused their weapons. The warriors removed their headgear. Mr. Anshu glared at Ms. Hethyr. Now that Jhee saw both their escae, it confirmed neither were of barbarian descent. Though, with Mr. Anshu and the younger merchant in her field of vision at once, she could not help but notice a similarity to their eye coloring and ears.

The announcer took center stage with a little laugh. "Such a spirited performance. Now, Mr. Anshu and Itzil shall perform a reenactment of the Taming of the Shell Drake and the Storm Child's Lullaby."

Ms. Hethyr smiled at Mr. Anshu, gave an exaggerated bow to the audience, and left the stage. Now alone on stage, Mr. Anshu had switched to glow fans, which had small glow orbs instead of live fire. A growl came from the performers' entrance.

A Zicarian bull hound, a tusked canine the size of its titular bovine, burst onto the stage. Jhee gasped. She drew on the prime forces within, and her hand went to the sigil that bound her to Shep. He had already sprung from his seat and placed himself between the beast and Mirrei and Kanto.

No one at the high table or audience had made a move. Jhee turned her attention back to the stage. The bull hound came to a full stop at Mr. Anshu's command. He stomped and shouted another command. The bull hound rose up and towered over him, its paws nearly the size of his head.

Jhee slumped in her chair. "Whelm and waves."

"Forgive my lapse, Justicar. The bull hound is Mr. Anshu's companion."

Mr. Anshu and the beast performed a dance full of gentle, rhythmic movements where he appeared to lull the animal to sleep with the fans. He tucked his fans under his arm and bowed to the head table. The hall erupted into applause.

Mr. Anshu petted the bull hound then fed it some land meat from a nearby bucket. Jhee drew in a breath. Her attention snapped back to her cohort in the boxes. Shep sat rigid in his seat; his eyes firmly fixed on the pair on stage. Her conch pulsed. She jumped in her chair. He turned to her, his ordinarily amber eyes a duller shade. He forced himself to relax. The sigil on her arm had gone cold and still.

The fear, having already shaken her wits and sharpened her senses, clarified her resolve. The more she thought, the more Ms. Hethyr's mask focused her on the scene from the courtyard. She excused herself from the table to check her conch.

Found storeroom, my lady. Storage for troupe's costumes and props. Nothing else, Bax's message read.

Inquire about troupe member Hethyr.

Jhee returned to her seat. She did a double-take when she realized the other gallery box had now emptied. "Who were the other guests in the boxes?"

"Mr. Pol, a pious widower and his son, Akesheem. The young man is thinking of taking vows. Displaced or wealthy families seek the honor joining our prestigious abbey confers. And to divest themselves of surplus males." A chair scraped across the floor. The woman from earlier staggered to the pulpit. The abbess narrowed her eyes and took a long drink from her cup. "Or mere surplus. Case in point."

"Two, two by Chance, a recitation by yours truly Raigen," the drunken woman said, her words loud and slurred. "Two mothers by chance, by rites. One bears the day, and one bears the crypts by nights. Two warring duchesses dance an extended caper. Abstinence. Humility. Hospitality. Three vows as binding as vapor. Four elements: air, fire, water, earth. The drakes' eyes shall witness their rebirth."

Drunken ranting described the recital better than word-smithing. No one applauded. The banquet hall began to empty. Raigen stumbled back to her seat beside the prioress.

The golden hue to the abbess's eyes had gone fifty fathoms deeper. "Shameful."

"Truly," Jhee agreed. She glanced at her cohort. Shep still sat stiff-backed.

"Raigen seeks to take vows at the deathbed request of her mother, the former governess of the district. A request I'd deny had she not once been amongst our strongest supporters. In life, she gifted us many relics, she bequeathed us more should her daughter become Professed, which I do not see happening. If you'll forgive me, I need to properly thank and provide homage to our true entertainers."

"Excuse me, as well. I would like to check in with my household."

The abbess swayed slightly as she got up from the table. "Of course."

Jhee's conch sounded again for a live message. "Speak."

"Hethyr was not with the other performers. No one seems to know where she went."

"Whelm. Meet me outside the banquet hall."

5

THE FEAST II

∼

The Poetess

Jhee joined her cohort at their box. "Alas, my dear cohort, I'm glad everyone got to see the feast performances."

"That Mr. Zane was quite handsome and skilled," Mirrei said.

Kanto folded his arms. "If you are into such unsophisticated fare. Could you believe that poetess, denye? So embarrassing."

"I was embarrassed for her," Mirrei said then shrugged. "A welcome diversion after the bull hound. I near died of fright here on the spot when Shep leaped up. Do you think they'll be animals like that at court?"

"I hear the Imperial families keep pygmy shell drakes as pets," Kanto said.

"No."

"Oh, yes."

They continued to giggle and gossip while Shep kept watchful eyes on the entrances and tugged on his forearm hairs. As Jhee approached, she heard him talking to himself, "Walls to our back good. Walls to the side. If cornered, the only way out is through, though. Confined space. No room to maneuver."

"Shep," she whispered so she would not startle him. He turned to her

45

and smiled as if nothing was amiss. "What of you, dear heart? How are you faring?"

"Much better now that you're within arm's reach."

Jhee stroked the ridges of his ears with her thumbs. "I was in no danger."

He brought her hand to his eye scar briefly before standing. "Best to be cautious."

They returned to the younger spouses. "Did you have a chance to try the Tranquility Gold? I'm sure it must have met with even your high standard, Shep."

"It was decent. I don't get the fuss."

"Who convinced whom to attend the feast?"

"We wanted to," Mirrei said.

She and Kanto locked arms. "We said Shep could stay if he wished."

Shep pursed his lips. "You could very well not attend the feast unaccompanied yet alone go about the halls by yourself, denyes. Hence, we all attended."

"We would have been fine," Mirrei said. "Perish the thought of any of us having time to ourselves."

"Indeed," Kanto said.

Jhee sighed. "Shep did the right thing. We are guests here. It's perhaps best if we stick together in this unfamiliar place."

Shep and Jhee made pointed eye contact. She tucked her hands into her robes and touched the sigil. He glanced at the exits. "Fine, then we should all retire to our quarters. Yav-yav."

Bax entered the hall. Jhee remained in place in contravention of Shep's attempt to herd the lot of them towards the door. He caught her eye again.

"I have an invitation to tea with the vizier. Return to the room. Hopefully, I won't be long."

Shep folded his arms. Mirrei degenerated into a coughing fit. Kanto provided her a steadying arm. Shep cast a stern glance at Bax then escorted the other spouses out. Jhee's heart tightened as she watched them leave. They passed the poetess, Raigen, who grabbed a wine pitcher from the tray of a Prospective clearing the high table.

Bax came over. "What now, Justicar?"

"All the men of the Abbey appear to be accounted for."

"There is a population of refugees nearby."

"So. With buildings such as this, there may be a multitude of hidden ways in and out. A small matter to find one and bring young men in and out."

"These are professed Drakists, Justicar!"

"One of the eternal dichotomies of celibacy. Make further inquiries into Hethyr. See what you can learn from the performers and Mr. Pol and his son."

"Aye, Justicar."

Jhee paused about to say something else when she noticed the proximity of the poetess. She sat at one of the seats at the high table, checking the cups for dregs. "We'll speak more later."

Bax excused himself. Jhee glanced the way her cohort had gone and thought about Mirrei. She did not like the cast to her pallor. She had hoped some time off the yacht would do her good. Jhee should have joined them, but this was apt to be her last case as a field Justicar. There would be time enough for nesting later after she fulfilled her promise to their dames. She would see Kanto and Mirrei safely to the capital where they can decide for themselves what it is they want.

Raigen, who did not possess a fraction of the grace or poise Mirrei had in her littlest finger, continued to hover and scavenge the high table. How different the poetess was to her late mother, the governess. How different this drunken wastrel was to her Kanto and Mirrei. The poetess was about their age. She thought them a credit to the younger generation. They sought to better themselves despite the hard turns the sea had sent them while this embarrassment drank away her future and a possible cure to Mirrei's ailment. The wine being slurped by this wastrel could well hold the key to Mirrei's recovery.

That Raigen could so flagrantly disregard the rules of not only polite behavior but basic health and yet remain standing, defied Design. Her squandered potential stole momentum from the Divine Mechanism, where it might better serve those who needed it more. While Mirrei struggled to do even the minutest activities, this scoundrel wasted twice the energy stumbling about in drunken idleness. At the poetess's age, Jhee's oldest, surviving sisters had already begun to distinguish themselves in the navy. When Jhee reached that age, she had dreamed of following in their footsteps.

Jhee marched up to Raigen, who had produced a flask. The area around the table still smelled of incense, licorice, and burn cream. Given Raigen's state of drunkenness, she expected it to reek of a still. The poetess tipped the pitcher to her flask. "What you are doing is not only unseemly but unsanitary."

"What exactly is it am I doing, Justicar?"

Her words were clear and articulate. The poetess's hands were rock steady. She did not so much as spill a drop.

"You're not drunk."

The poetess put the flask inside her robes. "No."

"It was my proud pleasure to have met the governess. Why such a disgraceful ruse? Your mother's eyes are still upon you."

"It is because of her, I'm here. Fools can go about nearly invisible and inquire where others can't. Much like Justicars."

"So, there is more method than madness to your poem as well. If you have some proof of a crime, I'll hear it and render fair judgment."

"Proof. Therein lies the problem. I like my tongue and my head precisely where they are."

"I've made it my mission to ensure such harsh penalties are no longer imposed in the district. For slander or libel penalties to apply, a false charge would have to be leveled. However, gossip amongst bored residents is simply uncorroborated evidence, not an accusation." Jhee took the pitcher from the poetess. She squared her shoulders and added sternly, "Nor proof."

Raigen nodded. "Saheli and my mother served together, and they corresponded often. She was concerned about odd happenings at the abbey. Whisperings in the walls. Weird lights. Odd behavior amongst the staff and novices. She sent a communique where she stated another authority was undermining her. I questioned some of the staff and novices. A name continued to come up: The Mist Abbess. Saheli died soon thereafter. My mother succumbed to illness before she could inquire into it herself. Fresh Lung Sickness. I promised on her deathbed to investigate."

Jhee flinched. Her gaze flicked to where her family had left. "Most admirable. What have you found so far?"

"Taking vows here may become hazardous to one's health. At least if you're male."

"Someone may have taken it upon themselves to correct the surplus male problem."

"Three so far that I know of. All since the first quake. Who knows how many more there may be? I don't have the skills to investigate thoroughly alone. I am a simple poet. You have legal backing and Imperial authority at your disposal."

"Which also carries a decidedly higher profile and standard of conduct," Jhee stated.

"I implore you. If not for my sake, then for Akesheem."

"You sent in the complaint."

"I'm sorry I left it unsigned. Reliable off-isle communications went down around then."

"By accident or design?"

"I suspect the latter. But to be candid, it wasn't stellar before then."

That mystery solved, Jhee declared, "Leave it to me from here out."

A Simple Request

Before Jhee could inquire further, Pyrmo reentered the banquet hall. Raigen knocked over a cup and snatched the pitcher Jhee held.

"Justicar, you are still here." The abbess gave Raigen a look of utter contempt. "Is this wretched creature bothering you?"

Raigen uprighted the cup. Jhee took the pitcher back. "Just discussing proper conduct with our young poetess here and the vagaries of poetry."

Raigen's formerly alert gaze was now glazed over and unfocused. "It's nice to meet, meet a learned woman sophisticated enough to nuance my poetry unlike you rest of, the rest of your bores. Perhaps I'll go share my poems with the Honored Dead in the Coral Cloister. Perhaps they'll appreciate it more."

Raigen staggered away.

The abbess relieved Jhee of the pitcher. "My forgiveness for your being subjected to her."

"None needed. It was most illuminating. The poetess's carrying on has been most shameful. There are a great many young men and women here, and it's for those of certain stature to set the example."

"I shudder to think how the governess would have reacted if she were alive to see what has become of her only heir."

"No doubt she would have been most distressed. Perhaps the allure of your delicious wine overwhelmed her."

"With the exception of those who work the vats, Professed and Prospective alike are only permitted one tankard of our house wines a week or a thimbleful daily for health except on certain occasions. They may also partake of small amounts of kolal during services, but no other stimulant drinks. She appears to have found a way around our restrictions. I'll have to tell the staff to be more mindful. This is not the first time I've found her such. You know I even found going through my things and the wine cellar the other day."

"Truly. Truly distressing when such a compulsion drives you to such lengths."

Pyrmo studied the pitcher she held for a moment then placed it on the table. "I had hoped to teach her self-discipline, and in some small measure, our teachings would have a benevolent impact on her. In that, I am failing. Perhaps you may have more luck in straightening the young priss out."

"Is that all that troubles you, abbess? The deacons mentioned recent deaths."

"I appreciate how you were able to navigate the waters between those two."

When Pyrmo said nothing more, Jhee attempted a different approach, "During my stay, I was hoping to get a tour of the abbey. In addition to the archives and ingenious hothouses, I heard of your famous Coral Cloister and Crypts. For now, I'm afraid this beautiful abbey has me a bit turned around. Where might I find the vizier's room?"

"I can escort you if you wish. The vizier currently occupies our hermitage."

"My thanks. Such an intriguing design to your central hall."

The abbess walked her out an entrance different than the one which led to the main dormitories. "The abbey's layout follows the principles of sacred geometry. Six entrances from six halls to represent the six pillars of society."

Jhee jutted her chin at the chained door nearest them. "Where does that door lead?"

"The Corrections Hall."

"What of the other?"

"The other? The crypts. Both are off-limits. They sustained some damage during the recent quakes."

"I hope no one was hurt. That isn't where the young man died, is it?"

"Not there. Both had already been closed by then, the hall due to Saheli's order. She took a different view of discipline than past abbesses. As for the crypts, the risk of flooding has put them off-limits during the storms. The extreme moisture also interferes during the first few years of the preservation process we use on our honored dead, such as my predecessor."

"May I inquire as to how your predecessor died? Disease? Disaster?"

"Transfiguration. Her spirit ascended in light directly to the Maker Sphere, while several of us watched. A transcendent sight I might have questioned had I and the high clergy not witnessed it ourselves."

"Remarkable. What events preceded this extraordinary occurrence?"

"Saheli and I had spoken just that morning about abbey business. She pursued several crafting and artistic pursuits in the gardens. The weather that day was sunny, not wet and black like now. Professed as well as the visiting scholar, Sister Niza, also there for contemplation, later heard her performing alignment chants. Then the sound of her engaged in dialogue with the Makers."

"How can you be sure it was the Makers?"

"Those who saw her said no one else was there, and she sat alone on the bench, but she had completed the most exquisite sketch of her cat. No doubt, via the Makers' inspiration. She announced her intentions to take advantage of the clear weather and spend the rest of the afternoon in contemplation via construction in her favorite place, the Bridge tower. Some time later, she summoned me, the prioress, the deacons, and a visiting scholar, Niza. She delivered an hour-long sermon about the nature of cyphering and drawing with respect to the pillars of society. The Imperial Theological Department is even considering adopting it as a primary text."

"Impressive. To qualify for consideration means an independent account exists. Where might I view a copy?"

"The archives. Saheli preached with transcendent power and full of the most inspired and eloquent language the great thinker, Yrisa, upon reading Sister Niza's account, wrote a ten-paged annotated commentary of its allusions and symbolism. Those of us present felt the strength and power of the words in our bones. Her spirit became visible. A great beam of light appeared. She spoke her last words and passed out dead on the spot. With a great blinding flash of light, her spirit ascended the beam to the Divine Spheres. Before it disappeared, I touched it and was left with these burns."

The abbess displayed her hands, then tucked them away.

"I know you already think us backward and superstitious, but Niza witnessed it too. The recent deaths have quite upset the residents of Tranquility Bridge. Justicar, were you sincere about offering us your services?"

"Of course, Abbess."

"Being a woman of law and letters, I thought if you were to reassure everyone and find a more natural mundane cause, it would put many minds at ease."

"As a holy woman yourself, you see no work of Unmakers in this."

"I know Unmakers, especially the Unmaker, prefers to use mortal faces to hide hir true intent. Here we are. The vizier's chambers. Some of Saheli's artwork and writings were put in the archives. The rest of her belongings are interred with her in the crypts. Her remains and belongings may someday be counted as relics themselves on par with our other Honored dead. This right here is one of Saheli's works."

An etching hung beside a door illuminated by a glow orb. Jhee admired the workmanship.

"Superb. What became of the cat?"

"The cat? Oh, yes. We buried it in the garden under her favorite tree."

"I would very much like to read that account and the sermon if I may, but it seems as if Sister Elkanah has taken a dislike to me."

"Ask the vizier. Sister Elkanah holds her in high regard. Perhaps if she were to speak on your behalf, she might be more inclined to grant you access."

"Many thanks. Is there any opportunity for me to autopsy Saheli's remains? My duties require some training in forensic and mortuary sciences. My first husband and wife also have some medical training. I'd be interested in what the act of transfiguration does to our mortal form."

"Autopsy? The preservation process may prevent that, and as I said, the crypts are sealed right now. I'm also afraid I cannot allow a male to examine such a holy personage as our abbess or near our most sacred spaces. I shall consult with the prioress. I must leave you now and attend to other matters."

Once Pyrmo left, Jhee examined the etching once more. Exceptional work. The tiny pop of grit ground underfoot drew her attention. She paused to listen, then stared into the darkness beyond the orb. She waited for her eyes to adjust but saw no one. A whiff of the air proved equally fruitless. Because of the drenched poultice, all she smelled was mint.

6

______

THE AUDIENCE

∼

Teatime

On the other side of the door from the etching, the wall bore a panel with a placard pad. Jhee placed her conch against it and transmitted her social credentials. Pyrmo had not delivered her a formal invitation, so she defaulted to social protocol. The panel displayed the lady's seal, then the door opened. Jhee's position relative to hers did not require that.

Jhee entered and waited by the open door to be acknowledged. Every piece of furniture was black lacquer. No doubt brought with her from the capital. Nothing in the room was simple and utilitarian, as Jhee might have expected of someone who had retired to such an austere place. The vizier's chambers were adorned in antique instruments and battle regalia. Feathered animal headdresses. War aprons with the sea bat or silver fox. Obsidian spears with hardwood throwing shuttles. The gold and green tabards of the ancient warrior societies. Battle flutes. War drums. The trace of high-grade incense hung in the air. Along the walls, shelves stacked with books and seaweed parchments alternated with others containing chests and other curios.

Lady Bathsheba acknowledged Jhee's presence with a look and gestured to a small table set up in the middle of the room on an exquisitely woven rug. Jhee closed the door and seated herself properly. A gilded tea service crowned the table while the carpet ringed it with curved and repeating pattern borders popular with the great houses of the capital. The tea had a heavy, earthy smell more similar to kolal, likely a blend of the two. The lady hummed a little passage of music then finished a last bit of writing with her fingernail quill. She considered the page then smiled.

At last, she joined Jhee. As for the lady herself, she was an imperiously postured woman with high cheekbones who dressed in robes a step or two in finery above anything Jhee might have worn. Her hair showed the silvering of age, but just barely. Her esca appeared bright as ever. "Allow me to pour, Justicar."

The vizier poured the steaming kolal into the cup in front of Jhee. Jhee waited for the vizier to fill her own cup. She slipped the insulated sleeve over her cup then turned it thrice before picking it up in both hands. "Honors, Vizier."

The vizier turned her cup twice. "Honors to you as well, Justicar."

Jhee drank a moment after the vizier. "It's good to see the injuries you received in the quake haven't slowed you down."

"Thank you for your concern. You are familiar with high etiquette."

"I have been to the extended court in the Outer Reaches and the capital."

"Never long enough for it to sink in its claws, I'll wager. The politics takes its toll. Although it can be dull at times, and I had to seek my own amusement. Clever girl to stay out of depths you may not be prepared to handle. Keep above the waves as long as you can, I say."

Jhee smirked. She attributed the slight she felt to being called 'girl.' Some time had passed since anyone had dared. Vizier Bathsheba was likely to have been an adolescent when Jhee was born. "The storm shield has changed much. Alas, Vizier, as storm and sea reclaim the Reaches, it is my fate to be reassigned to the capital. It is now my honor to serve at court."

"And you stopped at our humble abbey along the way. Poor dear, allow me to put something stronger in that cup of yours."

"No need, my lady. I think I would like to keep a clear head after the day's events." Everywhere Jhee turned in the room, she found more treasures. She did her best not to marvel. "Vizier, I must admit to being in awe of your fine possessions. Especially the lute. My second husband also plays one and is an admirer of your work."

"A member of the Imperial family gave me that. May I ask what brings you to Tranquility Bridge?"

"Our vessel required repairs. Although I have heard some disturbing tales."

"Oh? Of what sort?"

"The prioress told me of the cloister ghosts while the deacons speak about malign forces and Unmakers, especially in the Zodiac Courtyard where the young man died."

"Worried you've seen some?"

"A place of such history must surely have its share. Of secrets as well. Then there is the abbess's remarkable account of the death of her predecessor."

"I too heard something of Pyrmo's account and read Niza's record. Your credentials. During my tenure, they still spoke of an Imperial wedding stormed by adherents of the monogamist school. Your grand dame preached with them for a time. She surely would have some words over your cohort."

"Grandmamere rejoined the Makers some years ago. I'm told all the most prestigious residents of the abbey witnessed the miraculous event. What's your recollection?"

"To be honest, I'm not sure. I'm not as religious or zealous as some. I do know we sat in a room for two to three hours with little in the way of food or drink under less than ideal conditions. Who knows what phantoms devout minds might conjure up?"

"You believe no transcendence took place?"

"Who am I to say? It is a matter of faith for each one present."

"But not you."

"I have become something of a hermit. I am here to meditate and reflect. My goal was never oneness with the Makers as some others. Nor did I seek refuge from the war mind. I contemplated service, you see. I wanted to participate in the effort to defend our lands and way of life as they tell us so often we should. In the end, I always chose not to commit. Yourself?"

"I, for the most part, saw no combat."

"But not for the whole part? Sounds like a story there."

"One I won't bore you with."

"As you desire. You're only in your position a few years I take it. Judging by accent and the style of robes from the Far Reaches and no doubt ambitious. I understand the desire to leave simple country ways behind. What are the lives of simple country folk compared to the thrill of court? Yet you remain humble and remember from whence you came. Hand-made robes and an unsophisticated head wrap. A traditional, provincial marriage cohort, two men, one woman. I'm surprised one so unestablished took on a full complement before you reached the capital where more opportunities for strategic marriages awaited. I don't envy you having to balance those responsibilities."

Jhee's fingers twitched. "Duty sometimes demands a different path."

"You are ambitious, looking to move up. Difficult to do with something like that hanging over you. New marriages hastily put together. I suppose to show up to court with only one consort would have made the wrong impression. A full cohort shows a break with your grandmere's monogamist beliefs."

"I am but a simple servant to the office."

"Forgive me. I did not mean to imply."

The urge to touch her head wrap or Kanto's repairs to her robe made Jhee focus all the more on holding her cup. She had been relieved to wear the simple, elegant gowns when she expected to be dealing with a hermit-like public tutor. She had not wanted to put on airs. Faced with the sophisticated, urbane Bathsheba of Toho, instead, she felt more a backward, country rustic. Fine. If the vizier thought her a backwater, she would use it.

Jhee pinched the bridge of her nose. "I did see something odd when performing devotions at the main shrine: a figure embracing a naked, one-armed man. This dreadful weather has given me the most egregious headache and possibly a cold. My eyes may not have been as reliable as they once were. Maybe enough to imagine that."

"Do you partake of a lot of kreel?"

"It's a staple of the signature dish of our district."

"It's been my experience that an abundance of kreel, in addition to sometimes turning you pink, can hamper mental functioning. In conjunction with tiredness or poor health, I'd say you have a recipe for hallucination."

"You sound like my wife with her dietetic beliefs."

"She sounds like a wise woman."

"Perhaps, indeed, you are both right. I rather prefer that to the alternative: vengeful spirits drawn by an abundance of death or unwed souls."

"I found a draught part Tranquility Bridge's orange cider, part signature nectar, part black orchid tea, very detoxifying and good for the constitution." The vizier hesitated and leaned forward. "Did your ship really need repairs?"

Jhee opted for caution in the event she had misread the woman. "Have I given you cause to think otherwise?" Jhee asked.

"An abundance of death. What an interesting choice of words. You've never seen fit to visit our abbey before. Three dead Prospectives would have certainly drawn the attention of an involved justicar. I would have thought rather than chasing after phantoms of the mind. You had instead come to seek my counsel on the deaths of those poor, unfortunate souls. I do admit I had an ulterior motive in inviting you here. To see if some word of our plight, and the fates of those three Prospectives, had made it beyond these walls."

Jhee sipped her kolal and tried not to take umbrage. The vizier at least confirmed Raigen's findings. The dead men were not refuge-seekers or lay brothers, but men who had committed to the Drakist way. "My office had no reports of three Prospective deaths."

"Yet here you sit. True, there is no reason the deaths should have been reported. One boy, attended by the abbey physician and myself, appeared to have died of sickness. The other two were likely accidents or suicide. One died in a cave-in. The other fell while walking along the bluffs. All autopsied by the prioress. The passing of poor rural boys of consequence to no none, even their officials."

Jhee's grip on her cup tightened. "What a lovely finger maze. Does the vizier indulge in the art of sequence and gesture puzzles?"

"A recent find from the archives. One piece of a larger set. I had been working on identifying it, though parts are missing."

"I've dabbled. May I?"

The vizier nodded. "I'd be interested in the assistance of someone so studied as yourself."

"This one appears to be missing the key, which tells you how to start."

"Would you care to try, anyway?"

Jhee weighed her desire to rest and extricate herself from the vizier's high-handedness against the opportunity to match wits with an early cyphering enthusiast. "I've taken up too much of your time, Vizier."

The vizier pushed the puzzle closer.

Jhee performed a few gestures and solved a few levels in before tripping up. "My that was a tricky one."

"Ah, delightful. Might I make a suggestion? Having finally seen it used by someone as skilled as yourself, I see it has something of musicality to it. Keep in mind rhythm and flow, and you should be able to progress further."

"How clever of them! To incorporate musical timing rather than geometric or trigonometric principles. Two simultaneous left-hand sequences. I think it may require more than one participant. Oh, I see you pass it along like a relay or rounds. This might require some time and assistance from my wife to unravel. I have to return to my cohort else they'll think I've gotten lost."

The vizier poured them another cup of tea. Jhee turned the cup then lifted it with both hands.

"I thank the vizier again for her invitation. Honors to your house and health."

The vizier raised her cup one-handed without turnings. "No need for such ceremony, and please, call me Bathsheba. I left court to get away from such formality. An acutely pleasant change. You'll have to walk me through how to use the finger maze before you leave the abbey."

Once Jhee matched her, they drank at the same time.

Jhee set down her cup. The vizier escorted her to the door. Jhee hesitated when she glimpsed the edge of Saheli's etching.

"Was there something else, Justicar?"

"I hesitate to impose more on you, Lady Bathsheba. This etching. What do you think of Pyrmo's account of the death of her predecessor? Is there anything you care to add?"

"I spoke to her as normal, and then we parted company before her noon meal." The vizier glanced about her again. "I hesitate to relay gossip. Saheli was prone to taking psychedelics around the time she took her images for the day. It wasn't unusual to hear her speaking with the Makers during her vision quests. Prospectives near her thought nothing of the conversation. As she frequently had them. What she was not in the habit of doing was giving impromptu sermons. The abbey is about personal reflection and inner peace. It came then as a shock when this one day she called upon the senior clerics to hear her preach. She gave the sermon and died. You should read Sister Niza's account as it is most illuminating. We have a copy in our archives."

"I would like to, but Sister Elkanah doesn't seem inclined to grant me access."

"Sister Serra used you to show her up, didn't she?"

"Afraid so."

"The pitching-and-yawing between those two. The previous abbess had to do an intricate balancing act to keep them from tearing the abbey apart. They are very protective of their respective fiefdoms. If you desire access to the archives, I might be able to arrange it with the archivist. Consider it done. On one condition."

"If it is in my humble power to do so, I shall."

"You simply must consent to be my guest for tea again soon, along with your lovely household. It is rare I get to converse with such learned and higher-class individuals as yourself. I also welcome the opportunity to meet a fan."

Jhee was loathed to expose her cohort to the woman's snobbery. Yet, an outright refusal would be an insult. Not only would it hamper her investigation and prevent her from examining the archives, but it might also follow them to court. "We had a hard journey. I will see if they are up to it."

"Splendid."

Jhee affected a meek air. "The abbey appears to have been constructed in accordance with sacred geometry tenets, overly elaborate and confusing as if designed by building over serpent trails. That's ascetics for you. Celibacy. A natural crime if you ask me."

Lady Bathsheba laughed. "A natural crime, indeed. My secret. I use maps. One perk of my position as librarian is access to the old building records. I'll ether you a copy."

Jhee's still too full conch refused the transfer.

"Allow me to get you a hand map and a torch." The lady rolled out a digital parchment and transcriber. "A physical copy will serve you better in this weather, anyway. Though it won't have live position tracking. Your recognition of the sacred design of the abbey is correct. We are here now at the Bridge wing off the Prime axis. These are your quarters in the opposite wing. You'll have to cross the central hall again to reach them."

Jhee touched two of the marked openings. "I saw these barred doors in the banquet hall."

"The Corrections Hall. Part museum, part throwback to a stricter time in the Drakists' history where they kept misbehaving Prospectives and Professed. Quite lurid tales of what transpired there exist in the archives. Forbidden orgies, naïve juveniles forced to perform blasphemous rites. Imprints left from the previous residents or maybe even your ghosts. The other leads to the crypts."

Jhee laid a finger on the side of her nose. The abbess had told her the truth. Jhee rolled up the map. "I thank you for this, Lady Bathsheba."

"You'll need a provision card for the storehouse. It also includes an invitation key for your next visit. Remember, orange cider is the key."

Outside in the hall, Jhee adjusted her head wrap and consulted the map; sacred geometry indeed. A quick count and some reasoning revealed the square and hexagon layout of the abbey's original structure to be an unfolded, truncated octahedron. She traced the route to the lady's note marking the guest quarters. Then she traced another to the wing running beside the courtyard. She had no quarrel with Bax's thoroughness, but she wanted to see this windowless storeroom for herself. Her duty demanded she investigate these matters thoroughly for the good of her constituents.

Jhee set off down the hall. A noise swished after her. She whirled. Again, she found no one there.

The Storeroom

Jhee expelled a satisfied sigh at seeing the storeroom entrance. Not bad for a provincial magistrate. She strode boldly into the storeroom, On the way in, she bumped a shelf. A mask of Cheiropthys, the bat-faced Exemplar, fell from the shelf to the ground. She yelped but took a deep breath, so she did not flee the storeroom as boldly as she entered it.

Racks of robes and costumes lined the room. Masks and props hung from any fixture that would hold them. A quick examination of the accessories, hoods, and capes turned up nothing which matched what Jhee saw in the courtyard.

Jhee thought for a moment. She moved aside a chest stored against the outer wall made of coral cement blocks. A good solid thud met everywhere she rapped the pale blocks with her knuckles. She tapped a few more areas and pushed against every visible join, testing for voids and weaknesses. She even ran her fingers along the tiniest cracks and crevices.

The vizier's remarks had hit upon a concern Jhee had tried to suppress: her preoccupation with the capital and personal matters had caused her to fail her constituents. Jhee was hard-pressed to think who had been more self-righteous this evening: her, Lady Bathsheba, or the clergy. She needed to moderate her behavior and remember she was a guest in their place of worship.

A pebble skittered. Jhee reached into the sleeve of her robe for her knife then formed a defensive cyphering gesture. "I warn you I am versed in the combat forms. Best you show yourself now."

Jhee heard movement and whirled around. Bax held up his hands in a placating manner. "Please, ma'am, it's me. Stay your fury."

She slipped her knife back into her robes. "What?"

"Try as I might, I didn't find Hethyr herself. This." Bax pointed at a rack. He held up a pelt and tabard like the one in which Ms. Hethyr had performed. "This, though, was not here when I first checked."

"Without her make-up and costume, Ms. Hethyr may have been hiding in plain sight this whole time. She must have returned here while I tarried with bullies and fools."

Bax frowned.

"Not you, Bax."

"If I may, Justicar, your reaction seems to be extreme?"

Jhee was glad he had the courtesy not to say angry or even shaken. "Feh, this evening had tried every component of my patience. I have a constant feeling of eyes upon me other than my ancestors. To the more immediate matter, other than her costume, what else have you to report of the woman?"

"Ms. Hethyr is, at best, an irregular member of the performance troupe. A vagrant who joins up from time to time, sometimes in the familiar company of Mr. Zane."

"Odd comings and goings. Without other identifiers, we cannot be assured of her identity. The entertainer persona makes a perfect guise for an individual to come and go as she pleases to whatever purpose."

"You think she may be disguised as clergy or a lay sister? You suspect her in the killings of those young boys?"

"Yes." Jhee paused and realized she had not told Bax about that.

"The staff, Justicar. Always talk to them first. Cooks, maids, footmen, and the like will know all the gossip."

"Good to know." Jhee massaged her brow. "Do you know where the performers are staying?"

"Yes, Justicar. Permit me, ma'am. You've had a long and trying day. I pray you to return to Mr. Shep's ministrations."

"I fear he will have cross words for us either way. I cannot rest with my mind bedeviled by so many questions. And if these young men are the victims of some foul play, they've waited for justice long enough."

"You owe them the full power of your faculties, Justicar."

Bax played with the pouch on his belt as if deciding whether to push the matter. Short temper often meant short sight. She decided to rest. "Continue your inquiries with the staff then get some rest too."

He expelled a breath. "Yes, Justicar."

To Jhee's surprise, Kanto awaited her, not Shep. He had moved the glow lamp to the space by the window where he lounged in a dressing robe curled up with his conch on a salon chair, which had replaced one of the stools. With his brow furrowed as he perused his screen, and in the unassuming, dressed-down attire, he looked less the dandy and more the scholar. Mirrei stirred fitfully in the bed, while Shep snored lightly from a billet on the floor. Kanto looked up when she entered the bedchamber.

"Reading a juicy scroller, husband?"

"It's a copy of the Education Bureau report. It got copied over with the judicial archives."

"What might you be doing with your eyes glued to that?"

"I'll have you know I'm interested in cultural things such as ballet, opera, and education. I rather fancied once we reached the capital I could be appointed to an Arts or Education Council."

She quirked her head at the last. "Why stop there? Why not Education Vizier?"

"Why not, indeed?" He set the conch in his lap with a crisp snap and gave a disdainful stare down his snout at her. "Arts and their appreciation are underfunded in our educational programs, especially in places like the Far Reaches. Not everyone can devote as much time to following them as I can. If you're going to make fun, I'd just as soon you direct it elsewhere. We should have Mirrei fix whatever we did to our conchs. Some of your updates keep getting mirrored to mine."

Jhee lowered her head. She sat beside him and touched his forearm. "I'm sorry for being glib and presumptuous. It was disrespectful."

"You're in a foul mood. What has you troubled?"

"Feh, almost too much to list. To start, it seems as though I received a preview of what awaits me at court. A lesson I intend to take to heart."

"How was your tea with the vizier?"

Who do you think gave me the lesson? Jhee bit her tongue before she read statute on the vizier and her elitism. "It went well enough. I did my best not to embarrass you."

She removed her robe and put it on the chair. Kanto held up the dusty, stained clothes. He wrinkled his nose. "Ugh. Really, denbe? Again?"

"My apologies. I pursued a theory *after* tea."

"Fruitful?"

"I don't know yet."

Kanto sidled closer. He gestured at the robe. "Would you like to make this up to me?"

"If I can."

He played with the neckline of her undershirt. "Speak to the vizier about education funding. Find a way to fix it. Being a tutor herself and one of music no less, surely, she can put you in contact with the right people. At the capital, you can impress upon them its importance."

"If I can."

"You could ask her the next time you see her."

She still regretted her dismissive words to him. He was such an admirer of the vizier. His more substantial ask had such a long term, she owed him more immediate amends. "Would you like to ask her yourself?"

"Me?"

"I told her of your respect for her work and your skill with the lute. She asked if our household would like to attend her later."

She handed him the invitation key. His eyes lit up. "I'll start composing a reply immediately. And locating appropriate attire."

"Hold until the morning after we've had a proper tuck away."

7

THE SPIRES

~

The High Spires

"We have tea with the vizier tonight, don't forget," Kanto reminded her in the morning.

"Dinner with a vizier and famous music tutor," Mirrei said. She popped a saline pill. "How exciting."

"Tonight?" Shep asked.

"Yes, it's a family night," Kanto said.

"Jhee swapped days so she could deal with yacht repairs."

"No one told me. It'd be an insult to cancel now that we've confirmed."

Jhee covered her esca. Yesterday had been Shep's day. They had swapped it with her open day, which should have been today so she could attend to the yacht repairs. She often spent the free days with him anyway. She had only glanced at the invite key since she had not intended to accept. She took Shep's hand. "Are you up to this?" she whispered.

He glanced at Kanto and Mirrei discussing outfits. "You don't suppose he did it deliberately?"

"Regardless, I will respect your wishes. Insult or not."

"Mirrei's perked up. They're both so looking forward to it. I've had years with you all by my lonesome, I can spare some of it for them."

"You know, I hadn't wanted to do this at all. One tea was enough, but I erred with Kanto and thought this would smooth it over."

"Shall I draft marriage contracts and bring quills?"

"For the vizier? I should hope not. Besides, do you want to be the one to explain to Lady Kaydence how we married her precious jewel to a cloistered hermit?"

Shep grimaced. "Good point."

"Fancy some investigating together like we used to?"

"I wouldn't feel comfortable leaving them unguarded. See to your duties, Jhee."

Shep patted her hand and joined the others in picking out clothes.

Once Jhee and company had eaten a light morning meal, they took advantage of the Maker Shrine in the designated courtyard to do their morning devotions. Kanto sketched off alone by himself while she and Mirrei did their lessons with Shep as their pacesetter.

"What did you and Kanto quarrel about now?" Mirrei asked. "His mood changed suddenly. He's been rather sulky, not his usual upbeat self."

"No crosstalk," Jhee replied.

"My time. My topics."

"We've only spoken or even seen each other today in passing."

"In passing, today. Not so last night."

"Nothing is happening with us."

Mirrei raised an eyebrow. "The root problem. Make something happen. Put aside your reservations. Teach him casting."

"I'm hardly a proper teacher."

"It hasn't stopped you with me."

"Men, men are different. Besides, I can hardly do so here, can I?"

"Sounds like excuses."

"I'll talk to him later, though, if it will ease your bothered mind."

Mirrei tapped the tip of Jhee's nose. "It would. That is all I ask. We shall speak no more of the menfolk for the remainder of our appointment."

"Clear and center your mind," Jhee said.

Jhee and Mirrei shook out their arms. Jhee instructed Mirrei how to plant her feet wide and drop her weight in to ensure she could not be uprooted while cyphering. Using his old battle drum and heavy striker, Shep beat it to set the tempo. They practiced grounding themselves for several minutes.

"Focus on directing your weight down through your anchoring gears."

When she instructed Mirrei in the cyphering forms, the forces trembled and echoed. Some residual effect from the tremors on the subtle energies. If the healing powers of this place weren't pure fancy, what impact might it have on the prime forces one drew on while cyphering? Was there, more method than mania to the restrictions?

Flowers and Maker geld decorated the rubble in a section of the courtyard with no effigies. Was this where they found the Prospective crushed by falling debris? No trace of high velocity spatter. Jhee shielded her eyes as she scanned up the length of the spires. They cast long shadows. Brilliant, emerald and ruby coral clashed with those ghastly statues. Her mind began to work out the angles and trajectories required for anything which fell from a tower to land here or in the water.

Next she knew, she had her conch out. Mirrei and Shep cleared their throats. Jhee tucked it back in her robes.

Mirrei hugged Jhee's arm. "Someone died here."

"You'd be hard-pressed to find a patch of ground on or over which someone hasn't died," Shep replied.

"At some point," Kanto said, "but not weeks ago. No wonder the residents whisper about hauntings."

Jhee narrowed her eyes at the courtyard's far wall. Had she merely imagined what she saw at the courtyard shrine?

"Spirits and echoes of the past abound here," the prioress said.

The prioress approached Jhee.

"The abbess instructed me to give you a tour of the abbey," the prioress said. "She said you spoke about it after the feast."

"That we did."

The tour began at the gardens near their courtyard. They found Sister Serra overlooking a sparse contingent of Prospectives tending an herb garden.

"Justicar, what a lovely surprise. I was just about to make my rounds of the orchards and vineyards. Would you like me to explain to you our operations?"

"Please, denbe, can we?" Mirrei asked.

As much as Jhee would have liked to, she thought about how it might affect Mirrei to take a long journey in this damp. She wished she had had the presence of mind to see the litter prepared for their excursion. "Perhaps later."

Mirrei pouted.

Sister Serra took notice of her reaction. "A tour of the agri-pods then?"

Mirrei glimmered her eyes at Jhee. Jhee smiled. "Lead the way," Jhee said.

"One thing first." Sister Serra pulled out a magnifier and examined a vine bearing shriveled grapes.

"What are you looking for?" Mirrei asked.

"Noble rot."

Shep whispered to Mirrei, who asked, "For a new wine?"

Serra raised her head from the bunch. "Might as well put this mold and mildew to productive use. You know about viticulture?"

"Not as much I'd like. Why a new wine rather than increase production of Tranquility Gold?"

"The soil tutelaries responsible for the unique flavor of Tranquility Gold only inhabit the slopes. Not only is that area hard to work, but it's also at capacity. We can add the sweeter wines, which can only be made from grapes afflicted by a certain fungus, to our list of offerings."

Sister Serra winked. Jhee moved forward. Shep laid a hand on her wrist.

"Very sensible. I'm most interested in your sustainability and vertical farming."

"Blight destroyed part of our crops last year. Some affected fields became rice paddies. If we can increase the yields on the pods, we can protect them from the extreme weather."

Jhee stopped at a trellis of beige, wrinkled melons interlaced amongst spindly, vivid sea-green vines. The lattice occupied a sunny corner of the garden, not far from an apple tree and work shed. Underneath the tree, a stone memorial bench had been erected.

"Ha, lace root melons," Kanto exclaimed. He slipped between Jhee and Shep.

"This was one of Saheli's favorite spots."

"Secluded," Jhee said.

"She used to counsel many Prospectives here in private."

"Not entirely in private," the prioress said.

"Private enough. I didn't mean it like that."

"I'm sure you didn't."

"It saddened me to hear of Saheli's passing," Jhee said.

Their tour group rode a hand-operated lift up the agri-pod tower.

Sister Serra pointed across the way. "I saw her up there that day. She hailed me in the pods as normal. Then like that, she passed to the Makers."

The prioress scoffed. Jhee faked astonishment. "Is that where…?"

"A storm blew in after Saheli made the climb. We checked on her and found her passed out with the tower door open. Nectar drink and sticky paw prints everywhere. Drenched cat tore up the herb garden while we helped Saheli. It was good about keeping the crab-rats out but ate almost anything."

After Serra showed them about the agri-pods, they returned to the herb garden.

"What's up next on the agenda, Justicar?" Serra asked.

"The archives."

"Lethys's luck to you with that. Careful Justicar, you committed the most grievous of sins. You failed to condemn me one too many times. You'll be lucky if she lets you anywhere near the reliquary now."

The Middle Spire

The prioress brought their group to the archival wing. While there, Jhee decided to improve her map. A structure this old and storied was bound to have many hidden architectural features. She had best get started learning them now. She might be able to find the building plans, island survey maps, and tide charts somewhere in their records. By the time their company reached the archives, Jhee had to keep her hands tucked in her robes to keep them still.

The archivist popped her head out from behind an enormous book stand when Jhee and her entourage entered the library. The archivist's desk guarded the staircase to what appeared the only entrance to the library and reliquary proper. Anyone who wanted entry had to go through her.

She sniffed. "You."

"Sister Elkanah," Jhee said.

"What do you want?"

The prioress answered, "The abbess asked that I give the Justicar and her family a tour of the abbey."

"I, also, thought perhaps you might show us around your magnificent archive," Jhee said.

Sister Elkanah sniffed again. She directed a most scathing glare at the two men in Jhee's entourage. It wilted in comparison to the one she reserved for Jhee.

"We're quite busy."

Jhee glanced around at the mostly empty library. A few Professed and the odd Prospective occupied the rows of desks which at one point might have housed hundreds. Many tables bore scratches and peeling surfaces. One section, though, boasted new, gleaming counters with good indirect lighting.

The archivist tucked the book she had been reading under her arm. As they passed by the head desk, a knot formed in Jhee's stomach when she saw the archivist had several copies of Jhee's fictionalized account of her travels with Jeja of Marpele, "Dispatches from Arrow Point," arrayed on it.

"I take it you had time to review my requests again."

"I have. I had some concerns." The archivist stopped at the threshold of the archives and faced Jhee, the book she carried now fully visible. The faded cover of her grandmamere's screed on marriage, politics, and race confronted her. Jhee's stomach dropped through the floor. She almost smelled her hopes of extended time in the archives going up in smoke. "Quite controversial notions to be exposed to so young. A concern I had when I initially viewed your proposals."

"You looked into my family history."

"I was made aware of it and yours." The archivist held her chin up high. "Seeing firsthand, you do not hold to your family's controversial views on marriage, at least, has assuaged them. Nothing leaves the archives."

"May anyone who takes holy orders access the archives?"

"Yes."

Jhee continued when Sister Elkanah didn't elaborate. "I couldn't help but notice your carrels and duplicators. You do transcription and manuscript copying. I wondered if I might copy some of Thaedra's works. I understand you have some of the original founding texts, as well as one of the earliest reproductions of Thaedra's cyphering manuals and schematics. I heard of its famed translucent pages which glimmer in the light."

"Exposure to light and the elements can be extremely damaging to the text. Access to it is even more restricted. Duplication is on a case by case basis. While we have duplicators and conch image capture stations, not everything can be exposed to such direct lighting."

"Understandable. I might be honored to even see it from a distance."

"It's best not to be too enamored of the trappings of earthly wonders. The true wonders are the miracles of the Makers. Thaedra's schematics, while impressive, are the work of mere mortals. I debate they should even be housed with our most sacred of relics."

"You hold, then there is no divine inspiration to her discovery."

"We must concern ourselves more with following the path, which leads to reconciliation with the Makers. They are mostly secular works and, as such, must be put in proper context with respect to the teachings of the Makers. No males allowed in the arcane archives whatsoever or near our most sacred relics."

"Not even to provide more hands for transcription and preservation."

"The rough handling of their coarse, ungainly hands is as liable to pulverize as preserve our sacred relics. Women's slender, more graceful fingers are perfect for capturing the nuances of scripture and formulae and the fine art of restoration. No, the most sacred books and relics are reserved for the eyes of women alone. Particularly given the vast array of arcane knowledge they contain."

Jhee tucked her hands in her robes. This place and their backward rules. Kanto tugged on Jhee's sleeve and shook his head.

"My family and I considered an outing to explore the grounds and island a bit. Would it be possible to view any survey maps of the area? Or travelogues and traveler's accounts?"

"This isn't some holiday resort and the library some brochure center."

Sister Elkanah was pricklier than a pufferfish. Jhee usually had wheedled her way to the off-line catalogs by now. It didn't help the woman pierced her pressure points.

"What of the works of previous abbesses? I saw an example of Saheli's artwork outside the vizier's chambers. I heard some of her artworks along with her final sermon are housed here in the archives."

Kanto nodded at Jhee.

"I'm afraid males are not permitted to enter this part of the sanctum. Your husbands are welcome to wait here for us. We can circle back and pick them up later."

Kanto stepped up, "Denbe, denme and I need to choose outfits for tea with the vizier."

"The vizier?"

"Oh yes, Sister Elkanah," Kanto said. "My esteemed wife took tea with her last night. She invited us to dine with her tonight."

"Well, if the vizier, will allow you around her antiques, she must be reasonably confident you won't damage them."

"Nice to see the archives suffered minimal damage in the quake. Were you there during Saheli's final sermon?"

"All the most prestigious residents were."

Sister Elkanah drummed her fingers against the cover of grandmamere's book.

"Forgive my overstepping at the feast, Sister Elkanah. Sometimes my passion for Mechanism gets the better of me. What I really might like to read are histories about the island and the Mist Abbess."

"You'd do better to read the Cyclogenesis Sermons."

A recommendation tantamount to calling Jhee impious. She counted to three before she spoke again. "Who's your preferred sage? Kaerderon's my personal favorite. Perhaps you'd guide me to where they're kept."

"I don't have time for you now."

"It's important work you do here. Preserving all this history." Jhee moved to some structure prints and arcane manuals on a carrel stand. "Are these old, renovation plans for the abbey? This must be the original designs of the Coral Cloister. And this, the vertical farming tower. Does this describe the preservation process?"

Sister Elkanah slammed the screed on a desk. "I thought you were taking a tour. Then be about your business and leave me to mine."

Access to the archives had been within Jhee's grasp. She cast a forlorn glance at them and the archivist as the three left. Was Sister Elkanah's extreme reaction to the topic of the Mist Abbess more sinister than pious?

The Twin Spires

Every time Jhee wanted to inquire more into the details of the deaths, she remembered she had Mirrei with her.

"Are there lifts in the spires?"

"Stairs," replied the prioress.

Mirrei's labored breathing filled the corridor.

"Star Mirror," Jhee said, using Mirrei's outside name, "would you like me to have someone escort you back to the room so you can prepare?"

Mirrei curtsied. "If my denbe thinks that's best."

"I do."

Mirrei took her leave.

"I'll show you where Saheli died."

Jhee's conscience tugged at her start with the Prospectives' deaths. She considered exploring the isle and the place where the Prospective had drowned, but she should stay within the grounds so she would not be late for tea. "Would you show me to the Beach Tower?"

"Saheli collapsed in the Bridge Tower."

"I'm aware."

The prioress brought her to the Beach axis of the abbey, where they climbed the long, spiral stairway to the top. She unlocked a door, which led to a rotunda. Archways had been carved out and fitted with ornate railings to prevent mishaps.

"Is this door locked at all times?" The door did not show signs of forced entry. It had a flimsy lock that would not have taken much effort to prize it open.

"Usually, but it would not take much to open. We find many Prospectives and Professed come up here to think and reflect. Much like the *other* spire, which was one of Saheli's favorite places to seek solitude and contemplation."

Thick layers of pollen covered everything. Most of the footprints weren't recent, with Jhee's and the prioress's the only new ones. Jhee trailed her finger through the pitted, green dust covering the railing. That spoke of several cycles of rain and drying since anyone had wiped it. She tried to conceive a logical explanation. "You did not think it unusual for the Prospective to have come up here alone?"

"Alone, yes. If I may be candid, some come up here for much more unseemly pursuits, which is why we had to start locking it. The abbess and I possess the only keys and sign it out as needed to those who petition for its use."

Jhee dusted off her hands. The pollen had begun to bring tears to her eyes. "Are we so sure he was alone?"

"I keep the bed check. All the other Prospectives and Professed were accounted for."

"What of the senior clergy?"

"What exactly are you implying, Justicar?"

"I'm trying to learn the positions of bodies in the system." Jhee thought of what she had seen at the shrine. "All Prospectives are accounted for now?"

The prioress sucked her teeth. "Yes. And none are missing limbs, either."

"Mind if I have a moment alone to explore the spire a bit?"

The prioress gave a curt bow before stepping out. This spire afforded a fantastic view of the glory and majesty of the sea, the only power greater than oneself. Isles dotted the landscape off until forever: The Blessed Isles. She savored the salt on her lips. The view used to be all crystal blue waves and white sandy beaches at this time of day. She imagined how calm and meditative this place would be in clear weather.

The Blessed Isles. How many of those isles would remain once this was done? Lost to wind and erosion from the drenched shield. She remembered how far out you could see from the top rooms of her mountain home. No, she thought. They needed the shield to protect them from invaders who would violate their water boundaries and terrorize their lands. The barbarian threat was real. Yet, should they fight their own brother and sister races? Is that really part of the First Maker's Design? The shield was best for them and us. It removed the temptation to war.

Jhee pulled out her conch to note her findings. No signal and still almost full. She peered at the hillside underneath the spire. Around the edge of the bluff, she thought she could see flickering lights. The sea wisps?

She joined the prioress on the stairs. "Show me the Bridge Tower, please."

The prioress brought her to the other high spire. So many stairs. The space atop its height resembled the other except well kept. Archways had likewise been carved and fitted with railings. All except one which led to a little overhanging platform. The wind howled and rain pattered against the roof before accumulating to drip down onto the floor.

A view, as breathtaking as, the climb greeted Jhee. Jhee rested against the low rail. One overlooked nearly the whole isle from here. This spire's twin and the taller Storm Light Spire partially blocked the view. No doubt from the storm light deck little escaped notice. Mighty sea. High bluffs. Wetlands.

The Far Reaches, her household's home district or *nome*, existed near the recently constructed perpetual Storm Shield. It was remote even by the Outer Reaches' standards, quite literally the far end of the Reaches. It came as a shock to no one that the first phase of the Storm Shield project would run through their waters.

The billowing mass of the storm shield dominated the horizon. Lightning flashes from within brightened its ever-present glow. She squinted against an occasional glint from the solar array field when lightning escaped the bounds of the shield. Beautiful, vibrancy hid underneath new and near-constant fog and mellowing gray. The bright, cheery isle now plagued by storm and rain. Even when not storming, claustrophobic cloud cover persisted. How much more spectacular the view must have been before the shield? At the right time of day, in better weather, the light would be perfect for painting and photography. "Saheli made this climb, how often?"

"Every day, including the day of her transfiguration."

"She must have been most fit." Jhee pointed at scorched roofing tiles. "Is this where she ascended?"

"No, sometimes the reflections from a misaligned solar array get too hot."

Jhee held tight to the rough, coral arch as she inched out onto the overhang. She found paint splotches and some scratches from Saheli's easel and tripod. A little lean—more than Jhee found comfortable—gave a good over-view of the domed hothouses. She gave a sigh once safely back on the landing.

"Fit and fearless." Further in the distance, away from the town proper, ramshackle huts and cook fires dotted the landscape. "Those are the refugee camps?"

The prioress's perpetual frown deepened. "The loss of landmass and rapid erosion near the storm zone has driven many closer and closer to high ground such as Torilsisle."

"The same happened on my home isle." Jhee remembered the prioress's comments about supplicants. "Many seek to take holy orders?"

"Saheli encouraged it. Pyrmo has been more restrictive. Males in particular."

"Strange so many young men taking vows."

"Those refugees left their homes for better lives. As a larger isle, Torilsisle has game enough and land for crops and flower beds. It is in no danger of being lost to the sea, which is why it sees so many on their way to elsewhere. The capital will not be able to accommodate them all. With proper education and training, some may find work on the shield or in mining. Some have made the calculation; it might be better to stay at places such as this."

"I've seen some of the places in the Far Reaches. The abbey is indeed an improvement from what many might normally expect."

The prioress expression and tone softened. "More than that, Justicar, as laypeople or charity cases, what we provided them was much more limited. Many joined the abbey to have full bellies. The abbey makes use of who it can. The refugees are cheap labor for fishing and farming. As Prospectives, they get an education, better quality food and accommodation, and to serve the Makers as they will."

"In that light, it does make much more sense." Jhee noted this on her conch. She returned to the platform and held her conch aloft. "High spires. High bluffs. So many dangerous heights on this isle."

"It protects our privacy and allows us forewarning should trouble come our way. With enough of us being veterans, I suspect any coming to do us harm as in the raiding days would no longer find us such easy prey."

"I suspect not. How long have you been prior?"

"I was raised to the priory upon Pyrmo's appointment as abbess. She held the position before me."

"Was it you who found Saheli collapsed?"

"Sister Serra. I arrived soon after. The horticulturist claims she came to return her cat. I insisted we take Saheli to the infirmary. Both claimed it unnecessary. Perhaps if I had been more insistent."

Jhee noted that too. Another failed transfer notice greeted her.

The prioress scowled. "Am I boring you?"

"I'm listening. I thought maybe I could get a signal out. Any updates on the antenna?"

"It's been too overcast. For a strong signal, try the solar array fields or storm light tower."

"Would you show me to where Saheli transcended?"

The prioress's stern expression returned. "This way."

The Coral Cloister Lesson Hall presented such an unremarkable backdrop to such a remarkable event. Clean-boards for instruction faced worn benches and chairs. Jhee considered how one might get from here to the courtyards or the abbess's chamber.

"What time of day was it when she transcended?"

"Afternoon."

"Any idea why Saheli collapsed?"

"Heatstroke? Dehydration? The double sunlight can become intense on clear days."

"Forward-thinking to have fruit beer on hand. Saheli must have gotten so engrossed in her work she forgot to drink some. What do you think about these rumors of the Mist Abbess?"

The prioress's face lost expression. "The abbey's history has not always been a peaceful one. When the barbarians sacked it, they slaughtered lesser spouses and children who had hidden here for safety. Prior to that, it was controlled by the Middle Pillarists during the atrocities. In those days, it was called Swordbridge. The Drakist Adepts renamed it along with what we now call the Beach Tower."

"Adepts? Yet, you eschew arcana."

"Our abbey was originally founded by ex-soldiers who had turned to the ways of spiritual reflection. Yet the space remembers. They say the barrier between the first realms of the dead and last realms of the living is thin here."

Jhee started calculating angles of reflections. "First Maker's Folly, is that the time? I'm afraid I must interrupt the tour. Would we be able to see the storm light tower tomorrow?"

"A second day away from my duties is unacceptable."

"Thank you for your assistance. I shall let the First Makers' Design guide my steps then."

8

FAMILY TEATIME

~

Make for Make

"You're late," Kanto said. "And you look a fright."

"I know, I know."

The small washbasin on a nearby table showed he had anticipated tardiness. Kanto spared her a frown but did not pause the painstaking process of lacquering Mirrei's nails. His had been freshly touched up and colored to complement his turquoise outfit. She cleaned herself while the rest of her cohort dressed in silence. Every now and then Kanto set the lacquer bottle down with a punctuated thud.

Kanto approached to brush her hair. Her headache had returned. When she began favoring the bridge of her nose, Mirrei appeared from nowhere again with the poultice.

After eying the poultice briefly, Kanto checked the time and sighed.

"You wore one the last time you saw her. We'll pretend it's your look." He found a scarf to match the robes he had chosen for her. "Early is on time and on time is late. I swear if we insult the vizier…"

Despite Kanto's fears, they arrived fashionably early. However, Mirrei alone spoke to her during the trip. Kanto was giving her the felled fish routine while Shep was Shep. He detested visits such as this. Both had brought an item to showcase their talents: Kanto his lute and Shep his kalacha war club, a further reason for him to be ill at ease.

Lady Bathsheba welcomed them with the more formal bows rather than forearm clasps.

"Your prompt response to my invitation was an unexpected delight. The watermarks, so elegant: Star Mirror, Bright Harmony, Dawn Wolf. Outside naming. Such formality. You are, indeed, a quaint cohort. I took the liberty of having a meal prepared."

"All honors to you, Lady Bathsheba, and I took the liberty of providing entertainment."

Make for Make. The tea table had been extended to make room for five. Opposite the table, a little performance chair had been set out. Kanto and Shep displayed the lute and kalacha on it for later. Lady Bathsheba gave Jhee and her senior spouse pride of place to either side with her juniors seated farthest away. Kanto offered to pour the tea. After tea and pleasantries, her spouses set up to perform.

Mirrei performed a Stations-of-the-Moons cypher. Jhee mouthed along as Mirrei performed each station flawlessly as they had practiced so many times. When she found herself miming along as well, she stilled herself. While the cypher was overly elaborate for what it did, it demonstrated many of the fundamental skills and techniques of the craft. At the close, the vase emitted a shower of shimmering cherry blossoms instead of the usual sparkles. Translucent blossom illusions evaporated as they landed upon the rug. The Stations-of-the-Moons was one of the required entrance cyphers for the magic program at the academy. A wide grin overtook Jhee. She, Lady Bathsheba, and Shep clapped in appreciation. Jhee perhaps with too much animation. She calmed herself when she saw Shep snicker. Kanto hovered about the edges, appearing whenever their teacups emptied.

Shep came to her aid with a distraction. "I must compliment the vizier on your collection of relics. Is that Hymn to Toril scrollwork on those aprons?"

"Indeed, it is. You have a discerning eye."

Next, Shep took center stage to perform a battle stomp. Kanto had retired to the wings to sketch and prepare for his performance. Shep looked to Jhee before he began. She gave a slight smile and nod of encouragement. He performed one of the stomps their old unit did for inspections or when dignitaries came to visit.

"Your performance of Stations-of-the-Moon was simply masterful, my dear."

"The vizier is most kind. It's thanks in no small part to denbe's excellent tutelage." Mirrei gave Jhee demure eye twinkles then a wink. Perhaps the young woman laid it on a bit thick.

Lady Bathsheba unfurled the finger maze on the table. "Justicar, I hope you don't mind me bringing out the finger maze you admired so much on your last visit. You and Star Mirror might be interested in trying it together."

Jhee and Mirrei finger cast through the levels of the finger maze. Lady Bathsheba watched with a visage of barely contained excitement. "She hopes to teach my fellow junior spouse as well. Denye's as likely to flourish under her direction as I am."

Lady Bathsheba regarded them with a bemused expression. "Nonsense. The subtleties, the nuance, the grace required of cyphering is too taxing for the male character. Common elemental grunt work is the only training suitable for men. Could you imagine if men were as proficient with fire as women? They'd fireball everything in sight."

"Yet, some men are proficient with fire and have yet to burn the place down."

"I owe that to most of the empire being on water."

With the question thoroughly answered as to whether Mirrei and Lady Bathsheba would get on, Jhee changed the subject. "How long have you resided here, Lady Bathsheba?"

"Longer than I want to admit. I retired from court after the death of my third husband. What a talented cohort you have. You have your males well-trained and well-appointed. A state I had not expected given our previous meeting. The traditional figure of your anchor spouse shows the markers of virility and fitness. I never quite went in for silver fangs myself. He does, however, make me see the appeal. Shame about his eye, though. Was it a consequence of his military service?"

"The vizier is quite astute."

"His tattoos and the recognition of the scrollwork. I've been around quite a few veterans."

Kanto began a performance of Freedom Flight, a challenging piece meant to impress.

"Your Kanto, on the other hand."

They lapsed into appreciative silence while he played. Kanto finished with a flourish. Lady Bathsheba clapped thunderously.

"Thank you, my dear. Your playing…. There are no words. Handsome, talented, and a connoisseur of tea. Such talent and good breeding. Rare jewels found in such a remote district. You will fit right in at court."

"Thank you. Such high praise. The vizier is most kind," Kanto said. He and Shep bowed then returned to the table.

"Come. Sit beside me." Lady Bathsheba and Kanto turned Jhee's way. She inclined her head. "Where did you learn to play so brilliantly?"

"Tutors. Though I am largely self-taught. Our corner of the district is so far off the main lanes. Not too many tutors were willing to make the journey. Certainly, none as brilliant or prestigious as you, my lady. My family could spare the expense. I was an exception. My dames were always great matrons of the arts. I was talking to my honored wife about improving the state of education in our district, particularly regarding art and music."

"Talented and civic-minded. This one is such a flatterer. Makes me feel almost like a young woman again. Justicar, I might have to borrow him from you." Lady Bathsheba drank from her teacup and nodded approvingly. "A perfect pour, precisely spiced. Hard to do with this blend."

"Thank you, Vizier. Black forest tea has such a dominant flavor; it must be delicately treated, so it does not overpower."

"My goodness, I just noticed the lovely foil work on your nails. I'm amazed it didn't get damaged in your playing."

"The trick is to apply another layer of lacquer once it has properly set up."

The two laughed and got on famously. Whenever the Lady so much as held out her cup, Kanto rushed to refill it. Shep from his newly demoted position gave Jhee another smirk. Perhaps Jhee had been too fast to rule out a match between Kanto and the vizier. Yet, she imagined the conversation with Lady Kaydence. Trapped at the isolated abbey with these sexist women was surely not what his grandmamere had in mind. The abbey was a woefully inappropriate place for him. This place is too small for her husband. She was too small for her husband. And if she were to be so selfish, the match held little socio-political advantage for her.

Jhee occupied herself during Lady Bathsheba's distraction with a closer look at the room details. The martial theme to the decor had not been what she expected from a music tutor. A jostle caused the finger maze to slip. She caught the finger maze and placed it with some architectural plans for an archive expansion on a nearby table. The speckled texture of a ritual collar gave her pause.

"Such sumptuous robes, this time, Justicar. Was it something I said?"

"No, Lady Bathsheba," Jhee said, then finished in her head, *it wasn't one snobbish thing you said it was everything.* She returned her attention to her companions. She hid her mouth with her cup so Lady Bathsheba would not see her frown. The Lady Bathshebas of the world did not worry about having much younger husbands. They viewed husbands as pets. There would be more women like this in the capital. Not the ideal situation she wished for Kanto. In the end, it would be his choice.

One insurmountable concern outweighed the others for Jhee. Someone here may have killed Saheli and the young men. Even if the deaths weren't murders, the clergy had little love for anyone save themselves.

"In my indelicate way, I thought I was doing you a favor. My warnings about court were not hyperbole. I also sought to test you. Conscientious officials are not always the norm. Are you also, a veteran?"

"Intelligence pool."

"Wealthy enough for your family to position you away from real danger." Jhee sipped some more tea. "Please, don't take that wrong. As an official, a vizier, I had a way out of combat. Like yourself. Someone as fearless and civic-minded as yourself, I might have thought you'd get a commission to the navy."

"I prefer solid ground."

Lady Bathsheba studied Jhee for a moment. "I continue to scandalize you. A privilege of getting older is no longer concerning yourself with trivia, niceties, or conventions. Those are young woman's cares and concern of court. I live a more rustic life here."

A Gracious Host

Their assembly ate a most excellent meal of crispy pork, braised rice and onions, yams, kale and fennel salad, and a marvelous poached tuna, accompanied by a humble decanter of Tranquility Bridge's Light. As expected, Mirrei favored generous helpings of salad and heavily salted pork in avoidance of the starch and other animal proteins.

"Pascoe standards. No land meat. Did I get it correct?"

Jhee dabbed her mouth with a napkin. "You did, my lady."

Lady Bathsheba addressed Mirrei, "Your wife mentioned you are into dietetics. Are you whose palate we are accommodating?"

"I'm afraid I can't take all the credit, Vizier."

"Was everything to your satisfaction, gentlemen?"

"The crispy pork was cooked to perfection," Kanto said.

Shep nodded enthusiastically. "It helps when you start with such prime cuts."

"It seems the privation which hit the rest of the isles has yet to do so here," Mirrei said. Jhee winced. Kanto pinched Mirrei just under the table. She twitched. "Everything was wonderful, Vizier."

"Yet, you did not touch most of the dishes."

"I'm watching my saline levels."

"Fresh Lung?"

"A mild case."

"Your Star Mirror is a true daughter of the sea, Justicar. Did you try the draught I suggested? I hear it works wonders on Fresh Lung as well."

"Not yet, my lady."

Lady Bathsheba twisted her napkin. "Make sure you do so soon."

"Have you spoken to the archivist yet?"

"It might take some more time. Elkanah has proved obstinate. You must have really barnacled her keel."

"Thank you, Lady Bathsheba, for hosting us," Mirrei said. "Might I ask from what home isle do you hail?"

"I am from Wilobeia."

"Of course! home isle of this magnificent tea. And if I remember my biology and geography correctly: Cheiropthys, the batfish or batwing maye, and Maate-Kheru Wilobeian, violet harvest nut, one of various plants called seed of enlightenment. Isn't everything on Wilobeia poisonous? My biology tutor joked it was like everything on the isle was trying to kill everything else."

"A studious one. I see why you and your denbe are so well-suited. How are your cyphering studies? Are you familiar with the basics of gyration?"

Mirrei grinned. "Complete with veiled hoods and protective circles for the menfolk. Talk about your ancient knowledge."

Jhee swallowed her bite of yam and wiped her mouth. "It's the tradition. I'd do you a disservice if I didn't instruct you in the proper forms and etiquette. Though, I try to adhere to more modern Mechanist methods."

"Ancients sometimes have knowledge we don't. We weren't here first. There are beings older than us. Forces beyond our comprehension. Not just in this abbey, but in the cosmos; beings older than when we emerged and slapped the title of Maker on everything. Remember it wasn't us who aligned the worlds and the moons."

"You speak of the First Ones, the Prototypes. A closer stream of distant knowledge intrigues me more. I heard a strange term, Mist Abbess. Does that mean anything to you?"

"A mythical figure who once ruled the island. I hear tale of a resurgence in her blood cult. They seek to revive the practices of the old days and bring back the sacrifices and orgies. There are tales of strange figures walking the halls at all hours of day or night. Perhaps these are the ghosts that you claimed to have seen. Nothing supernatural. Simply all too mortal beings bent on resurrecting their heretical deities. Rumors abound of strange lights and figures seen about the abbey and on the island. Hints of cultish, pagan rites being performed in the now."

"Surely you do not believe in the Last Hunt, Lady Bathsheba?"

"I believe they believe it. Which is more than enough."

"For someone who doesn't believe, this appears to unsettle you."

"I don't know about the deacons' malign forces or restless spirits, but I do know something's amiss here with respect to casting. You've been practicing here. Have you noticed the difference to the prime forces?"

"My cyphering did feel off."

"The abbey's restrictions on arcana have deep roots."

"How so?"

"The coral edifice showcases examples of the earliest preserving arcana used to speed the mineralization process and fetter the dead. The reliquary, much like shrines, serves to accumulate ancestral power. This abbey is a giant spirit battery, Justicar. Perhaps the lights seen on the marsh was just illicit revelers and pranksters. Or perhaps it's from some far deeper and darker powers from which this isle draws its healing energy. The ichor of a power which sleeps beneath the isle."

Jhee took the initiative to lighten the mood and steer the conversation toward less existential topics.

"Husbands, if you would delight us again with your skills."

"It is my honor, denbe," Kanto said. "Any particular piece?"

"Do you perchance know The Strawberry Letters?" Lady Bathsheba asked.

Kanto tuned his lute. Shep took up a position beside the chair.

"Would you happen to have any maps of the island?" Jhee asked.

"I have. Over here."

"I'd be delighted to see them, Lady Bathsheba."

Lady Bathsheba walked Jhee to a corner of her chambers. She opened a giant sharkskin bound atlas and leafed through it. "Do you still have the map I gave you? I have a few landmarks you might find interesting."

"Indeed."

"Here, have a close look at this one." Jhee leaned toward the bound volume. The vizier marked the map with several court symbols. At Jhee's puzzled look, the lady whispered, "We're not alone. I suspect I'm being watched. I've heard odd sounds while supposedly alone. You must forgive my behavior in our previous meeting, Justicar. I didn't know who might be listening or if you could be trusted. I thought it better for eavesdroppers to think us at odds."

"The lady is most wise," Jhee said. She glanced around now, suddenly paranoid rather than annoyed. At Jhee's nod, Shep whispered in Kanto's ear then performed a simpler, but louder battle stomp as accompaniment.

"The atmosphere here changed once Saheli was appointed. We had all expected it to be Pyrmo. I don't think the high clergy accepted the Chief Abbess chose an outsider. Beyond fell rumors of orgies and malign forces, the name you mentioned, the Mist Abbess, resurfaced shortly thereafter."

Jhee pursed her lips.

"I discovered these poking around the archives after we last met."

Jhee looked closely and found a proposal and blueprints for commercializing the orchards and vineyards, submitted by Sister Serra.

"Who else knows about these?"

"If I found these in the archives, it would be the easiest task in the world for Elkanah to as well." Lady Bathsheba quickly rolled up the map and snatched up the glow orb. "No. I've said too much."

Jhee gently touched her arm. "No. Please, continue."

"There's a possibility I hesitate to entertain. I'm not so sure my accident was an accident."

"Forgive my impertinence, Lady Bathsheba, but I must ask. Where were you during the other deaths?"

"Of course. I would expect no less. I was here in my chambers."

Jhee frowned and said, "All three?"

"Not a very good alibi. I know. Wait, when Prospective Leigh drowned, I had jammed a toe and was being treated at the infirmary. The physician or her assistant should be able to verify I stayed there until morning."

"I will check this out and get back to you."

"Please, do. The sooner you rule me out, the sooner you can focus on who might have committed these horrible crimes."

Mirrei's eyelids fluttered. She slumped in her chair. Jhee immediately rushed over. "Are you unwell?"

"Just somewhat achy and light-headed. I must have eaten something that didn't agree with me."

"Perhaps we should retire for the evening?"

"Will you be able to manage by yourselves, or should we seek out assistance?" Lady Bathsheba asked.

"I can make it," Mirrei said. "No need to fuss."

Before they left, Lady Bathsheba pressed several signets into her hand.

"Justicar, you might need these, if you're serious about education. For as long as you are here, feel free to visit and talk as you desire. I enjoy the reminders you give me of court. Such a joy to have those closer to my station to converse with and possibly a kindred spirit. Now, you must go quickly and return to your husbands and wife. Hug them and cherish them for dark days may be upon us again."

9
—————

THE CLERGY

~

The Infirmary

As their cohort journeyed back to their room, Jhee kept a slow pace. Kanto and Mirrei had their arms linked with hers. Shep lagged. Jhee mused on the details of the case in between checking on Mirrei. Kanto was all grins and had a bounce to his step.

"No need to keep such a slow pace for me," Mirrei said. "I'm feeling better already."

"No rush after such an exquisite meal," Jhee said.

"Too exquisite."

Kanto eyed Mirrei. "A shame we had to cut the evening short."

"I, for one, had had enough. Not the least because of all those ghastly relics and artwork on the walls."

"Reminders of a more savage time," Shep said.

"Now you sound like the lady," Jhee said.

"I have a small confession to make, denbe," Mirrei said. "I thought you could use a reason to leave."

"I knew it," Kanto said. "You little liar."

"It wasn't quite a lie. Her outdated views and elitism had begun to make me ill. You wouldn't believe the things she said while you and Shep performed. I wasn't sure if I could stomach another moment of flattering her."

"Clever girl. I had grown rather tired with the evening myself."

Mirrei feigned shock. "No? Your eyes kept going that shade they do before you lose your temper."

Kanto snuggled closer to Jhee who patted his hand. "Lady Bathsheba thoroughly and entirely creeped me out with all her talk of ghosts and evil forces at the end though," he said.

Mirrei coughed. Jhee squeezed her arm in response. "She creeped me out with all her leering."

"Perhaps it was best we left before you descended into a self-righteous lecture, denye. I think we made a good impression anyway. Signet codes of introduction."

"Thanks to you, husband," Jhee said. A blush pinked his eyes. They exchanged smiles before he faced away. Jhee quickened their pace.

At the room, Jhee plopped in the chair. She fingered the access writ Lady Bathsheba had slipped in with the list of education contacts. If indeed Lady Bathsheba aimed to come off as a sexist snob and give the impression they were at odds, she had more than succeeded. She regretted her earlier ungracious thoughts which had accused Lady Bathsheba of snobbery. Reconsidering the meeting, Jhee may have taken the lady's words and actions the wrong way due to her beleaguered state of mind.

"You're the one looking wave-worn, now, denbe."

"I've been climbing stairs and visiting musty and moldy spires all day. While you may not have a headache, I do."

"I'd refresh your poultice, but our herbal stores are low."

Jhee changed from her robes into simple evening attire yet left the wrap in place as the poultice did help. She ran a thumb over the textured access writ. "Give me a list. I've meant to visit the infirmary, anyway. I'll see if they have some remedy for my sinuses as well."

In the hall, Jhee hesitated. She weighed the writ in her hand against Mirrei's list. Lady Bathsheba had drawn her attention to the storehouse at least twice. She consulted the map. The storehouse and the infirmary were on different axes of the abbey. One Prospective had died of sickness. They must have been tended by the abbey physician. The infirmary may also be where Saheli got her meditation aids. Jhee headed there.

A young, male Prospective sat the reception desk drawing anatomical drawings or nudes. No one else occupied the infirmary. He scrambled to his feet, shoved the parchments aside, and bowed, a protocol neither Jhee's office nor social status required. Nudes, then. She caught the whiff of robust, woodsy cologne. "Justicar, what ever is the matter? You've not taken ill, have you?"

"Not as such. I've been in and out of dreadful weather. Along the way, I developed a terrible headache. I also hoped to procure medicinal supplies. Is the physician in?"

The young man's eyes flared wide. "You actually want to see the physician? Perhaps, the Justicar, would rather see if it goes away on its own?"

"I'd like to see the physician this instant. Will that be a problem?"

"No. Not at all."

"What do you do here?"

He glanced at the pile where his parchments nestled. "I'm the infirmarian. I see to the non-medical needs of those confined to the infirmary."

A crash sounded from behind the physician's door then something thudded to the ground. The Prospective knocked. The door flew open. He jumped back as a short, graying woman barely taller than a shark dog stumbled out. "How many times have I told you not to move my equipment? And what's all this whispering out here? You best not have your friends here shirking their duties."

The infirmarian glanced at Jhee.

"Oh, a patient." The physician spat in her hands and slicked back her hair. She straightened out her robes before rushing to greet Jhee. A wave of the most horrendous body odor came with her. Jhee preempted her forearm clasp by initiating a bowed greeting. "He's as lazy as the refugees. I'm not like these other Sisters. I expect my assistants to work. These young men coming through today are nothing like they were in my day. You must be the famous Justicar? I'm Sister Zalver."

"I'd hardly say famous," Jhee said.

"Only to those such as myself, I suppose. I subscribe to the judicial law wire, followed the write-ups you did for Jeja of Marpele in Frontiers in Arcane Forensics, and read every 'Dispatches from Arrow Point' story twice. I absolutely loved your ingenuity in The Twelve Murders in The Manor. What brings you to seek my humble assistance?"

"That wasn't—. Never mind." What was she going to say? *That wasn't me; it was my literary counterpart.* Her fictional account had supplanted the truth in the popular imagination. Much as Jeja had wanted it to. "I wanted to pick up some supplies and perhaps get something for a headache."

"Come have a seat here." Sister Zalver urged her to an exam table. Jhee sighed with relief when the woman put on gloves before timing her pulse.

She had Jhee's eyes forced open before she knew it. "Eye color bright and shiny. Good. Here, drink this draught."

"What is it?"

"Tranquility Gold mixed with ippi extract. Opens the blood vessels, gets the circulation going. Do be warned. It does have a purgative effect."

Indeed, ippi extract did. Drunken vomiting while light-headed was one way to alleviate a sinus headache, but not how Jhee wanted to conclude this evening. Sister Zalver was either a squib or charlatan. Jhee checked for the neutralizer inside her sleeve in case the physician poisoned her accidentally.

Jhee faced away to avoid her fetid breath and spit out the draught. "I don't recall seeing you at the feast."

"Slept through it. I've dealt with enough real barbarity to not want to watch fools play at it. No time for that nonsense."

"Since I've arrived, I've heard too many disturbing tales of the abbey's history. From massacres to the Mist Abbess. Have you heard of her?"

"More nonsense."

"I also thought I might ask you about the Prospective who died."

"Which one? Ha." She slapped Jhee hard on the back.

"Prospective Yaou. The one you treated."

"Oh, yes. He volunteered here from time to time. Sister Elkanah brought him in unconscious."

"Was his illness sudden?"

"Sudden upon learning the magnitude of his work. The number of men who come in here and then make miraculous recoveries. They fake illnesses to bypass their studies and chores. Well, I set them straight. Some even left the abbey never to come back."

"Yet this one died."

"True. Sad case. The young man's weak character and fragile nature caused him to nearly wither away."

"Do you know from what?"

"No doubt some mystery ailment brought by the refugees. Saheli allowed too many to take holy orders. I've treated quite a few. Mostly for mild cases of Fresh Lung. Though I did see a rise in the cases of coruscate syndrome and sprained middle toes. A simple draught of one of my Tranquility Gold remedies and they're fine to go about their duties."

"Coruscate syndrome? That's quite rare, isn't it?"

"Which is why I questioned if they were sick at all. Squalid camps are a spawning bed for disease and sedition, though. Yaou's case was different. I suspected Fresh Lung at first. Very similar to chronic wasting sickness."

Chronic wasting sickness the favorite diagnosis of many family physicians in the Far Reaches. Often it meant they had no idea why someone was deathly ill. In more extreme cases, it said they were too lazy to find out or paid not to disclose the true one.

"He was a refugee?"

"One of the good ones. Hard-working. Conscientious. Not like a lot of these other lazy Prospectives, I could name who seek accolades without putting in the work." The physician raised her voice at the last. "Sister Serra, the vizier, even the prioress, and Sister Elkanah consulted, yet still couldn't diagnose him. Rather than admit the work too stressful and his constitution too frail, he worked himself to death. Most tragic. Gave up the will to live poor thing. But that is the nature of the male disposition."

"You said you treated Saheli. What can you tell me of her health?"

"Healthy as a sea ox. I was monitoring her for acid reflux and a mild case of Brine Lung, which I treated with barley and morning seed."

Brine Lung was the complement to Fresh Lung, which afflicts those from inland or higher elevations when they move to the Outer Reaches.

"As for supplies, nothing doing. Our stores are low too. Someone's been stealing them." The doctor pitched her voice at the infirmarian. Zalver leaned forward. Face and breath mere inches from Jhee's nose. Jhee's eyes watered, and she held her breath. "Can't be too careful. Spies. Everywhere."

The infirmarian peered around the corner his face full of empathy and concern. Zalver wandered away. Jhee hied to the waiting room. The infirmarian inched a cologne bottle and manta silk handkerchief he had taken from a drawer towards her.

"I'm sorry, Justicar. I tried to warn you." The infirmarian lowered his voice. "Most know to seek others if really sick. For supplies, it's best to ask Sister Serra."

"Serra?" Zalver yelled and trundled into the room. "Speaking of lazy. That dirty, smelly hedie. All she does is tempt and indulge. You watch that one. Medicine isn't the only thing she grows in that hothouse of hers."

"Did I hear my name?" Sister Serra strode in with one arm balancing a cask on her shoulder while wheeling another after her. "Which is it today? Am I stealing your drugs or growing my own?"

"Both. A bit late for a delivery."

"I wanted to get an early start on tomorrow. I thought you'd appreciate an early resupply."

"That I would." Sister Zalver licked her lips and rubbed her hands over the spirits the horticulturist had delivered. She grunted. Zalver wheeled out the casks. "These feel light. Stealing this like you've been stealing my medicines, you drugged-out hedie."

"Clam up, old woman. No one's been stealing your drugs." Sister Serra turned to Jhee. "My deliveries are less frequent. Our cash crops haven't been the only things to suffer from the weather. We also keep the heavy pharmaceuticals under lock and key."

"I've got my eye on you," Zalver shouted.

"Well, remove it. I'm leaving, you old goat." Sister Serra lowered her voice, "Come to the pods later. I'll give you some real medicine."

"Bye, Sister Zalver," Sister Serra yelled on her way out.

Jhee turned toward a cordoned off infirmary section. "What's this area over here?"

Zalver guffawed. "At the moment, quarantine. It's where Prospective Yaou stayed while ill."

"Usually, a quiet room for patients," the infirmarian said. "Or where staff nap when we're busy."

"If the doctor would allow me?" Jhee asked.

The physician tossed Jhee a fresh pair of medical gloves and an infection mask. "Do be careful, Justicar. We don't know what he died of."

"I will."

"Did he leave any belongings?"

"His effects are over there. They were meant to go to the mortician," the infirmarian said.

"Should be the incinerator," Zalver yelled. "I meant to take them myself. I intend to fumigate everything when I get the time, but it's been so busy here."

Jhee contemplated the abandoned infirmary again.

"I've already disinfected it. Several times over," the infirmarian said.

"Like I'd trust you to do a job like that right."

Once Zalver wandered off again muttering, Jhee searched the sickroom's plain bed and chest. The same rough, simple sheets as the other Prospectives. Jhee flung open the wardrobe against the far wall. The interior held a few day robes. Their hangers scraped along the clothing rod as Jhee browsed through them. Plain, but fashionable. Not the sort of clothing clergy or laity would wear. "When was the last time someone stayed in this room?"

"Just before your arrival."

Jhee pitched her voice low. "Passing strange Prospectives chose to put themselves under the physician's care when they knew to go elsewhere if truly ill."

"Not everyone stayed away. Abbess Saheli for one. Vizier Bathsheba stayed here after her accident. Sister Elkanah often complained of cuts and rashes from dealing with the archives."

"Naturally, she wouldn't seek out Sister Serra."

"Her injuries reminded me more of those the gardeners get."

"Oh? The Prospective she brought in, what was his condition like?"

"I'm no doctor."

"You tended him nonetheless."

"He didn't seem sick. At least, not until the end. I think he may have been hiding."

"From who?" The infirmarian kept his eyes to the floor. Jhee approached him. "If you know something, you should tell me."

"On several of Sister Elkanah's visits, I found her in here. The last time was just after he died."

"Who does the bed checks? You or the doctor?"

"Sister Zalver, but she logs it. If you could not tell, she prefers I not perform certain duties. I checked the logs, though, none of our patients went missing."

"According to Sister Zalver. And her questionable faculties. Thank you." Jhee raised her voice, "Sister Zalver, I'll take these off your hands."

"Please, do."

~

The Morgue

Outside the infirmary, Jhee quickly went through the box. Nothing except a basic Prospective's robe and shift. Cologne emanated from the box and its contents. The infirmarian must have doused everything in the infirmary with it. When she shook out the clothes to check for hidden pockets, a peculiar woven bracelet with a thin coin-shaped charm clattered to the ground. She did not recognize the decoration on its faces. The likeness of some Lesser Island Maker or ancestor, no doubt, perhaps even Maker geld.

"Has that half-blind goat got you running her errands?"

Jhee vaguely remembered the mortician as one of the clerics who had danced and sang at the feast. "I volunteered. I was there seeking relief already."

"Brave woman. Worst smelling living person I've ever met. I asked for his personal effects days ago. Put them over there with the others."

"Zalver wanted to burn them. She thought they might be infectious. Did you perform autopsies on the bodies?"

"Pursuant to the Justicar's new directives. The prioress and I did. One showed the markers of being crushed by rubble. Prospective Yaou asphyxiated. Evidence of cyanosis. No fluid in the lungs."

"Abbess Saheli?"

"As best I could. Her remains were quickly interred in the crypts given the miraculous nature of her death, and the necessity to embalm before the crypts became inaccessible."

"Anything unusual about the body? Any signs of violence?"

"Nothing not in keeping with the spirited nature of her last sermon. She looked quite peaceful. Not like the poor Prospective who drowned, though. Crabs had got at the body. Hard to tell if he died of something else. I could send you the autopsy images."

"Dear Makers, no. I mean my conch is almost full, and I can't signal out to ether out my data. I'd like my senior spouse to review them, however. I'll give you a routing code for his device."

"If ya like."

Jhee noted the dates on the boxes. "Are these the effects from the others who died?"

"Ayup."

"May I?"

"If ya like."

Jhee recoiled from the mildewed smell of Leigh, the drowned Prospective's belongings. Her headache worsened. "The prospective who drowned. Where was his body found?"

"Out past the breakers on the far side of the isle."

Drowning. Breakers. Jhee cringed. Perhaps she would investigate into that locale later. "Ever heard of the person called the Mist Abbess?"

The mortician chuckled. "Zalver can't help yammering about conspiracies and secret cabals, can she? A tale to frighten misbehaving novices. Obey the rules or the Mist Abbess will get you."

Jhee closed the box. "Is this all their effects?"

"The abbey sells or salvages what we can. I do keep a log." The mortician brought Jhee her records. "Yes. Yes. I remember this. The one who drowned was found with a sizable quantity of minted shell on his person. As well as an antique chest containing more in his trunk. It's not unusual for refugees to have hard currency. It's traditional to donate it to the abbey, though, upon taking orders. Such a large amount of it though. I informed the prioress, and we logged it into the treasury. I believe I still have the chest as I was waiting for the rest of his effects. It seemed valuable like a family heirloom of some sort. I kept it in case we located his family."

She had seen stamped shells, the former hard currency, more and more. With the shield wreaking havoc on inter-isle communication, centralized banking and currency transfer had become less reliable. Shell promissory notes and markers had regained popularity.

The mortician led Jhee to a locker and pulled out a black lacquer chest of exquisite make. While she did not have Kanto's eye for finery, she admired the angular, scrollwork and craftsmanship.

What would a novitiate be doing with this? A holdover from the days prior to starting down the cleric's path? A prospective monk should have either left such items with family or given them to the abbey to do good works. She delved further into the man's belongings where she found a wrapped bundle of delicate and expensive silk containing another of those coin bracelets tied to a single shell of currency looped through with leather cord. She sniffed the cloth, a trace of musky perfume or cologne. Why would a novitiate have such an item? What manner of unnatural acts went on at this retreat?

Jhee held up the two bracelets side by side. "What do you make of these?"

"What have you got there?"

"I found them among the other Prospectives' effects."

"Maker or craft geld of some sort? I haven't quite seen this one before."

"Me neither. Mind if I hold on to these?"

"If ya like. Could they be from the reliquary or archives?"

"How would they gain access?"

The mortician chewed on her finger quill. "This is a peculiar structure honeycombed with nooks. During renovations, we often find old caches of weapons and food, sometimes valuables. The earthquake also uncovered a few more of its secrets."

"The minting marks are too recent."

The mortician chewed her quill more.

"What is it?" Jhee asked.

"I'm sure it's nothing."

"If you've thought of something, please."

"I didn't actually see the prioress log the money into the treasury."

"Why should that cause you concern?"

"I'm loathed to relay gossip, mind."

Why should anyone stop now? Jhee bit her tongue even though she wanted the mortician to be out with it already. "No, please, do."

"I heard Saheli caught her stealing."

Jhee pressed against her nose in hopes from some relief from the pressure. "You've been more than helpful."

"Sinuses?"

"I got a powerful whiff of the mildew."

"Go see Sister Serra. She grows the medicinal herbs for the infirmary, and I dare say she'd be better at fixing what ails you than Zalver."

"I'll take your advice. Soon. The prospective who they found crushed. What can you tell me about his death?"

"Buried by falling debris in the courtyard when the tremor hit. Suffocated, poor thing. Interesting if you think about it all three lost their breath."

Jhee went to note her findings and noticed her low battery. "Mind if I induct for a bit."

"If ya like."

Jhee input her notes manually. Dictation required power and space her conch lacked. And she still couldn't transmit.

"You'll not get nothing down here. Best try the storm light spire."

A long, arduous trek to the top of another spiral tower ranked low on the list of actions she wanted to perform. The prioress did mention the solar arrays.

Jhee charged her conch a few more minutes before heading for the nearest wing to the solar array. She stared at the door hearing the rain and crying winds outside. The Storm Child's rage had quieted some since she arrived. It was still guaranteed to be wet and miserable out, though. She clutched her robes about her and sighed before she stepped into the elements.

On a storm-rent night, the panels were a nightmare of reflections and shadows. The eyesight played tricks. Difficult to tell if someone stood amongst them. With an overactive imagination, perfect fodder for more eerie sightings. Jhee sheltered by the arrays for some protection from the wind and rain.

Creatures dashed this way and rustled that way through the weeds amongst the solar panel bases. Jhee hoped. The moisture beaded off them or ran to the ground in rivulets to puddle underneath them. She held her conch aloft. At first, she saw nothing then a single pip faded in. It acted a guttering candle flame in the wind. She exclaimed with excitement.

"What was that?" a snatch of words on the wind said.

A disjointed reply came chopped and sliced by the wind. "Nothing… crab-rats."

One of the eponymous crab-rats scurried by Jhee. She pressed her mouth closed to stifle a yelp. Who would come out here now aside from her? Those who wanted privacy and nothing but the winds and willows to keep their secrets.

Jhee doused her conch within her robes and dimmed her eye color. It took a moment for her eyesight to adjust. A little way off she saw the prioress talking to Raigen. Jhee murmured a concealment cypher. Before she completed her eavesdropping formulation, the pair separated.

The abbey door clanked open. Raigen went inside while the prioress remained a glow orb in one hand and a large bundle in the other. Jhee huddled closer to the solar array. The prioress went to the far edge of the array before giving a sharp whistle which cut through the storm noise. Another figure came from the mists, and she handed the bundle off. The prioress stopped before the door to the abbey and gave another quick look around. She peered in Jhee's direction for a long time then turned and went inside.

Jhee used the delay to examine the Bridge Tower from this vantage. A discolored patch corresponded to the scorched section seen on her visit. After some quick and dirty triangulation, she traced the faulty section of the array. Several had bent struts smudged with soot, a short-circuit perhaps. She captured an image with her conch. Saheli may have collapsed from sunstroke. Had Saheli's transcendence taken place in the tower, this may have accounted for the brilliant flash of light.

Jhee waited a little longer before she headed for the warmth and dryness of the abbey. Her measly long-range signal pip had gone almost immediately once she was inside. She contacted Bax and set him about the task of trailing Raigen.

Jhee yawned. Anything else she might do must wait until tomorrow, though. She returned to her spouses, soaking wet.

"Were the supplies underwater?" Shep asked.

"Don't even get me started. The physician tried to give me an emetic."

"Vomiting? For a headache?" Mirrei asked.

"Tomorrow, I'll inquire about topping up our stores with the Mistress of Horticulture."

10
—————

THE ISLE

～

The Shed

Early in the morning, Jhee sought out the horticulturist. A few Prospectives who had been standing around talking hurried back to work. Jhee paused to have a gander at Saheli's favorite spot. Her mixed company on the initial tour meant she had not been able to investigate it as thoroughly as she wanted. Jhee rested on the bench and cast about her. White flickering from the ajar shed door drew her attention. She moved closer.

Sister Serra slapped Jhee on the back. She gasped hard to get her wind back. "None the worse for wear for your visit to Sister Souse, I see?"

Jhee felt a sharp pinch on her wrist. She found a bog gnat making a meal of her. She flicked its squished remains away. "Indeed. Your arrival was quite timely."

"I have standing orders with her assistants to call me if they're concerned. Try this. It's a mild analgesic."

The horticulturist handed Jhee a tube of spike leaf ointment.

"Zalver mentioned something about missing drugs."

"Not missing. Rationed. Besides Sister Souse isn't licensed to prescribe. Even if she were, we have doubts about how many of the pharmaceuticals would reach the patients. The prime suspect in the matter was the good

99

doctor herself. She may have been a good doctor once until her senses started to go, and the self-medication. We cut back her supplies after a few mishaps."

"She's still allowed to practice. Why?"

"Same reason she got assigned: nepotism. We've been waiting for a replacement almost two long-years. Many doctors are moving inland. The Soothbringers have been offering free healing lessons. Penance they say. They charge no fees to learn or for their services. Though, the healing does involve the new science. We are an order who eschews arcana. Most healers have incorporated at least some of their techniques into their work. It's getting harder to find doctors who don't in some way."

"To hear her tell it, she still does a brisk trade."

"Sister Zalver's favored remedies use spirits of the alcoholic kind. In particular, she views our select blend as a cure-all. I suspect it's the only reason anyone still seeks her out for 'treatment.' Most learned to come to me or the prioress. Now, I have an extensive selection of mood-adjusters, medicines, and herbal remedies. Fill me in on the nature of the complaint, and I can narrow it down for you. For nightmares and trouble sleeping, I suggest tharos root, though it does vex the ability to cypher. For shakes and tremors, lilac acid tincture. Night flower for mania and midnight bloom for melancholy."

While her herbalism and pharmacology were a little oxidized, Jhee found no quibble with any of those suggestions; unlike what the physician had recommended. Jhee might consult an expert, Mirrei, or bring her along on a return visit.

"Something scholarly, perhaps. A study aid. I have several preparations good for memory and focus. Others which make one more receptive to learning, and creative and imaginative thinking."

"I think perhaps I should just stick to the items on my list."

"Your choice. If I may?" Jhee handed Sister Serra her list, who touched her chin and bobbed her head in approval. "Lashotic remedies. Solid choices. Portable and easy to store. You'll want them pre-dried and ready for transport. We'll have to go into the apothecary stores."

"If it's not breaking any confidences, mind if I ask what you prescribed to Saheli?"

"I'm no doctor. Simply a gifted amateur. Verdale, where I'm from, was teeming in plant life. A lot of it useful. A lot of it hostile. Mistake brightshade for blightshade, you'd regret it."

The bog gnats continued to buzz around Jhee. She swatted them away. "Am I clear on understanding that Saheli partook of brightshade?"

"Just so. It's one of those study aids I mentioned. It does have hallucinogenic properties though and is best not taken alone. Saheli took two seeds twice a week under my supervision for meditation purposes. We sometimes sought the four conjunctions together which lie deep in barbarian lands. All save one have fallen into their hands. The only way to visit them is via the use of ecstatics to open the mind and commune with the Makers through visions. Though, she had begun to develop a tolerance to it."

"Is that why you went up the spire to check on her and didn't want her to go to the infirmary?"

Sister Serra took up a glass pipe and packed the dried leaves into it. She rubbed her fingers together, which produced just enough flame to heat it. She took a deep drag and held it before releasing a voluminous cloud of smoke. "No one in their true mind wants to go to our infirmary. Saheli humored Zalver to make her feel useful. However, she also knew her, the prioress, and Elkanah to be tiresomely orthodox and inflexible. When I glanced over and found her gone, a closer look revealed her on the floor. You are right I did rush to the tower to search for any trace of seed of enlightenment, so they wouldn't know. Meanwhile, the cat licked everything in sight, including her spilled drink. It escaped when I opened the door."

Serra offered the pipe to Jhee. Jhee refused. The horticulturist's pungent scent and smell of smudging stick made more sense now. "I didn't realize Drakists were allowed to partake."

"They're not. I'm Pluralist. One of the few left here. The remnants of my order merged with the Drakists when our monastery was overrun. I hope I didn't overstep offering you the wine."

"Not as such."

"Demand has spiked, but I'm eager for more independent research on its healing properties. I admire anyone who would take a pleasure cruise on these waters." Sister Serra leaned over and whispered to Jhee. "Must make for passionate times with the adrenaline and fear. Your full marriage cohort indicates you to be a woman of appetite. One spouse no doubt deft and experienced; two whom you can groom and teach. Always mind the quiet ones."

Jhee waved away more gnats. Sister Serra looked unperturbed.

"I saw you grow lace root melons. May I make an addition to the list?"

"Feel free. Unlike my colleague, who is stingy with the fruits of her labor, I prefer to be generous. I consider mine a gift to all those who would ask."

"Would you have any of the taffies?"

"Another of our most profitable exports. I can't get enough of them myself. Here you are. Added to your requisition writ. If you'd like some now, I'll give you some of mine."

Jhee slapped her arm as another bog fly got her. Sister Serra produced a candy dish from under the workbench, and they each had one. "You were right about Sister Elkanah."

"She didn't let you anywhere near her precious relics. Once that humorless shrew makes up her mind, that's it. You're better off. Archives, relics are about death. My domain is alive."

"I came across something interesting, though. Plans to turn this into a health resort or commercialize the vineyards and orchards."

Sister Serra coughed. The pipe slipped from her hands. She reached out but nearly dropped the pipe again. She bounced it a few times before she found a cool place to hold it. Serra placed it on the workbench then blew on her hands. "Unmake me! Justicar, if you would be so kind as to pass back that spike leaf ointment."

Jhee handed Sister Serra the tube. The ointment's scent was sharp and bitter. Pyrmo's burn cream had a similar smell. "On second thought, I may take some brightshade."

"Like I said. A woman of appetite. I'll give you some from my own private stock. I appreciate your challenging of Elkanah's perspective. Smaller tin next to the taffies there."

Sister Serra indicated the tin under the workbench. While Jhee set about locating the tin, she examined container labels. No marked pesticides or substances which might be used to poison someone. "I also learned something of the Mist Abbess."

By the time Jhee rose, Sister Serra had brought out a wave skimmer. "I have to get going. The Wave Witch's up and the weather's decent enough. We should go skimming sometime. I know all the best spots."

"Wave skimming? That would be a hard pass."

"Suit yourself."

The horticulturist hurried off with her skimmer. Jhee muttered an oath at the closed and locked shed.

～

On a Mission

Jhee sought Pyrmo out next. "Blessed are the First Makers, Abbess."

"How goes your investigation, Justicar? You visited quite a number of our facilities."

"I wanted to get a proper sense of the abbey's arrangement. To grasp the design, you must first understand the system. The prioress was most helpful. A shame her duties prevent her from helping me today."

"Duties? The prioress asked for the day off today. I assumed to assist you."

"Perhaps I misunderstood."

"Par for the course nowadays. Unfortunately, she has become increasingly erratic. Pity. When she served under me while I held the position, she was quite reliable. I think she was more affected by Saheli's death than she cares to admit."

"Oh? Were they close?"

"Hard to say really. Saheli was a very hands-on abbess. She frequently counseled young men personally. She was very friendly, but not without secrets."

"Like most. Would it be possible for me to look at the treasury logs or perhaps the inventories and manifests?"

"Why look at those?"

"Simply being thorough. A routine question came up, and I want to verify it."

"Those records are confidential. I might be able to answer any general questions."

"The mortician said you sell off anything valuable the clergy possess when they die."

"Generally, yes. The Professed bequeath their belongings to the abbey. The situation is more complicated for the Prospectives. We generally give the family an opportunity to claim them. Although, with the large number of refugees fleeing most have no family to contact. Often their only belongings are sentimental."

"Anything that's not gets logged into the treasury, yes?"

"Yes."

"You said Saheli's belongings were interred with her or donated to the archives. What about the Prospectives who died? Were their valuables logged into the treasury?"

"The Prospectives? Valuables? Most are fisherfolk or shepherds. They had nothing more than a few trinkets. While every bit does help, their possessions were meager."

"No large amounts of currency?"

"Currency? No. Why would Prospectives have that here?"

"Why, indeed? Another curiosity came up during my investigation. I heard a strange term, the Mist Abbess. Does that name mean anything to you?"

"A story to frighten young novices. There's a possibility I hesitate to entertain. The rumors of the Mist Abbess's return didn't happen until Saheli's appointment."

"Thank you, Abbess. With your permission, I'd like to continue my investigations."

"Of course."

The prioress had lied to Jhee about her activities. She never logged the large sum of cash the mortician found into the treasury. She also kept the tallies from bed check. The prioress's talk of ghosts could have been meant to scare Jhee away. Could she and Raigen have conspired in sending Jhee on a wisp chase? Perhaps Jhee would delve deeper into the prioress's activities.

～

Ask the Servants

"Ask the servants did you say, Bax? Lead the way," Jhee declared once she located her invaluable helper and family friend. Bax made as excellent a Justicar's assistant as he once made a criminal.

"They won't talk to you like that," Bax said.

With Kanto's help, Jhee had found her more unadorned day robes. She weighed the ability of her official robes' authority and dignity to loosen tongues against blending in. For now, she removed the sashes and any insignia of rank. She left her head wrap in place.

"It'll do."

After a few discrete inquiries, Jhee located the prioress by the storehouse. The prioress visited various provisioners and clothiers at the abbey and eventually the docks.

"I miss good old, grain bread. More and more it's that rice powder nonsense," said one fishmonger.

"Tried sopping up stew with it? Falls apart. Turns the whole bowl into mushy garbage," said another.

"Don't let it sit too long or dry out. It gets sticky. Like cement. Took two days to clean the bowl my youngest hid cause she didn't want to eat it."

"The trick is not to substitute direct," Jhee said. "Rice flour needs more yeast and starch. Coconut flour is very absorbent. Use less or put in more liquid." The fisherfolk glanced at her dubiously. "The First Mister likes to cook."

They nodded sagely. That rightly made more sense to them than a Justicar who might know how to cook.

"Bax, show me where the leaf mongers partake if you would." Bax led her through the hallways down to the cooking chambers to a rear enclosure sheltered from the elements. "I'm going to investigate the prioress. You keep following Raigen."

An overhang ensured privacy from the clergy's prying eyes. It also made an excellent vantage from which to mind the receiving area and await her quarry. A muddy well-worn path led the way with an occasional stubbed out butt. A few lay brothers and sisters toked on smoke root. When she entered, the nearest one dropped his and tried to stamp it out.

Jhee held up a placating hand. "I wondered if you might have an extra."

The staff paused dumbfounded. Then one stepped forward and handed Jhee an unlit, freshly trimmed root.

"Thank you." Jhee put the root between her teeth and used the young man's striker to light it. She dragged deep and tried not to cough. "My cohort doesn't like me to partake, especially on the yacht."

"One of the co-fathers was a stickler," another staff member said. "Drove our mother and the other father to toke in secret. When they had to get rid of theirs quickly, left a lot of half-smoked ones for me to clean up. Which I did."

The woman took a deep draw and raised her eyebrows.

Jhee nodded. "My grandmamere used to say smoke root kept evil spirits at bay."

"If only. It was spirits what got those boys. Maybe even the abbess," the second staffer said.

"Just the other day we had two Prospectives lured to their deaths," a third staffer said. "One got lured into the locked spire where he fell to his death. The door had been locked for some time, and there was still thick dust upon the ground. Now, how could that have happened save ghosts what led him there I tell you?"

"It weren't ghosts. It were the sea wisps. They led those poor men to their deaths. These young men about have them in a sore frenzy I bet you. They will take them under the sea to be their sea kings and spawn the next first fathers I tell you. Sea wisps beckon us back to the sea where we belong," the first staffer said.

"You don't really believe we were descended from mayes do you?"

"I believe what grandbabere and grandmamere told me. She said we were born in the sea and it ain't natural for us to be upon the land. That's what wrong with the barbarians. They don't spend enough time in the waves, and it has caused them to become uncivilized, especially the sky singers."

"The sky singers. You don't believe those old legends, do you?" the second staffer asked.

"I know we have the sky singers, the ground pounders, and them mixed fire children barbarians. That's what all I know."

"While I was out on the bluffs, I saw a pterosaur-like creature. One of the Unmaker's minions. I swear," yet another staffer said.

"No, it had to be Cheiropthys or the Wave Witch. Only she had the power to summon winged creatures."

The first staffer leaned in. "They say the blood cults are back and it's the Mist Abbess what leads them."

"Feh," the second staffer said, "best not to tarry with the Unknown Maker or worse the Unmakers."

"Sea wisps lured that boy to his death," said the first staffer.

"No," the second staffer said, "it was ghosts. They must have chased him up to the tower. How else could he have gotten in?"

"And caved in the cellar on that other one," agreed the third staffer.

"Did you hear one wasted away of fright?"

Jhee took a drag from her smoke root. "Ghosts. I think I may have seen some myself when I first arrived here. In the Zodiac Courtyard."

The second staffer nodded sagely. "Their favorite spot. They say that's where the Mist Abbess liked to perform her blasphemous rituals. That's where one Prospective died. Ill omen. It's the curse."

"The curse?" Jhee asked.

"The curse of the Unfettered Dead. I swear I can hear them whispering through the walls," the second staffer said. "Ghosts of those who died here don't like all these new, crude men."

"Reminds them of what they once were before they were cut down by the barbarians. Makers make the shield," said the third staffer.

"Makers make the shield," Jhee and the others repeated.

Had she seen an echo of some long-ago blood cult dismemberment ritual? The system remembers, and those who tinkered with the forbidden were most apt to leave traces not easily forgotten.

"This place sounds more frightening every day," Jhee said. "The abbess's death. These three unfortunates. You said sea wisps misled the one who drowned?"

The first staffer replied, "Wisp lights on the heath and the bluffs. Wisp lights have been seen for quite some time here. Boats used to be driven to their ruin on the breakers." Jhee closed her eyes tightly and shivered. "They say it was the ghosts of those massacred here in the past."

"The wisp lights led many a poor body to their death here. The young spouses and children who never got a chance to grow and play, now grow and play with the living to their detriment," said the last staffer.

"I've seen their lights out on the fields and bluffs myself. Especially the wood," the first staffer said.

The second staffer glanced back at the abbey. "The storm light's meant to drown out the false light of the dead."

The third staffer stamped out a root. "Best to ask the bilge workers near the harbor entrance. They found his body caught in some lobster traps."

The lights Jhee had seen from the first spire came to mind. "Did you know anything about him? Was he particularly careless?"

"Not more than most young men. He liked the bluffs though. He volunteered for any errands that took him out there."

Another staffer grinned. "Was it the errand location or the errand dispatcher?"

Jhee cocked an eyebrow. "You suspected him of an affair with the staff?"

The first staffer shrugged and gave a little glance up to the main abbey.

"Fraternization?" Jhee asked.

"Far be it from me to speak ill of the clergy, Justicar. But the horticulturist sure did need a lot of things from the seaport."

"Both deacons did," said the third staffer.

"More like the one wanted to know what the other was about. The Prospect who got sick worked at the archives off and on. Sometimes the agri-pods, too."

All staffers murmured agreement.

"What about the one crushed?" Jhee asked.

"He bounced around here and there. Restless sort. Not sure if this life was a good fit for him. But who am I to question the Makers' plan?"

At last, the prioress appeared. Jhee snuffed out her half-finished root. "I have to get back before I'm missed. Thank you, ladies and gentlemen."

The second staffer waved a smudging stick over her. "It'll cover the smell, Justicar. To protect you from the wrath of witches, wisps, and disapproving spouses."

Jhee gave a polite bow.

~

Blight and Bilge

The simmering sensation behind Jhee's eyes grew to boiling as she shadowed the prioress the rest of the day. The prioress paid the merchants and fishmongers with shell currency, no doubt the money stolen from the unfortunate, wretched Prospective's corpse. She did her best not to let outrage overtake her and confront the woman.

Finally, the prioress returned to the abbey. Enough time remained before dinner to undertake a visit to the bilges. The weather lightened to trickles, and the clergy went out to the fields to harvest what they could. Jhee conducted a personal walking tour of the island. Trailing the prioress had not presented the opportunity to appreciate its features. She strolled through the fields of grain. In the images she had seen, they were two or three times this height. For every cleric working, she saw one or two refugees. Some clergy even milled about and watched as the refugees worked.

She passed by the threshing shed and granary. What should have been floor to ceiling stacks of drying straw were barely half that. Refugees and clergy shoveled green, blighted plants into an incinerator. She picked up one of the stalks, some of them contained purple club-shaped growths: blightseed.

Some folk fished, lobster trapped, and hauled in the kreel nets. Others worked on a new drainage system for the bog trying to reclaim wetlands for expansion and to host more people.

The First Makers' Design guided Jhee's path to the bilges. The horrid, sweetly rank scent made the air a miasma. She covered her face, so she did not gag. She wished she had brought a smudging stick with her. She found the bilge workers on a break. She offered one her half-used root. She leaned forward and sniffed it deeply but waved it away. "No sparks or open flames while down here, Justicar."

"Of course. Later then?"

"Much appreciated, ma'am, but the smell gets in everything after long. What brings you down here, Justicar?"

Jhee put away the root as smoothly as she offered it. "Ghost stories. You know about the Prospective who drowned?"

"The morning crew found 'em. Glad it weren't mine. At least they found all of 'em. Sometimes you only find part. Finger. Toe. Dentures. You see a lot when you muck out the storm drains and inspect bilges."

"The staff thinks ghosts or sea wisps drove the young man off the bluffs or made him jump from the tower."

"Not sure how much ghosts had to do with it. Begging the Justicar's pardon. They found him beyond the breakers caught in some lobster traps wedged between rocks. He couldn't get that far out from even the storm light tower."

Jhee cringed, rocks, breakers. "The current, perhaps?"

"It's counter current. Only a few places he could have fallen to catch the right waters. The sloped vineyard, the bridge access way, or the lee of the isle. Most those is jagged rocks. Nothing can walk there but sheep and the surest of goats. He would of have to have been a ghost or wisp himself to survive walking about there."

"He didn't survive, did he?"

"No, ma'am, suppose not. Blessed be the Makers." The bilge worker locked her hands together.

Jhee did likewise. "Blessed be the First Makers."

11
———

GHOSTS

~

The Beach

Jhee awoke crammed between Kanto and Mirrei with the latter's arm flung over her face. She extricated herself as peaceably as she could. Her day robes and traveling robes had gone missing. She dug through the luggage around the room for anything resembling a simple wrap. The only other clothes of hers she turned up were the formal ones. She checked the dryness on her evening robes which hung near the fire. They were still wet. Beside them, the robes Kanto made had been cleaned and were dry as dust.

She found a fresh poultice waiting neatly on the table beside a full, clear, Adept teapot. She smiled and drew the teapot to heat the water. Shep joined her. As they drank the tea and perused the autopsy images, they sat hand in hand. He occasionally stroked her knuckles with his thumb. One Prospective had a peculiar tattoo on his wrist. Each had the more traditional jubilee tattoos which indicated the celestial phases and alignments of their birthday. Evidence of a brand which resembled those of the Medical Protectorate caused her and Shep to tense. It wasn't one, thank the Makers. Jhee brushed her fingers lightly over the failsafe sigil implanted in her arm. They touched escae before she left.

Planting herself outside the prioress's cell, bore Jhee the fruit she hoped.

III

The prioress wandered to a side door in the Shrine Courtyard. One not on Jhee's map. No wonder she had tried to warn Jhee away from the place. It led to a little-used delivery canal under the abbey for cargo and fresh-caught sea meat. The channel must, also, serve as escape route or means to come and go from the abbey unseen. A scruffy old man awaited on a skiff piled with boxes and crates. The prioress boarded, and they pushed away from the landing.

Jhee examined the canal area. Not another vessel nearby. The spit of landing ended at the canal entrance. From there, her options were wade or swim. In either case, she could not keep up with them.

"Psst!" A sound came from the shadows deeper in the abbey's bowels. The drip and splash of a pole in water preceded a skiff piloted by Bax and Raigen gliding up to the landing. Jhee surmised Shep had Bax keeping an eye on her regardless of whatever other tasks she set him. However, why despite her charge did Bax and Raigen occupy this craft together? She had no time to ponder it now. She boarded, and they pushed off before the illumination from the skiff's lantern left sight.

The haggard man looked over his shoulder often. By the First Makers' whim, a light mist rolled in. She drew it to conceal their pursuit. The fog had the power of the great storm in it, she realized after she had extended herself to it. It tugged and fought and tried to wrench itself from her grasp.

With a last effort, Jhee prevailed. She sat back and rested. Bax and Raigen proved adept at navigating the shallows and masking their passage through the water. Her concealment was by no means perfect. They would be seen if anyone looked hard enough. Or if the mist wights inhaled. Had she also wrestled the last breaths of the dead as Reach lore would have it?

Their journey came to an end when the skiff ahead came to a stop on an isle no more than a sandbar. Gruff folk met it. Bax and Raigen broke off pursuit and put in at a nearby inlet out of sight.

"Get out here. We'll stow the skiff and meet up with you," Raigen said.

Jhee hopped out, flipped her robes inside out, and removed her insignia of rank. She remained overdressed anyway as she tried to blend with the crowd gathered to meet the skiff. These haggard folk were refugees. Burly refugees in clothes slightly less bedraggled than the rest helped the prioress unload the boat onto nearby sleds. Excited murmurs grew as refugees crowded the landing area. To Jhee's astonishment, a suspicious handful of aid workers drew the sleds away from shore. They came to a stop at a nearby supply depot. The prioress clapped, and the refugees queued up. A table had been set up where workers already started a sorting line. The prioress opened crates and boxes to reveal food and clothing. She distributed them to the line of refugees. Every now and then she pulled out a toy and presented it to a child.

A sizable crowd remained once the prioress's provisions came to an end. She shook her head and rested her head in her hands. After a body-shaking sigh, the prioress went amongst the crowd distributing the only goods she had in infinite supply, prayers and blessings. Even without supplies, a crowd pressed in on the woman, and Jhee lost track of her.

The refugees had noticed the fineness of Jhee's robes even inside out. Their lean, starved faces pleaded with her. Jhee gave what she had on her person Maker geld, medicines, her medicinal inhaler. She even parted with as much of her clothing as was decent including Kanto's beautiful robe. She lost her poultice too. The crowd parted enough for Jhee to glimpse the prioress again.

In the confusion, the prioress disappeared once more. Jhee broke free of the crowd. She scanned the pathways through the tents and ramshackle huts. Most barely kept out the rain. Without her robes, she blended in better. She walked a few of the pathways between the tents. The sand was muddy and discolored. The air stank of urine and feces. A few aid workers distributed tarpaulins and beeswax to seal the plain cloth tents.

A gap opened between one set of tents and another. She spotted the prioress surrounded by a group of young men and women. They went to a flat bit of shore tamped down by many feet. Another crowd already awaited. The prioress clapped, and they formed ranks. Men, women, and children proceeded to do mediations in motion. The meditations Jhee did to clear and center herself for cyphering. The prioress made no effort to separate the men or boys.

The participants performed larger, more exaggerated gestures at full extension like the articles suggested. However, a beach full of people was much, much larger than the recommended five to six-person class size. Despite the admonition against cyphering and murky laws, the prioress proceeded to teach any and all cyphering, even men.

The sequences and cyphers were a hodge-podge at best. A pastiche cobbled together from many journals and articles about male cyphering. Jhee had planned on using many of the same moves in the system she considered for Kanto.

This close, there was no mistaking the aid workers' Pillarist garb; another reason why the prioress would not want her activities known. The aid workers were Soothbringers at least. The Doombringers had all but been eradicated. The Soothbringers had folded themselves into various other orders such as the Drakists and Beacons of Lost Sparks. Who else would be most equipped to teach cyphering indiscriminately?

The Middle Pillarists, more specifically the Doombringer heretics, were the reason for the cyphering laws in the first place. Technically, the rules against male education had been lessened and, in some cases, abolished. Poor men did not cypher and barely drew the elements. Much of the local populace still held to the traditions or distrusted male artificers. They looked askance at anyone teaching men such even though it was something the rich had done with their sons for quite some time now.

Gears ground and hitched in the environment. The unbalanced prime forces set Jhee's teeth on edge. Too many artificers in such a concentrated space. She hastened to test the air quality. The too sudden movement drew the prioress's attention.

The prioress gasped upon recognizing Jhee. She attempted to hide her motions.

"Justicar, please, I can explain," the prioress stammered.

"Later." Jhee queried the divine mechanism. Her mentor, Vizier Jeja, had been an arcane outreach counselor paid by the Central Authority to demonstrate the safety and benefits of cyphering. She had learned the signs when the environment spoiled, the symptoms of cyphering sickness. She had thought the program at the time had been meant to enrich the lives of the people. What it really was about was the Empire needed more artificers and adepts to work on the shield.

A man dropped to the ground and clutched his head. He convulsed. Jhee examined the man and cleaned the froth from his mouth. The air had the same wrongness, and depleted quality Jeja had taught her to look out for. They tended the man until he ceased his shaking and screams. Incidents like this only increased the stigma with regards to male cyphering.

"He should be fine. Cyphering is done for the day."

The prioress bowed profusely. "Justicar, if I may ask a favor. "

"You may ask."

"The clinic. Afterward, we can speak in private, and I will answer your questions as honestly as I can."

∼

Mist Blind

The prioress escorted Jhee to a makeshift field hospital. For those taken by diseases, such as Fresh Lung, Jhee could do nothing. She healed apparent surface infections first. Then Jhee mended cuts and scrapes, a few broken bones and more apparent wounds. What truly ailed them she could not fix.

A group of grateful leaders met her and the prioress outside. They brought them to their meeting tent and fed them a thin groutfish stew and a hard, crumbly chunk of bread from their meager stores. It tasted the greatest of feasts to Jhee. She washed it down with a swig of the refugee's strong homemade liquor, squelch. It burned all the way down. She gasped and pounded her chest until the inebriation settled over her.

Jhee remembered the tattoo she had seen in Leigh's autopsy images. She noted similar ones on several of the people she treated. The thought of the autopsy images made her appetite flee. Another swig of squelch helped that, too.

Jhee listened politely and respectfully while her hosts talked.

"Our livelihood is dying. That drenched Shield. It scares the fish. We can also no longer go out as far for whale and other sea meat. Only the big ships with passes from the Imperial Authority. Makers make the Shield, anyway. Let's see if those stipple bastards can get around that."

"The whale and manta are being driven inland where they strand, or the ranchers get them. We could find more out further to sea, but we are humble fisherfolk who can't afford the license fees to venture beyond like the big ships can."

"Not unless we go in on the fishing combines."

"The rep from the fishing combine was here again."

"I'll be unmade before I let some inland bureaucrats tell me what to do on my own ship. No, ma'am. Begging your pardon, Justicar."

"I used to think they were a joke. I had my own ship. Why would I want to give that up to have someone else tell me how to run it?"

"Or worse, work someone else's so they can get rich while you break your back."

"I don't know anymore. The Imperial Authority doesn't seem to care about the little fish anymore. Only the whales."

Another elder drunkenly interrupted, "Arcana. Feh. I know how they built the shield. They used necromancy and deep magic to rouse the shell drake what lies at the bottom of the sea. It now circles about the isles churning the waters into this Maker-forlorn storm. That's what caused them quakes."

"They awoke the Storm Child in hir fury. We had two tremors and wyrm waves."

"The Wave Witch and Wind Witch have quarrel again."

"No, the Storm Child rides the shell drake."

After the second or third time losing the thread of the conversation, Jhee knew she needed to leave before she passed out there on the beach. She swayed as she rose and made her farewells.

The elder shoved a small carved piece of driftwood in her hands. "Be safe. That place is full of restless spirits."

Jhee reached into her devotion pouch for a tiny shell she had carved with Maker runes and cyphering primitives. She touched it to her esca then handed it to the elder in trade. The elder acknowledged the exchange with a nod. Make for Make.

As if Jhee were not already tired enough, she still had the prioress to deal with. A hollow stare was all it took to get her speaking.

"Allow me to explain."

"The mortician said Saheli caught you stealing."

"For this."

"You also took the cash from the dead Prospective's body."

"To buy more provisions. He was a refugee too once. When I revealed to Saheli why I stole, she understood. Saheli and I both thought the laws governing the teaching and education of men backward and archaic. Even when it came to cyphering. We resolved to teach any who would be willing to learn, and so we did."

"But your order eschews cyphering."

"We were encouraged by our success with the mundane educational program. This is our pilot program. With a fixed, controlled group, we hoped to better understand the dangers and the risks. Our first obligation and duty are to our community and the welfare of all the Makers' children. The knowledge could be used to better the lives of themselves and others, which is our foremost obligation. As clergy locked behind our walls, we sometimes become blind to the suffering of the people around us. These refugees reminded both Saheli and me of that. She even sometimes visited the camp herself. I do what I can here, but it's still not enough. Not only were we going to teach, but we were also going to lessen the tithe as a show of goodwill."

"I can only imagine how well that would go over."

"Which is why Saheli wanted it kept quiet until she was officially ready to announce it. Perhaps we could shame the other orders into helping. Once the decree went public, there was virtually no way to take it back."

"Save for the appointment of a new abbess."

Such a move narrowed down the suspect pool to any overly proud and comfortable cleric at the abbey. Jhee stroked her nose which the working conditions had shifted toward a muzzle. Rapid minor adaptations were a consequence of the shifting weather conditions this close to the Shield. Before the Storm Shield, it used to be subtler and more gradual unless you were adept at skin slipping.

"I kept track of every shell I took; all sales and philanthropy. And so did Saheli once she knew. We drew the money from a combination of slush funds, petty cash, and her revenues as abbess. We started tracking after we took over the books from Pyrmo. We almost had to. They had not been kept properly in years, perhaps decades. Inventory and audit were next on the agenda. Thanks to the current insinuations, all Saheli's reforms are now under evaluation. Some, if not many, are bound to be discarded. Pyrmo has already cut back on our charitable giving to the poor, and she never would approve of cyphering lessons."

"Or working with Soothbringers."

"These people are desperate. The traditional orders are failing them. Nearby cities consider them a nuisance. As do most of my fellow clergy. The other monasteries have largely ignored their and our pleas for aid. Only the Soothbringers have done anything for them. As a result, more and more follow them. Can you blame them, Justicar? Saheli and I tried to get them to join the Drakists instead. We could be doing more. Refugee housing programs. Or have the Professed and Prospectives help them build homes. Instead, we're hiding behind the walls of the abbey."

"I am not unsympathetic. The restrictions regarding this sort of thing have become more social than legal after the reforms of the Rescission Councils. Much as you informed me regarding your vows, this is a matter between your conscience and the First Makers. If you are going to continue the cyphering lessons in whatever capacity, you should consult with someone who has actual experience instructing others to cypher."

"Proper teachers cost money. Look around, Justicar. They can't do lengthy apprenticeships or hire enough teachers for the recommended student ratio."

The education report and the signets of introductions Lady Bathsheba had provided her sprang to mind. "A few isles have pooled their resources for cyphering instructors. I, also, have the personal contact information for Imperial Education Secretaries. A similar arrangement might be set up throughout the camps. In the interim, I offer my counsel. I'll instruct you in a few more healing cyphers and the warning signs for cyphering sickness and pollution. We can discuss a curriculum and a funding stream for both their supplies and education."

The prioress gave more profuse bows. She extended her hands to Jhee. They clasped forearms and touched foreheads. Jhee did not mind such a familiar gesture in such a circumstance. She felt the situation more than warranted it. The prioress hovered her palm over Jhee's esca. "The Makers' blessing to you and yours. We may not have always agreed, but I respected Saheli. She genuinely cared about the poor and not lining her own pockets or puffing herself up. Do you really think she was murdered?"

"All I learn makes it more and more likely."

On the beach, a leader, much younger than the others and who had spent most of the conversation silent, stopped Jhee.

"I have not heard anything from my brother. A man came to the camps. He claimed he could get him good work in the city as a cook or servant."

"I'll see what I can do."

Jhee watched the refugees with fatigue. Their blank, worn faces continued as an endless sea. She imagined this must be what the inhabitants of Antasia who tried to hold back the sea on their own or the lone elemental practitioners who tried themselves against the storms felt like. Would it ever be enough? Could she ever do enough? Her stomach felt knotted, and she wanted nothing more than to sit down and close her eyes to everything.

"Justicar, we should go," Bax said.

"Yes." Jhee turned for a last look over the camp. She faced the dim glow of the storm shield. The barbarians awaited on the other side. She must remember that. "Raigen?"

Jhee had meant to ask where the woman was, but that's all she managed.

"Later, Justicar. Later."

~

The Ghost Stories

Jhee slipped back to her room. Once again, Kanto remained awake, but this time with an audience. By the fire, her three spouses gathered with bowls of pork and rice. Shep perched on the edge of his seat. Mirrei clutched a pillow tight.

"What of the wicked monk who had mocked the Makers and aided the raiders?" Mirrei said.

"And the greedy priest?" Shep asked.

Kanto set down his bowl and leaned forward. Mirrei and Shep did too. "A cave-in had blocked one exit. The servants they mistreated sealed the other after them. They say they lost their way in the crypt depths amongst the very honored dead they betrayed. On many days, if you listen closely, you can still hear them searching, searching for the way out."

The three fell silent as if to listen.

"Let me out," Jhee whispered.

Her spouses jumped. Jhee gave a weary smile as she stepped into the room. Mirrei groaned and tossed her pillow at Jhee.

"Not. Funny," Shep said. "Did you two plan this?"

Jhee chuckled. Kanto gave a hearty laugh until he noticed her appearance. "My word, denbe, what happened? Your robes? The poultice? Were you robbed?"

"That pork and rice looks delicious," Jhee said.

"Sit here. Let me get you some," Kanto said. He sniffed her several times. "Is that liquor? Are you drunk?"

"Long story. Thank you."

Shep set down a washbasin and a cleaning cloth. "You're not hurt, are you?"

"No." When Kanto returned with a bowl of food, she devoured it. The water in the basin was too cold. She gazed at the fire yet did not have the strength to redirect it. She'd be surprised if she could even get a spark from an Adept stone.

"Look at me," Mirrei said. Her usually light and demure tone had gone replaced by one which Jhee could only describe as motherly and stern. She held up a finger and moved it in front of Jhee's eyes. After one or two passes, Jhee had to stop. "Jumpy tracking. Pale. Low body temp. Shallow breathing. Cyphering fatigue."

Kanto hovered and frowned, followed by dragging Shep aside for an animated conversation outside her hearing. Jhee picked up an uneaten roll.

"Wait," Shep said. Jhee bit into it and practically chipped a tooth. She tapped the roll against the table. It sounded fit for an Earth Adept's use. "Not everyone has adjusted their recipes properly for non-wheat flours yet."

She sighed. "Do we have any broth or soup?"

She put the roll into the soup and consumed it piece by piece as it softened.

"Kanto, not now," Shep said.

"If not, now, when? Before or after she slips away again without a word? Only to turn up like this? Or should we wait until she turns up dead?"

"Fine, we'll change the schedule. Here. How's this? The past couple of days will be my days or off days, and Jhee has my full permission to spend them how she wishes. Mirrei's days will be next since it's been a while for her and Jhee."

"For Makers' sake, Kanto, if it's that important, take my day," Mirrei said.

"All right Kanto then Mirrei. Agreed?"

"Agreed."

"Jhee?"

"Yes. Yes."

"There. Now everyone's happy or equally miserable. Take your pick."

"Shep, Mirrei, I ask a moment of denbe prerogative?" They had taken enough of the ire meant for her. They went to bed, leaving her and Kanto. "I'm sorry I left without a word."

"The timing on your return couldn't have been better, though," he said.

She quirked her mouth. "Where'd you learn that story?"

"From the Prospectives. You didn't expect us to stay shut inside the room all day while you run around. Don't worry, I had a clerical escort. I didn't realize how many of them came from isles like ours."

"Is that your way of saying you want to become a Professed?"

"And scandalize these poor, sheltered women?" Kanto made a grand sweep of his hand over himself. "They couldn't handle this. This is also not to be hidden away under ill-fitting cowls and cassocks."

Jhee rolled her eyes. "Spheres forfend you smile at one. She may faint."

"Wouldn't be the first." They laughed. "Denbe, I don't want to fight or nag."

"No, I have to do better by you." Jhee touched her chin then patted his hand. "Learn anything else interesting on your outing?"

"Here listen to this."

Kanto played recordings from his conch. Notes from a lute quavered and echoed in a way she never quite heard before. It sounded as if wind chimes accompanied them. Jhee squeezed her eyes shut. Men chanted. The sonorous tones caused her to think about a home by the sea, about footsteps that echoed in the too empty house. Jhee pressed her hands together in front of her trembling lips. Once she regained emotional equilibrium, she opened her eyes.

Kanto quickly glanced away. "The first is me in the Worship Hall. Eerie?

The acoustical properties of the abbey are extraordinary. Our practice court-yard has a whisper wall where you can stand in one corner and whisper yet be heard by a person at the opposite corner. There is a certain step where you can clap and get an infinite echo. The weird shape of the building plays all sorts of auditory tricks. The wind blowing through an odd window or cracks might very well sound like moaning or scratching at the walls."

Jhee listened as further into the recording, the chants became sea songs and shanties. The refugees and the Prospectives were men like Kanto. The parallels between the missing young men and the deaths of the Prospectives weighed on her as much as her family duties. Refugees had gone missing, and no one noticed. Men died, and their Justicar had not noticed. Kanto had long felt neglected, and she had not noticed either.

Jhee folded her hands and faced away from Kanto. "Between Mirrei's health problems and Shep's episodes, you were the one I never had to worry about. I sometimes forget that you require my attention too, and for that, I am truly sorry. I never had to worry about you, and I took it for granted that I never would. Forgive me. We have not had a day together in a while. I intend to correct that. When your day comes, it will be your day and yours alone. We'll do whatever you want."

"Promise?"

"Promise."

Jhee had worked this all wrong. Despite the vizier's rebuke, she had still focused on the wrong death. She had avoided it, but she needed to plunge down into the drowned Prospective's death. She had set it aside long enough.

12

WISPS LIGHTS

~

A Goat Path

Jhee shielded her eyes to gauge the position of the dual suns. She might have time to check out the lee of the isle. She found the aforementioned goats and let them lead the way. The terrain became rockier and more treacherous as she approached. She turned to glance back at the abbey. Its shadows loomed large, yet not enough to reach this far. Even the storm light spire.

The small herd of goats wandered by her further out than she dared. They stopped and chewed on the hard scrub grass right on the verge of the cliff. One disappeared over the edge. The screech of child cut through the night.

Jhee whipped around to determine the source. The screech came again. It had come from the edge where the goat had fallen. She hastened over, summoned her courage, and peered over the edge.

The goat stared up at her from a series of steps carved into the cliffside. It gave another disturbing bleat as it descended further. She slumped her posture. The other goats trotted by her oblivious.

These steps may have been where Prospective Leigh fell. What was at the bottom? Jhee gathered her wits and courage to take the first step down. She thought to take the wet steps backward so she could look up instead of down. Or better still, eyes closed. Her Maker Within told her what a horrible idea that would be. Instead, she hugged the cliff and prayed the goat did not change its mind about its direction.

A fell, rain-soaked wind kicked up. Jhee accidentally glanced out over the steps to the breakers. She flattened back against the wall. "Not today, Storm Child. Not today."

She brought her focus back to the stairs. She murmured the phrase her grandmamere had taught her for when the seas got too rough over and over as she descended. The peculiar way the waves broke seemed wrong to her. The closer she descended to the shoreline, the better visible a subtle glow from a nearby inlet became. A yellowish glowlight bobbed in the water atop a small buoy tethered in place.

At the bottom of the steps, there was no mistaking the opening in the rocks to a smugglers cove. A sea vessel, not imposing enough to be a pirate ship and devoid of ship-to-ship weaponry, moored at a makeshift dock. A few glow orbs lit it from inside. She crept along the cliff base towards the lights. She caught a strain or two of shanties. A group of smugglers loaded the ships hold with crates and several of the metal-bound casks with the Tranquility Gold, double-Drake brand burned into the oak along with some bearing the black label and orange brands. No sign any were armed.

Jhee crept closer. A gull bird nesting in the side of the cliff flew from its hiding place. The smuggler nearest her position gave the alarm. One grabbed a cargo hook.

She drew in her breath and took hold of the nearby winds. A gust sent them flying into the water. She felt the pullback as one or more tried too. A three-way struggle ensued between them and the storm. They were practiced, probably from wielding it to speed their passage. However, she gained her experience in battle. She allowed the storm to do much of the work, only insinuating herself when it turned the winds in her favor. Anyone who had not fled was now in the water.

With a lull in the winds, she had nothing to work with. The smugglers, instead of seizing the advantage, fished each other out. One, though, had fallen farther away than the others. The one she knocked in the water first had drifted away from the dock and headed for the breakers. She struggled and gulped.

Jhee froze. A young, teen's image begging for her help replaced the smuggler. Jhee was a pre-jubilant again, clinging desperately to a rock while the waves buffeted her. She began to shake.

Not today.

Jhee tore free from her memory-induced paralysis and thrust her will into the water. Against the arcane infused waters, the best she managed was to prevent them from drifting farther out. The other smugglers threw a line to the one struggling in the bay. Jhee collapsed to her knees. With their compatriot rescued, they turned her way again. She offered no resistance. She merely focused on the sea and the breakers. One of the smugglers raised a hand to strike her.

The Cove

"No," the smuggler who had nearly drowned yelled. She coughed and sputtered. "She saved me."

"Saved you? Captain, t'were her what put you in the sea, first," another smuggler said.

"Ain't Makerly to kill a magistrate. We're not murderers."

"What you propose we do with her?"

"Are you all right?" Jhee asked.

The captain nodded. She gained her feet and shook the water off her body hair. "Thank you, Magistrate."

Both smugglers had sea dog accents and pale body hair. Their eyes were a lighter more amber shade than those from around here. Jhee indulged her curiosity. "You are from the Gray Dale, captain …?"

"Yaren. Aye, that I am. Pardon, the reception, mum. You surprised us is all. What might a magistrate be doing about the beach in this weather?"

"I might ask the same of you fine folk."

She tugged on her ear. "We got slips. All forms and whatnot proper-like if you want to see them."

"Please."

The smugglers released Jhee. She dusted herself off as Captain Yaren led her to an alcove with a driftwood box. She opened it and pulled out a tiny, credential chip and a conch. At the bottom of the box, was some hard, shell currency. When she attached them, a manifest appeared. "There you are, Magistrate. As ye see, all taxes and duties, paid rightly."

Jhee gave the manifest a once over. The header was crooked. It had Penstock Freight's name, the shipping company it purported to come from, misspelled. The signature belonged to a notoriously corrupt dock master who had died two years previous. "What I see is a mediocre forgery."

Captain Yaren's eyes went wide, and she played with her ear. "Me crew have nothing to do with it. They loaded what were by their reckon a proper manifest."

"I'll take that into consideration should your help with another matter yield dividends."

"Aye, ask, and it be my humble honor to comply."

"Are you aware of the young man they found on the rocks?"

"We ain't had nothing to do with the death of that poor boy. We're Makerly devouts, we are."

"He had to have gone in the water around here. Any idea why he might be out this way?"

The captain tugged hard on her ear. "Admiring the view."

Jhee shoved her hand in her robes. "You try my patience, Captain. Your crewman's inner wrist bears a tattoo though he tried to remove it like the one on the Prospective's body. Likely a gang marker."

The captain's eyes flared. "Gangs?"

"That currency at the bottom of your chest matches the minting shape and denomination of currency also traced to the Prospective. Did you and your crew find him wandering out there and seek to rob him? He struggled, and you flung him to his death."

"Bite your tongue. None who be here is thief or robber of men. We're decent Maker folk. You ask the abbess. It were she what gave us the wine."

"Pyrmo?"

"Saheli. We're Makerly devouts, Magistrate. The tax on the wine were better spent on good works. We shared our custom and plied our trade to the benefit of Tranquility Bridge as much as our own. The abbess reckon it no crime we kept ourselves and our families fed. She saw we said prayers, made our offerings, and did our penance and devotions regular."

"Regular? How often?"

"Once or twice a long-tide until recently. Now it's that sour-faced woman what comes. Or we meet her by the solar arrays."

"The prioress."

"Aye, that be her. We sought to aid that boy's troubled soul. He paid us fair sum to take passage on our next lay out. Our lay out come, he never showed. We sailed ahead of a nasty squall. Not till our return did we learn his fate."

"Because of your operation here, you chose not to share your arrangement with the young man with the authorities."

"Beg pardon, Magistrate. Weren't our business. We told Saheli, and that were the last we heard of it. No other authority know enough to speak to us. We won't do it for them."

"Do you know why the young man wanted to leave?"

"Nay. He did seem sore troubled, though. We did our humble part to be fishers of our fellow folk as the abbess taught us."

"And for a nice fee."

"We do have families, mum."

Jhee imagined Saheli sitting up in her spire engaged in her works, seeing the strange lights as Jhee had. If she also had full access to the archives, she would learn the isles many secrets and inlets. An operation such as this would not escape so an involved an abbess as her. If Saheli not only benefited but supplied the smugglers, she had no incentive to turn them in except in the direst circumstance. And they had no motive to do her in as long as their arrangement held. It made it hard to believe they would kill Prospective Leigh for catching them. Why not merely tell the abbess and have her deal with it?

"How did he even know you were here?"

"A good question, mum."

The crewman Jhee singled out for their tattoo tried to hide behind another. "You there. Would you happen to know how he knew?"

"The abbess did not always come herself for the items she needed. She sent him down to procure them in her place."

"What items?"

"Fancy, expensive items. Sometimes… intimate items."

"I'll hear no false talk against the abbess," the Captain said.

"It's true, captain. The boy came here regular with a list and payment to get personal goods on behalf of his abbess. His words. I never brought it up with her myself due to the intimate nature of some of the items."

"He booked passage for himself and no other?" Jhee asked.

"Aye, mum."

"Thank you."

Jhee stroked her chin. The captain cleared her throat. "Magistrate, what might ye be doing about me crew and my humble person?"

"For the moment, nothing. Remain here should I have need of you again. If you flee, do know I have what I need to track you down."

Jhee touched their sailing vessel and performed the full hand cypher for a temporary illumination. The smugglers gasped. None of them seem to know the difference.

"Aye, Magistrate. Best hurry, mum. Begging your pardon, you ought not be out on the heath after dark. If not for sheer treacherousness of the footing, but what with the spirits and wisp lights about like what lured that poor, troubled boy to his doom. Best take a light and this sage."

Jhee tried to wrap her head around what she had learned. The Prospective wanted to leave the isle. Where had he acquired the currency to book passage and still have such a significant sum left over? Pilfering was not out of the question. He had a pipeline right here. His tattoo showed he had some form of gang affiliation. Could he have been profiteering off the refugees? Did they have those sums of money?

The missing men from the camps. Might Prospective Leigh have something to do with it? Trafficking? The same brand of robbery she accused the smugglers of.

~

The Wood

Armed with a glow orb and sage, Jhee made her way back up the stairs. She kept her gaze focused up and away from the breakers. It was almost last-sun or second sunset when she reached the top. Alone on the bluff, the goats have gone on along their way, she felt like relighting the sage. It had gone out during the climb though it continued to smoke. With the smugglers, prioress, and formerly Saheli running around here at night, she saw now why everyone thought the place infested with sea wisps. She gazed up at the moons in the sky. Full bright, when the largest shined its fullest. Sister Serra's talk about astrological alignments and unleashed evil forces came back to her.

The dim-day—time between sunsets—had turned grayer. Jhee held her orb aloft to fight the gloom and made her way back towards the abbey. She thought of the sightings of spectral lights out here. Likely only the glow orbs of all the travelers between the abbey and the smugglers cove no doubt. Combine orb lights with a few mist reflections, and you had a recipe for sea wisps. Not to mention any gases which leeched from the wetlands or from underground mineral deposits.

In addition to the light and sage, the captain had explained to her the quick way to the side door by the solar arrays. The shortcut offered a different approach to the horticulturist's shed. Sister Serra was quick to illuminate the failings of others. What might she have to hide out there? Jhee examined the shed by the herb garden and the door that led to the solar arrays. She couldn't help but notice twice Sister Serra had prevented her from seeing inside. Serra was also rather cagey about her whereabouts.

Jhee glanced out into the gloom and thought she saw a light. She stared back at the warmth and safety of the abbey. Dare she? She did not believe in ghosts and spirits wandering about the grounds. If anything, her locating the smugglers, had made the notion less plausible. Regardless, she felt better with the sage in her pocket. She set off.

Clouds rolled in obscuring the moons. Light rainfall began. Despite the downfall, the vineyard remained clear of fog and mist. The light was definitely on the move. She maintained a constant distance. A concealment charm would not work in such an open setting. The night made a music all its own full of cheeps and chirps. Outside the range of her orb, splashes paralleled her. A frog loudly croaked its annoyance she had disturbed it. It hopped off to join its fellows in their night songs.

Jhee glanced frequently back at the abbey. She pretended she had not spent the day investigating the misfortunes of someone who may have stumbled or been pushed to their death. Possibly after being led astray by mysterious lights in the dark.

She swept the light frequently between the ground and the way further forward. She consulted her conch to gauge how far she might be from the edge of the bluffs.

The light ahead stopped. Jhee hid her orb in her sleeve and shaded her eyes. Whether what she followed was some moor phantasm or a more mundane entity, she preferred not to announce her location so clearly. Jhee held still. After a moment, the light began moving again. Jhee now proceeded with her orb partially hidden. If she stumbled and broke a bone out here, her cohort would never let her hear the end of it.

Amber-lit trees appeared in the distance, the orchard. The light continued toward it. As they approached, brighter lights flickered amongst the trunks. Murmurs and chants carried on the wind. Backlit by the counter light, Jhee's guide light became not a spirit or wisp, but a robed silhouette. Anger for even entertaining the notion fueled her pace. This accursed abbey and this drenched isle with its superstitious residents had her so wound up.

Jhee hid her orb able to navigate by the light from a bonfire amongst the trees. Rather than follow directly behind the figure, she followed at an angle until they reached a clearing. She flattened herself against a tree just beyond the ring of light. Robed figures circled the clearing, hands linked. Beside the bonfire, crossed beams bore a man strapped to them. A central figure in an elaborate headdress waited beside it. The headdress bore white on black markings with the cephalic lobes of the giant maye. The rear sported a whip-like, spineless tail. Jhee could not be sure, but she thought it was a represen-tation of the Maye Queen.

The figure Jhee had followed presented the Maye Queen with a chalice and dagger. The Maye Queen held them up for all to see. Another figure poured burgundy liquid into the goblet. The Maye Queen went to the man on the cross beams. She cut the air in front of him with the dagger then tipped the cup to his lips. He drank deeply, gaze fixated on the masked figure. Once he had swallowed his fill, he ran his tongue over his lips and waited with parted lips.

With a last brandishing of the dagger, the Maye Queen slashed his chest. The man cried out. Jhee dropped into her first stance but hesitated. The man's cry had more the sound of ecstasy than pain. He still stared at the Maye Queen without fear in an almost trance-like fixation. A trail of blood opened across his chest. He even bit his lip as she drew the dagger over his flesh two more times.

The Maye Queen held the chalice to the wounds. She sliced her hand and dripped her blood into the vessel, too. She drank and then handed it to the next figure. They drank then passed it on to the following who drank as well. The Maye Queen pressed the blade to his lips. After he licked the blood, he arched his back and moaned.

The robed figures passed the chalice and chanted. They intoned a sequence Jhee had never heard before. After the attendees drank, they swayed in time. The Maye Queen tilted her face to the man on the beams.

"Warrior of Pain come to us. Warrior of Pain come to us," the figures chanted.

Mist snaked from the man's mouth to the Maye Queen's like reversed inspiration. When the Maye Queen stepped away, the man sagged against his restraints. Was this the Mist Abbess of which so many had spoken?

The Maye Queen's assistant presented her with a bit of cloth. They sang healing sequences and dressed his wounds. The Maye Queen placed a similar headdress with a tail spine and black-on-white markings, the Maye King, on the man.

"The Warrior of Pain is with us," the man said.

"The Warrior of Pain is with us," the circle of figures repeated.

The Maye Queen and her assistant cut the man down. Several figures with long staves pounded the ground. The other figures cavorted around the fire. Lady Bathsheba spoke of blood orgies. The Baqairu Blood cult rituals had been infamous for extreme bloodletting and cannibalism.

The capering figures stripped off their robes. Raindrops hissed on the bonfire turning into a woodsmoke-scented mist. The participants of the ritual began kissing and fondling each other. Scandalized, Jhee backed away.

This was just a bunch of dabblers partying. These people did not seem to be interested in kidnapping and killing Prospectives and refugees. Certainly, not secretly poisoning the former abbess. One of their revels may have gotten out of hand. A Prospective who partook too much stumbled off and slipped to his death. The theory still left the problem of the abbess and other two Prospectives. She saw no one involved who was not a willing participant. This made it no matter for the law. Jhee turned around and went back quietly the way she had come.

13

———

THE TEMPTING GARDEN

~

The Garden

The next morning Jhee found Shep sitting in the gardens. She tensed and froze when a salamander hopped away as she neared, but Shep didn't startle. He only turned her way, beaming. Her sigil remained inert, so she sat the bench beside him.

"Morning, dear husband."

"Morning, dear wife."

"How is Mirrei doing?"

"She seems better. She and Kanto are off exploring the courtyard."

The rains had picked up again today. The skies strayed beyond a mild overcast, but nowhere the previous days' gales. The Shield had added an extra layer of unpredictability to the weather. The high artificers had yet to perfect the formula. Artificers were still required to keep it operating efficiently. Soon enough, they expected to complete the perpetual motion sequence to make it self-sustaining. The derivations would be reintegrated every now and then, but it would hold on its own without constant tending. Barbarian raids and the need for measures like the berserkers, siren modules, and the other Medical Protectorate experiments would be a concern of the past.

133

"How are you faring?" Jhee asked.

"Dari and I went out for a run earlier this morn."

"Good."

Jhee expelled a breath relieved Shep answered the question she had not asked. The cramped confines of the yacht may not have suited him, but he had not complained. The weather had not afforded Dari or Shep enough time and space to roam as they would and relieve some of the pressure. They had needed more time above deck.

"We all needed off that boat."

"Did we? Or was it another way of avoiding Kanto?"

"You seem to have more than made up for it."

"My conversations with him regarding you are not substantively different than my conversation with you regarding him. He's young, healthy, and wants to please you."

"He was a fitting choice as second."

"Kanto deserves a say."

"What of the conversations between you and Mirrei?"

The look he returned had a tinge of anger mixed with bewilderment. "There are no such talks between Mirrei and me. That I leave to you. As that arrangement was made without my input, your other plans for her should be too."

"We owed them."

"Did we?"

"I owe them."

"I re-submit my previous response with the pronouns changed. Mai made her own choices."

Mai: their nickname when they were young for Mirrei's mother.

"She and her family were finally out of our lives." Shep's arm tensed. "One of my sisters contacted me the other day."

Jhee chocked her teeth together then pressed her mouth into a flat line. He did not need to clarify which; the one who had sided with Mirrei's family against them. If he wanted to depth charge the conversation, he could choose no better topic. "The archives were extraordinary. I think I may have scuttled my opportunity to visit them again."

"Well, dear wife, it's lucky I proved more charming. While you ran about the isle, I viewed the autopsy images and secured permission to perform an autopsy."

"Good on you. Aren't you industrious?"

"Isn't that why you keep me around?"

"Oh, is that why?"

Shep reached out and tickled the small of her back. She slapped his hand away with a laugh.

"Don't think I'm not angry with you for telling him about that place on my back."

"I see myself in him. I took pity on him. He wants to please you. You should let him."

Jhee and Shep had spoken of finding a training husband. She had agreed reluctantly, but she had still not thought Shep serious until he returned with Kanto in tow. "He's so young. They both are."

"Those are good things. New energy to revitalize the household."

"It's not that I don't appreciate their refinement and vigor. My tastes have always leaned towards a more rugged handsomeness." Jhee winked at Shep. He smirked. "I'm late for my lessons with Mirrei. Would you fetch us some breakfast and some treats? How about the lace root melons we saw during our tour?"

"I'll see to it."

Jhee and Shep held hands before she left.

$$\sim$$

The Refectory Incident

"I wonder what's taking denme so long with breakfast?" Mirrei said after the lesson.

"Perhaps he got to talking with the clergy. Many are vets," Jhee said.

Kanto scoffed. "Denme? Talking?"

"Fine. Grunting in the affirmative," Mirrei said. They giggled.

"Be nice, you two," Jhee said.

"Yes, denbe."

Jhee wondered as to Shep's whereabouts herself. He went to fetch their breakfast some time ago. The sigil on her arm itched. She pulled out her conch. It had died at some point during the night. Kanto offered his.

Bax answered instead of Shep. "Justicar, Makers' thanks. The refectory, quickly."

Yells and roars let loose in the background. The conch screen's image devolved into streaks and blurs. Jhee rushed to the abbey entrance.

Mirrei and Kanto had gathered their things. "Wait for us."

"No. No." The sigil on her arm burned enough to cause pain now. Jhee dared not bring them into a dangerous situation blind. She glanced around the courtyard. Their room would be more defensible, but dare she send them back unguarded? "Stay here. Don't leave unless, Bax, Shep, or I come for you."

"If someone's hurt, I can help," Mirrei said.

"Do as I say! Stay here. Both of you. Watch for anything… strange."

Mirrei and Kanto clutched each other. Jhee strode from the courtyard.

"Demons!"

"The Unmaking!"

Clerics and laypeople ran by her and away from the din of fighting. Jhee skidded to a stop at the refectory entrance. Several tables had been upturned. More diners sheltered behind them.

Shep whirled on her, his eyes fiery orange, teeth elongated. His nostrils flared. Deep, rapid breaths expanded his chest. His muscles had thickened, and his bulk had increased. A bench scraped against the floor stones. Shep spun towards the sound. Several clerics hurried away. Others had taken defensive stances. Shep hunched. His fingernails formed now into deadly sharp claws.

"No one move," Jhee said. She slipped a hand inside her robes to the sigil. "Shep, look at me. Please."

He snapped his head back in her direction. The Professed rushed him. He flung two aside then roared. His skin had taken on the black and sleekness of the orcinus, the whale crusher. More Professed surrounded him. He grabbed the heavy wooden table and hurled it into their midst. They scattered.

A few older Professed grabbed mugs which they struck against the table while they grunted in time. Shep paused.

With shaky gestures, a Prospective prepared to draw fire.

"No," Jhee yelled. Shep put himself in between her and the threat. He drew back to strike. Dari bounded into the refectory and hurled herself into Shep. He crashed backward. Dari planted herself in front of him with a warning growl. A Professed warrior tackled the foolish Prospective to the ground. Others piled on Shep. Jhee dug her nails into the sigil to activate it.

A dog-like yelp came from Shep. He stiffened then fell to the ground. He rapidly returned to his normal state. Jhee rushed over and cradled his head. Dari whimpered as she curled up beside them.

Sister Serra and several Professed came over. She held her hand above Shep's head. Dari snapped at them. "May we?"

Jhee nodded and petted Dari's head. Sister Serra examined him while the others locked their hands and chanted. Shep's eyes opened. They helped him to his feet.

Sister Serra and the Professed escorted Shep to the side.

The abbess arrived. "What has happened here?"

"I beg your forgiveness, Abbess. My husband, Dawn Wolf, had a mental crisis."

"Crisis? He went feral. I've seen it before," Sister Elkanah said. "You have a duty to report this."

"He did not go feral." Jhee paused to mitigate her tone. "I will, of course, report this."

"Must you really?" Sister Serra asked. "Your own husband."

"Because he is my husband, it is more incumbent upon me to pursue this. I must render judgment under the law without fear or favor even to him. I'll recuse myself from the case and call in another Justicar to render judgment once communications return."

"What if he regresses again?" Sister Elkanah asked. "Justicar, is he not guilty of crimes under the law? This man endangered the life of a government official as well as senior members of the abbey. He should be confined, not coddled."

Sister Serra tsked. "What of compassion, mercy, second chances, forgiveness, Sister? Do these mean nothing to you? Do the ways of the faith mean so little to you? This is a place of refuge for those with pasts they would rather forget."

"It's prophesied. The signs of the Unmaking. Saheli one who died by divine fire, the one who died by water, the one died by wind, and the one who died by earth. The last martyr, the last prophet. I don't want anything to happen to the pious souls who reside here."

"Neither do I," Jhee said.

"As you love and worship the Makers, your duty under the law is clear. As well as to the pious souls who reside here. Can we be sure he won't harm them?"

"Abbess, a statement from you will mitigate Dawn Wolf's sentence. In the meantime, may I have your permission to have him brought to the gardens? It will ease his recovery."

"He belongs in the Corrections Hall," Sister Elkanah said. "It was designed for situations such as this."

Jhee felt defeated.

"Justicar, if I may." To Jhee's surprise, Lady Bathsheba stepped from the shadows. "The abbey is located in a relief zone which places it under the Sanctuary statutes, am I correct?"

"Yes." Jhee's shoulders felt lighter. She repeated stronger, "Yes. Pursuant to the Fair-Weather Statutes, this is one of the few instances in which the Imperium does not maintain total sovereignty. The communications blackout or state of emergency means jurisdiction over certain acts reverts to local authority. Since I did not draw my weapons and no weapons were drawn by others. With no one killed or seriously injured, this is an ecclesiastic matter. This puts the crime in the sole jurisdiction of the abbey, more specifically the abbess."

They turned to Pyrmo. She squared her shoulders. "Then, I declare an apology and our forgiveness, constitute sufficient punishment."

"I must protest, Pyrmo. Are you to be as lax as Saheli? Shirking off serious infractions. No wonder why nether forces have taken anchor."

"Enough! I've made my decision," Pyrmo said. Lady Bathsheba and Sister Serra nodded approval. Sister Elkanah glared. "However, after some time to collect himself via reflection and communion with the Makers, he is confined to quarters for the rest of his stay. Except for an hour a day, in which he may visit the Maker's Shrine in the gardens."

Sister Elkanah gave a grudging nod. Jhee turned to thank Lady Bathsheba only to see her slipping from the refectory. She checked her pockets and found a message. The abbess collected Sister Serra, and they spoke to Shep at length. Tears formed in his eyes. The Professed Shep had injured joined those around him. Her view of him was now blocked. Jhee stepped forward.

"Here, Justicar, drink this," Bax said. He handed her a cup. She recognized the peachy smell of Tranquility Gold. She took a drink. Even watered down, the wine still tasted delicious.

Prospectives and staff had already started cleaning the mess. A growing pool of red liquid with bits of land meat on the ground caught her attention. The spilled contents of Shep's porridge bowl mingled with it. Blood. Shep had eaten blood porridge.

A cheer went up through the hall. Jhee whirled on her heel. The Professed and Shep took turns, consoling each other. He smiled and wiped his eyes. He headed her way.

"One moment," he said. He squeezed Jhee's hands before continuing passed her.

The abbess led him to the front of the hall where she announced, "Our guest has something to say."

"I would like to apologize to everyone for my disturbance, and I humbly ask your forgiveness in the Makers' names."

"I accept. Blessed be the Makers," Pyrmo said. She clasped forearms with him and winced.

Another Professed, one he had attacked, followed suit. "Blessed be the Makers."

After those he had injured had embraced him, a slow clap began. The clergy took up the applause. Jhee approached Shep, the abbess, and the horticulturist.

"Thank you for your understanding, Abbess."

"Understanding? Yes. I'd hate to have your explorations about the abbey hindered by a divided focus."

Jhee searched for Shep again. The horticulturist stopped her before she left.

"I have those supplies you wanted," Sister Serra said. "Stop by the agri-pods. I may be able to provide additional help."

"Thank you, Sister Serra."

~

The Temptation

After Jhee and Bax collected Mirrei and Kanto, they found Shep in the garden once again.

"So, what is my fate, Justicar?" Shep asked then tugged on his forearm hairs.

"This matter fell under the abbess's jurisdiction. She won't pursue any additional punishment. They explained the terms?"

"They'll give me until the rest of the day out here to reflect, but they have asked I remain in our room until we leave." Shep stared out into the distance. "A fair ask."

Jhee sat the bench beside Shep. She stroked his face. He kissed her palm and traced his eye scar with her thumb. He froze when he saw the discolored sigil on her arm.

"How bad?"

"Level two."

He stifled a sob. "I'm sorry. You and the others might want to secure separate rooms for yourselves as a precaution."

"No, dear one, no. The dish you grabbed was blood porridge."

"Makers." Shep tugged the hairs of his arm. "I like it here. It's very peace-ful. A great many veterans reside here. It's good to be around others who know what it's like."

"Indeed," Jhee said. He took her hand and gently squeezed it. Despite what happened, she liked seeing how easy and untroubled he was. Her care-taker. Everyone's caretaker. She only wished she looked after him as well as he did the rest of them.

Jhee took a stand and dusted herself off.

Shep did too. "Let's go for a walk."

They walked through the courtyard and gardens. Shep's hands clasped behind his back and hers dignified and tucked into the sleeves of her robes. The minutes' respite, the privacy, the open space, and the beautiful surroundings emboldened her. She slipped a hand over and looped it through his arm. She kept public displays of affection to a proper minimum nowadays. She never wanted to make Kanto and Mirrei feel uncomfortable or left out, so she tried to maintain a certain equanimity to how she behaved towards them. Yet, her urge to be fair sometimes shortchanged Shep. With the junior spouses elsewhere and the location so secluded, she indulged herself. Droplets of moisture glistened in his blue-gray body hair. Mindful of prying eyes, she reached over and stroked his forearm.

Shep pulled her into one of the alcoves. Jhee taken aback gave a quick glance around. They ensured no one watched before he slipped an arm around her waist. She and Shep nuzzled their noses together gently, before succumbing to a kiss. Jhee squeezed his upper arms for encouragement.

"I miss being alone with you," she whispered.

"Me too."

"One room. We'd have to be quiet."

"As I recall, I'm not the one who had trouble keeping quiet."

They shared another deeper kiss. Then stood for a moment with their escae together.

"Sometimes I can't breathe for wanting you."

They could find a discrete place now if they wished to find a few moments pleasure with each other. Behavior as fair to no one as it was improper. She had to conduct herself with the honor and decorum required of her office. She had to respect the abbey's rules. He deserved more than a few stolen moments.

"It's so tranquil here," he said.

"Perhaps we should forget the capital and simply take up on one of the nearby isles."

Shep smiled. "Yes, and we could work the seas and dive like we did as children. We'd fish and build a good home just the four of us with none of the pressures or intrigues of court."

"I don't know. For myself, I think I'd set up a cyphering school or a more permanent judicial arrangement helping refugees secure aid along with work credentials. Perhaps a tailor's shop or music school for Kanto. For Mirrei, a lab. No, a community center or garden where she could sell embroideries, do light healing work. It would be just lovely, don't you think?"

"Yes. Yes, it would."

Jhee and Shep stared at each other. Neither seemed convinced. She saw his scars, and he saw hers. As quickly as they had abandoned decorum, they regained it and want back to their proper distant postures. Nothing but a respectable married couple. The look on their faces returned to somber as the dream of a simpler life flew from their minds.

"Could you imagine Kanto here? Stuck on another rural isle too small for him or his vision?"

"No. No, I can't. He'd be bored beyond belief within a long-month."

"Less."

"He deserves a say."

It still felt surreal to be the head of household. Jhee's inheritance a fluke, the result of various coincidences and tragedies. She was not even supposed to be a justicar or magistrate. Her plan had long been to become a professor or fellow at some academy branch. Those were in the days of the Arcane Rehabilitation and Restoration Initiative. Before she enlisted in the military to follow Shep. She had been so young and naïve. True, the intelligence pool was usually a nepotist scheme to avoid heavy combat. It had been the best place for her considering. She took the work seriously, which did not go unnoticed. Her head for details landed her several, critical military intelligence assignments despite the cloud surrounding her. Perhaps even because of it. For information the Central Authority did not wish to entrust to conch, ether, or parchment, they used ciphers she designed and her encoding skills to hide their messages.

14

———

BROKEN PROMISES AND REMEDIES

~

The Fallout

Jhee stared at her conch, sitting alone on the charging station. Kanto and Mirrei had slipped out some time during the night. She paced and tapped her conch against her hand. Where were they likely to have gone?

Jhee yanked open the room door. They walked into view, giggling.

"Morning, denbe," Mirrei said. "We charged your conch for you."

Jhee turned the conch over and over in her hands. She still had not left the doorway. "Thank you."

The junior spouses' faces sobered as they brushed past.

"Mirrei agreed to take a look at our conchs."

"Where were you two? I thought I warned you not to go wandering about alone, especially you Kanto."

"Denye wasn't unaccompanied. He was with me. Kanto and I ate with the laypeople. Not everyone can be so lucky as us to eat from the high tables. What they have to eat was a water's worth less lavish than what we've eaten over the past few days."

Kanto wrinkled his nose and looked ill. Eating from the high table suited him fine. Therefore, it had to be Mirrei's half-drowned idea.

"Do your poverty tourism another time. I am well-appointed, and you

143

are provided with the finest food, clothes, and medicine. And you always will be for as long as I can sustain it. You know how lucky you are. Can't you just enjoy it?"

"Pause, respite. Mirrei, could you give me a moment with our denbe?"

"Fine." Mirrei stomped into the next room.

"I suggested we give you and Shep some space," Kanto said.

"You should have informed me of your whereabouts regardless."

"Had you kept your promise, you'd know our whereabouts."

"My promise?"

"Whose day is it?"

The indignation which had stiffened Jhee's posture and made her so haughty drained away.

"You don't remember, do you? Today is Mirrei's day. Yesterday was mine. We moved around the days. Remember? Did it even cross your mind to ask me?"

"To spend the day with Shep? He was in crisis."

"About anything? You think me petty or insensitive. I am not without empathy. All you had to do was ask or inform me even. But I didn't even cross your mind. It was our day, and I got to spend it watching you sharing passionate embraces with another while plotting to send me away."

Jhee deflated even further. "The whispering wall."

"You're going to send Mirrei and me away once we reach the capital."

"It's more complicated than that. That was always the arrangement. In the capital, there will be those richer and more powerful than I. Or whose goals simply align better with yours. You want more than I can give you and you should have it. Politicking and power bring out the worst in me. My best life is a modest one. I'd still be a provincial official if I could. That would never suit you."

Kanto sighed and softened his tone, "How would you know? Did you ever ask, or did you just assume? I've committed to you and your household. A commitment I wish went both ways."

"Once we are somewhere with more options, I don't want you to feel obligated."

"Obligated? Neither Mirrei nor I want to be an obligation. What we want is your enthusiastic affection. What really happened to your belongings?"

"I gave them away."

"You what?"

"It had to be done. You wouldn't understand."

"What I don't understand is why you were wearing them in the first place. Those robes were not for running around in the dark or repairing ships. You even lost the poultice. Typical. It's not about the robes. It's not about days. It's about respect and consideration. You have no respect for the gifts we give you. You have no respect for us, or perhaps just me."

Kanto stopped. The truth of the thought fixed itself in his expression. Jhee realized too, seeing his reaction. He folded his hands into his robes and composed himself.

"I see," Kanto said.

"I've always been respectful to you."

He guffawed. "Proper, yes. Respectful, debatable. When we are together, you are always proper, a perfect gentlewoman. You were always perfectly proper. I could tolerate your reserve, your aloofness when I thought it simply your nature or a tactic. Some denbe do that, so none of their spouses know where they stand. In one glimpse, I saw otherwise. With him, you were vulnerable, open. I heard the desire in your voice. The way you spoke to Shep. The way you came alive in his arms for that one instant he kissed you. It's more than what I heard or saw. It's the affectionate and sometimes longing way you react to him. It's so effortless. He doesn't have to use tricks to stir passion in you. It's written in every way you touch each other. To sense the history there, to understand how he gets a part of you, I can never hope to…."

"Missing your day was unfair and inconsiderate. I remember we chose the day schedule because we thought it would be more equitable. Everyone received their own day instead of grouping it by activity. Fancy balls or political functions, which I hate and would have avoided, meant I might never spend time with you. I mishandled this. The respectful course would have been to ask to suspend the schedule during the investigation and not set up expectations for how much time I'd spend with you."

"Or as now, I'd be left the sole objector while Mirrei and Shep accepted it."

Jhee glanced at her personal effects where she kept the broken music box. It might make the perfect peace offering, but she judged the gesture too manipulative or worse, maudlin. Instead, she thrust a handkerchief at him. "What can you tell me about this?"

Kanto wiped his hand down his face then took the handkerchief with a sigh. "Nice scent, a Winter or Spring Forest fragrance, but the pattern's at least a decade out of fashion. Where did you get it?"

"I must have picked it up from somewhere. Is there anything I can do to make up for my oversight?"

"Is this where you attempt more matchmaking between the vizier and me? Or make another promise you break? Communicate with me honestly, so I don't have to assume or speculate and can serve your household properly. Unless... it's not about me, but you. You think I settled. You think this isn't where I want to be. It was. Until this moment. I'm not sure if I can do this."

"Will you be taking leave of us once we reach the capital?"

Kanto tucked his hands into his sleeves and stiffened his spine. "I haven't decided yet. If I may take my leave of you, denbe? Only to the next room."

"Of course."

"Thank you." Kanto stalked to the stool by the window and took up his sketchbook without further acknowledging her.

"Whelm!" Jhee said.

The Mineral Springs

Mirrei poked her head into the antechamber. Jhee remained in the antechamber where Kanto had left her, but she had settled into one of the tea nook chairs. He sketched furiously by the window.

Mirrei pulled up the other chair. "I trust you're in a better mood."

"Your trust would be misplaced."

"Let's relax with perhaps a soak in their open-air mineral springs."

"Open-air."

"It's not that bad out now. There's a nice mist to provide a little privacy. Hm? Hm?"

Mirrei leaned in and nuzzled Jhee's cheek.

"As you wish."

Eternal praises and the First Makers' blessings to the intrepid soul who had carved steps into some of the mineral springs. They made it so much easier on Jhee's knees and feet as she and Mirrei descended into the healing pools. After a few moments, her aching muscles relaxed. The young woman had been right, even with the drizzle and fog this had been worth the chance.

Jhee licked her lips. The minerals tasted sharp and salty, but sweeter than the salt taste of the sea air.

"Did you take your saline?"

"I must have forgotten in the excitement. Did you take your inhaler?"

"I must have forgotten in the excitement. Travel on the yacht had been so peaceful. To tell the truth, I had gotten rather used to not taking it."

The still, warm water had a particulate size too small to be detected by the unaided. Jhee murmured a basic cypher to enhance her sense of touch. Her skin tingled from the slight grittiness. Her imagination? The healing properties of the waters? She sighed. She might stay here forever.

Mirrei swam by her naked. On a sunny day, the waters may well have been crystal clear. Now, though, they had a grayish sheen which made them murky. Jhee barely made out the outline of her body. Wisps of steam rose from the pool's surface. Mixed with the fog, they caused a wavering haze which obscured the other springs. Jhee was glad Mirrei had the opportunity to take the waters with her. She only wished she could show her and Kanto the sights of the island. She felt terrible for them holed up in their room the entire time. And before that, cooped up on the yacht. It was bound to make them a little cabin cross. Here, she felt it a necessary precaution, though. She became all too aware of her bug bites again as the minerals irritated them.

Mirrei floated to Jhee's side. Her ears had perked up, and her pallor no longer quite looked so peaked. They shared a few kisses. "You're investigating a crime."

"A small matter."

"Murder."

"Nothing for you to worry about."

"Then why have you kept us locked away and under constant supervision while you run about the place tipsy turbulent?"

"I can't get anything past you, can I?"

"You don't have to hide it if you are."

"There seems to be something odd happening here. I'm just curious as to what. It will probably turn out to be routine. You know me. Looking for mysteries everywhere."

Mirrei tilted her head at Jhee. "You're a better liar than this."

"I found strange occurrences and incidents. Nothing I would stake my legal tabard and credentials on."

"Now, that was the truth." They left the springs and made their way to the nearby sauna. "Do you want another day off so you can work?"

Jhee grabbed a package of Tranquility Bridge's patented mineral salts. She poured the salts into the steamer and ladled water on to the warming stones. "That won't be necessary. The horticulturist offered me this. She called it 'seed of enlightenment,' a study aid."

Mirrei turned the plant over in her hands then took a good sniff. She wrinkled her nose. "Maate-Kheru Verdalia. Brightshade, sometimes called seed of enlightenment. A hallucinogen and natural insect repellent. Most plants of that Maker taxonomy are. Seems as though you should have taken some. You would have avoided your current discomfort. One of its derivatives also treats migraines."

Jhee put some spike leaf gel on her insect bites. "Explains why the insects swarmed me yet left her unmolested. Would you like to work the case with me?"

Mirrei swirled her hands throughout the steam. "I'm not sure what help I'd be. Another trip to the horticulturist is definitely in order. You look like you are in need of another poultice."

"I'm sorry I gave your previous one away."

"May I ask to whom?"

"Refugees. Their camps are on the beach on the far side of the fishing village. The conditions they live in… It'll break your heart."

"Then why should I mind if you gave it away? Seems they needed it more. Speaking of, don't forget to take your neutralizer and change out your spare."

Jhee had a quick puff while Mirrei popped a saline tablet. "Happy now?"

"Denbe, you told me the number one cause of death in our district was poison."

"Natural causes."

"You meant poison. Difficult to tell without autopsies."

"That it is. Good on you for catching that. Thank you for setting up that alert on my conch. For that and making me address them."

"If you are going to take the time to set them, you should not ignore them."

"I know. With the move and the travel, I had let them slide. Four people died in the few weeks before we arrived. According to the abbey's public records, the deadliest period since they had a boat capsize and a scaffolding collapse during renovations."

"Unusual enough for the search to catch."

Jhee smiled and nodded. Mirrei always the apt pupil. Jhee's quick praise of Mirrei made her pause.

"The poetess claims the deaths were murders."

"Do you believe her?"

"Unsure. What I do know about the poetess is she is an accomplished liar and Trouble Maker. I thought it best if I look into it."

"Flagging and addressing irregularities others missed or ignored is how you got your reputation."

Jhee sighed. "And our one-way trip to the capital."

"Who else can boast their wedding feast ended with half the guests arrested?"

Jhee shook the inhaler. It rattled lightly. "Don't remind me."

"Almost empty?"

"Ugh, greens houses again it is." Jhee dabbed gel on another bite. "Come with. You can pick up your supplies while I make inquiries and perhaps let me know what exactly she's growing in there."

"Thank you," Mirrei said.

"Thank me for what?"

"For losing that frown, that look. The piteous, worried expression everyone has around me."

"I'm sure they do not mean to offend."

"It's just tiresome. I do know what is going on with myself and my health."

"Do you feel I disrespect or am overly dismissive of you?"

"I know you can't abide foolishness. Foolish in your mind often equates to age."

Jhee took hold of Mirrei's dainty, slight hand and kissed it. It certainly felt a shade warmer and stronger than usual. "My apologies."

Mirrei tapped the tip of Jhee's nose. "Note, I only accept because I've seen improvement in your behavior. Towards me at least. Let's go."

∽

The Greens Houses

The pair found Sister Serra waxing her wave skimming board and puffing on her glass pipe by the shed.

"Decided to take me up on my offer, eh? I could give you some seed of enlightenment for your man there. It works wonders for those afflicted with the war mind. Saheli found it most helpful."

"He wouldn't take it."

"Too proud, I suppose. Perhaps an elixir for yourselves then. I have many."

The Sister propped up the skimmer and offered them the pipe. Jhee waved away the smoke.

"Do you not partake at all or just when you are investigating? You think Saheli and those other Prospectives were murdered. You've been running about the isle asking questions."

"You are very well informed."

"I have my ways."

The wave skimmer propped up beside the work shed fell over. Mirrei held up her hands. "Sorry. Curious and clumsy."

"My wave skimmer. Do you skim?"

Mirrei sparkled her eyes and blushed. "Me? I could never."

"You should. Can't skim much since the weather turned bad. Although, knew some suicidal skimmers who would try. Makers bless them."

"I adore your extraction setup. Is this where you refine your guidance-seeking tinctures?"

Mirrei spoke softer as she moved down the work area away from the skimmer and shed. If Sister Serra wanted to hear, she had to follow.

"I've also been studying the mold and mildew affecting the crops."

"I remember. Noble rot. For your new wine, correct?"

"Among other things. I'm corresponding with pharmaceutical companies about the blight and major farming operations about hardier crop strains."

The lock on the shed hung unsecured. Jhee peeked. A black and white bundle behind a curtain caught Jhee's attention. Jhee moved aside a bit of cloth. She recognized the Maye Queen's headdress and robes. Mirrei pointed opposite Jhee's direction.

"Is this good for migraines? Denbe and I get the most terrible headaches."

"How do you normally treat them?"

"I make a sweet-smelling poultice. Lashotic."

"Of course."

"My, that's a nasty scrape on your hand. How'd you get it?"

"Hm, don't know. Running around in the vineyard somewhere."

Jhee returned holding the Maye Queen robe and headdress. "Or cavorting at a bonfire in the orchard?"

"Makers' whim," Sister Serra said. "It was a lark. We found some masks and did some rituals to the Warrior of Pain. No harm done."

"Sister Elkanah might disagree. These belong to the archives, correct? Along with your ritual implements: the ceremonial dagger and chalice."

"I planned to return them. Eventually. Because of who they're associated with, she didn't guard them closely as the others."

"How did you gain access without being seen?"

"This place is honeycombed with passages and exits. Escape routes put in after the massacres so that the residents could always have a way out."

"Did Saheli stumble upon one of your revels?"

"No."

"You involved Prospectives in your little revels?"

"Yes."

"Perhaps some of your participants changed their minds or had an attack of guilt. Were the dead Prospectives part of your little cabal?"

"No."

"They threatened to tell Saheli."

"No!"

"Maybe remorse so overcame them, they wanted to go to Saheli and confess their misconduct."

"Please, Justicar. You have it all wrong. Ask the mortician. We were both at the rite the evenings of the fall and the first tremor along with a dozen other village elders. Despite my boasts, I don't hand out medicine to or revel with just anyone. With Saheli, I finally felt like I had an ally. She was willing to honor other aspects of the Makers than the stern disapproving ones. I think she was one of the few who truly understood my path as ecstatic rather than ascetic. Saheli was open to the ecstatic path. What worth is it to kill my most powerful ally? I think Saheli made her wishes clear. She saw the pods and farming as the future of the abbey, not Elkanah's musty, old books and bones. The copy I got hold of must of been an old one. Saheli showed me her plan to enlarge the agriculture operations. A tasting room and shop to bring in more funds for the abbey."

"You ran to Sister Elkanah to gloat about it."

"No, but she found out somehow. Imagine how well she took it. I saw them arguing, and I caught her following the abbess. She's who you should be questioning. With Pyrmo in charge, Elkanah has exactly what she wants. A more conservative abbess with as much greed for relics as her. The sick Prospective was her creature. She used him to spy among other things. That is when she wasn't doing it herself. I wouldn't be surprised if she poisoned him. You won't tell Pyrmo or Sister Elkanah, will you? If the Justicar would see fit not to… should the Justicar be interested perhaps in attending herself I'm sure we could come to some reciprocal arrangement."

"Stop right there, before you sail into a bribery charge. I'll confirm your story first then decide how to proceed."

15

——————

THE CHARMER

~

A Favor

Mirrei waited outside while Jhee got a quick confirmation of Sister Serra's whereabouts from the mortician. The woman perspired and stammered throughout but confirmed Serra's account of the revels in the orchard. She was full of profuse apologies for her behavior, regrets that Shep would not be able to autopsy the bodies, the state of the fields. Given enough time, she might have confessed to the assassination of Qamate. Perhaps indeed Serra and the mortician's frolics in the orchard had led to tales of the Mist Abbess resurfacing. With the two alibiing each other, there were two more suspects removed from her list. She might keep an eye on them all the same. There was still the matter of the contraband and wine smuggling.

"I hope that didn't upset you too much," Jhee said.

"You work is more exciting than I imagined. Who knew an abbey could be such a hotbed of intrigue and scandal? Fertility cults. Affairs. Rueful confessions."

Time to move on to Jhee's next likely suspect, the archivist. She had yet to speak to the woman since their first trip to the archives. Who would have thought she would have dreaded a visit a place full of so much history and knowledge? While she was there, she hoped to accomplish another task. Jhee needed a better map. This supposedly secure fortress of an abbey had more secret entrances and passages and back doors, so many no one could possibly know them all.

"I guess we better try to question the archivist now. I might prefer another stint with the bog gnats."

"You know it might calm the waters between you and Kanto if you ask him to help with the investigation like you did me?"

"I'm unsure. I tried to have him identify a clue, but just made muck of it."

"The last time we were at the archives, he buffered you and Sister Elkanah."

"Maybe you should ask him. I'm not sure if he's speaking to me right now."

"It will mean more coming from you."

Jhee and Mirrei returned to the room. Jhee sat beside Kanto. She cleared her throat and straightened her robes before proceeding, "Would you like to help me with my investigation?"

Kanto barely spared her a glance.

"I would like your help with my investigation. Please."

"To what end?"

"Sister Elkanah."

"Oh, so she is immune to your charms, then?"

"Please, be more reasonable than she is Kanto."

"I've been reasonable for months. Even after you married a new spouse before you'd even wiped our wedding contract ink from your fingertips. I've been reasonable when you flee my every attempt to woo you. Or meet it with panic or disinterest. I have tried base appeals to your lust. Flattery. I often wonder if you would have warmed to me if I held back or presented you more of a puzzle. You thought you had me solved the moment we met."

"People are dead, Kanto. I think we can agree that finding the killer is the priority."

"Well, I've been asking questions on my own, denbe, and you know what I found? Given her age and the other activities she got up to, it's no wonder Saheli died."

"Please, you mustn't go off investigating on your own. You have no authority to ask, and anything you find may be deemed unusable." Jhee added, "That goes for both of you."

"What do you want from me? I suppose you just want me to look pretty and act charming."

"No, I—"

"Do you remember our first tea? I dressed impeccably. For a change, I saw some glimmer of the attraction and fascination I was used to receiving. I was putting away the tea service after you left when I realized I had been sitting in front of grandmamere's antiquities collection.

"I'd hoped you'd be different than my mamere. House Kenyatta sires, denbe. Mamere was no exception. Officially, I have no baberes. Both sire and grandsire resided elsewhere upon the successful conclusion of their contracts. My dames had no use for them. Presumably, they settled down with those whom they loved and were loved by in return. My sire was particularly despised. He had produced female children for every dame except mamere. What she wanted was a daughter; a disappointment she never forgave my sire for or me. Being that I was not female, she had little time for me as well. Grandmamere, though, doted on me. She always kept a pouch of lace root melon taffies. Every time I told her something new and interesting about the people who visited us, I got one. I've always known what likely paths lay before me. From the moment, I understood what my chastity tattoo meant. I will not be treated as my sire was."

"My apologies. I have much to learn about having more than one spouse and many other matters. Please, help me with Sister Elkanah, and show me what you can do. That woman was insufferable."

Kanto chuckled. "Where would I have gotten in life if I didn't know how to flatter conceited old women? She's a territorial, rigid, self-important academic. It's no wonder you don't get along. On our way then. I'll help navigate these rocky waters. But you'll owe me."

"Owe you what?"

"I'll think of something."

Kanto's smile filled Jhee with the notion she'd made a Dismantler's Deal.

~

The Archives

The archivist popped her head out from behind the large book stand when Jhee, Kanto, and Mirrei entered the library. She sniffed. No one, least of all a Prospective, gained entry without her notice, yet somehow Sister Serra managed it when she stole the Maye headdresses and robes.

"You. Again," the huffy sister said.

"Sister Elkanah."

"What this time?"

"Might I have access to your archives?"

"Didn't your man just tear up the refectory?"

"Yes, but—"

"You must understand my first thought must be for the archives."

"That was an exceptional circumstance."

"I can't take that chance."

Jhee clenched her teeth then gave Kanto a pleading look.

"I understand your reluctance, Sister." Kanto cast his eyes down. "I assure you I have no interest in arcana or the like. My grandmere always said it was not gentlemanly to cypher. It's sage advice I've done my best to heed."

"Your grandmere sounds like a sensible woman, unlike some others. Come then."

"We weren't the most Makerly household, but we did have a collection of antiquities and relics for our Maker shrine as my denbe here can attest."

Jhee rushed to capitalize on the opening Kanto had provided. "I am given to understand you have a small library on local laws and ordinances."

The archivist snorted. "And you wish to view them?"

"I thought perhaps I could contribute: a small gift of my own writings on the subject and a few relics from my personal collection."

The archivist's eyes sparkled and widened. "What kind of relics?" she said with measured pauses between her words.

"Hand-carved, late century adjudication weight and scales set given as a gift to the third prefect."

"I am not interested in pagan idols. It would be inappropriate to have such things amongst our holy relics."

"These though are purported to have been blessed by Canon Oandzo."

"You have the provenance?"

"I have the signed note she sent along with the gift."

"I'd have to have it authenticated. Which texts were you interested in viewing?"

"A few manifests which may be vital to my work, some reference books, and perhaps Sister Niza's account of Saheli's death."

Sister Elkanah cut her a dubious look. "Make a new, formal request, and I'll consult the abbess and the vizier on it."

"Time is a factor."

Jhee fished the access writ the vizier had slipped her from her sleeve and placed it on the book stand in front of the archivist. Once the archivist verified the card, she snorted at Jhee again. "Hopefully, this one is better trained. The same rules as last time. Nothing leaves the archives. Duplication is on a case by case basis. We have a station for conch image capture. However, not all items can be exposed to such direct lighting. No males allowed in the arcane archives whatsoever or near the bones of our honored dead."

Glass doors which led to the staircase hissed open. Jhee and entourage crossed the threshold and traversed the steps to the library spire. Two paths flanked by tall stacks of shelves floor to ceiling diverged from the entryway behind the archivist. Jhee touched her palms together at angles for the First Makers' clasp. She brought her crossed hands to her esca before proceeding.

To Jhee's right, shelves bore every manner of chest and box. Stone, wood, polymer, colored glass. Some plain, some gilded and gleaming with jewels behind glass walls. Coffin-like chests. Funerary jars for the remains of the honored dead.

The right wing bore books in an endless array. Short, tall, fat, thin. Loosely bound sheaves of parchments. Document boxes. Aging conchs. Carved stones and shells whose weight and rough texture she already imagined in her hands. Or the slight scratching of parchment paper between her fingers. The joy Jhee experienced in the mineral springs did not compare to what she felt now. In this archive, she might genuinely remain forever. Hour upon hours spent with tactile, visceral representations of history held in her hands. Such fragile treasures like the heart of a lover.

Jhee inhaled deep the air's slight fishy tang. No doubt from the seaweed paper. A hint of decay and must from the flesh and blood and bones of canons and paragons reportedly housed here floated to her. Maybe the trace of an alchemist furnace or reagent created the sub-scents. One report she read of the archives said it housed the bones of a celestial.

As much as Jhee wanted to grab the nearest book or treasure and study it, she limited herself to the abbey's records and histories. She, Kanto, and Mirrei began to pore over books.

"Pirates and raiders destroyed or overran many other area monasteries," Kanto said. "Tranquility Bridge survived due to its unique location and large number of fighters. The Abbey of the Broken Sword was originally founded by ex-soldiers who had turned to the ways of religious reflection. They changed the Pillarist name Swordbridge to Broken Sword."

"And from that to Tranquility Bridge," Mirrei said.

Jhee turned a page of the text she read, records of building supply purchases. Curiously she could not find the architectural drawings she saw her first visit. "The Abbey of the Broken Sword at Tranquility Bridge. Technically, Tranquility Bridge is the name of the bridge, not the abbey."

"It says here that an untold number of spouses and children took their lives rather than be taken by the barbarians," Kanto said.

"That's the romantic interpretation, anyway. I doubt the children committed suicide. Which alone means whatever the prevailing narrative, the truth is there were a lot more murders than there were suicides. I suspect reluctant adults were helped along too."

"So, a massacre either way."

Jhee could not cast aside the notion she had been toyed with, led around. She had run around the isle chasing down every half-poached, fish-brained rumor when she should have been thinking smaller, simpler. Her curiosity had her chasing phantoms and tales. She must return to first principles.

One moment, it seemed as though the key to this case was Saheli's death. The next, one of the Prospectives. Somehow, she had gotten off course. Was she too focused on heresies, scandals, and grand conspiracies? Back to basics as her mentor Jeja Marpele would say when Jhee went too far chasing wisps down sea wormholes. First principles: most murders were simple. Committed by simple people for simple reasons. What came after was complicated. What was the simple truth here? Were these murders? She had yet to make that determination. She had lots of oddities and unanswered questions, but no definitive evidence. Nevertheless, her Maker Within whispered to her something didn't add up.

"I'm still not sure what we're dealing with," Jhee said. "One could have been an accident. One may have committed suicide. One may have been killed by an incompetent physician."

"And the abbess?" Mirrei asked.

"Possibly a heart attack or maybe she did ascend to the Maker Sphere in glorious light. Everyone loved Saheli. Loved her so much they can't help but make insinuations and cast aspersions."

"Well, denbe," Kanto said, "what I heard from the Prospectives is that the men who died were friends. What if Saheli killed them to hide she was having an affair with one of them? It proved too much for her fragile health, or maybe she committed suicide."

"A good theory I entertained, but one or more died after Saheli," Jhee said.

"Faked her death?"

"Reasonable premise. How?"

Mirrei jumped in, "Phosphorous or another volatile chemical. She may have had help. To refine brightshade into liquid form requires one of its derivatives. The horticulturist would have some if she cooks it herself."

"Volatile chemicals could cause too much heat and be too dangerous. Performers do use smokes and powders to make themselves disappear." Jhee tapped the side of her nose. "If perhaps she had a secret way to and from her chambers through which she sneaked the young men in, she could also slip away with no one the wiser."

Kanto said, "Pyrmo could have been in on it or knew about it. Staging it is how she burnt her hands. Now, that the abbess's chambers are hers, she would know of any such back exits. She and Saheli could have finished off the others."

"What if Saheli did not fake her death? What's the motive then?"

"Retaliation for the others? The drowned Prospective killed the others then Saheli or some combination thereof then committed suicide by flinging himself from the tower or falling off the bluffs while trying to make his escape."

"Also, another theory I entertained until I learned of his plans to run away. I, also, considered accidental overdose, due to Sister Serra's mention of her resistance but dismissed that too after more thought."

"Why?"

Mirrei answered without looking up, "Because it's next to impossible to overdose on that class of drug."

Kanto furrowed his brow, then propped his head up on the desk. "You make this look so easy."

Jhee set aside her book. "Likewise, your flair for style and diplomacy."

Jhee and Kanto locked gazes then hands. They shared a tentative smile.

"Aw!" Mirrei said.

Jhee cleared her throat and went back to her research on plant toxins. Brightshade which she knew the horticulturist grew. Or the blightseeds from the ruined crops. The archivist had access to the very text she read. Jhee eyed various places from which one may listen to anything they said.

"Makers' Mark, denbe, listen to this," Mirrei said. "'The big and sweeping movements are in keeping with the simplistic grandiosity of the male character. The subtlety and refinement of finger cypher are not suited for their clumsy, intemperate nature.' Now, I know where the vizier gets her backward ideas."

How many times had Jhee read some similar sentiment yet glossed over it? Now, confronted with an abbey full of women like this and the real-world effects, she had to grapple with how her silence aided the damage those attitudes caused.

"Are you aware Saheli was one of the leading signatories to the Nahele edict asserting there was no doctrinal or scriptural basis for the exclusion of men from cyphering?" Mirrei asked. "The abbey's practice of no cyphering began in their cloister school, was enacted to ensure a gender-neutral curriculum rather than directly challenge the inherent inequality of the ban. If they had included the practice of cypher in their studies, they would have been forced to exclude males from entry like the Tihalmec Imperial Academy. They maintained low-cost, high-quality education because they did not have to maintain the facilities for or hire experts in magical instruction."

"Seems she also sat on the Rescission Councils that overturned the bans. I may have even seen her there," Jhee said.

"You attended the Rescission Councils, denbe?" Kanto asked.

"As a member of Jeja's legal envoy. The law they passed to enact the ban had serious flaws which made their legitimacy shaky. This is the woman everyone is trying to convince me was a sex fiend of the highest order, who hated relics, was anti-education, and wasted the abbey's money. Either on the impoverished or expensive items for herself?"

"The aspects are not mutually exclusive. It could be how she expected them to show gratitude."

"True. She could have felt owed for her magnanimity. She would not be the first. If Saheli were this fiend as I've been led to believe, how could she have ascended in light to the Maker Sphere?"

"If you're interested in the arcane, denye," Mirrei said, peruse this."

"Mirrei, don't," Jhee began.

The door to the reading room burst open. Jhee tucked a ledger under her arm and jumped to her feet.

"Out," Sister Elkanah said.

16

—————

COLLECTIONS

~

An Unfortunate Relic

"What? Why?" Mirrei asked.

"I'll have no fraternizing, inappropriate contact in my archives or ill talk of the abbey's esteemed leaders. Most of all no showing of new science texts to men. I warned you."

"How would you know if we were fraternizing or what we were discussing?" Mirrei glanced around. "Because you were watching."

"What of it? I told you my first concern was the proper reverence of the manuscripts and relics. I thought it prudent given the feral behavior your other husband displayed."

"Dawn Wolf did not go feral. Bright Harmony, Star Mirror, gather your belongings. We're leaving."

"No, you stay," Kanto said. "I'll leave if it will alleviate the Sister's concerns."

"And you with all your tempter's talk of not being interested in artifice."

"Get this through your narrow-minded head," Mirrei said. "You better get used to the notion of men cyphering, as the time's coming when as many men as women know how. And there won't be a single thing you can do about it."

161

"What a vile, disrespectful creature you are. You have no idea the disaster you court."

"Star Mirror, please," Jhee said. "We're leaving."

"Your spouses need discipline. I see where they get it from. If you weren't such a weak denbe, you would keep them in line. A few swats of the scourge or board might teach them some manners."

Jhee took a measured breath and initiated the tricky procedure to focus her siren module's calming abilities on herself, without making herself too docile. She suppressed the urge to use it on the archivist and be done with her once and for all. Any evidence gained through non-consensual use of the module gave instant grounds to appeal her ruling.

"That's enough, Sister Elkanah. Mind how you talk to my spouses and to me. I am still an Official of the Court."

"And nobility," Mirrei said. She folded her arms and raised her eyebrows. "Shame on you for turning away or trying to have imprisoned those like the refugees or our denme who need your help."

Sister Elkanah snapped her mouth shut. So much for trying to charm and back current information from her.

"Sister Elkanah, can you account for your whereabouts during the deaths of the Prospectives Leigh, Yaou, and Imsu?"

"Prospective Imsu died during the first quake at which time I and several others were trying to secure the items in the archives. Prospective Yaou's happened under Zalver's care, and she assured me it was some natural disease."

"I understood she treated you for scratches and skin irritation."

"Serra sometimes thinks it's funny to put itchweed on my finger quills."

"Did she do so while Prospective Yaou was there?"

"Yes."

"So, that means you would have had an opportunity to check in on him while he was there?"

"But I didn't."

"Wasn't he your assistant? I was under the impression he volunteered at the archives?"

"What of it?"

"You didn't want to inquire about the health of someone who helped you maintain the archive?"

"What if his ailment was contagious? An infection or mold might have detrimental effects on the collections. I didn't want to risk it."

"Then why were you repeatedly seen in the quiet room with him."

"Who told you that?"

"What of Prospective Leigh?"

"I'm not sure. I think I was performing devotions."

"In your room?"

"Yes."

"Alone."

"Yes!" Sister Elkanah snatched the ledger Jhee had slipped under her arm and jabbed her finger at the door.

Jhee stormed out of the archives. She would not be lectured about marriage by celibates. She could think of few practices which dishonored the Makers more.

"A celibate presumes to tell me how to treat my spouses. Kanto, you can have all the adept and cyphering lessons you want and more. I owe you that and another apology. I'm surprised anyone had bothered to report these young men's deaths at all. As they viewed them as too stupid or useless to be of concern."

How could she have contemplated for even a moment leaving Kanto here at the mercy of these fishwives? Mirrei suppressed a smirk.

"This isn't funny."

"No, it isn't." Mirrei continued to smirk. "Such a collection of bigoted women."

"These were my peers. Would I have even noticed a few years ago?"

Kanto snickered. As he continued, Mirrei and Jhee gave him dumbfounded looks. "I had matters well in hand with the archivist until you and Mirrei got up in your ether with her. Is this what it takes for you to respect my intelligence? Other women belittling it. The pattern emerges. You have no desire for pleasure or procreation with me, yet you feel free to hypocritically lecture the clerics on the celibate lifestyle. I'm leaving. Not that you'll have further need of me."

Kanto tromped off down the corridor.

At last, Jhee's anger flowed away. "It's getting late. That's enough excitement for today. Allow me to escort you back to the room."

"Where our adventure ends for the day?"

"I have a few more lines of inquiry to follow. It would put my mind at ease to know you are somewhere safe."

"Implying you will be somewhere not safe."

"I'm amazed at how quickly you've come to know me."

"Do remember I was a guest at your house for some time before our betrothal."

"How could I forget?"

Jhee and Mirrei returned to the room arm in arm.

"Kanto hasn't returned? He left ahead of us."

"Bax has eyes on him. He's talking to the Prospectives," Shep said.

~

The Storehouse

Jhee examined the procurement writ. She supposed now was as good a time as any to check out the apothecary. She hoped whatever Lady Bathsheba had tried to draw her attention to was still there.

A bored Professed unlocked the stores. "We're on the honor system for most supplies. Come up front when you're done and close the door after yourself. If any provisions you want are locked up, scan them, and I'll get them for you before you leave. Then I'll scan and close out your writ for you."

While nowhere near as magnificent as the archives, the shelves which lined either side of the storehouse boasted as much abundance. Jhee captured an image of the storehouse map posted by the door then set off down the aisles. Storage units brimmed with boxes of herbal and floral extracts. Dried leaves hung from hooks or vine ropes on every vertical. She used the illumination and magnification function on her conch to read tags and box labels. A thick layer of dust showed some had not been touched in ages. She had to dig through a few shelves to find the supplies on her list.

First things first: her promised casks of that most delicious Tranquility Gold. Mostly for her and Shep. A wine which surely should have met with even Shep's high standards. Though, she was disappointed he had not enjoyed it as much as she did. To be honest, the second taste she had the morning of the incident had been underwhelming. She located a cask, tapped the writ against it, then pressed a tag on it. She also wanted some of the must and unfermented nectar to study. She pinched the bridge of her nose. She gathered more raw ingredients for Mirrei's poultice.

Lady Bathsheba's draught recipe came to mind. She already had the nectar. What else did she need? Jhee snapped her fingers. Orange cider and black orchid tea.

Why had the Lady intimated she visit the storehouse? Why call her attention to the tea so ostentatiously? Was it meant to be a clue as to the doings of this murderer who stalked the abbey? Jhee would get to the bottom of it. If only because of professional curiosity alone. It was also her duty.

If only adhering to Jhee's familial duties came as easily to her as duty to empire and profession. How much misery would she have avoided if she had married a Crag Hall sibling as her family asked, not gone to war, or followed Shep? Uncharacteristic rebellion. She had thought to get a rise from them. She had always done as they wanted until she could not take it anymore. She had once sought to escape her rural district for life at court. A favor here; some discretion there. Which is how she acquired ministry connections at the capital. Then Central Authority had recalled the officials from the border districts as the Shield went up. All officials had to report to the court as soon as they could. And she did. She did as she was told. When Miramar learned of her assignment, she asked Jhee to take her daughter with her.

"You owe me, Jhee."

Their home island had half sunk into the sea by then. Jhee's home, which was on higher ground remained, but the displaced and homeless had grown. Miramar's house had sunk, and out of friendship and kindness and duty and loyalty, Jhee had taken Miramar and her daughter into her home. She gave them food and shelter. Jhee supposed it was why Miramar thought it was only natural to propose the match she did. Jhee out of friendship, also, chose to ask no giving or receiving of boons. Mirrei had much of her mother's looks. A fact which made the decision much easier on Jhee. She had been wary of taking a female consort at least before she had settled into her new assignment.

Jhee initially held the traditional, last position in her household for a more political arrangement at court similar to the one she had with Kanto's family. However, Kanto's social savvy and discontent with a modest life indicated he was already halfway to shore. She did not expect him to stay with her long once they reached the capital. She just hoped he would help her arrange his new situation. That way, she could reap a political benefit. She would probably do something similar with Mirrei. She would find them both spouses more suitable to their age and ambitions.

The orange cider Jhee spotted in a neater, more frequently used part of the storage room then scanned it and put a non-procurement tag on it. The black orchid tea she found by the lace root melon taffies in a locked, glass-front cabinet.

Jhee was in the middle of the pecking order and was not as overly ambitious as some. When opportunities presented themselves, she took them. She did not force them or jostle for position as others did. She rather liked her job as magistrate. She traveled from place to place on isles too small for much in the way of permanent structures. Especially with the Great Barrier Storm, those islands had become increasingly isolated, especially given the storm's effect on communication equipment. A measure designed to confound the barbarians' navigation systems. From time to time, shipwrecked barbarians washed up. They were also her duty to hand them over to the body catchers for transportation to the capital. She wondered what they did with them. Perhaps they would use them for the Medical Protectorate experiments instead of noble warriors like Shep.

Jhee contemplated the taffies, or if she truly wanted them. Did she really hope to buy Kanto's forgiveness with candy? It was the gesture she thought. A symbol to show she listened and was not wholly uninterested in him as a person. She tagged the sweets.

A door opened. Jhee assumed the storekeeper had come to check on her. Cool, outdoors wind moistened her face. Jhee stopped on the verge of calling out to the new arrival. The breeze, heavy with the scent of the smudging stick, whispered down the aisle. Shuffling footfalls, their gait halting, approached. The horticulturist? The poetess? Jhee doused her conch and ducked down an aisle.

The Complaints

A figure garbed in clerical vestments dragged a hefty, black keg over to the case. Still oblivious to Jhee's presence, the person stumbled to one of the giant barrels of beer and poured a tankard from the tasting spigot which she chugged in one go. She removed the stopper and used a sampling pipette to fill a flask she produced from inside her robes. She took a quick swig before screwing on the cap. Jhee followed the figure to the locked cases where she produced keys and unlocked them.

Behind the tea, rested more giant black kegs. The figure thumped a few before one had a hollower, heavier sound than the others. She paused and touched the scan tag Jhee had left. She spun around.

"Looking for me?" Jhee emerged from the aisle.

The figure lowered her hood. Pyrmo glanced at the flask she held then shoved it into her sleeve. She sighed, shook her head, and took it back out. "Alas, you've discovered my dirty little secret."

"May I ask what that actually is?"

Pyrmo's attention went to the black keg. "Tranquility Black. Moonshine. My own private stash. I am ashamed to have you see me like this."

"Let only those whose feet have never been wet lecture someone else on how to keep theirs dry. I'm afraid I will have to ask you a few questions regarding the death of Saheli and the Prospectives."

"Ask. Whatever answers I have, I will give."

"I've heard your account of when Saheli died. I'll need your accounting of the times leading up to the deaths of the Prospectives."

"My accounting? It's hard to say. I was well into my cups then. The night of the storm where the Prospective fell, I had been drinking particularly heavily. Likewise, the first tremor. As embarrassed as I am to say, I made quite the spectacle of myself. Far more than ever, the poetess did."

Jhee laid a finger aside her nose and tapped in thought. Pyrmo's contempt for the poetess then lay more in the distaste of seeing one's own flaws reflected back at you. "Can anyone confirm this?"

"Confirm? I would think half the abbey could. To the specific, though, the prioress was called to put me to bed like a child. Not my noblest moment, Justicar."

"I will confirm this with her."

"Of course."

"Did you have occasion to visit Prospective Yaou?"

"I did."

"May I inquire what you spoke about?"

"I am afraid, on that, I must be oblique. As the communication happened under the veil of counsel."

"He confided in you something for which he wanted absolution or advice."

"Why does it feel as if I am being interrogated?"

"Four people have died here in the past few months. To faithfully execute the task you set me, requires my due diligence."

"Your thoroughness is appreciated. Though had Saheli's miraculous death not had such a thorough accounting by so many witnesses, I might not have thought her long for this world. She was on the aged side. As for those poor, young boys, life is always short and harsh for those such as them."

"Still, I want you and the residents of this abbey to know you are not forgotten. To do less, would be a disservice to you and my duty under the law."

"I see. You shame me once again with your insight, Justicar. My personal failings have led to my not being as concerned with the affairs of those beneath me here at the abbey. I think we should both strive to do better by those under our care."

"I am glad you would agree."

The abbess unscrewed the flask's cap and proceeded to the nearest drain. After she dumped out the contents, Jhee nodded. Pyrmo grabbed the black orchid tea. "I will require this to sober up. I'd also appreciate your discretion."

"Once I have satisfied certain curiosities, we shall speak no more of this."

The abbess set aside the tea to clasp forearms and touch foreheads. The overly familiar gesture between them more warranted this time. Though the reek of smudge thick on Pyrmo—which now made more sense—worsened Jhee's headache. Despite that, the smell of burn cream and licorice overpowered it.

Jhee twiddled the letters on her conch to log the abbess's statement longhand, glad to have enriched someone's life. Given her domestic blunders of late, she luxuriated in a rare feeling of competence.

Although, if Pyrmo's alibi checked out, she might have been on the verge of eliminating her major suspects. What was it Raigen said Saheli suspected in her letter? Another authority undermining her. If anything Sister Serra said could be believed, Pyrmo made a prime candidate for this Mist Abbess character. If she and Sister Elkanah disapproved so strongly of Saheli's methods, Jhee could see them staging a coup. Though, would they have gone as far as murder?

Back at the room, Mirrei prepared Jhee another poultice. "Try not to give this one away."

Kanto returned to their chambers. "Mirrei, may we have the room?"

"Sure," Mirrei said. "Keep it civil, you two."

"Shall we try this again?" Kanto took the other chair in the nook. "I feel like you think I'm some kind of fool. I don't like you looking at me that way."

"From what I can tell, you are quite intelligent in your own way."

"My own way? What way is that?"

"Emotional. Cultural—"

"You made some impressive strategic moves in the positioning of your house like coming to the aid of House Foster in exchange for half their holdings. Underwhelming ones too such as not crushing House Diamante when you had the chance. How many times have they encroached on both your sea lanes and spawning beds since? You were an academic, though. Women like grandmamere would eat you alive. I would be the secret ingredient."

Jhee viewed him anew. What could she say? She had never discussed household strategy with him, yet he knew about some of her more oblique maneuvers.

"Nothing to say to that. Of course not."

Kanto rose.

"The choice to marry you was mine. Though, if grandmamere disapproved, she would have found a way to talk me out of it and likely make me think it was my idea. She is well versed in the art of letting other people have her way. Grandmamere still got the better of you in our marriage negotiations. Yet, she was impressed with how hard a bargain you commanded."

Kanto glided from the nook as Jhee continued to sit mute.

17
———

THE GUEST WING

~

The Performers

According to Sister Niza's account of Saheli's death, all senior clergy were present and in full sight of the others. While it's possible they were all part of some conspiracy, Jhee doubted it. With so many factions, the likelihood they conspired to protect the guilty party was nil. If either the archivist or the horticulturist had an advantage over the other, they would use it.

First, Jhee must confirm or deny the abbess's alibi before she entertained other theories. She tracked the prioress down in her cell.

"I caught Pyrmo sneaking liquor. She claims to have been drunk the night Prospective Leigh drowned and that you put her to bed."

"I did. It explained much. She was prioress before me. Saheli's indulgences extended to more than the deacons. She took the hands-on approach as abbess. No disrespect intended to Saheli or Pyrmo, but the abbey's finances were a mess and Pyrmo a disaster as prioress which makes more sense considering her problem. I may not have always agreed with Saheli's choices, but I trusted her judgment. Still, Saheli should have found a less challenging position for Pyrmo."

With each of Jhee's prime suspects providing alibis for different murders, perhaps there was some elaborate scheme by which they all did it. A cabal

171

that conspired to keep the truth of Saheli's death private? While dramatic, with these players unlikely. A bit of the "Dispatches from Arrow Point"-era Jhee's mindset had sneaked out. She had proceeded with the hypothesis that if Saheli were indeed murdered the perpetrator had to be a clergy member. Strangers such as the performers or refugees could not get close enough. Though, having learned of Saheli's personal approach to running the abbey invalidated that premise. Which raised another possibility: what if the principal victims were the Prospectives?

The suspect pool opened much wider. She may have been too quick to narrow her focus to the high table. A mistake she would now correct.

Performers do use smokes and powders to make themselves disappear.

She thought of Shep, Mirrei, and Kanto's admonishments. Had she been too quick to dismiss the Prospectives and the refugees based on age or gender? Or even the performers? She had been ready to condemn Lady Bathsheba for snobbery, but what of her own. She knew how easy it was to lay blame for everything at the threshold of margin dwellers. Maybe she was making the same mistakes with the perpetrator as she had with the victims. If not for suspecting them first, but for perhaps dismissing them as not smart enough. Members of the camps. Smugglers. Performers. She had cast aside her doubts on them for dubious reasons.

"What do you know about the performers?" Jhee asked the prioress.

"Not much. Some of them were refugees, and they sometimes did free shows there. They usually stuck to the port towns."

Jhee remembered the tattoos on the members of the camp, the smuggler, and yes, of course, one of the performers. This abbey had secret ways in and out aplenty. There existed smugglers and contraband. All that was required was someone on the inside. What better way to smuggle contraband or people to and from the abbey than via the performance troupe?

The prioress kissed her Drakist effigy. "The things they're saying about Saheli aren't true. She was good folk. Yes, she had her own ways of doing things, and even I didn't always approve. While her emphasis was on good works and labor, she valued knowledge too but understood formal education wasn't for everyone."

"'To every part, its place in the Design.' Thank you for your candor."

Jhee found the rather storm-tossed appearing Pyrmo in the Worship Hall praying. The black orchid tea rested beside her on the bench. She placed a gentle hand on the abbess's shoulder. Pyrmo started and gazed about her wildly.

"Justicar, why are you here?"

"Sorry to disturb you, Abbess. I had a quick question about the performance troupe."

"The performance troupe?"

"Did they perform here frequently?"

"Not at all. I believe this was their first time although the abbey is on their route. Though it was not my idea."

"Why the change?"

"The troupe leader's request. I thought with the special occasion, why not?"

Jhee tapped the side of her nose. "Thank you."

On Jhee's way to see the performers, she visited Lady Bathsheba to thank her for access to the archives and for her help in the aftermath of Shep's incident. She also might glean more information about the initial state of the system.

"You would have thought of it yourself eventually. You were under enormous pressure at that moment."

"Thank you then for hastening my recollection of the law. One more thing, whose idea was it to have the performance troupe play the feast?"

"Saheli and I entertained the idea. We knew they came through the area often. Pyrmo made it happen, though."

Jhee contacted Bax. "Have you found out anything new?"

"More gossip mostly. I've tried sending you field reports, but they've bounced."

This storm-blasted communication blackout had struck again. Laughter and clinking glasses carried through the connection. Were Jhee a less charitable sort, she would have suspected him of having been drinking it up this whole time. "Could you arrange for me to meet with the troupe leaders?"

"Of course. They were just here."

"What's your location?"

"We're in the hostelry near the guest annex. I can meet you and provide introductions."

"Splendid." Jhee whipped out the trusty, invaluable map and set off.

Scrapes and the odd rattle shadowed Jhee, as she met Bax in the guest wing. The troupe leaders were a married couple, the announcer and the assistant who held the fire blanket during Mr. Zane's performance. They greeted her with hearty smiles and wide arms. A distinct change from the other receptions she had received these past few days.

"Welcome, Justicar. Welcome." The announcer kicked out a seat and had already poured her a cup of whatever they had already been drinking by the time Jhee sat. "No empty cups at my table. One. Two. Three."

The announcer, her husband, and Bax knocked theirs back then slammed their cups down on the table. Jhee took a deep drink. She ascribed no other distinct taste to the alcohol other than burn. She squeezed her eyes shut to stop them from watering. The liquor paled in comparison to the refujuice she drank the day previous. She covered her cup when the announcer went to refill it. The obligations of politeness had been met.

"To what do we owe such a distinguished visit by such an important person as yourself?"

"I'm in need of some quick answers if you don't mind."

"Of course, not. We'd be happy to. Ask. Ask."

"How was it you came to perform for the feast?"

"I'd think many of the troupes which passed by this place had wanted to. We'd often bypassed it ourselves. We might've done so again if two of our number hadn't mentioned their anniversary celebration."

"Two?"

"Yes, both Hethyr and Anshu mentioned the feast. They'd been after us to visit for some time. Although we'd make a few shell at the nearby town, it hadn't made sense until now. Holy places can be some of the cheapest patrons. There's something about celebrations which can prize open even the tightest clams."

Jhee nodded and took another polite drink from her cup. The announcer bobbed her head with satisfaction. Jhee's shoulders loosened as she settled more into her seat. Either the alcohol or the announcer's warm, melodic voice had wrapped a sense of welcome around her. "Do your performers give lessons or work by private arrangement?"

The announcer raised an eyebrow. "Some have been known to. Mr. Zane, for instance. Mostly, by prior arrangement."

"No chance of calling upon them, now."

"They may make an exception for an official visitor. The hall across the annex. Men on the left and women on the right. Ms. Hethyr and Mr. Zane are at the far end."

Jhee wrenched herself free of the camaraderie and rose to leave. Bax stood too with a slight sway. "Hold, my lady. Mr. Shep would have my hide if I let you go alone."

Bax, who had gone bright red and sweaty from the effect of drink, would be of no use to her in this condition. "In your current state, Bax, what help do you think you would be? No, Bax. Stay and partake with your friends. I only have a few simple inquiries. I don't intend to be long."

The performers' quarters were located across the annex from the owners. At least she did not have to ascend or descend steps. She held her glow orb aloft as she crossed the cloister, a long walkway of alcoves and columns, many filled with grotesque statues. She paused to examine one. They were eerily life-like with a similar finish to that of the abbey. She shivered.

The patter of footsteps came to a stop an instant after hers then went quiet. A drip of water rang oddly warped by the annex's weird acoustics. Had Bax chosen to follow her anyway? If he had, why would he not announce his presence?

Jhee tucked the glow orb in her sleeve and ducked behind a column. Once her eyes adjusted, she noticed a shadowy shape stealing down the annex. She waited for the figure to pass then doubled back along her route a few columns. She peered out again.

The whiff of something akin to sickly-sweet fennel came to her nose. A sharp strike to her head caused a flash in her vision. Her head struck the column. She swayed and slumped to the ground.

~

The Actor

Jhee awoke in a strange room. A young man, in a dressing robe, filed his nail claws at the desk beside the bed. He set aside the file to daub himself with cologne. "Oh, good, you have awakened."

She glanced around the room. One corner held hoops and poles wrapped in wick or topped with glow orbs. "Mr. Zane? How did I get here?"

"I heard a thud outside my door. I opened it, and there you were. I initially thought you had passed out drunk."

He addressed her with a tone, while demur, deferential, also conveyed no hurry or concern for having found a strange woman at his door. Jhee's head had the dull throb of a headache which had been her constant companion since her arrival. A hazy recollection of being struck returned. "Let me smell your cologne," she ordered.

"A fair thank you for someone who may have saved your life."

The room had the sooty smell of accelerant and old fire. It made her nauseated. Jhee clenched her mouth shut. Her head exploded in pain. She probed the tender spots on her head. "Do it this instant, young man."

Mr. Zane gave a crisp snap of his sleeve and held over with the small, cologne bottle. He removed the cologne's stopper and wafted the scent towards Jhee. Then he leaned in to let her catch his scent. Both scents bore cucumber undertones. Not a match for what she smelled before she had been struck. "I've known men who've received expensive jewels in return for less."

"Thank you. Forgive my rudeness. You should not have been the recipient of my ire. This stay has been bothersome in the extreme through no fault of yours."

She lurched to her feet. The room shifted as her perceptions righted themselves. The tenderness at both the front and back of her head stopped at the edge of her head wrap. The poultice must have cushioned the blows she took. It may well have saved her life.

"You should be compensating me for all the liberties you're taking, Justicar. What has you creeping about so late?"

"I was hoping to speak to Mr. Anshu or Ms. Hethyr. If you could point me towards Ms. Hethyr."

"Hetty." Mr. Zane rolled his eyes and adjusted his robes. "A subject of little interest to me anymore. She's a crude, stupid, ungrateful, clumsy beast."

"Yet, you did keep company?"

"When it pleased me. Which it no longer does." Mr. Zane moved aside the collar of his robe to reveal old burns where someone attempted to leave a drawer's mark or cypher's sigil. "She was abusive and consorted with criminals."

"She sought to bind you?"

"Don't all artificers."

"Only the weak ones."

"Fortunately for me, she has her sights on another."

"Mr. Anshu."

"He recently joined the troupe. Right before our arrival here."

"Is he any more receptive to this attention than you?"

Mr. Zane slipped one of the arm hoops from the corner over his forearm. He moved his arm in a circle until the hoop spun. "You would have to ask him."

The spinning hoops made Jhee dizzy. She stilled them by reaching out, then flopped back down on the bed. "I have asked you."

Mr. Zane sat beside her feet. "Justicar, may I talk candidly to you?"

"By the Makers, it's time more did."

"I imagine your position has you hear a great many shocking things?"

"On occasion."

"I couldn't help but notice your household arrangement. Mr. Anshu has drawn more attention than Hethyr's. I have found that I am fond of him as well, a fondness I believe he returns. An awkward situation has developed between Hethyr, Anshu, and myself. The fondness between Anshu and me has drawn Hethyr's notice to the detriment of her behavior."

"Oh." Jhee rubbed her hands against her thighs to give herself a moment to think about this new dimension.

"Hethyr is not the first of my admirers. They all, however, have been women. This affection for Anshu has upended me. I suppose for branch Drakists who'll take no mortal lovers of a different gender, there is no scandal. Although for the celibates here who take no mortal companionship at all, both paths make a widow of the life mate the Path Maker intended for me. I had never supposed a situation like this would arise outside of a household."

Jhee cleared her throat. Of all those to consult in affairs of the heart, Mr. Zane had chosen the poorest of experts. She should have excused herself and made an instant bid to leave. Yet, he had sought her counsel, and she owed him some answer. "Give it some time, and perhaps the feelings will pass. A string of admirers suggests dissatisfaction with each. Mr. Anshu presents an element of mystery and the unknown."

"You suggest perhaps my affection stems from routine and a desire for something new." Mr. Zane placed a hand on Jhee's forearm. He glanced down as he brushed her robes then up again at her. "Perhaps the attentions of a more established, smarter woman might snap me out of it."

And wealthier. Jhee had no doubt which trait of hers interested him most. "Even if the affection lingers, you must find your own path."

"You wouldn't find it a hindrance to my obtaining a proper place in a household. Say, yours, for instance."

Jhee removed Mr. Zane's hand from her robes and placed it demurely with his other. "I have no doubt of your resourcefulness to find a situation befitting whatever path your preferences dictate. My advice, being something of a traditionalist, would be wholly traditional and not as befitting the free-spirited nature to which you are accustomed. These cannot be matched to the mutual bonds within a household which are born of deep affection and a commitment to child-rearing. However, the law has minimal judgment to render on the mutual affections of informed adults. Now if I may, might you point me in the direction of Mr. Anshu."

Jhee hoped she had made seeking a placement with her sound suitably dull and proper.

Mr. Zane smirked and squared his shoulders at Jhee's uncomfortable reaction. "I thank you for your most learned counsel. Second door down. I would prefer it he not know what I confided."

"You can count on my discretion, young sir."

Jhee removed her head wrap and tucked it under her arm. She owed her continued health this evening to the young and love-struck. They had proved her the foolish one many times for discounting them. She had a duty to her constituency. One she had neglected too long. This made her all too cognizant of the trade-offs Mirrei and Kanto made to join such a household as hers.

Jhee had to do better by all those who depended on her, from the forgotten young men to the members of her household. She would uncover whatever unscrupulous behavior was going on at this abbey. She would deliver Mirrei and Kanto to the capital where they can reach their full potential and spread their wings and fly. Then she and Shep would return to licking their wounds together.

She made haste to the hall where she enacted a mild healing on her head injuries.

~

The Animal Handler

Jhee scanned her surroundings and kept constant watch about her as she went to Mr. Anshu's room. Due to the abbey's odd acoustics, every drip and scrape echoed and magnified, assaulting her hearing from every angle. She kept her hand on the knife up her sleeve. Some fiend had caught her unawares once. There would not be a second time.

No light came from Mr. Anshu's door. She knocked anyway. Her patience was thin, and she meant to have answers from someone, anyone tonight. "Mr. Anshu, this is the Justicar. I wish to speak with you."

Shuffling came from within followed by an unintelligible moan or grunt. Jhee took that as leave to enter. The room smelled of animal musk. The bed lay empty and undisturbed.

A shadow rose beside her. She turned, glow orb and knife at the ready. Pale eyes peered out from a dark corner. Too pale to be folk. Itzil, the imposing bull hound from the feast performance, crept forward with a low growl. The buckles on her harness clanked on every motion.

Jhee reached for the door. Itzil raised up on her haunches and loomed over her. Its bulk filled the entire space between Jhee and the door. Itzil growled in warning. A rudimentary attempt to soothsay it with Earth also elicited a warning bark. Jhee closed her eyes and focused on projecting a calm voice.

"Easy, Itzil. Easy." Her voice came out calm and disappointingly normal, without a trace of reverberation. She tried again. Pain shot down her spine. She saw stars. The blow she took must have activated the anti-tampering protocols on her siren module.

Jhee hazarded a glance behind her. A driftwood wardrobe stood open. Discretion being the better part of valor, she ducked inside. Through the sword-shaped openings carved in the doors, she watched Itzil, who returned to all fours. Itzil curled up in front of the wardrobe doors and blocked Jhee in.

Any movement Jhee made, the bull hound barked or snarled. The moment Jhee squatted down, Itzil became quiescent.

Jhee must have drifted off to sleep because she awoke to the sound of jingling bells. She peered through the wardrobe openings.

Mr. Anshu entered the room. He jingled the bells at Itzil who sat up and panted. "Good girl."

Mr. Anshu took a seat at the dressing table and turned on the lamp. He took up the nearby towel and wiped down his face and muzzle. He removed his hairpiece and placed it on a wig stand. He unbuckled the straps on his armor to remove his cuirass and pauldrons. He scratched his scalp then dug at his golden, sparkling esca. Part of it came off in his fingers. Jhee fought back the bile rising in her throat.

Itzil growled at her movement. Mr. Anshu grabbed a knife and faced the wardrobe. No blood or fluids dripped from the esca. It was intact. Except now it showed its actual shape, the divoted star of a woman. Mr. Anshu appeared not to be a mister.

"Pardon me… ma'am."

"Who's that?"

"The justicar. I'd appreciate it if you called off your companion."

"Itzil, go."

The bull hound bounded to its bedding in the far corner. The animal handler opened the wardrobe. Jhee let out her breath. "Makers' blessings upon you, madam. Or should I still address you as sir?"

"The clothes are the lie, not my body. Please, explain your presence in my wardrobe."

"It was the safest place I fear from your companion's wrath. I barely made it with my life."

"If Itzil meant you true harm, I assure you would not have. She must have liked your smell or was otherwise feeling playful."

"That was playful?"

"You are still intact, aren't you?" The animal handler leaned in and sniffed. "Minty. A raw undertone. Do you own pets?"

"A shark dog."

"Shark dog musk. That must be it. Itzil is very docile with respect to other hounds, especially sharks and—" The animal handler's eyes brightened. "The man at breakfast. Your husband?"

Jhee nodded then sought to change the subject, "Perhaps I would have done well to bring some shark nip with me."

"Be lucky you didn't. Itzil detests shark nip. You still have not explained why you're here."

Jhee pointed at the knife the animal handler still held. "If you would. I have a few questions I wish to ask."

The animal handler lowered the knife but did not put it away. This close and without all her gear on Jhee again noted the similarity of hair color and ear shape to her glimpse of Mr. Akesheem. "You are some relation to Mr. Pol and his son?"

"I'd pity anyone with that bottom feeder as a father. I am Djet Anshula from Ebbingsisle. Aki is my brother, Djet Akesheem. Mr. Pol is no one's father least of all ours. Astute guess."

"The calibrations or alignments are the key. Alignments: You carry yourselves similar. Coloring. Ear shape. The unique shade of your eyes. Calibration: At the performance, also, Akesheem expressed no distress over Itzil's appearance. Yet, terror at every brush of Ms. Hethyr's flames."

Ms. Anshula fondled Itzil's chin and scratched her chin while she secured her harness to the wall. "My brother's met Itzil before. You had other questions?"

"First, how did your brother come to be here without you and in the care of one you describe as a bottom feeder?"

"Akesheem, in despair over a matter of the heart, left home. He struck up a friendship with Mr. Pol, who agreed to transport him to the capital and get him proper work papers without our parents' permission. If not work, then he would find him a wife or other accommodation. I understand his impulse. Our family is poor. Both our leaving provides relief to our family. More for our siblings' dowry. We could not afford dowries for them to marry."

"Dowry? Rather than boon exchange?"

"Things are becoming hard in the Outer Reaches."

Boon exchange was more common among those not well off. Despair over a matter of the heart. Jhee understood that kind of despair all too well, though.

Jhee rubbed her muzzle. Her thoughts went to Kanto and Mirrei. "This disguise?"

"Recruiters came to our isle offering work grants. The work grant was only for men who could already artifice. My parents could only afford teaching for me. My primaries are Earth and Water. A helpful recruiter suggested I disguise myself to participate in the free work exchanges where I could get advanced training with drawing to work on the wall. She got another recruitment bounty. While I assumed one of my other brothers' identities to support myself during my search."

"Earth and Water. Hence your rapport with Itzil."

"That and some early volunteer work with veterans. Itzil and I traveled, moving from work camp to work camp. I hired myself out as a drawer until I joined the troupe. There Itzil could be part of my act. I soon learned my brother had resolved to take vows."

"You asked the troupe owners to visit because you are of a mind to talk him out of it."

"If I can. To look after him, if I cannot. There is also the matter of a recruitment fee Mr. Pol paid my family. My parents wanted to make sure they would not have to give back the money if Aki took vows."

"So many amateur investigators running about, I feel I am redundant. Two by chance. One here for her mother. One here for her brother."

Ms. Anshula smiled. "The poetess. My brother's reaction to her has bolstered my hope of dissuading him from celibacy. A fact I just discussed with her."

"Feh. Celibacy. Does no actual meditation and contemplation take place at this abbey? What of Ms. Hethyr?"

Ms. Anshula snorted. "Hethyr? That brute. You won't find her here. I have seen Mr. Zane's 'love bites.' It requires much restraint on my part when I am in her presence. Just as well she has kept her distance from me."

Jhee tucked her hands in her sleeves. Then Ms. Hethyr had an independent desire to visit the abbey.

A knock came at the door. Raigen burst in trailed by Mr. Zane and Bax before Ms. Anshula responded. Itzil perked up.

"Itzil, down."

Raigen spoke, "Forgive my rudeness. We are looking for the justicar."

Mr. Zane stopped short at Ms. Anshula's appearance.

"It appears your dilemma has answered itself, Mr. Zane. So much for your attempts to scandalize me."

"Pity. I had begun to warm to the idea of something different."

"Off with you and your pretense of decadence and sophistication. It grows tiresome. Now, what has happened to put you in such a state?"

"Sister Elkanah has accused Sister Serra of heresy and wants to call the Invocation. The whole abbey is in an uproar. She has cited you as a witness."

"Me? Forge my patience in flames. This woman."

18

———

THE ACCUSATION

~

The Unmaker's Work

When Jhee entered the main hall, the abbess registered a mix of shock and relief at her arrival. Jhee took a position off to the side.

Sister Elkanah held the floor. "Serra is from Verdale where they still practice the blasphemous worship of those such as the Maye King and Maye Queen or their so-called Deep Makers. Here are some of her indecent effigies."

"*Toki* dolls. You plant them in the field for a good harvest," Sister Serra said.

"Profaneness and heathenism."

"It's no secret the Maker selection and exclusion process was largely political. I didn't know what else to do. I went with what I knew. The fertility rituals of my childhood isle. Maker geld and effigies and buried toki shell figures. Yes, I borrowed a few of Sister Elkanah's texts and researched a few more rituals. I figured what could it hurt. Ceremonies and sacrifices to honor the Maye King and Queen and the Warrior of Pain."

"Virgin sacrifices?"

"Yes."

"You see Abbess and Justicar? She admits participation in vile blood rites."

Sister Serra cleared her throat. "Not that kind of sacrifice."

The physician suppressed a chuckle.

"Oh," Jhee said.

"It is the Unmaker's work," Sister Elkanah said. "You shall not profane this holy place with such infernal practices. No wonder the abbey has been plagued by death and demonic forces. I call upon the Invocation of Xendatia to cleanse this holy place."

Everyone gasped. Professed and Prospective alike whispered amongst themselves, even the remaining senior clergy. The physician began to rock back and forth in her chair, shaking her head. Jhee had an accountability chain: audits, review boards, Chief Justicar councils. The Invokers did not. They worked by patronage. Once invited in, the Invokers would not stop.

Pyrmo stood. "Silence. I'm sure, Sister Elkanah, you did not mean that."

"This is not a laughing matter or a matter for play. You do not invoke the Unraveler on this sacred isle."

Pyrmo shook her head. "A member has called for the Invocation of Xendatia. I will retire to consider the matter."

"What is to consider? These fiends invoked the Unmaker on our isle. We must have a cleansing."

"You are not the abbess here, Elkanah."

"Perhaps I should be. I once thought your leadership would bring about a return to tradition and decency. Yet, the Unraveler's influence continues to rise. Perhaps I was wrong to support you."

"What of your sins, Sister Elkanah?" Jhee asked.

"My sins?" Sister Elkanah sputtered. "My-my sins are not at issue here."

"Unraveler? An interesting choice of appellation for the Unmaker. One I believe favored by the anarchist wing of the Pillarists. Whom I seem to remember you called the Doombearers instead of the more common term Doombringers."

The archivist's eyes went wide, turning a dark umber in the process. "How dare you?"

"How dare you, Elkanah?" Sister Serra said. "Everyone knows how jealously you guard the archives. Care to explain how I could have gained access to the archives under your watch?"

"Upon occasion, I had need to counsel one of my assistants. One evening after our conversation and prayers, I returned to find the archives had been breached."

"Conversation? Is that what you call it? In your chambers, no doubt," Sister Serra said.

"I am not on trial here."

"Perhaps you should be."

"I admit to one night having succumbed to the affections of one of these wicked, wicked men."

"Who?" Jhee asked.

"Prospective Yaou. I later realized someone had taken relics from the archives. My activities with the Doombringers were misguided. My sins, though, are not why we're here."

"All our sins are," Sister Serra spat. "The land suffers for our sins. The constant storms are drowning the fields, poisoning the crops and sea life. You'd know that if you poked your head out of the archives long enough to experience the world around you."

"I've experienced the ills of this world aplenty. This is about you and your shameful, wicked ways. If you had perhaps stayed on the true path instead of these false ones, the Makers would see fit to reward our isle with an abundance of something other than misery."

"Idolaters. You with your lust for relics and false piety. You've sown the soil with fallowness. The Makers want us to make, to produce. Yet you worship relics of the dead and practice celibacy. Then we threw up that blasted shield. And the land withered. Archives, relics, crypts, are about death. The fields, the orchards are life."

Pyrmo's hands shook, and her eyes smoldered almost orange. "Must I remind everyone final authority to start an invocation rests in my hands alone? I will give the Justicar some time to find out more before we have the whole isle crawling with Invokers and go staking people out to be godsparked. Most of us have seen enough death. Before we invite more, we must see what else there may be behind these deaths. The Justicar assures me there is no evidence of Unmakers and that what has happened was solely a mundane matter. Now, if you will excuse me."

Pyrmo left via the clerical door and jerked her head for Jhee to follow. Once inside the abbess's office, Jhee closed the door firmly behind them. Pyrmo collapsed in her chair. "I need a drink."

Jhee stepped forward.

Pyrmo tucked her shaking hands into her sleeves. "That's far enough. I've been true to my word and haven't touched any since you caught me. Please, if there is anything you can do to avoid our having to call the Invokers or the exorcists. I will not have them running through here, causing hysteria amongst the clergy. Have you made any progress?"

Jhee hesitated to voice her current inquiries into the performers. With the archivist on a tear, it would be too easy for them to become the shark's bait. If one did murder, only that one should pay. "Some, Abbess."

"Could Sister Elkanah be right about Sister Serra? At least for the murders."

"Possibly. For me to pronounce sentence yet or even make an accusation now, is premature."

Pyrmo brought her hands to her esca and murmured a prayer. "In exchange for the understanding and discretion you have shown me and my problem, I'll allow you more time to complete your inquiries and hold off on charging Sister Serra or calling in the Invokers. But please, I urge you to hurry, before this mess boils over. Sisters Serra and Elkanah publicly confessed to serious breaches of the abbey rules. At the very least, I'll order them confined to quarters where they can't antagonize each other. However, if anything else untoward happens, I'll be forced to Invoke the Xendatia Cleansing."

Jhee and Pyrmo returned to the main hall. The abbess announced she would not invoke a cleansing until Jhee concluded her investigation.

The Penitents

Sister Serra was taken away to be put under guard. She stopped Jhee as she passed. "Watch Elkanah. You surprised me in the pods when you said you found expansion plans for the archives. After Saheli died, I switched out the compromise plans for mine."

A tapestry at the far end of the auditorium rustled. Jhee crept toward it. The decoration flung aside, and the vizier beckoned her.

"Lady Bathsheba? What are you doing here?"

"I didn't hear back from you regarding my message. I wanted to speak to you about something I found. It's a matter of some urgency, but not out here in the open. My quarters. Meet me as soon as you conclude your business here."

Message? In all the commotion, Jhee had forgotten about the note the lady slipped her. Lady Bathsheba hurried off.

Sister Elkanah tried to slink away in the interim. The prioress met her at the entrance. "I suspect the Justicar has some questions for you."

"Thank you, prioress, I do. You uncovered hothouse expansion plans."

"Yes."

"You killed Saheli because you thought she was going to gut the archives and expand the fields and orchards."

"No. At first, that's what I thought. After I had confessed my transgressions to Saheli. She showed me the full expansion plan, including those for archives. True, I felt her too lax, but the dead cannot be improved only remade. A lesson I punish myself for not learning sooner.

"I understood the hard position she was in. It could not have been easy taking me in and keeping my secret. Was Saheli too lenient with the clergy and novices? Yes, but that was her way. Those writings, that heretical trash, could ruin her reputation. I should know. As a Doombringer, I thought I was on the side of the Makers, but now I see I was doing the Unmakers' work. I didn't want Saheli to go down that path. The Makers gave men and women roles and arts, and it was a mistake to force a misguided notion of arcane equanimity on them. One they were not ready for."

"Those writings? The missing sermon and Sister Niza's missing account?"

"What do you mean missing?"

Jhee held up the empty folder. "Quit your games and stalling. Show me that sermon and Scholar Niza's account, now."

"No," Sister Elkanah said. "No. It must be here."

"Check for yourself, if you don't believe me."

"That's not right. The boards, the papers on her desk were full of cyphers."

"Sister Elkanah, you've gone through quite an effort to conceal her final Sermon. Perhaps to cover up your part in her death."

"No, but I feared the roots of Unmaking taking hold. I won't deny being glad Saheli can't cut archival spending or sell my collections, only to see the monies diverted to the hothouses and fields."

The prioress clasped Elkanah's hands. "And outreach. Saheli wasn't anti-knowledge. Indeed, she had taken great pains to enhance our learning facilities. Overhauling our fee structure. Reducing both the tithe and the tuition. She wanted to make it more affordable and accept more male students. Maintaining the archives was expensive. By enhancing our crop production and selling off some of the relics and books, she could subsidize the classes. Pay more attention to the living than the dead and relics of the past. Divest some rare books in favor of textbooks. She planned to use the sale of rare books and relics to finance the purchase of textbooks and modern equipment. Workshops, labs, vocational facilities, adepts, and cyphering teachers."

Sister Elkanah snatched her hands away. "She wanted to dedicate more and more resources to refugees and teaching men arcana. I won't stand for it! It is because of my past I know the dangers and wickedness unleashed by teaching men artifice. She could not see what a dangerous path that was. I thought as she did once, except I was trying to doom the worlds. Then the first alignment came, then the second, and then nothing. The third and fourth Doombringer rebellions had accounted to little more than mobs and riots. Though still deadly."

"Now, Sister Elkanah, tell me about this stolen antiquity."

"I realize now I was being lured away from the archive. A few items were stolen: an early uncensored copy of the Grand Design; a gilded metal and hardwood strongbox with some personal papers and family tree; inscribed ivories; some drawing puzzles; and parts of a Pillarist, arcane polyptych. When I caught Yaou with a triptych—a piece of the polyptych—and the strongbox, he threatened to reveal our indiscretion unless I taught him how to decode and perform the cyphers therein. Saheli came upon us soon after and confiscated both. I couldn't very well tell her how he obtained them. Saheli already knew about my past with the Doombringers. She said this abbey was a place for second chances and atonement.

"Later, I confessed my transgressions and urged her to burn the triptych. An act I found myself unable to do. She could not either, I suppose. To destroy a relic, even a blasphemous one, was anathema to us both."

"And her missing sermon?"

"Being both familiar with male cyphering and having read the triptych myself, I recognized the source of her inspiration. She had taken the theorems and built on them. All believed she had transcended to the Spheres, while I knew the Makers struck her down for her apostasy. I returned later to destroy it and retrieve the strongbox. I found the triptych and strongbox missing. That profane relic. We should have destroyed it. It's dangerous. Anathema."

The sister's body language showed no indications of lying. "I'll discuss what to do with you with the abbess later. In the meantime, perhaps you should retire to your cell until then."

"You have no authority—"

The prioress touched Sister Elkanah's elbow. "Please, do as she suggests and don't force the matter."

Sister Elkanah stiffened her posture and strode from the auditorium.

Jhee pinched the bridge of her nose. "Still no closer to finding that storm drenched sermon."

The prioress contemplated the floor, then mumbled, "I know where it is. Or I did. I saw Sister Elkanah take the sermon. I used my master keys to take it from her cell, where I also found the account. To protect Saheli's reputation. I'm sorry, Justicar. I knew she'd destroy it. Maybe I should have let her. They'll use it to ruin Saheli's reputation."

Jhee huffed. "Where are they now?"

"I put them in the crypts for safekeeping."

19

────────

THE EYE

∼

Shapes in Fog

Jhee met Lady Bathsheba at the hermitage near the springs.

"Did you come alone?" Lady Bathsheba asked.

She peered out into night behind Jhee. Jhee did likewise. "As far as I know."

Lady Bathsheba pulled Jhee inside. She brandished an amulet. "If you be a spirit or demon, this talisman of the Wave Witch compels you to answer me now in the affirmative."

Jhee fixed the woman with an exasperated look. She brandished the amulet at Jhee again. "No. I am not a spirit or demon."

Lady Bathsheba visibly relaxed.

Jhee and Lady Bathsheba sat at the tea table assessing the merits of the tasty cod the monks caught today. The delicate, moist flesh practically melted in the mouth. It was so incredibly juicy. Jhee quite thoroughly enjoyed it. "Shep is a great diver. He has never caught something as succulent as this. But close, very close."

"Fresh-caught. I bypass the kitchens and pantries and acquire my food straight from the docks and market. More so recently. As a precaution."

The land meat, rotisserie goat, smelled like roast perfection. It's scarce she had any; even then seldom so rare. She had loved it as a child. The dietary minefield she had to navigate with her household made it simpler not to have any. Jhee closed her eyes and savored the delicious taste. If only it were rarer. She had it so infrequently, even more cooked than she liked, it was divine. "Divine."

"Glad you enjoy it."

They partook of some white abalone. Jhee politely held her wine cup. Between whatever she had drank with the performers and her blow to the head, she needed to keep her head clear. "I wanted to thank you so much for your help, Vizier. Especially with Shep's troubles. You mentioned a matter you wanted to bring to my attention."

Lady Bathsheba coughed. "You are welcome. It's been good to get out again. I swear I feel years younger. It's a good thing I'm not. I might well give you a run for your money with Bright Harmony or even Dawn Wolf a run for you. Were that I were a few years younger and not a hermit here, I would certainly have to steal him. My reclusive lifestyle is not a good fit for such a bright treasure such as him."

Jhee thought back to Miramar, Mirrei's mother and once her closest friend, standing alone on the docks the last time she saw her. That is who Lady Bathsheba reminded her of. The defiant Miramar. So many regrets. Nothing to be done about it now except move forward and try to do better. Jhee wiped her muzzle with the napkin.

Lady Bathsheba coughed again. She covered her mouth with a fist. "Pardon me. Something must have gone down the wrong pipe."

She took another drink from her wine cup. A coughing fit overtook her. Her pallor changed. Beads of sweat broke out on her forehead. Lady Bathsheba stared at Jhee with panic then gaped at their wine cups. She dropped hers and knocked Jhee's from her hand before falling into Jhee's arms. Her skin had turned a purplish color. She clawed at the collar around her throat.

Jhee produced her inhaler from her robes and gave the Lady two puffs. Lady Bathsheba calmed down. Her breath came in a steady though wheezy tempo. It took a few minutes before her color turned back to a color resembling normal. The lady reached out a shaky hand to the emergency call button.

Jhee brought out her conch as she went to the call button. She pressed the button several times. Nothing happened. Jhee swore. She got no response from Bax or Shep. She slipped Lady Bathsheba's arm around her shoulder. "You need help."

"Where?"

"The agri-pods. We need kinberry to counteract the effects of the poison."

Lady Bathsheba struggled against her. "Not Sister Serra. Take me to the infirmary."

"The infirmary then. I'll have someone meet us there with a counter-agent."

Jhee flung open the Lady's door. A figure in a bat-faced Cheiropthys mask stood there. The garish tongue hung out underneath a crest of extravagant plumage. There came a whir followed by a hiss. White smoke billowed from the mouth. Jhee coughed and waved her hand in front of her face. Warmth crept through her head. Her vision skewed. Jhee sank to her knees. The figure brushed past her. She reached feebly at a hem. It shook off her limp hand. Jhee captured an image with her conch before falling against the wall.

Consciousness came and went. Jhee felt like she was being dragged and sometimes carried. Drizzling rain driven by a chill wind passed over her skin. A cry went out. She found herself dumped on the wet, muddy ground. The air held the slight scent of sulfur and effervescence.

Raised voices argued. Then a loud splash. More cries.

Jhee stumbled to her feet. She could not tell if the fog came from her mental state or the weather. She staggered among pools of water. A satin bubble, brightly-colored, caught her eye in the nearby spring: Lady Bathsheba's robe.

The strands of the elements slipped through Jhee's mental grasp. She gathered enough to bring Lady Bathsheba within arm's reach. With a great heave, she pulled her from the water. Jhee collapsed backward, unable to do much else.

Weird phantasmal shapes in the fog swam before her in the mist. The image of that fiend, Hethyr, approached her out of the fog. Fiend. Abuser of men. Sister Elkanah burst from the fog. Jhee's eyes became too heavy to remain open.

Jhee sank under the ocean again, drowning. She couldn't touch bottom. The waves battered her about. Every now and then they slammed her against hard, sharp rocks. The impacts forced the breath from her lungs. Her limbs were so heavy. She could not fight anymore. Mouth clamped shut, lungs burning, she contemplated the briny depths below. As she decided to let go, an enormous, brilliant, scaly eye opened, bathing her in light. She opened her mouth to scream. Ocean poured in. A hand grabbed her collar.

～

Shadowed

"Justicar. Justicar. Wake up. Wake up."

A hand tapped Jhee's face repeatedly, but gently. She groaned and opened her eyes. The infirmarian's face hovered over her. She uprighted herself.

Lady Bathsheba lay on the bed in the quiet room. On the exam table beside Jhee, resided the prioress.

"Are they?" Jhee croaked.

"They're alive. Barely. Praise be the Makers."

"Blessed are the First Makers. What happened to the prioress?"

"No one's sure. She came to the infirmary shortly before you did complaining of shortness of breath."

"Similar symptoms to Prospective Yaou?"

"Maybe."

"Justicar?" Lady Bathsheba called out in a meek voice. She held out a hand to Jhee who took hold of it. "Thank you."

"Please, don't try to speak. I never thanked you for intervening on my husband's behalf. Thank you."

Jhee sat vigil by the Lady's bedside pondering the questions. This abbey, this place of rest and quiet contemplation hid so many secrets. If this was the prelude to the capital, the lessons learned here, she would not soon forget.

The door to the infirmary banged open. Sister Elkanah strode in triumphant with the remaining senior clergy. "Good. You're awake. This time I have proof Sister Serra is the fiend," she proclaimed.

She thrust a bit of torn silk at Jhee. "What is this?"

"I tore this off your *masked* attacker when I saved your lives. You should count yourself lucky Zalver and I had decided to shadow you to ensure you remained on a righteous path."

Jhee's face burned. "Is that so? What if I hadn't?"

"Then it would simply be more evidence for the Invokers of the Unmaker's work."

"I see."

"I'll summon the abbess and have her put Sister Serra in the Corrections Hall at once."

"On what proof?"

"I gave you the proof."

"You know this is Sister Serra's how?"

"I don't—. The mask."

"I assumed you inventoried your masks."

"Yes."

"How many were missing?"

"Three."

"You retrieved how many from the horticulturist?"

"Three. Which I put in the custody of the prioress."

Jhee displayed the images she had captured on her conch to Sister Elkanah. "Was this one?"

"No. But you saw—?"

"I saw a masked figure and at some later point you."

"Me? I rescued you. Why are you questioning me?"

"What proof do I have you weren't the one who attacked us?"

Sister Elkanah regarded the rest of her mob with a pleading expression. "Serra had the masks."

"Thanks to your accusation Sister Serra was under guard, which meant she could not have attacked us."

"An accomplice. One of her fellow debauchees. Several masks were missing."

"Which don't resemble the one in these images taken during the assault. May I further submit ghosts and demons don't have separable garments?"

Sister Elkanah tried one last feeble excuse, "But she stole my relics and violated the sanctity of the archives."

"A courtesy you no doubt repaid when you and your minions trashed her hothouse. Or do you claim to have neatly turned it upside down searching for your flimsy evidence? Her mischief and yours are matters for the abbess, not me."

Jhee marched to the dejected archivist. Her nostrils flared. She took a good whiff.

"What are you—?"

Cold and musty like her relics. It was not her. "Thank you for my rescue. Now, go before I change my mind. Be lucky I am more considered in judgment than you. I'm going to ask the abbess to confine both you and the horticulturist to quarters until I resolve this matter. Try my patience, and I'll have you confined to the Corrections Hall you clamor so much about with only a copy of the Cyclogenesis sermons."

"You can't do that."

"Try me."

Jhee ruled Sister Elkanah out as the person who bashed her on the head and nothing more. The scent of the attacker was so familiar. Yet, so far, she had not matched it to a culprit.

20

THE UNEXPECTED GUESTS

∼

The Actress

Now that Jhee had dealt with both the archivist and the horticulturist, she needed to collect her thoughts and resume her investigation. Before all this nonsense began, she had been investigating the performers. Jhee replayed her misadventures in the fog. She had seen various figures: Sister Elkanah. Ms. Hethyr. With her compromised mental state, she was not sure which were real or imaginary. What she did know is, she had no good intelligence on Ms. Hethyr's whereabouts since the storeroom after the fire show and her heated exchange with Ms. Anshula.

Bax met her inside of the infirmary, grim and stone-cold sober. "I failed you, my lady. You'll go nowhere without me anymore."

"Ms. Hethyr's room. We'll get the prioress's keys to gain us entry if need be."

"At once, Justicar."

Jhee stalked over to the prioress. "Now, as for you. Niza's account mentioned calculations and a board full of equations. Yet, the images I acquired from Sister Elkanah show clean boards."

"The servants say the words faded away with her transcendence, leaving us with only the accounts of those present as to what was said," Bax offered.

Jhee fixed her gaze on the prioress who turned away.

"I wiped the boards and hid the images and calculations in the crypts. I knew what it was, but it was so brilliant I didn't want Saheli's last great contribution to the world destroyed. But if anyone else found it, it would jeopardize her legacy and consideration as a Canon."

"I'll need your master keys for the hostelry. Is every scrap with the sermon?"

The prioress placed them in Jhee's hand with a sigh. "Yes, I planned to move everything once the weather got better."

"Saheli wasn't talking about the pillars of society, she was talking about the pillars of arcana as envisioned by the Middle Pillarists."

"Now, you see why I hid it. Given Elkanah's past, likely she knew it for what it was, too. Who knew what she might do with them?"

They left the prioress and made their way to the performers' quarters. They knocked. Jhee double-checked for wild beasts before using the prioress's key to unlock the door. The room was sparse with very little personal in it. It had the same air of old smoke and oils as Mr. Zane's room. It contained a much more extensive collection of burn tools than his. Jhee sniffed among the few toiletries she found. Nothing matching what she smelled before her blow to the head.

"You should see this, Justicar," Bax said. She abandoned her search to kneel beside Bax and the open footlocker. She gave him a questioning glance. "It was open."

She hoped the footlocker contained nothing of actual probative value or else she might have to exclude it from her deliberations. "What did you find?"

Bax held up a simple woven shift like the ones worn by the Prospectives. "It is as you suspected, Justicar. Hethyr must be disguising herself as clergy."

Jhee laid the shift down and scrutinized it. It smelled of cologne. She found a name written on the inside of the collar. "There's a name written here."

"Prospectives are responsible for the washing of their own garments and vestments. They wouldn't want to get them mixed up."

"Leigh."

"The drowned boy."

Jhee dug around the chest to see if she might find one of those bracelets. Nothing. She paused to think. She pulled out her map. "Follow me."

"Where to, Justicar?" Bax asked.

"To the only places in this warren I haven't traversed back and forth a dozen times over now."

Outside Ms. Hethyr's room, they bumped into the trio of Raigen, Mr. Zane, and Ms. Anshula.

"I went to confront Mr. Pol and reclaim my brother," Ms. Anshula began.

"Mr. Pol and Akesheem are missing from their rooms," the poetess said. "It is as I feared, Akesheem shall be the next mysterious death."

"If he has harmed my brother," Ms. Anshula said.

Jhee held up a hand. "Do not finish that phrase."

Jhee attempted to reach her cohort via conch. The signal pip came and went. Ms. Anshula gathered a few weapons from her room. Jhee eyed her.

"A precaution," she said.

"To my room."

"What?"

Ms. Anshula's eyes widened. Jhee held up her hand. "First and foremost, we ensure the safety of those whose location we know. Come with me. I must check on my cohort. Then we formulate a plan."

Jhee took off, expecting them to follow.

～

A Game Interrupted

"Will denbe be here soon?" Mirrei asked.

"Soon. Never you mind. She has a great many duties to attend to, but she always returns safe and sound." Shep placed his next tile down. "Try that, Sprite."

"An amateurish mistake, Pup." Mirrei smiled and made her play. She knighted a single capture tile next to his stronghold tile. "Breach."

Mirrei turned over Shep's stronghold tile so, the bright side faced up. With that, she had him. He scratched his head and hunched his shoulders. He had missed her stealthy positioning of the capture tile. "Well, would you look at that? You have much improved since we've first played."

"Why do you think I never play her anymore?" Kanto said. He punctuated the statement with a few notes on the lute.

Shep smiled at his two junior spouses. He tried not to let on how worried he was for Jhee. He had not heard from her or Bax in quite a while. Usually, he'd be out there with her. He needed to be here though to protect them.

She'd had multiple attempts on her life, yet insisted they were the ones in the greatest danger.

The conchs sat on a table near the one charging station. Not only was the amount of power the station put out barely a trickle it had to be split between three and four devices when Kanto did not monopolize it. He should check for a message from Jhee, but they had a strict no-devices rule during tiles.

Kanto and Mirrei cast frequent, furtive glances at each other throughout the evening. They reminded Shep of him and his sister with how they could bicker one moment then be back to school fish the next. He had not entirely worked out what mischief they had gotten up to. All he knew was they left early with Bax and returned late without him smelling strongly of drink. In the meantime, he had not been able to contact anyone to learn what was happening.

Mirrei laughed which soon degenerated into a coughing fit. Kanto gave her his usual sidelong glance. The coughing fit lasted a few moments longer and sounded wetter than usual. Shep reached out and felt her forehead. If he weren't so familiar with her condition, he might have attributed her turn for the worse to a hangover. Kanto ceased playing.

"We shouldn't have gone out today," Kanto said. His face concerned and perhaps guilty from having doubted her.

"You were right. I am the one confined here, not you."

While Shep did not say it, he second-guessed letting them leave the room. He should have stood firm against their pressure. Jhee had been worried enough by what was happening at the abbey to insist they always had an escort. With her and Bax indisposed and him obligated to stay in the room, he felt guilty that they had to stay by his side. They were back safe. He supposed that was all that mattered. He had needed the time to himself, too, to ensure if he was in the right frame of mind to protect them.

Rapid footfalls approached. Shep caught a muddle of unfamiliar scents. His tattoo tingled. His ears flattened against head.

"Both of you get to the far side of the bed away from the door." He motioned for Kanto and Mirrei to place the bed between them and the door. He rushed to his war chest. His war club lay on top since tea with the vizier.

The doorknob rattled and slowly turned.

～

The Dropped War Club

Jhee and company burst into her rooms. No one sat by the fireplace. A game of tiles remained unfinished on the tables. An unmoving shape lay on the bed. The sigil on her arm ached. Her heart dropped. She rushed forward. A grunt behind her caused her to turn. Raigen lay on the ground, disarmed. Shep stood behind the door, poised to strike again. His hands shook. His chest heaved. Sweat beaded on his face while his breath came in snort-like bursts. A dull red-gold fury glowed in his eyes.

"Shep, they're with me." Ms. Anshula inched back, palms wide and empty. She formed the first gesture of an Earth drawing. Jhee stroked the sigil on her arm gently. As she sang a few notes of Shep's favorite song, his eyes returned to their standard golden color. The war club dropped from his hands. They embraced each other. "It's all right. I should not have made you worry."

Jhee pulled against Shep's embrace. He held tight. Kanto and Mirrei poked their heads out from behind the bed. The tension drained from Jhee.

Hacking came from Mirrei who tried to suppress it. Jhee rubbed Shep's ears. He indicated his calmness with a curt nod then dropped to his knees. His hands raised in supplication.

Raigen got up, brushed herself off, and shook the remaining vapors from her head. "Justicar," Raigen said, "please. Time may be running out."

"A moment please." Jhee ushered Mirrei to the bed where she removed the pillows they had used as decoys.

Raigen held out her flask. "Try this."

"Why?" Shep intercepted the flask and had a tentative sniff. He and Jhee had more experience than they cared to admit with mystery flask games. His expression softened. After a taste, his face lit up. "Whoa, that's delicious. What is that?"

"Tranquility Gold."

Shep cocked his head back. "I had Tranquility Gold. That wasn't it."

"This is the Tranquility Gold served at the head table. Try this. This is probably what you had. And this, this is the Tranquility Gold being sold to merchants."

Shep tasted the second. He gagged and nearly spit the second out. "Oh, that is disgusting. Bleh. Those aren't the same. The second's watered-down garbage."

"What they sell to the general public is even worse."

Shep eyed the third cup before taking a sip. He spit it out immediately, wiped his tongue with a napkin, then washed it down with a drink of water. "That was like vinegar. That can't be from degradation of the harvest due to weather. Those were more what I expected from the first flask. It's been blended with low-grade wines."

"We can only hope. The squelchers on my isle used to get very creative."

Shep waved for Raigen to give him the first flask. He sipped the contents until his grimace went away. "Now, I understand the fuss."

Watered-down wines. Jhee cast her mind back to the storehouse and her discovery of Pyrmo there. "Could it be for themselves?"

"At the scale I uncovered, it would be a drinker on the order of Lethys and the Rum Toad," Raigen said.

Jhee guffawed. She supposed Pyrmo or Sister Zalver might have drunk a river of alcohol over the course of years. "Then the culprit must be pocketing the proceeds. Or putting them to other use."

"Perhaps I should not have sought Mr. Akesheem's help. It may be what caused those fiends to turn on him."

"Doesn't this give Sister Serra motive to kill Prospective Leigh?" Shep asked. "Tampering with the wine jeopardizes its imperial certification as a noble blend."

"Either he found out and was going to expose her," Jhee speculated and nodded.

"Or she learned he sullied the brand which she takes so much pride in."

Jhee integrated this new component of the machine. Pyrmo as prioress for years had been an excellent position to run such a scheme. Yet, as Jhee had learned, she must not be too quick to eliminate the others. The horticulturist was exceedingly proud of the abbey's wine. Would she dilute the reputation of the brand? The archivist might, both to embarrass Sister Serra and put the monies into the archives. The prioress and Saheli might have done the same. Hadn't the smugglers confirmed as much?

"Ms. Anshula, you and Mr. Zane stay here. Raigen, Bax, and I will continue the search for your brother and Mr. Pol."

"I'm coming with you," Ms. Anshula said. "Your male possesses a kalacha and the full gift of skin slipping. He can protect your cohort on his own."

Shep had returned to supplicating kneeling.

"He was a war chaplain and needs to recenter. I'll say no more of it. Please, I'm entrusting you with the protection of those who mean most to me."

Jhee took in all the faces in the room, especially the young ones. Her spouses who bore the hopes of their families. The dutiful daughter looking out for her family. The would-be lovers. These people had put themselves in her care. She did not intend to lose a single one. She strode into the hallway. Bax and Raigen fell in behind her.

21

SECRETS OF THE DEPTHS

∿

The Halls of the Tortured and the Drenched

"Another elementalist might have been helpful," Raigen said.

Their selected party, Jhee, Raigen, and Bax, headed for the central hall. Jhee compared her map to the one she had copied while in the archives. "With as wound up as everyone is, I fear what may happen if the wrong pairs of people interact. Where we find Mr. Pol, we may encounter Ms. Hethyr."

"Ms. Hethyr?"

"Merely a hypothesis. I suspect perhaps some alliance between Ms. Hethyr and Mr. Pol." Jhee traced a finger along a faint corridor not shown on Lady Bathsheba's map. "Now, follow me."

The archivist had been right about one detail. There had to be an accomplice. Her current surmise led her to believe more than one person perpetrated these crimes. Whatever scheme had befallen Saheli and these young men involved multiple people.

"Justicar, where are we going?" Bax asked.

"The crypts."

They journeyed back to the Prayer Hall back through the central hall. Jhee flipped through the master keys. None of them seemed to match the locks on either barred door. She returned to the first barred exit from the banquet hall.

"This way leads to the Corrections Hall," Raigen said.

"According to my examination of these maps," Jhee began, "there is an entrance to the crypts at the other end of the hall."

They stood before the massive door to the Corrections Hall. Jhee jangled the rusted lock which secured the chain wrapped around the handles in place.

"It's been locked and closed for years," Raigen said.

"Will that be a problem, Bax?"

"No, my lady." Bax knelt in front of the lock. Jhee moved the glowtorch closer so he could see better. Bax reached into his waist pouch and pulled out a fastened kit. He rubbed his chin, then produced a pipette and vial from the wallet. A thin trail of smoke rose from the lock as he piped a few drops of liquid into its keyhole. Jhee's eyes watered. Her pores burned. She covered her nose and mouth as the foul odor reached her. Bax placed an awl in the lock's keyhole. A solid hammer blow shattered the whole lock. The chains slid to the ground.

Raigen gave Jhee a confused look.

"Bax came before the judgment block as a thief," Jhee said.

"To spare me a more traditional punishment"—Bax held up his hands and showed them off front and back—"the Justicar paid my fines and took me into her service."

"Seems as though I'm not the only one who wants to keep their body parts intact," Raigen said.

Jhee pushed open the doors to the Corrections Hall. The miasma of dust and decay greeted them. An eerie silence hung about the place. They crept forward as anything else seemed disrespectful. An automated light guttered to life then returned to power conservation mode. She swept her glowtorch over the exhibits. They pushed forward.

"I was born to murder the world," a recorded voice blared from a loud-speaker.

Jhee yelped but had a cypher at the ready. The three faced outward in combat stances. Ominous, red light flared in the nearest exhibit. The shadowed forms shuddered and moved. It took a moment to realize the display was automated.

Horrible, garish creatures glowered at them from frescoed reliefs. Carved hands clawed from pits in the ground as if beseeching the passerby for deliverance.

Figures painted like barbarians, their faces formed into the most horrid expressions, wielded wicked-looking weapons as they disemboweled or decapitated warriors who tried to fight them. Their tongues lolled, and malachite eyes looked lustily at captured spouses and children.

They formed up their ranks as they continued. "You said you suspected an alliance between Ms. Hethyr and Mr. Pol," Raigen said.

"The performers' route provides a perfect trafficking route, and her tattoos tie her to local gangs. Mr. Pol has access to a steady stream of young men via the camps and the abbey. Ms. Hethyr might even be the Mist Abbess. Also, who's to say the Mist Abbess must be a woman? Anshula proved with some basic make-up and the right demeanor, people saw what they wanted to see."

Further along, the next exhibit gave the dangers of the Baqairu blood cults who, led by the Mist Abbess, had resolved to end the Flower Wars and bring back the days of the hunt and battle through sacrifice. The priest figures in their headdresses and masks cut and ripped hearts from bare chests and sucked the marrow from their victims' bones. Priestesses sucked the faces off victims and stole their breath or used fire and godspark to cleanse their bodies. The scene she had stumbled on in the wood had made a hedonistic mock of it.

Another voice-over kicked in when they reached the next exhibit. "The Final Sword. Even beyond the Baqairu death cultists, were the doomsday cultists. They wanted to end all existence, and their instruments of destruction were artificers. All who practiced magic in numbers saw how the lands and the areas around them suffered from excess cyphering. The Middle Pillarists known as Doombringers, based on the forbidden sequences from Thaedra's portfolio, innovated particularly devastating sequences that when used by male artificers left miles of destruction in their wake. They made no effort to preserve the environment. They encouraged male and female artificers alike to burst cypher. A process which often killed them and anyone in the area immediately around them. The area remained deadly for years afterward. Not a plant would grow, not a creature could flourish. To even move through the area, one could not survive. The land itself was hungry and drank the very life from any living thing unlucky enough to enter it."

A reverse spirit battery of sorts.

"My lady, what do you make of this?" Bax asked. He held his glowtorch over a giant, rectangular void in the dust in front of the Middle Pillarist exhibit. Jhee peered closer. The pattern in the dust came from something woven. Nearby a discarded Middle Pillarist prayer cloth and glow orb stands had been kicked aside. Brown droplets flecked the ground, ripped bits of fabric and scourge thorns scattered among them. The minute scratches on Sister Elkanah's arms and shoulders flashed in her mind.

"Sister Elkanah. She appears to have a different idea of how she should atone than her former associates."

The exhibit beyond this one came almost as a pleasant relief, depending on one's feelings about flying rodents. Cheiropthys the bat-faced Lesser Maker, his symbol, the sky fox, a gigantic, bloodsucking bat which dwarfed many hounds. The sky fox hailed from one of the aboriginal isles. A more tropical equivalent of Verdale with its host of deadly plants.

Next, came scenes of the counter inquisition's torturers. Then the Medical Protectorate doctors whose experiments and excesses had created unfortunate programs like the berserkers. Jhee turned away. Bax's torch swept over a scene of a physician dismembering a young man. He stifled a sob and covered his mouth in horror. She placed a tender hand on his forearm.

"You know the other name they had for the Corrections Hall," Raigen said. "The Halls of Torture and the Drenched. A holdover from another time when we focused on the fear of the Makers rather than the love of them. The custom was to lock young Prospectives in here to contemplate their sins."

Even as a learned woman, if locked in here long enough, Jhee would certainly rethink her life. This hall must have its own emergency power source. First Makers forfend these exhibits not work when you wanted to frighten prisoners or young Prospectives. Another pit of grasping hands bookended the displays. "Pleasant. Come, let's leave this foul place as quick as possible."

"Agreed, Justicar."

~

The Crypts

They found an archway at the far end with a pressure sealed gate. As Bax worked, vermin most likely crab-rats skittered in the darkness behind them. The wind outside had picked up. Loose tiles in the heights of the ceiling rattled. The blowing wind sometimes sounded like a whistle. Other times it affected the moans of the drenched.

The pressure seal disengaged with a hiss. They entered an airlock on the other side without a moment's hesitation.

"Reseal it. Pyrmo said the salt air could contaminate the crypts."

What Jhee really wanted to do was seal herself off from the images in the hall.

The airlock's dim, low-level lighting made a bright white contrast to the blood reds and fiery umbers of the Corrections Hall. Sea and storm air made a welcome change from the mustiness. A series of wind shafts and fans whined and groaned with every spin as they labored to keep a steady flow of air. The door out of the airlock showed more recent and frequent use likely for maintenance.

Steps beyond the door led down into the depths of the abbey. Jhee took the vanguard with her glowtorch outstretched. A fog, the folkloric last breaths of the dead, covered the lowest steps.

Warm, misty air tickled her cheeks. The back and forth seawater flow and air pressure gave the impression of the cave itself breathing. Jhee found focusing on the walls hard. The stony surface wavered as illumination sparkled through moisture droplets. Faint, cyan light emanated from the rocky strata comprising the vaults. She clutched her robes and recited statutes to her Maker within.

"Mr. Akesheem. Mr. Pol," Jhee called.

Frogs and water drips gave the only replies. They continued calling out for the missing men as they pressed forward. Dank air brought the swift return of Jhee's headache. Their footsteps sloshed through the water. Something brushed her legs. She did not even want to think about what sorts of unseen creatures swam at their feet. They turned a corner.

A sharp pain knifed through her esca and the back of her neck. What was it about this isle that made her head pound so? She squeezed her eyes shut.

Open your eyes and look, her Maker within said. When Jhee opened her eyes again, she was enveloped in mist. She must have gotten turned around in the fog.

"Bax, Raigen," Jhee called.

The breathing of the cave had grown louder. Caves, mineral springs, earth gases, bizarre construction. All manner of causes to trick the senses. Add in being primed to see oddities by all the rumors. No wonder rumors of the abbey's haunted nature persisted.

Emissary.

The mist grew deeper. Jhee forged ahead. She reminded herself of the weirdness experienced at the mineral springs. The sigil on her arm throbbed. Jhee thought it was because of Shep for a moment. Shep made it itch or burn. This sensation was different.

The bridge or the sword. Until all are one.

Jhee's ears rang. Her head pounded. It felt as if the world itself quaked.

A frog leaped off a most hideous green statue like those in the cloister and on the edifice. Jhee started.

Bax and Raigen called her name.

"Here," Jhee answered.

"We got separated in this labyrinth," Raigen said, as they joined her.

Bax clutched his thieves' tools. "Blessed Makers, places such as this are favored by bogglies and swamp goblins."

"It's just a statue. The hall we just went through should provide proof enough there are things far scarier than bogglies or swamp goblins."

Peculiar statues in shades from white-green jade to brightest emerald lined the passage. Unlike those on the edifice and in the cloister, these appeared more malformed or half-formed and melted. They moved further along. Raigen, who now led the way, gulped.

"Maker's Mark, that's disgusting." Raigen glanced around the passage her color turning ashen then covered her mouth as if choking back vomit.

"What is it now?" Jhee snapped.

"These aren't statues."

Jhee stepped in front of her. A placard which read "Saheli" hung above an alcove. The former abbess's body sat propped up on a pedestal, her mouth a rictus. Bits of skull poked through the face. Glittering, green coral and barnacles had grown over parts of her. In places, patchy fur and pale brown skin shown where the creatures had yet to take hold. Within a few more months or years, her mortal remains would be grown over as solid as the other residents.

"The 'honored dead,'" Jhee whispered.

Bile rose in Jhee's throat. She recited more statutes to remain composed in front of the Raigen and Bax. She set her jaw and cleared her throat. A chest Jhee presumed contained Saheli's belongings rested at the foot of the corpse. A mix of live and dead barnacles covered it. "Bax, open this if you would."

Bax gave her a wide-eyed stare but broke open the chest anyway. He scampered away. Jhee pulled out Saheli's scrolls, paintings, and crafts, one of which appeared a companion piece to the work outside Lady Bathsheba's chamber. Something nagged at her about the pieces, yet she could not quite place it. Opened eyes.

"Look at this etching. Do the cat's pupils strike you as particularly large?" Jhee asked.

For the pupils to be that large, the etching had to have been painted somewhere dark, somewhere unlike atop a sunlit spire in the afternoon—

unless something else caused them to dilate. She gave a last look at Saheli's semi-encrusted corpse. The process appeared patchy and uneven as if a morbid piece of rock candy. By reflex, her hand went to her bruised head. Sights, smells, and sounds associated with her attack flooded back to her.

"You were right, Raigen. Saheli was murdered. We've had our audience with the mother who bears the secret of the depths. Now we need one with the mother who bears the secrets of the spires. We'll leave by the main entrance and drop off these troublesome items."

"My poem? You insisted we come here. Now we're leaving? What about Mr. Akesheem and Mr. Pol?"

Jhee rolled up the scroll with the sermon and Scholar Niza's account of Saheli's transcendence and replaced them in the small chest. She shook out a handkerchief. Jhee averted her face as she collected a handful of the dead barnacles. She grabbed her glowtorch as she hurriedly led them out the main entrance to the crypts. "There is nothing more we can learn here. I had thought Ms. Hethyr would have brought them here or the Corrections Hall as they are the only places forbidden to all. I assure you we will find them."

Bax and Raigen stared at her oddly.

"Your esca?" Bax said.

"What do you mean?"

"It's silver," Raigen said.

"What? I don't know. I must have been exposed to something in the crypts."

"Ours are fine."

Jhee took a moment to examine her sigil. Its color had changed too, having become silver and iridescent. She quickly covered it back up. "Problem for another time."

Her mind contemplated the geometric nature of the abbey again. This crystallizing embalming process sought to use the spirits of the dead to protect the abbey. The crystal coral may have explained why it felt so odd to cypher here. Were they atop some giant spirit battery? If so, what did it feed or power? Was this abomination Doombringer or Baqairu witchery?

They headed back to the room. Jhee dropped off Saheli's chest while ignoring the reactions to her esca.

Mirrei forced a smile. The one Jhee returned was equally forced. She had thought time off the yacht would do Mirrei good. Instead, Mirrei appeared to have gotten worse. Had this been Jhee's doing? Was the trip to the climate-controlled archives or exposing her to substances in the agri-pods too much for her delicate constitution?

Kanto double-glanced at Jhee but gave his seat to her without question. She picked up Mirrei's practically untouched kale and fennel salad. "You really must eat something," Jhee said.

Mirrei averted her head from the forkful of salad Jhee held out. Even Jhee blenched at the sickly-sweet licorice scent of the fennel. Mirrei managed a few sips from the cup of wine Shep handed over. A quick aroma of peach identified it as Tranquility Gold.

Mirrei licked her lips. "I input that I was sick out into the system, and the Makers implemented my design. I'll be fine. I feel stronger already."

Jhee patted the young woman's arm. She caught the smell of the fennel again. Jhee's hand went to her bruised head.

"Foolish. Foolish. Foolish," Jhee said. She hurried from the room. Bax and Raigen caught up to her. She swept across the hall and through the north courtyard. "I've had too many voices in my ear since I arrived."

"What?" Raigen asked. "Justicar, please."

"I allowed myself to be pulled into the deacons' drama and missed the obvious. I predicated my investigation on a false assumption. Namely, whoever killed the Prospectives killed Saheli, and whoever killed Saheli must have killed the Prospectives. Ms. Hethyr and Mr. Pol might have free access to the Prospectives, but even an abbess as open and friendly as Saheli would be cautious of them. Only someone Saheli trusted, with access to her food, and who knew her habit of communing with spirits in the spire could have killed her. It had to be a member of the senior clergy. Many of whom I mistakenly eliminated based on alibis for the Prospectives' deaths."

"Saheli died in front of many witnesses."

"Poison knows no hour." Jhee paused at the top of the Prime spire to catch her breath from the anger-fueled pace she had set to reach here. Once she had composed herself, she banged on Pyrmo's door.

22

SECRETS OF THE SPIRES

~

The High Chamber

Pyrmo opened the servant's door with a look of astonishment. "Ah, Justicar? Raigen? Why have you arrived via this entrance?"

"We've been to the crypts where we've searched Saheli's burial items and seen her corpse. I'm here to inform you of my current progress in the investigation and make an accusation."

"I suppose you better come in. I was deciding if I should have some tea." Pyrmo wandered away from the open door to make herself comfortable in her chair. A tea service and the box of black orchid tea sat on the lacquer table beside the chair. After she waved away some steam, Pyrmo sniffed it deeply. "Almost perfect. Now, what are you going on about?"

Jhee set her conch to record at the most space-conserving setting possible and handed it to Bax. "We've come to make you answer for your crimes. These two shall act as witnesses."

"Witnesses? Crimes? You'll have to elaborate."

"I have concluded my investigation into the death of Saheli. I'm here to hear your defense against the charge you murdered your predecessor, Saheli. Do you deny it?"

The trial in extremis was a few of the responsibilities of rural magistrates such as herself who needed to travel the Outer Reaches. She did have to record and send her records back to the capital for the legal archives.

"Who accuses me of such?'

"I do. Do you deny the charge?"

Pyrmo winced as she picked up her cup and spoon. "It's best if I drink this before it gets cold. I'll have to make sure to drink every drop, so I don't leave a mess."

"You also stand guilty of the crime of assault against an imperial official. It was you that struck me the blow to my head."

"Blow to your head? Where are my manners?" Pyrmo offered Jhee some tea.

Jhee refused. "Do you deny these charges? Do you deny you are the Mist Abbess?"

Pyrmo took a sip of her tea. "I assume you have proof. Or is it your habit to go about spewing slanderous claims?"

"The matter of the Prospectives remains an open question. I shall lay out my case if you wish. My primary concern is the location of Mr. Akesheem, who has gone missing along with your confederate, Mr. Pol. I shall show leniency provided we find him quickly and unharmed. You and Mr. Pol conspired to traffic folk and illicit goods, namely skimming and counterfeiting Drakist wines."

Pyrmo pushed her tea aside. She took out a flask and had a long drink. "Mr. Pol is a procurer. He lures innocent young people to the city with the promise of work. Then he sells them to any willing to pay. Artificers. Wealthy patrons. Middle Pillarists…. Medical Protectorate."

"For you as well?"

"Those were wicked boys who engaged in the most sinful of acts on this sacred isle," Pyrmo yelled.

Flecks of spittle flew from her mouth. She wiped it away with a sleeve.

"With this Mist Abbess or a senior member of the clergy."

"Malign practices and the lustful abound. It is their fault for having succumbed to the material temptations of the world, it was their duty to resist. If they had not indulged in such wickedness, they would still be alive."

"What of yourself and your love of drink and relics? It was your duty, your responsibility to care for them. The protection of all under this roof is your responsibility."

The abbess returned to drinking her moonshine with more speed and vehemence. "Celibacy and chastity keep the essence pure. I see no use to waste it on relations with the wicked. I may have failed much and not been as devout in my adherence to all the Drakist tenets, but I hold our vow of chastity most sacred. It is the fount from which the others derive. I heard some of the acts these boys were alleged to have engaged in. I assure you I would never sully myself in such a way. We even had to lock the towers to prevent their misbehavior. Disgusting. Wickedness, though, reaped its own harvest."

"Where are Misters Akesheem and Pol?"

"I'm afraid I have no answers to give on that subject. So comfortable." Pyrmo nestled into her chair and drank her flask slower. "I'm still waiting to hear why you believe it is I who has knowledge of these transgressions."

"Once I realized you were the one who tried to kill me, the rest fell into place. I was confused by the smell you see. The odor of the smudging stick and spike leaf ointment dogged me since the night of the feast even though I did not realize it. A similar odor I smelled once more when I was struck. Both you and Sister Serra reek of them. In my various interviews with you, I kept noticing it. However, because Sister Serra and the previous Abbess were both in the habit of taking 'seed of enlightenment,' it made their scent sharper and more pungent and them like giant pest repellents. You, on the other hand, with your licorice moonshine and mints to cover the scent of your drinking, had a sickly-sweet smell. Much beloved by the insects. When you called me into the office post-trial, it was the only time I have smelled you in isolation without my poultice. The poultice I used for my headache masked the scent most of the time. The same dressing saved my life from your murderous strike."

Pyrmo's flask cap clinked against the flask body as she continued to drink. "I fail to see how that connects me to the murder of Saheli. My, that tea seems more appealing all the time. Perhaps it is a good idea to finish that instead. How could I have killed Saheli in front of the senior clergy without a hint of violence?"

"Here is where you were most clever. Saheli was not some frail, old woman with one foot in the grave as you tried to get me to believe. She daily climbed to the top of the Bridge Tower to paint and meditate. Having done it myself, I know the climb is indeed arduous. Anyone who spent much time up there, especially in warm weather might like to have a pitcher of refreshments with them. You also knew of her habit of taking brightshade. You knew she would bring something to quench her thirst while she did her crafts and surveyed the isle. You spiked her fruit beer with the similar, yet deadly ordeal oil or nightmare blight extracted from the infected crops. Among its effects is dehydration. To be sure she was quite thirsty, you also adjusted one of the solar panels to point at the tower. The warmer it got, the more she drank. The more she drank, the thirstier she got. Unfortunately for you, a sudden storm blew in. The horticulturist and prioress checked on her and found her alive with her cat lapping at her spilled fruit beer. She passed out but survived due to a combination of her good health and being on conflicting courses of treatment from the physician and the horticulturist. One treatment caused her to retain water, and the other acted as an antidote. I imagined you must have been shocked when Saheli came down from the spire and summoned the senior clergy into a meeting. You must have thought she was on to you, so you set about covering your tracks. You returned the volatile chemicals you used to concoct your deadly brew in the storehouse then ran out to the solar array to return the errant panel to its original position."

Pyrmo grunted. "You may indeed have me stuck at that. These are good supposes but supposes, nonetheless. I suppose you could autopsy her, but I suppose the encrustation process might make that quite difficult."

"Your cleverness failed with the quick embalming. You hoped it would hide the evidence of your crimes. Instead, the preservation revealed it." Jhee set the handkerchief with barnacles on the table beside Pyrmo. "Remember, how I noted the tendency of pests to be repelled by those who partook of brightshade. As you said, the barnacles and coral involved in the preservation process only thrive in a certain environment. Saheli's tissues proved to be too hostile for them to take hold. Even proved toxic to some."

The abbess slurped at her flask. A few rivulets slid down her chin. As she drew her sleeve across her mouth, her hand trembled. She held up her hands out, palms up. "You can't prove anything with a bunch of dead sea critters."

"Ordeal oil has similar effects to seed of enlightenment. If anyone did a toxicology, they might dismiss it for the more benign brightshade. The excited utterances Saheli made before her death. The talking to herself. Your ten-page commentary was nothing but the dying utterances of a madwoman high on a mix of hallucinogens. Your miraculous burns came not from the glorious light of transcendence, but Saheli's literal fiery speech igniting the chemicals you spilled in your haste."

Pyrmo had broken out into a sweat and looked distressed. Proof positive of her guilt. "You are that confident of what poison was used."

"You know what I did not find in the crypts with Saheli? The remains of her cat. It is a small matter to find where it's buried. Under her favorite tree, was it? Another effect of ordeal oil is dilated pupils. An etching I did find caused me to realize her cat may have ingested whatever Saheli had. I may not be able to autopsy the former abbess because of the preservation process, but I can necropsy her cat. Pyrmo you are confined to quarters for the attempted murder of an Imperial Official and the death of Abbess Saheli."

Pyrmo grimaced.

Jhee stroked her muzzle and conferred with Raigen quietly. "She made no mention of Ms. Hethyr. Help me search this room. There must be a clue here somewhere."

A Glamor

When Bax, Jhee, and Raigen's search turned up nothing of note, they left the abbess's chamber via the main door.

"What now, Justicar?" Raigen said.

"Mr. Pol. Bax, take her master keys. Secure this and the servant's door, so she doesn't leave until we return."

They searched Mr. Pol's room. They still turned up nothing.

"I must think. This all began when I saw the figure with a mask struggling with a naked, one-armed man. It did not match any of the ones we recovered from the horticulturist. It did not match the one in the image of my attacker."

One of them did, however, match the Medical Protectorate masks from the Halls of Torture and Drenching. Like that one-armed body on the table in the hall.

Jhee thought about the hall and the moaning of the wind and further to her encounter in the crypts with the breath of the isle. She shuddered. When had she decided to name what she encountered? A name tamed it, made it more tangible. Tangibility might also give it more power. The moaning winds became a more pleasant thought in contrast. The moans of the wind? The moans of the trenched. "What a fool I've been! We need to go back to the Corrections' Hall."

Jhee brought up the rear as they rushed back to the Corrections' Hall. Strapped to the table in the dismemberment scene which had so horrified them earlier they barely glanced, they found Mr. Akesheem.

Raigen gasped. "That fiend Ms. Hethyr has chopped off his arm and foot."

"Get him down quickly." The stumps appeared clean, with no outward sign of infection. Jhee geared up for a formulation which blended cyphering and fire drawing. "I can cauterize the wounds to forestall infection or sepsis.

We're unlikely to find anyone capable of limb regeneration this far from the capital."

Jhee laid her hands upon the arm stump. Where she expected empty air, she contacted solid, soft flesh. She probed further until she felt the full outline of Mr. Akesheem's arm. She checked the space where his foot would be.

"How bad are his wounds?"

"His limbs are there. It's a glamor."

"Praise the Makers."

"Praise, indeed. Let's get him down." Jhee tried her conch. Low on power and barely any signal. "I'm unable to contact the Central Authority. With the abbess relieved of duty, who assumes control over the abbey?"

"I'm unsure. I'd suppose one of the senior clerics."

"Who are all under confinement. Save the physician."

"We have to take Akesheem to the infirmary anyway."

"She's as likely to kill him as cure him. Take him to my rooms. With Sister Serra unavailable, Shep and Mirrei might be the best healers at our disposal. I'll go seek Lady Bathsheba and the physician at the infirmary. One of them is liable to know how to bring up the antenna. We must inform the local peace-keeping authorities and the Chief Abbess at once."

~

The Uncomfortable Room

Ms. Anshula's head tracked Mr. Zane as he wandered to the fireplace where Kanto's robes hung. Mr. Zane raised the hem of one and let it fall. He addressed Kanto, "Beautiful work. Yours?"

Shep compared the performer to his co-spouse. Handsome. Sleek, athletic builds. Pampered and flawlessly groomed. Traits they shared with Akesheem from what he remembered.

Kanto looked up from his sketch pad. "The design and construction are mine. The embroidery. Star Mirror did that."

"The cuffs are perfectly shaped. I've tried starch and interfacing. What's your secret?"

"Wire."

"Wire? Yes, obvious and ingenious. The Justicar's feast robes caught the eye. Your work too?" Kanto nodded. "Bold designs for a bold denbe. Doesn't it worry you what she gets up to out there at night? It would worry me."

"Denbe can take care of herself. What do you know of what she gets up to at night?"

"Nothing except your wife found herself in my room so many times, I may ask to be put on the marriage charter."

"When was this?"

"Yesterday. She didn't tell you?" Kanto glared at Mr. Zane then at a handkerchief on the bedside table. "She was the perfect gentlewoman and took no liberties. Neither did I. The blow to the head she took that landed her in my room could have killed her."

The two men sized each other up. Eye contact passed between Ms. Anshula and Mirrei showing they shared the same opinion on the posturing.

"I could not abide a woman who kept my beauty hidden away for her eyes alone or would not let me use my own name around strangers."

"So, you claim Mr. Zane is your birth name?"

"Such nice clothes. And your denme here doesn't look like he has missed too many meals. You don't get a husky figure like his eating kelp and plankton. It requires lots of calories and protein. Your whole household seems well provided for."

Shep tucked a little coverlet over Mirrei who had retired to the bed with Kanto beside her on a stool. She looked paler than before but made no complaint.

"Sprite, I thought I asked you to keep Tunes here out of trouble."

Kanto grabbed Shep's forearm and held his gaze. Shep patted the younger man's hand for comfort, before returning to their guests who occupied the salon chair together. Shep went to the table and reset the tile board.

"May I interest either of you in a game of tiles?" Shep asked.

Mr. Zane rose. The animal handler, Ms. Anshula, held his arm. He sat back down. "Mr. Zane, perhaps you'd be more comfortable on the chair with me."

"Madam Anshula?"

"We're fine as we are."

Shep sighed. He prepared a cold compress and took it over to Kanto and Mirrei. As Kanto arranged it on her fevered brow, she assured them she was comfortable. The animal handler took a keen interest in Shep's every move. He approached her. She tensed and formed a rudimentary base for a cypher.

"You don't have to worry. I am a danger to no one here."

Ms. Anshula's expression remained hard.

"If it concerns you so much, play tiles with me. I find it calming and meditative."

Shep returned to the tea table. He placed his first tile then gestured at the empty seat opposite him. Ms. Anshula joined him. Mr. Zane stretched out on the salon chair with great ceremony. Kanto spared a last glance at Mr. Zane before jamming his conch's earpiece in his ear and snapping open his sketchbook.

Ms. Anshula cast a speculative eye at Shep and matched his opener.

"I know what you are: an augmented, skin-slipper. I worked with some on our home isle." Ms. Anshula jerked her chin at Dari. "Therapeutic companion?"

"You could say so. Is that how you came into possession of your rapport with Itzil?"

"My village had veterans, even those who went through the process you did. They made frequent use of my skills to reintegrate. Their hands did not shake like yours. I heard about breakfast."

"Their eyes likely have not seen what mine have seen. The trigger is unfamiliar blood. Strange environment. I know your scents now. You are also a command female...and an animal handler. If something were to happen, my instinct would be to obey rather than attack you."

Ms. Anshula played as terse and reluctant as she spoke. "All the same. The Justicar did not want to leave you alone with them."

"You're so sure it's me which worried her? Should you encounter Ms. Hethyr or the one who took your brother what would be your response?"

"No less than they deserved."

Yet, Shep was the one confined to quarters. "Consumed. That's the match."

"What?"

Ms. Anshula grimaced at the board. All her tiles had been captured or turned.

"No, that's not right," Kanto said.

Shep thought he meant how he had beat Ms. Anshula. When he faced Kanto, though, the younger man had his head buried in his sketchbook and an earpiece in his ear, brow furrowed. A slow smile appeared on his face. He nodded more and more then snapped his fingers. "Denbe's going to love this."

At last, Kanto pulled out his earpiece. He met Shep's gaze with a smug smile. Shep turned back to the tile board where Ms. Anshula still puzzled over her loss. Mr. Zane draped on her arm, stroking her hair.

"Denme, double-check this for me. So, I know I'm not imagining it before I show denbe."

Kanto thrust his sketchbook at him. Shep reached out. He did not know what meaningful input he could provide on a new clothing design or musical composition, but if it kept the peace, he was all for it.

A knock came at the door. Shep inhaled deeply. No alarming scents. He stood, but Ms. Anshula motioned for quiet. She positioned herself behind the door. He wanted to tell her there was no need. Yet, the doings at this abbey of late justified her caution. One might not be able to tell friend from foe.

Shep opened the door. Raigen and Bax bustled in with an unconscious Akesheem.

"Please, he's not well," Raigen said.

Shep checked the hallway. No sign of Jhee. A mere glance and Bax scampered out before Shep closed the door. He'd have his words with Jhee and Bax later. He directed them to the salon chair. "Here."

Mr. Zane vacated the spot as they laid Akesheem down gently. His sister gasped. "His limbs."

Shep's attention went to the young man's missing arm. Shep's hand twitched.

"A glamor," Raigen said. She poked the area. Her finger indented in the air.

Shep said a chant and marshaled himself to stillness. Had Mirrei not been in such a severe way, this glamor would have been of great interest to her. A quick examination showed the signs of dehydration, but no other illness or injury. Those glamored limbs though needed dealing with. "Raigen, have you any skill in elements or cyphering?"

"Some."

"I'm not sure if this is cyphering or a drawing trick with air. Work with Ms. Anshula to figure out how to undo it. I want to make sure he has no hidden wounds. The limb being invisible will make it difficult to decypher the sequences used to create such an illusion."

Shep provided the young man with a little reheated broth.

"Here give him some." Raigen handed Shep the flask. "You might want more yourself."

The wonderful peach bouquet met with his approval. He took a sip and found himself doubly stunned again. He administered some to Akesheem and more to Mirrei for good measure. They both quieted.

23

UNBROKEN CHAIN

~

Succession

Lady Bathsheba welcomed Jhee to the infirmary quiet room. Jhee's mind reeled from all the death and revelations. She only hoped her desk position at the capital entailed less such frightful chores.

"You look as if you should be the one abed, Justicar. Would you care for some kolal? It'll calm your nerves."

"No, thank you, Lady Bathsheba. I must inform you I've confined Pyrmo to quarters. It seems as though she murdered Saheli. I'm still unsure of her connection to the dead Prospectives, though."

Lady Bathsheba shook her head. "My word, that is dreadful. Truly. We were shocked when the Chief Abbess named Saheli, an outsider. However, it seems as though she was most wise. She might have known about Pyrmo's problem, or the firestorm if she had appointed either deacon. How may I be of help?"

"We need to raise the antenna, so we can inform the authorities. I'm also unsure of the abbey's succession hierarchy. I will likely need you to take charge of the abbey until a replacement can be dispatched or I sort out culpability amongst the senior clergy."

"Of course, I will do what I must. This is terrible business, really. I left court to be rid of such concerns, but duty is duty. How could these scandalous happenings have occurred right under my very nose? Had I paid more attention…. Instead, I chose to absent myself from the day to day affairs of the abbey. I believe some part of me suspected which is why I pressed you so on those three men's deaths."

"Please, Lady Bathsheba, there will be a time for blame, but it is not now."

"Yes. Yes. The matter of the missing young man."

"Missing? No, we found him. It will mean much if a former vizier, such as yourself, is there while Mr. Akesheem gives his recorded testimony. You may well have questions for him yourself."

"Indeed, I might. I have no doubt you will do a more than adequate job. However, I must see to the unexpected duties which have fallen upon my shoulders. Firstly, a headcount to ensure no others are missing."

"My thoughts precisely," Jhee said.

"With most of the senior clergy confined, I must wear many tabards from here out. So much to be done. So much to be done."

"It may seem a trifle, Lady Bathsheba, but the map you gave me proved most helpful."

"Sometimes it is the trifles which mean the most."

"Words to contemplate indeed. May I have your permission to grab some provisions from the infirmary's stores?"

"Yes. Yes. Of course. Whatever you need." Lady Bathsheba produced a set of keys from her robes and unlocked the cabinets for Jhee.

"Thank you."

"Now, you rest here and finish your kolal."

"I must return to my room."

"Stay here for a few minutes and catch your breath. You've had a hectic and punishing few days. Give your head time to clear before you return to your cohort. They'll need you at your strongest."

Jhee thought of Shep's disapproval, Mirrei's quiet admonishment, and one of Kanto's disdainful huffs awaiting her. "I suppose you're right."

After a few minutes of rest, Jhee rose. The prioress beckoned for Jhee to join her in the hallway. "I had another idea of how you can get a message out."

"Excellent. How?"

The prioress pointed to a view-screen half-hidden by an ornate drapery. "The old theological address system."

"Is that a viewer? Where is it getting its signal?"

"The short-range, inter-isle communication network. A holdover from the

Imperial literacy campaign. It uses a series of relays. Easily accessible in remote regions. We use it as a theological address system, now. I understand you believe us to be technology resisters, but we have it for the occasions when the Chief Abbess makes a convocation or edict meant to be implemented at once across the various cloisters and monasteries or for group prayer. There are a few circumstances where we need one. They're only tuned to one channel: the private frequency of the Drakist Hierarch."

"You work on that while we see Mr. Akesheem to wellness."

The Testimony

Jhee returned to her room. "Lady Bathsheba has assumed control of the abbey for now."

With all these people in it, it rather resembled the docks upon arrival of the noonday ferry. Mr. Akesheem laid fitfully on the salon chair. Meanwhile, Mirrei rested equally as fitful on the bed. Jhee considered them and where her higher duty lay. Shep and Kanto tended both.

"Welcome back, Justicar," Raigen said.

"Did you decypher the glamor on Mr. Akesheem's limbs?"

"The invisibility made it nearly impossible to back form; your man Dawn Wolf was most helpful. He's also awake, now."

"Is Mr. Akesheem able to give testimony?"

Raigen and Ms. Anshula were aghast. "He's in no condition."

"An account of his ordeal, as horrible as it was, and while it's still fresh in his thoughts, is paramount." Jhee turned to Shep, who stood beside the man ministering to him as he did to everyone. He frowned then nodded. "Ms. Anshula, as his dame in absentia, may I have your permission to inspire him?"

"Inspiration? What is that?"

"An interrogation method. It is a little invasive, but it won't harm him. You may observe if you wish."

Ms. Anshula wrung her hands. "I'm trusting you, Justicar. I'll call stop at the slightest sign of pain or discomfort from him."

"A fair ask." Jhee hit record on her conch. It refused with a space too low prompt. Then the low power indicator. She dug a thumb into her arm to suppress the swear which almost passed her lips. She swept over to Mirrei's bedside where she deposited the conch on the charging station. Her skin prickled from all the eyes on her.

"Here, take my conch," Kanto said. "It has the archives on it."

"Thank you."

Music played from the conch. It sounded familiar. Now, she remembered. The refugee camps. "Is this music from the refugee camps?"

"Yes."

"When did you record this?"

"During the heresy trial. Mirrei and I, we sneaked out."

Jhee bustled him out to the corridor. "You what? By yourselves?"

"Afraid some dastard might brain us over the head?"

"I should have told you about that. I didn't want you to worry."

"Shouldn't I be worried? It seems you should be the one kept in this room."

"Was this your way of getting back at me?"

His eyes took on the glaze of hurt. "Did I need to?"

"If you are upset with me, there's no need to take it out on poor Mirrei."

He turned away from her and whispered, "Oh yes, poor sweet, innocent Mirrei? Who we've been looking after while you traipse about strange men's rooms, picking up their favors."

"What are you talking about?"

"This." Kanto faced her, eyes brightened by red. He waved a handkerchief at her. "This isn't mine or denme's. The second you've acquired that I know of. Why not accuse me of making Shep feral too?"

"Did you? Sabotaging my night with him worked to your advantage. Why not go farther?"

The look of hurt appeared again. "Perhaps my intent with tea was to have more time with you in a setting which showcased my talents. My intention, though, was not to usurp Shep's time. Why not ask him if he did it to himself to ruin our day together? That worked to his advantage. It was my day, remember? Of course, you don't. Or else you might not have spent it sharing passion with another while plotting to give me away like a gift you don't want. To be clear, denbe, I am a gift. It's to your detriment you don't see that I could be your secret weapon. Just like you didn't bother to ask me to give up my day and look after Mirrei so you can tend to Shep. Just like you didn't bother to ask me if I want to be remarried. That's your default operating mode. But that's a discussion for another time."

"Indeed, it is. Now, if you'll excuse me."

Kanto smoothed his robes and softened his tone, "Please, denbe, wait. I think you should hear this. It's important."

"I'm sure you think it's important, but others need my attention right now. Least of all your denye because of your irresponsible behavior."

He narrowed his eyes. "My behavior? If you're not being attacked, you seem to be wandering about a number of strange bedchambers at night. Despite what you think, I'd never transfer my anger at you to Mirrei or Shep, least of all endanger them. Never." Kanto paused and took a deep breath. "I'm not trying to fight with you. I think I can help."

"Help? You can help me by keeping yourself occupied while I get the young man's testimony."

~

Tale of The Low Chamber

Back at Mr. Akesheem's side, Jhee noted those present and had Ms. Anshula reaffirm her consent to the inspiration procedure. Jhee took a deep breath and made herself as relaxed as possible before she began. She opened his mouth slightly and exhaled deeply. A shimmer of air passed from her mouth to his.

"Brave, Akesheem," she said in a mild and comforting tone. She heard the reverberation as expected and felt no discomfort of her own. She stroked his head and ears. "Hear my words, Akesheem, you are safe and in the company of those who care for you."

Tension drained from Mr. Akesheem. His restlessness quieted. When his eyes opened, they shone a color more silver than gold. Like hers. At least, in his case, it was explainable.

"What are you doing to him?" Raigen demanded.

"Quiet," Shep whispered. He gestured for them to be serene. "If he is to be calmed, we must remain calm."

"Brave, Akesheem, please, give as full an account as you can of how you came to be in the Corrections Hall."

"Having recognized my sister, Ani, I resolved to have it out with her. After her performance, I slipped away from Mr. Pol to speak with her. My initial intent was to send her away. Then I heard Raigen's poem. Between my sister's counsel and Raigen's words to me throughout my stay, I was no longer as sure of my decision to take vows. I found Mr. Pol and confessed to him my doubts and my desire to possibly return home. He grew furious. He yelled at me and called me ungrateful.

"'We'll see what the abbess has to say about this. A great number of preparations had been made to much trouble and great expense. I've already received payment for you and spent it besides.' He also explained if I backed out now, my family would be forced to repay the sums he had given them."

Mr. Akesheem's coherence impressed Jhee. Shep and Mirrei working together to treat him must have been the cause.

The sordid tale continued, "He pulled my hair then dragged me to his room where he locked me in. Some time later, he returned. I thought we were going to see Abbess Pyrmo. He pulled me through the Prayer Hall and through a courtyard then pushed me through a door. We emerged into a dressing room with a curtained bed. I had never seen such a luxuriously appointed room. A voice which echoed from everywhere called to me. It said I should join her as her groom as the Father Maker joins the Mother Maker. How could I properly decide if I would know no wife other than the Mother Maker unless I knew what it was I gave up?

"I refused. Mr. Pol grabbed a cane from the wall and then a branding iron from the fire. 'He is willful. I know how to ensure obedience.'

"'His skin is far too pretty and unblemished considering where he comes from. Unmarked, he may be of more use to us later. Put him to sleep where he can reconsider his options: my company or the brand.' A figure wearing a Cheiropthys mask stepped forward. Smoke emanated from its mouth. I fainted."

"At first, he had called the voice the abbess. I thought they sought to make me take vows against my will. Later, while I was stripped naked in that room, Mr. Pol called her the Mist Abbess. It was then I knew they had something far more diabolical planned. I despaired of my very soul.

"I awoke later only to see you and Raigen pass me by in the Halls of the Tortured and the Drenched. I thought all was lost. I too felt like I had been tortured and drenched. Then by the Makers' grace, you returned."

"You are very brave, Akesheem. No one has the right to enforce such indignities upon you. Now, this is very important, did you smell anything when you were in the room? Smudge? Licorice? Accelerants?"

"No—Wait. The lovely aroma of flowers and woody cologne. The beautiful fragrance mocked the misery the room must have seen."

"What about Hethyr? Did you see her or hear her name mentioned?"

Mr. Akesheem shook his head. Jhee furrowed her brow. She closed her eyes and drew a deep breath. The inspiration left him. "Very good, Akesheem. You did very well. Rest now."

Mr. Akesheem drifted off to sleep. Ms. Anshula looked away with moist eyes. Mr. Zane held her to him. Itzil roared in the distance. The sound broke the tension. "Itzil hasn't been out in a while. I need to exercise her. She likes the Zodiac Courtyard. That's where I'll be if you need me."

"I'll come with," Mr. Zane said.

They exited the room with haste.

"One of the many hazards of keeping a bull hound in your room," Jhee said. "Bright Harmony, you may have your conch back now."

When no response came, she faced those watching. Kanto wasn't present. He must have gone with them. She sighed. Shep placed a hand on her elbow.

"Mirrei has gotten worse," he whispered. "She is ill with fever."

"I checked on her. She is young and resilient. She assured me she is fine. I have no doubt you can and will tend to her."

"I *demand* of you little, but on this, as denme, I insist. Talk to her more. It may do her good."

Jhee inclined her head. She pulled up a stool beside Mirrei and adjusted her compress. "What's all this fuss? Think of the shame if we arrive at the capital and the first action we have to do is petition the Soothbringers for their cures. If you wanted my attention, you just needed to say so."

Mirrei smiled. Jhee returned the gesture. "So."

Jhee noted Mirrei's embroidery hoop lying beside her sickbed abandoned. Her smile faded. "This embroidery looks to be your finest to date. The poultice I chided you for proved pivotal in my investigation. It may have even saved my life. Between the journey and the single room, our time together has been lacking and for that, I apologize."

"No need."

"You have your denyes worried to waves over you. You were supposed to be resting, and they were supposed to be taking care of you."

"Please, don't baby me. Remember what I said about your ageism."

"How am I supposed to react when you both behave like disobedient adolescents? What else did you expect? Running around in the cold and damp?"

"No credible source says being out in the rain affects your likelihood of catching a cold."

"Exhaustion does. Besides, you don't have a cold. You have Fresh Lung Syndrome. This water is much too riverine for you to traipse about."

"Hence, why I wanted to see the Soothbringer healers in action."

Jhee pulled a faded, wrinkled parchment from her breast pocket. She placed the letter in Mirrei's chilly, dainty hands. "This is the letter your mother sent along with you before her passing."

Mirrei grimaced.

"She made me promise when she gave me your hand in marriage, I would see you safe and given a better life in the capital. Which is precisely what I intend to do. Will you make a liar of me and shame us both in her eyes?"

Mirrei shook her head 'No.'

"Good."

Jhee gained her feet. Mirrei grasped her hand.

"It's not his fault. I begged him to come with. He didn't even know where the camps were. I knew because you mentioned it then I consulted an atlas while we were in the archives."

"Nevertheless, he should have known better. You're in no condition to go traipsing around the island. Your delicate constitution is not suited for such misadventures. How could he have been so irresponsible to risk your health like that?"

"Makers, you didn't say that to him, did you?"

"Not in so many words. I know about his history with his mother."

Mirrei sunk further into the bedding in relief. "Good."

Jhee patted her hand. "Before you two came along, Shep and I were quite lax in our devotions. I shall go to the shrine and pray to Pascoe and Lashae for you. I shall input that you are well into the system, and I dare the Makers not to implement my design. You must heed me and your mamere's spirit and get better this instant."

Mirrei nodded. "Make time for him. You've made time for everyone else. Now, do so for him."

"Rest. We'll discuss it when I get back."

Bax reported back the results of the headcount. All were accounted for except the criminals, Ms. Hethyr and Mr. Pol. And now her husband.

"Where do you think Mr. Kanto went?" Bax asked.

"Likely sulking. Who knows? Maybe he went to Lady Bathsheba looking to trade up."

"That boy idolizes you, Justicar."

"I'm sorry. That was uncalled for. I'm not in the right waters for one of his moods now."

"Drench it, Jhee!" Shep said. "Are you this blind? What better way for you to think him capable and clever than to help your case and uncover the murderer himself?"

"He wouldn't be that reckless, would he?" Shep gave her a hard glare. A young man trying to impress would be precisely that reckless. She and Shep went to Kanto's seat by the charging station. "His sketchbook isn't here."

"He had been working in it while listening to his conch. Trench, he mentioned something he wanted me to look over before he presented it to you. I forgot in all the commotion."

"Maybe there's a clue on his conch."

Jhee tried to listen, but the room held too many distractions. "I must excuse myself, so I can think about how we are to proceed. Bax, with me. The rest of you stay here."

"Yes, Justicar."

Jhee and Bax headed out.

Mirrei took hold of her hand. "Go after him. Apologize. Pray for me together."

Mirrei closed her eyes. Jhee placed the embroidery hood and box on a stool for when she awoke. She used her sleeve to hide wiping away tears. She paused an extra moment to compose herself. Everyone in this room looked to her to maintain the systems. She must not fail them.

24

THE CLOISTER

~

The Coral Cloister

Kanto paced out the length of the Coral Cloister. He had left in such haste, he had brought no instrument to test his theory with save his voice. Not only that, he left his conch behind as well. He swallowed hard. He opened his mouth then clamped it shut again. Instead, he clapped. He took note of the sound of the echo and sustain. He proceeded a few paces. Then clapped again. He repeated the routine about half the perimeter of the Coral Cloister. Each spot sounded the same so far. He pulled out his sketchbook.

Tap. Tap. Kanto's knuckles rapped against an annex wall. He knew he was being a bit of a brat. But after weeks cooped up on that boat to see how denbe favored Mirrei. If only she knew.

With Mirrei's arrival, Kanto's calculations changed. He was no longer as sure of what his role was to be in their family as he once was. Perhaps he shouldn't fight denbe's plans to remarry him. But drench it, that was his decision, and she had not even bothered to ask him if that's what he wanted. His grandmere for all her cunning had at least respected him that much.

"She'll hate this," Shep had said. *"She'll hate that I'm here. But she needs a more suitable companion for the state dinner."*

The arrangement with Shep had been standard. Kanto was to escort

233

denbe to public functions and be the elegant, refined showpiece of her house in situations where appearances and tact mattered. Shep had no desire or inclination to do it himself. Having, also, heard about the refectory, if only secondhand, denbe could not risk such an incident at court.

Initially, it had been unclear if Shep intended romantic duties as well. Kanto suspected that had been an up-swell from grandmamere. He touched his side where the specialized, seahorse tattoo covered the nearly invisible scar from the "gentleman's" surgery he had as a child.

Grandmere must have up-swelled them as she had him. In the provinces, you sold excess. In the capital, they bought. *"No, he would not just be your companion for events or social secretary,"* she must have told them. *"Make him your husband. He would be your stream to riches. Claim his dowry and then remarry him for even more at the capital."*

Tap. Tap. The columns sounded fine. Kanto walked the Coral Cloister again as he checked his notes.

How easy Kanto had thought it would be to win promotion to first husband. It took mere moments in the company of the vain, preening Mr. Zane to realize that's what denbe thought he was. A clownfish paddling for a wave to the capital. He understood now he needed to impress her. If he helped her crack the case, it might crack the ice between them.

Why did Kanto fight her so hard on remarrying him? He would find a rich woman, who kept him finely attired and supplied with taffies and cakes. Until he grew aged and fat and she threw him aside for another younger and more fit. He did not think denbe so shallow. One had to cast their gaze no further than her current first husband.

Denbe thought him shallow. She thought it was about the material trifles. It was about respect. She was no longer going to be a field judge. She would have to sit on the bench and render judgment. If she showed up to a court function in ripped, dirty robes and disheveled hair, who there would respect her? If she had to attend higher-ranking officials, would they submit to the judgment of someone who presented to them as beneath them? No. When she got to court, he wanted them to see what he had seen their first meeting, the small, unassuming woman who nevertheless owned the room. The one who made Shep's eyes brighten and sit up straighter when he talked about her and being her husband.

Kanto huffed and grimaced at the grim statues. Scarred, graying like Shep. If grandmamere's information was correct, not spending nearly enough time in the marriage bed.

Grandmamere had known the ways to hook Kanto. She filled his head with tales of a loveless marriage, a marriage of convenience, how he could give her love and care, and most importantly, heirs. What he knew was denbe and denme were not on the same wavelength about everything. Kanto's introduction didn't seem a matter of sexual satisfaction, and Shep had spoken of children and family. Yet, those seemed the farthest notion from what denbe wanted.

"What had happened to saddle such a smart, passionate woman with such an unsatisfactory partner as Shep. If my inquiries are correct, he's barely able to perform his husbandly duties. I fail to see what use Shep provides her that mere hired brutes could not, yet she lavishes attention on him. She needs your political savvy. Younger, more handsome, more virile. It should be an easy task for you to become first. It should be child's play for you to supplant him."

Spousal promotion might have been an easy task if Kanto spent enough time alone with denbe. No sooner had they consummated, however, then Mirrei and Miramar arrived. He had made some measure of progress. He gained Shep's confidence enough to learn denbe's exciters and dislikes. He caught her eye more and more.

"Don't be another crisis she has to manage. I am the denme. If there is a problem, come to me first. I'll do my best to resolve it without troubling her."

What if the problem was the distance between Kanto and his denbe? Shep's attempt to be a well-meaning intermediary only heightened the problem. Could he even assure himself Shep meant well, though?

"Flatter her. Don't be a burden."

Shep's help always hung in the space between sabotage and self-destruction. Kanto and denbe needed to find their own accommodation. How to assert himself and his needs, though, without adding to her burdens?

Kanto wiped his forehead with a handkerchief only to realize it was the one denbe had 'picked up somewhere.' He shoved it back into his robes.

"Bright Harmony, what are you doing?" the vizier asked.

Kanto started. "Coming to see you," he quipped to cover his embarrassment and gave her a charming smile.

She tilted her head. "Is that so?"

He sighed. "There was something I wanted to investigate."

"Taking after your denbe, I see. I was on my way to speak to her. You shouldn't be about unaccompanied. Don't you know there is a killer about with a murderous desire for young men?"

Suddenly, Kanto felt childish and even worse foolish. What was he doing out here? *Well, denme, she'll hate that I'm here, too.*

"What was that?" The vizier clasped the codex and amulet closer to her body. She tensed upon scrutiny of every shadow as if expecting an Unmaker to leap from every single one. "Come, let us return you to her care forthwith."

She offered him her arm. He paused to consider if he should take it. The vizier was still a handsome woman. One, who were he still entertaining suit, he would not have accounted a hardship to be paired with. Yet he knew authoritatives like the vizier from years having to prepare and serve tea for grandmamere's visitors. To them with their cups held out, he was invisible except when they leered. He minded being invisible little. The better to serve his information gathering.

With denbe, Kanto minded being invisible much. He wanted denbe to see him and his worth. He had not accomplished what he set out to do. If he returned with nothing to show for his efforts, he confirmed his wife's opinion of him as shallow and frivolous. Maybe she was right. Maybe he was out of his depths. He was no investigator.

"I don't know about this, Bright Harmony. I think we should go. Now. As soon as possible."

Lady Bathsheba swiveled her head this way and that at the slightest noise. Kanto rapped one of the statues in an alcove. Tap. Tunk. A flatter thump than the others greeted him.

"In a moment, Lady Bathsheba. I want to try this one, last..." Kanto pushed. The statue rotated inward unexpectedly. He tumbled through the opening.

~

The Cellar

"I don't like this, Bax."

"Me neither, Justicar."

"Drench, foolish man. There's still a killer on the prowl."

With a taste for young men. Jhee and Bax made their way down to the central hall. She did not anticipate having to tell the vizier her husband had run off. Which outcome horrified her more? Him wandering around the abbey a step ahead of murderers? Or as she had wondered all along his interest in her had revolved around money and ambition? What if she did find him seeking the vizier's attention? She would simply have to manage.

Outside the annex, Cheiropthys emerged. From the Cheiropthys mask to the clothes, all remained as she recalled from when the character had taunted her and assaulted her amongst the mineral springs. However, he held Kanto's sketchbook. She gasped.

"Stop there!"

Cheiropthys dropped the sketchbook then turned and ran. Bax gave chase. Jhee paused to scoop up Kanto's possession. Their pursuit took them through the kitchens and across the courtyard. They ran the length of the outer perimeter. This time Jhee determined not to stop until she had unmasked that foul man.

She had to think this through and analyze the best course. With the abbey's layout, if they continued pursuit haphazardly, the figure could easily keep a step ahead of them. The same if she gathered others for a systematic search floor-by-floor.

In the cellar, they turned up the crab-rat they sought. Jhee charged. Cheiropthys fled. The fiend's shoes skidded on the rocks. She drew a burst of air. In the time it took her to stop and draw, Cheiropthys turned a corner out of her sight. The puff of air only blew around the dust where he had been.

She ran again. The glow orb lit tunnels meant she had no source of fire to use. His foot disappeared around a corner further down the hallway. They emerged into the cloister again, having traveled in a loop.

Columns and macabre sculptures surrounded the cloister. She stopped to draw. Cheiropthys dashed between the columns. The blast of air passed by him again. She ran to his former location. He crawled through a small archway in the wall. She squeezed through hot on his trail.

The archway led to food stores. Cheiropthys grabbed a rack of rice and pulled it down after him. Jhee scrabbled over it. Cheiropthys pulled more shelves of food down. Next, a rack of dishes. A few wooden bowls and utensils flew at her propelled by elemental force. She defended herself with a combination of covering her head and wind bursts. By the time she looked up, he had taken off again. Pots clattered to her left.

Cheiropthys made a whip-like motion. Pebbles pelted her. Many tiny without and much force behind them. She plowed through as another shield meant less speed. A small whir came from the mask. Jhee was ready this time. She spun aside and had a counter ready. She used an air gust to blow it back in his face. The masked figure leaped back. Only a thin, sputtering wisp of smoke came from the mask this time unlike the voluminous amounts previous.

Her attacker ripped off the mask to reveal an obsequious face with goatee. Mr. Pol doubled over coughing. He spared a frustrated glare at the mask before he hurled it at her. She ducked. He dashed down the hallway.

Jhee pursued again. His gender treachery and vile assaults upon innocent young men would not go unanswered. She would find Kanto even if she had to tear the whole abbey apart with her bare claws. Had Kanto's kidnapping been belated vengeance for spoiling their plans? Or as Jhee hesitated to entertain, a prize in and of himself. His refinement, his breeding, his gentle nature. To be despoiled by some cougar like the one behind the curtained bed. She had not appreciated him. She shuddered to think to what indignities the more aggressive deviants of the capital might put her poor Kanto through. Mr. Pol and whatever dark-hearted and cruel enterprise he served ended tonight.

At last, she corned Mr. Pol in the storeroom where the performers kept their costumes.

"You will answer for your crimes," she said. "Tell me my husband's location, and I shall be merciful and speak on your behalf in front of the Central Justicars."

Jhee gestured for Bax to circle around.

"Unfortunately, Justicar, I will not be going anywhere with you. There are far worse fates than imperial justice. You don't know the forces the one whom I serve can bring to bear. Look at what the Mist Abbess did to those who defied her. The previous abbess tried to oppose her only to be struck down, too. The Mist Abbess took us into the depths of the abbey and used her magical powers to influence our minds and see what she wanted us to see. She even roused the Storm Drake twice causing the earth to tremble and the waves to rise. I doubt I'd survive long enough to make it to trial. Forgive me if I pass on your generous offer."

Had Jhee seen such a creature herself, heard its snoring, felt its breath? What had she seen glimmering and shining on the walls of the crypts? Toril's resting place? The slumbering place of one of the lesser drakes? Some lesser kin to the Storm Drakes? If the greater drakes existed, it stood to reason the lesser drakes did too, perhaps slumbering beneath the isles. Alive or preserved as the honored dead were?

And once the fancy took her mind, she could not loosen it. Her vision sped down through the rocks of isle's foundation to some vast cavern to where Toril and his drake slumbered until the time of the great Unmaking.

"Please, I beg of you, tell me where my husband is."

Mr. Pol did not reply. More pebbles flew at her. His elemental skills were weak and overused. The bowls were probably the most damage he could muster. She might wrest control of the stones from him. A gesture not worth the effort compared to her air shields which he proved weak against.

Jhee, also, had a more mundane alternative. She reached into her sleeve for the handle of her knife. He proved to have no skill with air. If he wasted his focus on pebbles, he could not deflect her blade.

"You have nowhere to go, Mr. Pol. Please, surrender this instant."

He must be hiding in the niche. Jhee crept down the last few feet of the storeroom. She pulled out her knife. "Please, Mr. Pol, no games. All I want is my husband's safe return."

With a cry, she rolled across the opening of the nook; the empty nook. The yell died on her lips. Mr. Pol had gone.

She and Bax stared at each other. He could not have slipped past both.

"Perhaps he was taken by the ghosts."

"For the last time, Bax. There are no such things as ghosts."

"With all the strange doings around here and then, Mr. Pol disappears into thin air."

"I'll not leave Kanto in the hands of ghosts or whatever else arcane or mundane which haunts this place. Now help me search."

They tore the nook apart. Baskets and masks lay strewn everywhere by the end. Yet, not a single clue of where Mr. Pol had gone.

25

―――――

THE MIST PARTS

⁓

The Curtained Bed

Kanto favored his head which rested scant inches from open space. He scrambled toward the wall of the narrow landing. The Makers' grace alone prevented him from overshooting the landing to the steps or central shaft. He hastened to his feet and hugged the wall. What murderous architect designed such a stairwell?

He heard muffled voices the other side of the wall. He pushed on it. "Lady Bathsheba?"

Mumbled, distorted vocalizations answered him. He pushed on the wall again. He felt no other mechanism to open it. He turned his attention to the stairwell. The sensible course would have been to wait for Lady Bathsheba to figure out how to open the secret passage. Assuming she had even seen what happened to him. Or for denbe to find him. Dare he wait? This is what he had come to the Prayer Hall to discover in the first place, wasn't it? To investigate the discrepancy in the Prayer Hall's acoustics on his own and present his findings to denbe in a manner she would accept.

Kanto had lost his glow orb in the fall. After a moment, his eyes adjusted, and his esca provided a modicum of illumination. The gloppy contents of the broken polyglass sphere trailed down the stairs. A faint, warm glow emanated from below. He placed a hand firmly against the wall to his left and wriggled and shuffled forward. The coral rock walls scraped against his fingertips. He took the extra moment to test each step before he put his weight down. As he proceeded further down the stairwell, he regretted learning then retelling the ghost story of the lost cleric trapped in the walls. He started at the slightest noise. He repeated to himself the nature of the acoustics of the abbey. They magnified and distorted every drip or crab-rat shuffle into the roar of waves or footsteps of giants. Acoustic trickery. That's all it was.

Only crab-rats. Those were scary enough on their own. Kanto continued to feel his way towards the light. At last, he came to a wooden door. He pushed it open to reveal a curtained bed. A cozy fire burned nearby. Golden, glow orbs rather than the more traditional and stark blue were inset in sconces on the wall a giant, single glow orb in the ceiling. He expected a room like this to be cold and damp even with the fire. However, the Prospectives had told him in certain old parts of the abbey, the hot springs ran around or even through the walls.

Deep, high thread silken tapestries in green and golds hung from the rods near the ceiling. Furnishings made from hardwoods adorned the room, luxurious though dated. A cloying fragrance permeated the room combined with the smell of a mild, spring forest cologne, an expensive cologne with an airy woodsy scent only available via special order. Whenever Kanto smelled it as a child, he associated it with inland and the capital. A bouquet of sea roses graced the center of a black lacquer table.

The door creaked. Kanto whirled and ran. It shut and locked as he reached it. He tried the handle. It did not move.

The coral walls matched the color and orientation of the Prayer Hall above. A sideboard contained a staggering arrangement of food delicacies. Beside the bed, a clear decanter of Tranquility Red, the abbey's less well-known brandy, had been opened and allowed to breathe. A pre-packed glass pipe nestled next to an ash dish containing rare, aged smoke root shaved and rerolled into a tight tube. A silver tray bore Black Sea maye roe, white abalone, and algae toast points. The wall had made the passage to the Black Sea all but unnavigable spiking the price and dropping the availability of any products from the mayes of that region. Kanto's stomach growled. He scooped up some the roe with a toast wedge.

The table runner, with its dated scrollwork, caught his attention. He reached into his robe for the handkerchief. The pattern on it matched the runner. He sniffed the scarf. Woodsy notes. The curtained bed. Flowers. Mr. Akesheem's kidnapping account. The lair of the Mist Abbess.

"Please, indulge yourself."

The voice echoed from all corners of the room at once. Eerie screeches and deep rumbles accompanied by weird echoes. Acoustic tricks, Kanto reminded himself, due to the shape of the room and the Prayer Hall. Like the whisper wall. All the speaker had to do was stand in the right place.

"Where are you? Show yourself."

"In due time."

"Please, I wish to return to my family."

"Not quite yet. Soon I promise. Do not trouble yourself. For now, truly, indulge yourself."

The overhead orb faded out. The secondary spheres remained the only source of light along with a few companions on the table. He waited for a while. He took up one of the lamps from the table and went to the door.

Kanto examined the lock. A basic mechanical lock, easy enough to foil even if he did not have Bax's skill for it. He required something long and thin to work the tumblers. Mirrei had struck a deal with Bax. She formulated and supplied him with his lock-picking aides, and he taught them how to use them, including the mundane ones. The lessons their little secret because denbe would have been scandalized. Mirrei claimed you never knew when it might be useful. He, on the other hand, had done it to alleviate the monotony. Otherwise, he might have been driven mad with boredom while denbe tried to solve the world's mysteries. Mirrei turned out to be the one in the right.

Kanto scoured the room for something thin to fit into the opening and strong enough to manipulate the mechanics. He paused to consider how denbe might approach the search. He felt along crevices and walls and bedposts. He had much to learn from denbe. As he had from the hours he spent listening at his grand dame's feet. He sought to find interest in the subjects she found interest in. He sought to delight her with his stylish and bright clothes and his music playing. Some lessons went over his head. Many did not.

On the headboard, Kanto found a slightly raised lip. He worked at it a bit with a nail to reveal a small compartment. A thin bound notebook lay atop a sheaf of parchments. He leafed through them. Names, dates, a few symbols. The symbols must have acted as a shorthand for what they had done that his captor could use against them. He had found someone's favor lists, a potent leverage tool to share with denbe once he escaped. He tucked them away in his hidden, breast pockets. A tight fit as he had not made his as capacious as Jhee's.

Despite Kanto's ordeal, his robes while dirtied and muddied retained the impeccable shape to the sleeves had worked so hard to perfect. Wire. He picked at the stitching until he created an opening large enough to worry out the wire. He separated and twisted the wire into a shape suitable to serve his purposes.

Denbe's house needed him as well. She may have been an academic and not a politician, but it was a deficit he could help her correct if she allowed. On some sphere, she knew or else she'd never have agreed to the match.

As Kanto worked the lock, he glimpsed a brand beside the fireplace. He pushed away Akesheem's account. He shoved away the knowledge of the three dead Prospectives. A beauty such as himself did not come along often and would have been most valuable. The delicacies, along with his capture, proved the villain who held him, had some taste at least. He hated to think he would spend his last few hours with someone with bad taste. Simply unconscionable. He leaned into the lock picking. His pick bent.

Kanto swore. He calmed himself. He was Kanto, only son of House Kenyatta, son of Kaisonia, grandson of Lady Kaydence, and he would not die in some sleazy, underground boudoir decorated with dated, mismatched furnishings. His wife, the brilliant, powerful Justicar Jhee, would find him and make those who did this pay. She likely already searched for him. He refashioned the pick and tried again.

The proper clicks went off in the right sequence. The door swung open.

Kanto made a satisfied sound and stepped outside. A figure in a mask of the bat-faced Cheiropthys blocked his path. The figure chanted and gestured, a drawing. A small rock flew from the ground. He enacted a quick air burst. The drawing produced only an impotent puff which barely perturbed the rock.

The rock struck Kanto on the head. Kanto covered his esca. The figure closed the distance. A white plume of smoke emanated from the mask's mouth. The smoke hit Kanto directly in the face. He coughed. He felt light-headed.

"The playboy?"

"The favorite husband or the wife would have been better. Too late now. We'll make do."

The images and bright colors of the coral spun about Kanto. A moment later, he had a vague awareness of the hard-coral ground rushing to meet his face.

$\sim$

The Last of the Elixir

"Mr. Pol is still out there. And Ms. Hethyr. What if they have procured Kanto? He stormed off because we had cross words."

"It's not your fault, Justicar."

"Nevertheless, it is still my problem. Kanto tried to inform me about an issue important to him, Bax. I dismissed him. I should have listened. I should have made time. Come. We must hurry."

"Don't be worried, Justicar. Mr. Kanto probably just went to the springs or to visit with the refugees."

"My hope is you're right."

"Should we go back to the Corrections Hall?"

"No, Mr. Pol is unlikely to return there so soon. Not since we are likely to be watching it. Pyrmo. She may have answers."

When they entered Pyrmo's room, the former abbess was still slumped in her chair sleeping restlessly.

Jhee stalked over. When she touched Pyrmo's shoulder to wake her, she noticed Pyrmo's yellowish pallor. Her skin was cold and clammy. She shook and coughed.

"What did you take?" Jhee fumbled in her sleeves for her elixir. She had used it all on Lady Bathsheba. "Bax, hand me the spare elixir."

Pyrmo collapsed against Jhee. Jhee flipped Pyrmo onto her back. Bax handed her the elixir vial, and she tipped it to Pyrmo's lips. "Please, Bright Harmony and Mr. Pol."

Pyrmo coughed the elixir back out. "This life is just mist."

The abbess frothed at the mouth, shuddered, then stopped moving.

"No!" Jhee hunched over Pyrmo's lifeless body. "She was our last link."

Bax brushed her shoulder in reassurance. A flask weighted down a note on the lacquer side table: "Best not to leave a mess. You are shrewder and more resourceful than we gave you credit for."

Jhee examined the flask. It wasn't the one Pyrmo drank from earlier or in the storehouse. "This is a different flask. She was murdered."

She found the servant's door unlocked.

"I locked it I swear, Justicar."

Jhee believed him. They made a quick search of the crypts. Its mists now made her uneasy. A ringing, a quiver of eagerness filled it now.

Their urgency brought them to the mineral springs. Jhee's heart skipped a beat. She carefully examined each. Thankfully, she found them empty with no trace of Kanto. She breathed a sigh of relief. Now, they still had to hurry.

"Where else, Justicar?"

"Where indeed? This wind-blasted abbey has so many twists and turns and nooks to it. Let's limit his means off this rock then."

After Jhee and Bax alerted the licit boat captains, they rushed to the smugglers' notch. The captain and her crew worked the deck as if in preparation to leave. Upon sight of Jhee, the captain worried her ear. "Magistrate, we were just securing our ship."

"No lies right now, captain. You're clearly taking a lay out while the weather is passable. My husband is missing. Has he or anyone else approached you to book passage? You have seen no one unusual while you prepared?"

"Nay."

"May I have leave to examine your holds?"

"Now, wait one moment, magistrate. I reckon we've been more than accommodating—."

"As have I. No other authority has come to trouble you. If it were my intention, to change that I would have. I assure you my concern is larger than poaching or smuggling." Jhee and Bax did a quick search. They even ferreted out a few false panels and holds, much to the captain's chagrin. No trace of Jhee's husband. "Is the wine the only cargo you smuggle?"

"Nay. We do a little fishing what to feed ourselves and our kin with. Well, and the items what you already knows about."

Jhee cornered the gang-affiliated crewman she identified her last visit. "What manner of fineries did you procure?"

"All sorts. Caviar. Roe. Abalone. Forest Cologne. Sur Dale root and leaf. Jassar silks."

"Silks?"

"Aye, mum."

"Was it always Prospectives who came to procure the items?"

"No, mum. I weren't always required to bring goods in. Times they needed me to send items out. Them times it were either a man or a lady what gave them to me."

"Would you recognize either if you saw them again?"

"Aye, mum."

Jhee fished out Kanto's sketchbook. She leafed through the sketches.

"There, that be the man."

The crewman had stopped on the picture of Mr. Pol. Jhee continued to go through the images. "Her. She wore a cloak what kept her face hidden, but I recognize this symbol."

Rage threatened to consume Jhee. She resorted to counting and statute recitation to calm herself. Under the circumstances, she could not risk misusing her siren module on herself. "Captain, please, might you delay your departure in the chance I have need of you."

"Mum, we tarry for days at your say so while our family like t'starve and we sore miss 'em."

"I know, I know. Please, a little longer."

"An hour or two maybe, but after that, we will leave."

"If it comes to that, ensure none but your crew are on board."

"Ye have my word on it."

As Jhee left, the captain seized the crew member by the scruff and clout them on the ears.

~

Echoes at the Courtyard Shrine

Every distorted noise in the distance became the most horrid cries. What was happening to Jhee's rejected husband? What were those fiend folk doing to Kanto? Gentle souls like him and Mirrei would be mistreated by this world. The Makers put those like Jhee here to protect and keep them. She had failed. In her obsession with puzzles and the law, she had sore neglected both. Now Kanto had met an unknown fate because she could not spare him a few moments attention. She did not want him to die in fear and hurt thinking they had not cared. That he would not be missed. Shep's mental health and Mirrei's physical health had deteriorated. Kanto felt abandoned and unappreciated.

Jhee conjured an idealized image of Miramar, Mirrei's mother and her childhood friend, in mind. From that image her recollection went on to the complicated relationship between Jhee, Shep, and her. Then settled once more on the image of Miramar standing defiant against the waves. Miramar had wished to sleep under the waves which held her loved ones and families' remains. The same waves which had claimed their home atoll soon after.

Jhee erred. It had been her responsibility to see her cohort safely to the capital as she had promised Kanto's grandmamere and sworn in remembrance of Mirrei's mamere. She had pledged to Kanto's grand dame and Mirrei's dame they would have the best she had to offer. She had meant monetarily. Yet, that turned out to be a pauper's meal which had done nothing to nourish their essences.

In her search, Jhee found herself at the courtyard shrine. She knelt and removed her headwear. She clasped her wrists. "First and Greatest Makers, I beg of you, please, let me find Kanto safe and unharmed. If you do, I promise to honor him and cherish him as I do Shep. I promise to respect his wishes and not take him for granted."

Jhee breathed in the breath of the salt and sea. She got the sense of being watched. The Forebears. *Those in the waves and those in the sky gaze favorably upon us in the liminal realm until the time of our Remaking come.*

Of her spouses, Jhee understood Kanto the least. She and Shep were content to sit and enjoy each other's company. She didn't feel this pressure to do "something." She and Mirrei could talk books or arcana. She and Kanto fought or walked on new crab shells around each other.

What did Kanto get from their relationship other than the obvious? Jhee did not know what he saw when he looked at her. There was the core mechanism of it. Shep saw her with an old lover's gaze, one born of youthful affection and years of bonding. Mirrei saw her with gratefulness or as a successful older woman to emulate.

What did Kanto see when he looked at her? This woman he had been sold to. Sure, she and his grand dame had dressed it up in pretty words and a contract, with other particulars of the arrangement worked out by Shep, Kanto, and Kanto's grand dame. But it involved an exchange of value for him, though not monetary. She had bought Kanto. And she planned to sell him again once they reached the capital. Older women passed men and women as young and cultivated as him around like fine art.

Kanto's disappearance was the same as it was with those missing young men. We were so concerned with the death of the more prestigious individual, the fate and absence of the less prestigious nearly went unremarked and unnoticed. Another overlooked, passed over for more intriguing and immediate concerns. If some calamity befalls Kanto, I will never forgive myself.

"He hears things. He's very observant. Jhee, he's smarter than you give him credit for," Shep had said once.

What did Kanto see or hear that sent him rushing out into the night? Jhee brought out Kanto's sketchbook and conch. She cursed herself. She had predicated her search on Kanto's foolhardiness. What she should have done was trusted his talents, namely his ear and his eye. To combat the sense of impropriety she felt viewing his drawings, she skipped past any which appeared to have been drawn before their arrival. She came upon a sketch of the household in the courtyard. The illustration depicted her with the flowing hair of waves and seaweed common to the Lady of the Isles imagery from back home. He had drawn himself in lightly as a cupbearer with Mirrei and Shep as her standard-bearers. Roughed in around them were the wall with the abbey's sigil and the arches, pillars, and pedestals bearing several Makers' marks and offerings.

Jhee blessed him for his practicality and cleverness when she found a document entitled "Time Codes." Inside Kanto had recorded names and times codes for audio snips he had found interesting. The last two notes read "Whisper Wall" and "Dead Zone."

She listened to a few recordings of the Prospectives telling the stories of how they had arrived at the abbey. They relayed tales of tiny, overloaded crafts capsizing; the sounds of the screams and then the eerie silence; the image of hands scrabbling for any piece of flotsam only to disappear under the waves to never resurface. Jhee's chest only allowed shallow breaths. She imagined a calm shore to block out the images. She skipped ahead to the sea songs and shanties of the refugees at the camps. Waves and winds crashed in the background. She scrolled back to the Prospectives telling their stories. More waves and wind performed as undertones to their accounts.

She rewound again. The Prospectives stories had been captured inside the abbey either in the central hall or Prayer Hall as they undertook their duties. Where was the sound of waves and wind coming from?

Jhee stared at his sketch of the courtyard. Then she looked at the direction where she had seen the strange occurrence. The wall with the abbey's sigil. The bridge and the sword. So much had happened since she had arrived, she almost forgot about the mysterious sight she had seen her first night here. She examined Kanto's sketch again. In his drawing, the bridge and the sword were joined upright with the sword pierced through the bridge. The same as they were on the entrance gates. The mark she saw now, and on the first night, the sword and the bridge were separated. The bridge was oriented up and down and the sword horizontal. The crenelations atop the wall were offset from each other with one double row then a single. The drawing showed only two rows. It could have been a fanciful interpretation like his sketch of their family. Yet, he had been painstakingly accurate and literal about every other architectural feature he had drawn since he got here.

Lost Prospectives and whispers and music from within the walls. Walls more than two meters thick. Why build internal walls that thick? Jhee consulted her map.

Jhee approached the sigil. It was not single emblem hung or carved on the wall as she had assumed, but two pieces. She placed a hand on the bridge and the sword then rotated it.

"I have become something of a hermit."

"Sister Serra, the vizier, even the prioress, and Sister Elkanah consulted."

As Jhee turned, the sword and bridge rejoined. The wall reconfigured amidst a grinding of stone and dust. She rotated the emblem the opposite way. The masonry flowed aside to reveal a secret passageway. A slight breeze hit her face. From a few steps back, the wall appeared seamless except for the crenelations.

"I've barely left my chambers."

"The vizier and I consulted."

Jhee took up her map and a glowtorch. She passed through the opening.

When Jhee pocketed the conchs, her hand brushed the handkerchief containing barnacles. *"The second you've acquired..."* She compared it to Elkanah's ripped garment scrap. Similar, but not exact. She had gotten this one from Leigh's belongings. Where had the second come from? The infirmary.

The trick Kanto and Mirrei pulled with the pillows. *"...none of our patients went missing." According to Sister Zalver. And her questionable faculties.* How closely had she checked?

The opening led to a narrow corridor which ran alongside the principal axes. Jhee made her way along the passageway. Different colors and textures of stone composed the opposite sides of the passage. One side also displayed signs of weathering. The passage must have been added later. Every few minutes, she heard the sound of metal striking stone. As she got closer, the noises were preceded by a moist thud. Whack-shink-whack. Thud. Whack-shink-whack.

The passageway opened onto a hexagonal room. Just inside the entrance, a mechanized puppet missing an arm and foot lay propped against the wall. Meanwhile, the noises continued ahead. A figure in a mask stood before a coral altar. Her arm raised to reveal a bloody cleaver which she brought down on a slab of meat on the platform.

The masked figure doused the altar with rancid fluid from a black keg. She snatched up a cattle prod. Then with one swift motion set the table alight with godspark. Blue-green flames leaped into the sky. She removed her fanged, re-breather mask and apron which she threw onto the pyre. She spread her arms wide. The flames grew higher. She gestured in an upsweep. The fire consumed everything on the table and then vanished.

Jhee moved up behind her. Munching and squishing noises began.

"Nice trick. Since I doubt you discovered the secret of true making, I assume that leads to a waste chute. Am I in the presence of the Wave Witch, or should I say the Mist Abbess?" Jhee held her glow orb higher. "Or shall I call you vizier?"

26

THE LOW CHAMBER

~

The Low Spire

Lady Bathsheba turned to Jhee. She smiled at Jhee with a blood-stained mouth, a half-chewed heart in her hands.

"I have a flair for the dramatic. I do hope you were impressed." She gulped down the last of the heart. "Now, his spirit will serve me in the realms to come. Lady Bathsheba will be fine. I must congratulate you on finding my little hobby chamber. A gallery of horrors of some sort. I arrogated it for more pleasurable pursuits."

"I'm not so sure if the men you abducted thought so."

"Seduced. I'd never take you for such a prude, Justicar. You'd be surprised how agreeable they found my company."

"You or the gifts you showered them with?"

"Spoken with the contempt of finery and riches only capable by one who has never been without them. Rather than as achievements, comforts, you view my enticements as bribes. They're luxuries these men never hope to possess on their own; a glimpse of a life which under normal circumstances would never be theirs. Fine wines and delicacies. Delights they would have never tasted on their backwater, provincial isles. They were then more pliable and predisposed to the sorts of women they would meet in the larger towns.

Once having learned some grace or refinement, they would be better able to make their way in the cities. It's a buyer's market out there. Oh, to be there myself. It is very similar to the learning husband situation most were already accustomed to. It's obvious you had similar plans for Bright Harmony. Was what I did so much different from you? Was it also not how you married him in the first place? I gave these boys opportunities they would not have otherwise had. I was really doing them a service as well as my clients in the city."

"Spoken with the arrogance and self-delusion of every predator I've ever dealt with."

"Please, Jhee, I'm quite a cut above those provincial villains in your stories. Basic competence, let alone, dare I say it, genius, is a trait sorely lacking nowadays. Like Thaedra with her salon of great thinkers and talented students. The best and the brightest who drove each other to innovate and experiment. You yourself can attest to the insights we are still gleaning from their body of works. To be sure Thaedra was no Canon. I feel a kinship with her. You think Thaedra, surrounded by such young and vigorous company, did not succumb at least once or twice. I'm apt to think her salon was as much a dating pool as a place of study."

Lady Bathsheba bent by the puppet and deposited the recovered piece of the triptych or polyptych into a gilded metal and hardwood strongbox. The lady grinned and wiped her mouth with a silken, amethyst sash. A dark chunk fell from the altar with a wet smack: a partially charred hand. Jhee's heart dropped to the great depths.

"You fiend." Jhee drew the elements and slammed Lady Bathsheba against the wall with a burst of air.

Lady Bathsheba laughed and picked herself up off the floor. "You really must calm yourself."

The First Makers only knew what Jhee might have done if the altar were still ablaze. "Vizier Bathsheba of Toho and Wilobeia, by the power invested in me by the dual sovereigns of the Six Isles, I—"

"Please, Justicar, let's return to my chamber for some kolal before you finish your accusation."

Lady Bathsheba hitched up her skirts and walked past Jhee. Jhee opened her mouth to protest.

"I assure you it will be a career-ending phrase for you, not me. Shall we return to my chamber? I need to refresh myself."

Jhee stared at the smoking, blood-stained altar. She had promised his grand dame. His well-being had been her responsibility.

"They say this place was built by an evil necromancer, a rival of Thaedra.

I fell in love with the acoustics the moment I arrived. One of the few compelling traits this backwater boasts. Aside from the ghastly statues. Most remarkable. In the Corrections Hall, you must have seen some of the more salacious, sordid episodes in this place's history. I'd say my activities barely rate in comparison.

"Now that you have explored more of the abbey, you simply must tell me what you think? I would love to compare notes. I'm still impressed. I only discovered it myself recently. I thought you were clever. The moment I saw your pretense of sophistication, I said to myself that is one clever girl. I was assured of it once I met your lovely cohort."

"The embracing couple," Jhee mumbled.

"Your cloister ghosts. Yes. Via my blunder then. Your sudden arrival prompted me to clean up after myself. I had been using the puppet as a decoy to fool the bed check and give the impression certain places were haunted. Then Pyrmo informed me they hadn't let your vessel sink as I suggested. I improvised as best I could, but not enough."

"All the talk of malign forces was you giving a good show. The Mist Abbess rumors didn't start with Saheli's arrival. They began with yours some long-months before. With the crop blight and weird chemicals, ghost hysteria hit Torilsisle, and you were all too happy to capitalize on it."

"Quite the contrary. I caused it. You said it felt strange to cypher here. The tremors resulted from my attempts to perform the incomplete rites. I knew I had missed some nuance. I had thought to search the archives again while everyone was preoccupied with the banquet. It took some time to locate the missing start sequence. Thank you for oh so helpfully pointed out part of the instructions were missing."

$\sim$

The Unraveling Tale I

Stunned, numb, Jhee allowed the vizier to guide her back to the hermitage. She once again found herself laid bare and belittled at Lady Bathsheba's table surrounded by her terrifyingly beautiful things. The vizier cleaned up as the kolal heated.

Jhee had failed. Her responsibility had been to see her cohort safely to the capital as she had promised Kanto's grandmamere and sworn in remembrance of Mirrei's mamere. She could not pry her attention away from the purplish, blood-smeared, and dirtied sash. Her tabard of office weighed on her like an anchor.

"I meant to have tea ready, but you arrived earlier than I expected. Why so taciturn? I'd imagined you full of questions and more talkative than this. This is the part in your stories I always loved, where Jeja would sit down with the villain and allow them to tell the story of why they did it."

Lady Bathsheba noticed Jhee's gaze on the sash. She snatched it up.

"Ah, amethyst. Bright Harmony's preferred accent color. No. No. No. My word, you didn't think? Justicar, what good would that have done me? He is far more valuable alive. More so than the panicky Mr. Pol. Men like him can be replaced as can men like the Prospectives. Unlike the irreplaceable treasure you don't make proper use of. Your disinterest shall we say in his obvious charms impressed itself even on me. With the care and work he puts into his appearance, it's positively criminal for you to neglect his efforts."

"It was Mr. Pol?" Jhee mulled over the thought. The finger claws on the hand had been dirty and ragged, which could have happened while trapped. However, they lacked nail lacquer and foil work traces. The clothing and the thickened body hair color had not matched her husband's. "It was Mr. Pol," Jhee asserted.

"Hopefully, now you are in a better frame of mind to listen to what I must say. Please, if you have any questions for me, now is the time to ask."

"Kanto, where is he?"

"We'll get to that." Lady Bathsheba poured kolal into both their cups. Jhee did not touch hers. "I am not petty or vindictive. What do you take me for?"

"A perverter and killer of men."

"You have me there. You would already be dead if that were my wish. We need to come to an arrangement. I am being courteous to you because you have been a worthy opponent. You should not refuse my hospitality."

"With all the poisonings around here, you shouldn't be insulted by reasonable precautions on my part."

Lady Bathsheba picked up her cup and drank. She grimaced at her cup. "A little bitter. Forgive the bad pour. Nowhere near the skill of your husband's. My palate's been off since my little dip."

"You mean the night you poisoned us."

"A bit of theater. Nothing more. Nothing we ate or drank was poisoned. Harming myself once was enough. A little fireroot on the fingernail, dab some in your eye or another mucous membrane. Sweats, complexion change, palpitations set in. Very dramatic. I do need to thank you for my daring rescue. The intent was to disappear with you as witness, not drown."

"Staged. Just like your accident before my arrival."

"Not entirely. I didn't realize the archivist was stalking you. I fell into the springs by accident when she attacked Mr. Pol. That ninny was so determined to catch the Trouble Maker she ran after him and left us to die. I'd say that's enough time for me to be showing signs of anything you suspect I might have added to the tea. Now, please, have some. It's so nice to have a proper tea."

Jhee made a show of picking up hers and bringing it to her lips. She was, however, not foolish enough to drink.

"There. Civility. While it is a bit of a relief to have everything out in the open, I'm curious as to how you figured it out. Was it only seeing me with the puppet?"

"'Sometimes it is the trifles which mean the most.' It's rarely anything obvious. Anyone can reckon the obvious. It's the details, the minutiae. Small misalignments are the elements most people miss. Tiny parts of the mechanism out of place create a need in me to figure out where they fit. I sometimes lose sight of the larger device."

"Won't you at least give me one hint?"

"Despite your efforts to convince me you were a reclusive hermit, a paranoid shut-in in fear for her life, it never quite felt right. Everywhere, everyone from physician to abbess greeted me with accounts of your active hand and participation in abbey affairs. Almost as if you ran it instead of the assigned abbess, a Mist Abbess, in effect. I suppose you could have done it via messages. Much like you did with your acolytes. Your appearance at the refectory after Shep's episode rang most falsely. No one seemed shocked by your presence. As if they were used to it. Why did you have keys to the infirmary stores? Also, I never mentioned Mr. Akesheem was missing."

"Oh, so thorough. I like it."

"After Mr. Akesheem's testimony, the brand which I had initially taken as some form of gang marker, turned out to be the marker of a different illicit affiliation. That and the visage on the wergeld bracelets I did not recognize."

"Not only tokens of my affection and nefarious power, but trackers. The 'Talisman of the Wave Witch.' I had convinced them it would protect them from the nether forces of the abbey and the marshes. Proof of membership in my salon."

"Along with expensive silks and cologne. I must have picked some up from your other acolytes. The infirmarian for one."

"If memory serves me correctly, artifice marks were considered the preferred way to put arcane enhancements on males in days past. In order for Dawn Wolf to so much as think of cyphering or be released from berserker service, what manner of implants and trackers might he have on him? Bright Harmony likely has a paternity stamp somewhere. Others put their mark on their property, I put my mark on mine."

"Just how many others are 'yours'? You seem to have hands in every spire."

"My acolytes strategically placed throughout the abbey helped me obtain people, the odd relic or two, the occasional drug from the infirmary or agri-pods."

"Did we miss anyone in your salon?"

"With Mr. Pol meeting with the wind and waves, all dead. I find keeping secrets easier the fewer who know. Pyrmo's suicide and Akesheem's rescue sent him into a bit of a panic. Men can be so emotional, don't you think? It always falls to us women to do the most vital work."

Jhee scoffed. "Suicide?"

"Pyrmo and I discussed her options in the past and agreed it was best. I anticipated she might lose her nerve, so I did it for her. A much more painful end than Saheli's, which could have been avoided if she had done it herself."

"The black orchid tea. So, you meant to kill me too?"

"If you drank the tea by itself, you would have been fine."

"Until you chose to administer the chaser."

"If. Merely a precaution."

"Her moonshine, the tea; a two-part reaction of creeper toad venom and toadstools."

Lady Bathsheba clapped and beamed with delight. "That's exactly what I used. Well done."

Jhee studied her cup, doubly glad she hadn't drunk any. "Why kill the Prospectives? It seems you had found an equilibrium. What changed?"

"Lot Number Fifty-one or the request for it. Mr. Pol procured folk. I procured other items. Rare books and artifacts. Exotic medicines. One of our regular clients asked us to procure a collection not a person: The Eclipse Chest, or effects and paperwork collection Lot Number Fifty-one. Lot Number Fifty-one was a strongbox containing various papers, relics, and a dodecaptych, twelve-part arcane manual, gifted to the abbey and thought lost. It turns out the reason no one could find it was the lot had been broken into pieces first then archived."

"The stolen items from the archives."

"Then Yaou found that drenched triptych in the strongbox. An early arcane manual of some sort. I'm not sure of who the author was. Certainly, not Thaedra. Maybe her sorcerous rival. Almost certainly, someone of the Pillarist persuasion. Keep in mind this structure's history. I was curious."

"With the sudden interest, you wanted to peek and see if you could gain some advantage."

"It was an unusual request, after all. This particular client had always asked for people. What would they want with a musty old relic? In fact, I had two competing requests come in for it. I concluded it must have some sort of significance and that it could be worth far more than I was being offered. I was curious as to what the object was and investigated further. Imagine my surprise when it turns out that I may found the legendary Altarpiece of the Creed or at least an early reproduction.

"I managed to learn one or two techniques such as that glamor before Yaou absconded with it. Along with a ritual, which I enacted. I awoke something. I attempted the ritual again with similar results. It's then I realized the ritual was incomplete."

"Part of the instructions were encoded in the finger maze."

"Exactly. Now, you're playing your part. This is where you ask me why I invited your household to tea."

Jhee rolled her eyes. She knew why. "Why risk it?"

"I had read your requests. I needed our first tea to assess you. Were you a drunkard, a relic lover, lustful? I originally meant to scare you off until I realized you knew how to unlock the finger maze. The second tea for you to demonstrate how it worked.

"You are not mistaken in that most of my powers were trickery. While nowhere near as accomplished at the arcane as you, I do have some training. Mostly the parlor trick variety like your Star Mirror. I want to thank the two of you for showing me how to work the manual."

"I can't believe Abbess Pyrmo was a party to this."

"Don't be too hard on her. She was a thief and a smuggler from long back who was no good at covering up her affairs. She and Zalver had been pilfering from the abbey for years. Ever since she was passed up for promotion to abbess. Once she needed my help, I had her. It was a simple matter to compel her to kill Saheli once she had became suspicious. Then a recommendation to the Chief Abbess."

"You were able to assure the appointment of an abbess more accepting of your habits. The only snag was Sister Elkanah who continually wanted to confine everyone to the Corrections Hall."

"Then that Xendatia business. No one wanted Invokers running around. They only make a mess. She's been almost as much of a problem as Saheli.

Every time I thought the matter sunk, another piece of flotsam surfaced to cause trouble. So many meddlers between her and your whole household."

"Dawn Wolf had secured permission to autopsy the Prospectives. You slipped him raw, land meat to stop it."

"Technically, the mortician did. Though she didn't know what would happen. The incident also split your focus, bought time, and gave me a way to ingratiate myself to you by helping."

"Not many know what he is, let alone how to involuntarily trigger a slip."

"It's not hard to deduce if you know what to look for. His tattoos. His military service. Knowledge of Toril. An aversion to land meat. Not many know about the last. I don't imagine many berserkers are eager to tell given the results. I've had occasion to deal with the Medical Protectorate. In fact, it's dealing with them that instigated this whole disaster."

"What about kidnapping my husband?"

"The plan was to catch one of your other spouses, the ones of which you're most fond. On my way to finalize the details with my accomplice, who should leap into the net, instead? My personal favorite among them. A sure sign from the Makers."

~

The Unraveling Tale II

The lady was a good storyteller. Now Jhee understood how easy it would be for the sheltered and lost to fall under her sway.

"You pitted Saheli and her former prioress against each other. Just like you tried to pit her against the smugglers. There is where your plan fell apart. The abbess befriended the smugglers because, for all her flaws, she cared about people. She remembered the first duty of the abbey as a beacon. You then used that to frame the poor abbess and taint her legacy, using her sympathy and mentoring of young men to paint her as a maneater. Saheli befriended most of those you sent against her."

"All it takes is one. Such as one drunk bitter, she had been passed up for an appointment."

"And you as the caring and sympathetic vizier suggested what remedy the poor put upon pious clergy should use against the heretical, radical abbess. You made the ordeal oil. Pyrmo wasn't in the storehouse covering her tracks. She was covering yours."

"They didn't need all that much convincing. Despite being a thief, smuggler, and drunk, Pyrmo still felt she should have been named abbess. Between you and me, I think she was more than happy to be rid of the excess males. It almost became a race to see who did Saheli in first. Elkanah, the reformed Pillarist, wanted heretics. Zalver wanted a villain, and I gave her one. Zalver self-medicated because she was once a Counter-Inquisitor with the Invocation. Did you know that? I suspect part of her misses it. She much like you was oh so eager to see Trenchmasons everywhere. Conspiracies always made for so much more juicy narratives than the mundane truth."

"Once Saheli confided her expansion plans to you, you had Prospective Yaou steal a copy. You showed the deacons only the parts of the plans guaranteed to infuriate them. When she announced her new reforms, Pyrmo's lucrative sideline would be threatened as would yours."

"It was bad enough to be exiled here, but to no longer be allowed to live in the manner to which I was accustomed. Her foolishness had spread to even my salon, some were even contemplating taking these silly arcana classes of hers."

"You were everyone's friend and confidante, whispering in their every ear. Including mine."

"The traditionalist and the fanatic in their pride and arrogance over their priceless relics and treasures. Poor, good-hearted reformist trying to save the world. The hedonistic Serra always craving new sensations and experiences. Last, the stressed-out magistrate who wanted nothing more than a shoulder to lean on and a brief escape from responsibility."

"Raigen's recitation about three broken vows: abstinence, humility, and hospitality."

"I specialize in matriarchal issues, Justicar. Those starved for powerful, maternal approval like Kanto or those drowned in maternal affection like Mirrei. You and Kanto have more in common than you think. Empty, distant households where you always had to be the adult. Imperial spouses confined as they were to the Imperial isles have similar weaknesses. Sheltered. Often overlooked and underappreciated. Allowed few if any visitors."

"Except for tutors."

"Except tutors. Sister Serra was an amateur at a game I perfected there."

"Lure them in with drugs and liquor."

"I've been cooking up mood-adjusters since before you were weaned."

"Young, unsophisticated men whose minds were altered by your concoctions would be impressed and have no idea your magical powers were no more than tricks. Then what happened? The novelty wore off, and your hold on them began to slip? You read the triptych and thought here was your chance to impress them and regain your power over them. It worked too well. They became terror-stricken and ran over half the isle yelling about demons. You had to silence them or risk what you had been up to coming to light."

"It's my fault for encouraging them. I indulged them, gave them the finest of everything. A few I even allowed access to the restricted archives. I allowed them the run of the abbey, looked the other way as they practiced minor arcana. You did well not to do so with your husbands. The Sages were right. Nothing but disaster comes of it. Look no further than that abomination they've constructed out there."

"Much better to initiate your own abomination here, by practicing arcana you don't understand. You provoked the drake. Using the triptych like a toy killed Prospective Imsu."

"We were in the Low Spire altar room. I began the ritual, and a tremor hit. Part of the ceiling collapsed on Imsu."

"To cover up his death, you brought him to the courtyard and pushed some rubble on him."

"Matters deteriorated from there. Leigh panicked. I scared him, poor thing, and he wanted to leave the salon. Meanwhile, Yaou stole part of the triptych."

"He wasn't frightened?"

"Quite the contrary. Yaou had gotten a taste for the nether arts. I got the idea to poison him after the second novitiate's death. I used an aerosol poison. I was feeling a bit clever, and it made a bit of poetic sense. One novitiate died crushed by stones. The other by water."

"Saheli met quite the fiery end."

"Happy coincidence."

"Still, murder seems extreme if not wasteful."

"The client is a piece of work. Someone you don't want to mist off. It's why I took such extreme measures to get the pieces back. Yaou's curiosity did him in and Saheli as well. I had the foresight to booby trap the triptych when I saw his too keen interest in it. I turned out to be right. After he stole the book, he tried to get Elkanah to show him how to use it by blackmailing her over their indiscretion. She turned out to be smart enough not to handle it. I was sure the archivist had it until Saheli, and now the prioress turned up sick. That idiot Pyrmo botched Saheli's murder, and she returned before I retrieved the triptych. Somewhere in the ensuing chaos over the abbess's death, the triptych got lost. Thanks to your deft skewering, Elkanah bared her soul in the infirmary where I could hear."

"Here I thought you considered yourself the only competent person on this island."

"I am surrounded by incompetent crabs who consistently seek to pull one back into the pot with them. I would think the abbess's death would be something of a cautionary tale for you, Jhee. No one likes a reformer. If I may give you some advice, stay out of depths you're not suited for. Stick to the rivers and the lakes you're used to. Don't be a waterfall chaser or wave maker."

The lady didn't need to tell Jhee that. Her whole dashed tenure as Justicar had been an object lesson. By the time of her reassignment, she had almost welcomed leaving for the capital.

"Many powerful interests are often invested in the way circumstances are. Tangle with it at your peril. I hope this teaches you a valuable lesson. The next woman may not choose to give him back. Considering your obsession with policies or the law and minutiae, you might have been better suited for a position as a librarian or scribe. My advice to you, given your lack of ambition and cunning, is to keep your head down and enjoy the life of a bureaucrat once you reach the capital. Perhaps find a wealthier benefactor or matron to protect you or else they'll eat you alive. Also, learn who counts and who doesn't. A lesson I forgot once and wound up here. And not a lesson I wanted to learn again. If some people counted and some didn't, do you think I would have gone unnoticed for so long?"

The lady frowned and held up her hand. "Enough. Tomorrow, would you be my guest for a game of three stack or tiles? I'd be interested in matching wits with you on a smaller scale."

27

———

GATEKEEPERS

~

The Courtyard of the Zodiac

The hen chimes rang from the spires to mark the morning hours.

"Shall we get some breakfast, Jhee? It is so nice to have someone to talk to."

"I intend to see you brought before a tribunal for murder, rape, and abduction."

"My accomplices are all dead. The boys in my salon were more than willing. As for the others... The boys never saw me until I wanted them to, and by then they were under my total sway. What proof remains points to poor Pyrmo and Saheli. Your words against mine, sage and former imperial vizier. In a capital case with such flimsy evidence, I rather suspect the worst they can do to me is force me to retire to some remote monastery for quiet reflection. Wait, they already did that. Perhaps they'll move me to somewhere better than this. In that case, it will be worth it. Though, I will miss the unique construction."

"It won't just be my word."

"Because you're 'secretly' recording our conversation? It would have disappointed me if you had not. I counted on it. Have you forgotten the communications array is down? Your recordings will not be transmitted until it is in operation again. Assuming some unfortunate sabotage does not befall it. It will though be harder to explain your genetic matter on Pyrmo's flask, the black orchid tea, and the poisonous toadstools she ingested. The same tea and toadstools on your writ and for good measure your prints on the case in the storehouse. You must have thought her greeting of you overly familiar. Although, she thought I meant to extort or frame you for someone's else's murder."

Jhee remembered the esca touch. They entered the courtyard by now bathed in the new, bright light of day. The rains had stopped finally. It seemed a mockery after the dark and horrible events of the evening.

"What a pleasant day. I just feel like singing. Which brings us to the matter of Bright Harmony's return. Bright Harmony. Outside naming. A tool of economic control. Your spouses given no opportunity to grow their own names and thus their independence from you. Yet you would lecture me on the proper treatment of young men."

Jhee and Lady Bathsheba ventured further into the Courtyard of the Zodiac. "Enough. How do I secure Bright Harmony's return?"

"Oh, fine. You will find that most evidence points to the unfortunate Pyrmo. The only solid proof you have of my involvement is my confession. The antenna doesn't come up until I say so. In the meantime, one of my admirers implants a simple worm, and the data is erased. As for the copy on your conch, you're going to remove that and destroy any auto-copies. In exchange, I'll tell you Bright Harmony's location."

Tampering with Jhee's evidence register. The vizier couldn't have hit Jhee harder if she had punched her. She needed to catch her breath.

"That's it. That's the look I want. Let's finish up, shall we, so we don't waste this marvelous day. This interference has cost me greatly. It will be some time before I can rebuild my salon. I am nothing if not patient. Slowly bit by bit, I will rebuild. If as stated you consider the deaths wasteful, I can assure you they 're not. I will be much more selective, and I promise to more closely monitor my excesses and those of my salon members. I can assure you nothing else like that will happen again. Thanks to our postmortem tea, I now know how the mistakes I made helped you catch me. I can assure you I will take many more precautions next time. Fate is a cruel mistress, destiny's a bitch, and coincidence is monster. Waves always break at the worst possible point with the wrong amount of force and at the worst time. Such are the vagaries of the sea and the Wave Witch. Now, if you would sign me into your case files."

Jhee held up the conch. Her stomach felt cold and sour.

"Must I remind you I hold your husband's fate is in my hands. You've already had a taste of what it felt like to lose him. Would you like it to be permanent?"

With her heart heavy, Jhee entered her code.

Lady Bathsheba took the conch from Jhee's hand. "Goodness, Justicar, do you ever delete anything from this? No wonder I couldn't transfer my map with the malicious implant. I had to settle for a short-range tracker on the portable. I didn't always know your whereabouts but knew your position well enough to arrange several strategic run-ins. First, the recording of my confession."

She made the delete gesture. Jhee winced.

"That's pretty drenching. That's must go. Oh, yes, that too."

A rapid series of deletes followed. Jhee's head swam. She closed her eyes only to see the image of the blood-stained, charred altar where Mr. Pol met his end.

The lady frowned and then looked angry. "Now, that's just speculation and unkind as well. Gone."

Another delete.

"That can stay. It points to Pyrmo so no problem there. Now, this. Definitely can't leave this one either."

Another deletion gesture. Each one felt a tear at the fabric of Jhee's very being. Preserve life first. Let Kanto escape this unharmed. Let it not be in vain.

"Gone. Gone. Gone. Like words in the waves and kisses on the wind. You are quite the little detective, Justicar. If I had not had so many fail-safes and contingencies, you would have had me dead to rights on a couple things. This has been an amusing couple of days. The most fun I've had in years because of you. No one else could have done it.

"I do hope you won't judge me too harshly. One must keep oneself amused somehow. It gets so terribly lonely out here with nothing but the near tee-totaling monks and nuns. I just needed something to ease the boredom only a fraction. I thought I had it with the salon. Then with the forbidden arcana. None of it did anything. Finally, when the deaths started happening, I had not felt that alive in so long. You kept me on my toes, and for that, I thank you. Plus, the lovely diversion. It was the most beautiful thing ever.

"It can get so boring here. My amusement with these eager young boys makes it tolerable. Valueless males foolishly committed to celibacy. A natural crime, as you said. I share your contempt for the practice. Don't you have any hobbies or bad habits, Justicar?"

"Your dislike of this lifestyle makes me think your retirement here was not entirely voluntary."

"I once taught music and etiquette to the future emperors and empresses. Until I chose the wrong participants for one of my special engagements; someone's favorite son or husband. On occasion, I craved the extra bit of challenge and danger from seducing men of higher prominence. Now I reside on a rock with rabble and caught between two nitwits quarreling over whether rocks or weeds hold the true path to enlightenment. All because a few noble priaps didn't know their limits. A circumstance unlikely to occur here with so many young men coming through here. So wide-eyed and desperate. There are always more Pols and Akesheems."

Jhee scratched her nose. She had begun to shake. "They are all disposable and interchangeable to you, aren't they?"

"They are nowadays. I simply put out my net into the waters, and they all practically jumped into it. They would not have made it at the capital. None of you belong there. But what else are they going to do with you after destroying your homes? You should not blame me, but the foolish feckless officials who put up the wall."

"I have seen war if the Shield prevents it so be it."

"At what cost? A gimmicky boondoggle of a public works folly they claim will protect us yet has done nothing but hurt our own people. It has destroyed so many homes. The smaller isles subsumed under wind and waves among them yours. From the birth defects and pod strandings to the Fresh Lung Sickness, suffered by your very own Mirrei. All so those cowards could gut our military and cede the better part of our world to the barbarian hordes."

"They built the Shield for our protection."

"They built it for theirs. To hide behind like the clergy. To prevent the reunification. To prevent the resurrection of the lost god. The sword and the bridge. Two halves coming together."

Jhee twitched from her own helplessness. Itzil's roar reverberated from the pen where Ms. Anshula must have left her. The Storm Shield. The trenched Shield. As always, it came back to the trenched Storm Shield. "I'd build the drenched shield myself if it prevents more atrocities like the berserkers."

"I met one of the last surviving doctors of Medical Protectorate involved in that. Now, she was scary. I like your wit and your fire, Jhee. Despite your crudeness, in my marrying days, I could have molded you into a fine second. If you are going to survive at court, you'll need to learn who matters and who doesn't."

Lady Bathsheba handed Jhee back her conch. "He's at the bottom of the Storm Light Tower. Have your representative meet mine at the tower steps so he can be safely escorted back into your care. Try not to lose him again."

Jhee contacted Bax and Shep and gave them the location.

"Such a lovely day, I recommend the maye eggs and lamprey, one of the few flesh dishes available here."

Lady Bathsheba gestured towards the gardens. Jhee obeyed. The vizier's overconfidence was earned. Jhee had only hearsay left.

"Lady Bathsheba!"

～

The Gate

"Lady Bathsheba! We are here to make you answer for your crimes."

Ms. Hethyr appeared with several villagers and refugees. Each armed with clubs and farming implements. Ms. Hethyr, however, carried two swords with a series of holes along the blades, wind swords. They threw the beaten smuggler and the infirmarian on the ground in between their mob and the two officials. If they were here, where was her husband?

"Tell the Justicar what you told us," Ms. Hethyr said.

"Leigh came to the infirmary complaining of coruscate syndrome, the code for proper identification and transit papers to the capital. He offered me the remaining proceeds from his medicinal sideline and gave me a silk handkerchief and expensive cologne as down payment. He didn't have to tell me where he got the items from. I knew. The same figure had presented me similar gifts when I first arrived. I was so young and naïve. Seems like a lifetime ago."

"Who was the figure?"

"We called her the Witch because of the mask she wore. She also had another name, though, The Mist Abbess. She instructed us in the finer things in life. How to speak. How to dress. Few of us who graduated her course remained at the abbey. It was too small after having seen what the world had to offer for those of us who had never seen such things. I didn't learn her true identity until she showed up in the infirmary."

The crowd advanced.

"Ms. Hethyr, wait!"

"Step aside, Justicar. Our quarrel is with the so-called Mist Abbess. I knew if I followed you, you would lead me to my brother's murderer."

"The garment. Leigh."

"Yes."

The vizier prepped a cypher. Nothing happened. "Protect me, Justicar. I lied about your husband's location. If they get to me, he remains lost, too."

Jhee maneuvered Lady Bathsheba behind her. Ms. Hethyr leaped forward. Jhee grabbed a tall torch stand and blocked Ms. Hethyr's strikes. The clash of torch stand against sword produced a clank and the wind swords distinctive whistle. Jhee pivoted, keeping herself between Ms. Hethyr and Lady Bathsheba.

"Stop this!"

Lady Bathsheba fled. The crowd hesitated.

"What are you waiting for? Go after her. Don't harm the justicar."

Jhee took a deep breath and projected her voice toward the crowd. "Halt!"

The mob paused. They murmured and looked at each other in confusion. Ms. Hethyr narrowed her eyes at Jhee.

"Ms. Hethyr, I can't let you do this."

Ms. Hethyr flinched and shook her head. "You can. I saved you twice. Once when I brought you to Mr. Zane's door and second when Cheiropthys and the Wave Witch attempted to carry you off."

"You have my thanks and that of my whole house. Still, I cannot allow you to kill her. She has my husband captive."

"He is already lost as were our family members. Now let us do what needs be done."

Jhee leaned into the voice module. "Return to your elders. She belongs to the law."

The mob began to break up and wander off. Ms. Hethyr covered her ears and glared at Jhee. "Sorcery!"

Lady Bathsheba fled through the arch to the Zodiac Courtyard. "This way, Justicar."

"No, Vizier, wait!"

Jhee had no choice but to follow. One of Ms. Hethyr's blades whistled by Jhee's ear. She spun around with the candlestick and brought it up in time to block the second blade. She gripped the candlestick tighter or else she might go for her sleeve knives. Preserve life first.

Ms. Hethyr swung her wind swords. Jhee edged back from her to keep beyond the reach of her blades. The piercing sound of the whistle increased the faster Ms. Hethyr swung her swords. Her movements generated winds along with the high-pitched whistle. Jhee cleared her mind to grasp them.

One block and defensive counter after another, she met Ms. Hethyr's blades and attempts to blast her with winds. She edged herself and Lady Bathsheba back through a covered walkway.

"Remarkable," Ms. Hethyr said. "You are a demon and worthy adversary. But all this for her."

"She belongs to the law. It and only it will see her punished."

"I overheard you. She deleted all your evidence. She will never see justice, and neither will my brother or our families. Never."

They reached a closed metal gate, the only way out of the area they occupied.

"Nowhere left to go," Ms. Hethyr said.

Lady Bathsheba tried to cypher a few more times.

"Tharos root. Didn't you think your tea tasted a bit odd? I took a page out of your book, Mist Abbess."

Jhee seized control of the winds. She blasted Ms. Hethyr back.

Lady Bathsheba opened the grate to the side yard and slipped through. Jhee caught up to her just in time for the lady to barricade the gate. She shook the grate. "Listen to me, Vizier. Open this gate now."

Lady Bathsheba tossed a geld coin at her. "Thank you, Jhee. I will not forget this. If you survive Hethyr and the mob, put me on your favor list."

The crowd of angry relatives found them again, dragging the infirmarian with them. Jhee rushed through them to shield him. She grabbed him by the lapels. "Did she tell the truth? Is my husband at the bottom of the Storm Light Tower?"

The infirmarian started to cry. Useless. Jhee fought her way back to the gate. She rattled it again. "Vizier, get out of there!"

Ms. Hethyr groaned and advanced on them again. "I will avenge my brother. Even if I have to cut through you to do it."

Jhee dropped the torch stand. She took a deep breath and grasped her sleeve knives. For Kanto and her promise. Jhee's conch rang with Bax's tone. Then the sigil on her arm pulsed out a message.

Jhee dropped her hands to her sides. "No need. Put up your swords."

Ms. Hethyr stared at her, confused. "Pick up your weapon. I'll not slay you unarmed. In liking of your skill, you will not meet the Makers empty-handed."

"No. Put up your swords," Jhee commanded, changing the target of her inspiration to Ms. Hethyr.

Ms. Hethyr dropped her swords. The vizier grabbed the torch stand. She jammed the gate with it.

"Thank you," Lady Bathsheba said.

"Don't thank me. You are about to know what it is to be at the whims of animal appetites other than your own."

An ominous growl came from behind Lady Bathsheba. The smug expression froze on the vizier's face. Jhee withdrew her inspiration from Ms. Hethyr.

"Perhaps you can drug Itzil before she decides she doesn't like your stench any more than the rest of us."

"Shark nip? No, wait, she hates shark nip. You can't do this."

"You have a better chance than any of your victims."

Jhee folded her hands into the sleeve of her robes. She strode by a dumbfounded Ms. Hethyr. Lady Bathsheba's screams and the bull hound's roars echoed throughout the courtyard. Jhee winced at each one. The mob parted as she approached. They let her pass unmolested. Once out of their sight, she doubled over and emptied the contents of her stomach upon the ground.

Jhee read the message on her conch from Bax again. -We have him.

It did not note if they had found him alive or dead. She ran to the bottom of the Storm Light Tower. A group of Prospectives and Professed had gathered. She pushed through the crowd. The inner ring of the crowd consisted of those she had left in the safety of her room. They huddled around Kanto's blanket-wrapped figure. His skin looked deathly pale.

Her heart skipped a beat. Jhee dropped down beside him. "Kanto?"

For a horrible moment, nothing happened then his eyes fluttered open. His gaze focused on Jhee's face. He rubbed his wrists where he bore bruises from restraints. "I've found something new about an official we visited with. I'm going to want some melon taffies after this for sure. Melon taffies and little cakes."

Jhee laughed. She dug about in her sleeves and found a lone parchment wrapped melon candy. She placed it in his hand.

"And little cakes."

Jhee and Shep helped Kanto to his feet. They supported Kanto as they headed back to the abbey.

Ms. Hethyr and the mob had joined the throng of onlookers. Jhee paused.

"Now, you, Ms. Hethyr, have your own crimes to answer for. Not the least of which is your disgraceful treatment of Mr. Zane. At the very least you owe him an apology."

"I had been drinking, having just found out about my brother's death."

"That is no excuse. I'll withhold charging you pending Mr. Zane's input. I suggest you throw yourself on his mercy."

"I cannot face him."

"Try, and I may see fit to see my way to excuse your assault upon a member of the court."

Ms. Hethyr nodded.

Jhee and Shep returned Kanto to their room.

28

THE FIRST SPIRE

~

The First Spire

After Jhee had every healer on the grounds and even a Soothbringer examine Kanto, she remained by his side while he convalesced. Once he had a good meal, she brought him lace root melon taffies along with his little cherry, citrus cakes as promised. He also requested reading materials, namely later copies of "Dispatches from Arrow Point." Jhee, at last, had free access to the archives. She scoured their histories for any accounts that might shed light on what occurred in the crypts. Her search came up empty. Kanto ate his treats happily while he read, and they chatted.

"Definite improvement from your first ones." He set them aside. "I knew you'd come for me. I just had to have faith and hold out. Akesheem and I were lucky. We had people who cared enough to come looking. I think about others. The lost and forgotten. Victims of other Lady Bathshebas and Mr. Pols."

"One of the biggest tragedies about all this is that no one really cared about these men. No one took them seriously. They were dismissed, condescended to, and disbelieved. Had someone shown the slightest bit of concern, their tragedies might have been prevented."

"Isn't that what happened in the end, Jhee? Those who were concerned spoke up for them."

"Lady Bathsheba was right. It was my job to speak for these boys. A duty I plan to take much more seriously from now on. I'll count it amongst one of the many lessons she and you taught me."

Kanto snorted. He placed a hand on Jhee's arm. "This past day was nice."

"But?"

"It'll make it worse when you go back to barely tolerating or avoiding me. The only time I despaired was when I overheard my kidnappers' debate. They were disappointed they caught me and not Shep or Mirrei. Even strangers noticed how much more regard you had for them than me. Your history with Shep. The history between Mirrei's family and yours. I'm the only outsider here. You obviously mean Mirrei to inherit and Shep runs your household. Where does that leave me?"

"I hadn't considered that. My long view never accounted for you remaining once we reached the capital."

"These brutes bought and sold men. How did grandmamere frame selling me to you?"

"The Lady Kaydence had multiple tacks. A rescue."

"Grandmamere couldn't wait to get rid of me like you."

"Not that way."

"When you had no use for my savvy or physical charms, I thought perhaps what you needed was someone light and fun. Then you brought home Mirrei and proceeded to pass me over in household and political matters. I kept thinking it's me. I'm your equal, Jhee. I've read the accounts of your cases with Vizier Jeja. You know the power of expression and story to affect people. What is music and fashion if not another means of expression, of storytelling? I am a remora as attached to fashion and politics as you are to arcana and the law. I'm not some poor frail thing like Mirrei nor am I a sturdy pair of arms like Shep. What's more, you respect their interests more than you respect mine. Shep's interest in food and fauna or Mirrei's interest in medicine and flora won't be of any more inherent value than mine in music and fashion at court. The minutiae I value may be the only tool to help you survive there."

"This is precisely why I tried not to become overly reliant on your charms. I didn't want to build false expectations."

"Yours or mine? Consummation, instrumentation, and sensitization decrease your incentive to remarry me. At least, be honest about the true cause of your reluctance. You've always been of a mind for remarriage when it comes to Mirrei and me. Every night spent in your arms secured my place further in your household and hindered annulment, which makes remarriage for gain harder."

"You never answered if you wanted to take your leave once we reached the capital."

Kanto swept over to the hearth and gazed into the fire. "It's so easy for you to forswear our marriage. You're not invested. You never let yourself be. That stings most of all."

Jhee moved to stand behind him. She wanted to reach out, but it would just be too little too late. Maybe if she told him he was right. That seemed inadequate, as well. She balled up her hands and remained paralyzed by insecurity.

"'Don't be another problem she has to fix.' I've tried to play along with this idea you have of me as some empty-headed libertine. Perhaps I shouldn't have. It only seems to make things worse. You know you never had that way of undressing me with your eyes the way most of those who visited the grand dame did. I liked that about you. You literally liked your little obscure facts and figures, and it didn't matter what I looked like. I'm not sure if I'd ever experienced that before. When you visited our house to meet, I thought, me, you made a straight shark-line for our private antiquities collection. You were so adorable and awkward. Here you were, an accomplished official who had spent time at the capital, and you were so out of your depth but down to earth. Your head so full of facts and figures so full of the minutiae. That's how I first knew and saw the person who Shep described to grandmamere. I must admit to having been smitten. I decided then and there on the spot, I would marry you. Even if grandmamere decided against it. Do you know while she did want me to have a love match, she hedged her bets? She let it be known your house and mine might be coming to an arrangement."

"Plenty of takers I have no doubt."

"Plenty, too many to count. It was a bit of a frenzy for a while."

"No doubt, you could have done better than me."

"There you would be wrong; I could *never* have done better than you, because you were *my* choice from the very beginning, from the moment I saw you. Not grandmamere's, not Shep's. *My* choice. I know grandmamere, though. If she disapproved, she'd have found a way to convince me otherwise and make me believe it was my idea." Kanto hugged himself. "Jhee, where was this flattery months ago when it might have made a difference?"

"I don't know. I was just blind to your strengths, I suppose."

"I think it's more you don't reckon what I excel at as strengths."

"You know me so much better than I know you."

"Most assuredly from your lack of trying. Here, Jhee." Kanto produced a slim, leather notebook from an inner pocked and gave it to Jhee. "This is how the vizier kept herself protected. I planned to use these as part of my independence kit. Without me, you're liable to require them more than I."

"Favor lists?"

"Lady Bathsheba's. I've done my best to decipher them. I found them in that awful room she held me in along with her boudoir journal, where she rated the various merits of the men she 'seduced.' The possibility remains they are decoys or fakes so exercise caution if you choose to use them. Consider them a parting gift from me."

"I cannot even begin to account for all the ways I've wronged you as your denbe."

"You did the best you could."

"Thank you. May I give you a parting gift as well? Gift for Gift rather than Make for Make."

"As you like. Any gifts given I intend to keep, including clothes and other finery. The only matter I'll account you stingy is in your affections. Your other attentions were quite lavish."

"I thought you would want this. I should have given it to you long before this."

Jhee pulled out the cloth-wrapped bundle she had debated giving him so many times. The moment had never seemed right. Now, she no longer feared the gift might give the wrong impression. Since signs pointed to this being her last opportunity, now made as an appropriate a moment as any. She unwrapped the unadorned, freshly repaired music box and presented it to him.

Kanto's eyes went brilliant gold, bathing his face in a warm light. "Mamere's music box. It was smashed. Irreparable."

"With an isle full of Earth Adepts and enough motivation, even the most broken items may be fixed."

Jhee gingerly passed the music box to Kanto. He opened it and wound the tiny key. Bright, tinkly notes of an old melody filled the alcove. He choked back a sob.

Tears brimmed in his eyes. "Before she grew bitter and sick, I would curl up in her lap, and nestle my head under her chin. She would pick up the music box and turn the crank. The bright tinkly melody would float out. Thank you."

"Would you like to take the waters or a walk in the orchards? You and me. No one else. Right now."

"Include the Storm Light Tower, and I'll consider it."

Stairs and heights overlooking breakers. Jhee noted his folded arms. "Agreed."

$$\sim$$

The Dismantler's Deal

Jhee and Kanto walked through the Annex. Jhee's hands remained tucked into the sleeves of her robes while Kanto clasped his behind his back. "The building's structure, no doubt created with the tenets of sacred geometry in mind, played several visual and auditory tricks on the unsuspecting visitor," Jhee said.

"The Lady Bathsheba, armed with her theoretical music knowledge, was uniquely equipped to recognize and take advantage of it."

Jhee untucked her hands to initiate contact, then tucked them away again. "You were uniquely able to as well."

They concluded their walk on the storm light's observation deck and paused to watch the dual suns set. Jhee held back from the edge. Kanto offered her his hand. Gently, he eased her closer to the rail. Jhee gasped at the sight of the suns dipping below the horizon. They tightened their clasped hands.

"I asked one boon of Shep before he presented me to you. Non-negotiable. Tell me everything you love about her. I merely wished for you to view me with an inkling of the desire you have for him or even the way you do books in the library. I had hoped to substitute desire for respect. I am highly concerned with art and aesthetics. Pursuits you consider frivolous. I do understand weighty topics. Do you know the price my grand dame negoti-ated with Shep?"

It had not been money or wealth. Shep had the run of those. They had not decreased with Kanto's arrival. "Nothing monetary. He is a good diver."

"A bunch of sea meat is what you think you're worth?" Kanto sighed and shook his head. "You."

Jhee's mouth opened in shock. "Me?"

"He told her stories about you. She listened to the affection in his words. Her house is waning. Grandmere could have leveraged me. She had oppor-tunities to make arrangements with wealthier, more prestigious houses. Such arrangements are fickle and subject to whim. I am young and beautiful. Now. What happens to me, once they are bored or someone more youthful or attractive catches their eye? My only hope was to have given them favored daughters. My grand dame may have been tough as fellstones, but she loved me. Rather than barter me like a commodity to save her house, she arranged marriage to someone kind and fair. Someone who might come to love me. Someone who would be as committed to me as I would be to her."

"I did not know."

"You thought all I cared about was the trinkets and baubles. My mother had no female heirs. My idiot cousins have already blown through their inheritances and are waiting for grandmamere to die. I wanted to help you build your house. I've done my level best to meet you where you are. Shep does not play the game as well as I do. He does realize what you do not. It must be played regardless. You need someone better at it than you two. From the questions he asked, I inferred my purpose. When you took in Mirrei, it strengthened my resolve to nurture this house. You demonstrated both your pragmatism and your generous spirit. Giving the daughter of your child-hood friend a better life. Giving yourself a female heir for your holdings should you have no daughters."

"You never wanted to be married to a provincial official."

"Stop assuming you know my mind. Ask. What effort have you taken to get to know me? No, you assumed based on appearance. You did it to me, and those at court are going to do it to you."

"'Drown him in jewels and finery. Don't let him sit alone in a big empty house by the bedside of another dying woman.'"

"Grandmamere had just started using the chair before Shep's visit. She had a health scare."

"She said she fell on her way to religious devotions."

"She tried to feed me that hook too. She fell while visiting her lover."

"I suspect she'll outlive us all." Jhee ran her hands over the favor lists. "How would you do it?"

"Do what?"

"Test to see if the favor lists are fake."

"Call in a random marker. Nothing too big to guard against the list being authentic. Our dear departed vizier must have been embroiled in a massive scandal. These contain some powerful individuals. Court officials. Imperials."

"Either what she did was to someone of such stature, no one in that list could save her. Or of such a heinous nature, exile was her best outcome."

"Precisely. There's hope for you yet."

"We could exchange political lessons for arcana lessons."

"Do you not want to teach cyphering lessons, or do you not want to teach me? You haven't hesitated to teach strangers."

"Do you really want them? Or is it just a way to flatter me?"

"I've wondered what it would be like to learn. It is prudent to have options."

"I thought of something else we could do with these and her journals. Would we be able to track down where she sent the men she trafficked? Kanto, I don't know if there will ever be love between us. I will promise to no longer keep you at arm's length. I further promise to work harder to demonstrate the value and respect I have for you as a person. I'll first start with saying, 'Thank you.' Your skill and eye for details helped me dismantle the Mist Abbess's whole scheme."

"I suppose that's a start."

Kanto extended both hands toward Jhee's face. She stepped forward, and they briefly touched escae.

～

The Ferry

Jhee pushed open the doors leading to the docks. Sunlight and sea spray caressed her face. She breathed deep of the beautiful tang of the sea air. For the first time since their arrival, her sinuses were clear and her headache a memory. Eternal silence and the First Makers' curses to whoever designed this abbey. She swore by everything Made she might godspark the next person who so much as uttered stairs.

The foghorn for the ferry sounded. Between the weather and the uproar, the repairs to their travel yacht were still underway. However, if they delayed any longer, they would be late for festival season. The prioress followed her towards the dock.

"Thank you, Justicar, for all you have done on behalf of the abbey. I shall take over the running of the abbey until a new abbess is appointed."

"Think nothing of it. I shall tell the Chief Abbess she could do a lot worse than to perhaps appoint you."

"All honors to you, Justicar. You are most kind and gracious."

"I merely did my duty as an official of the court. Perhaps even my duty under the First Makers."

The prioress signaled a nearby Prospective to bring over the Eclipse Chest. "Here, Justicar, take this with you."

"Perhaps much grief and suffering would have been prevented if it were destroyed."

"Saheli wouldn't have wanted knowledge and history destroyed any more than you, especially on her account. However, it doesn't belong here. The temptation is too great. Raigen was right to mock us. Our order had three sacred tenets, vows to which we were to cling before all others: humility, chastity, and charity. We flouted them all with glee. We have already proved ourselves unworthy to safeguard them. You may be able to find them a better home in the capital."

"I'll consider the chest and its contents on indefinite loan."

Other lay folk loaded a supply of Tranquility Gold wine along with samples of the wild yeast cultures.

"Don't worry. Here's the bill. After all, that was the offer you made at the feast correct?"

Jhee steeled herself. She had seen the market prices for their increasingly rare noble blend. They might need to cart her to the infirmary once she saw this invoice. They should name it after her for the amount she was going to have to shell out. Jhee opened the receipt. A huge smile spread across her face.

The prioress grinned for the first time Jhee had ever seen. "I calculated the market rate for the wines and fees versus the industry standard for the services you rendered us."

Lay people loaded their belongings onto the ferry. Jhee tucked the small chest containing the relics, sermon, and triptych under her arm. The litter arrived bearing Jhee's younger spouses accompanied by Shep who had chosen to walk. Mirrei's fever had broken sometime during the night. The abbey's select blend had indeed worked wonders. And Jhee now had a container of both that and their traditional nectar to study or sample as needs be. The two couples, Mr. Zane and Ms. Anshula, Raigen and Mr. Akesheem, came down the stairs behind them to see Jhee and her entourage off. Ms. Anshula clasped forearms with Shep. She passed a vial to him which he pocketed.

"Are you sure we can't see you to the capital or perhaps another isle?" Jhee asked.

"No," Mr. Akesheem said. "I left home to find my way, and I have. Raigen has promised we shall build a new home and new birthline together."

"I have made similar promises to Mr. Zane. We shall go forth as a group of bright and brave companions to make our fortunes in the world. We will honor our parents and see their sacrifices earn dividends through our prosperity."

Jhee smiled. "I've often wondered at the romantic ideals of the young. You have restored my hope that indeed, romance has not died even in these changing times. I wish you all the luck and blessings the First Makers will see fit to have me give you."

Bax arrived.

"Is it done?" Jhee asked.

"Yes. The solar arrays have been recharged, and the communications array restored. You may transmit soon."

"Alas, what remains of my report to Central Authority isn't enough for Lady Bathsheba's full crimes to be known."

"Do you anticipate trouble?"

"Perhaps. Which is why I sent a copy of my report of the fate of a certain vizier to Jeja and asked for advice. She has agreed to act as my advocate should anyone become too curious about it. I also learned that she wasn't the only one to shed shark's tears at the news. She said, 'You should have spoken to me first, Jhee. I could have told you Bathsheba was a well-known predator.' Which leaves the matter of you."

"Me?" Bax stepped back and asked, "What?"

Jhee folded her arms and grinned. "I thought I set you to follow Raigen, not work with her."

"She... caught me." Jhee heard the hitch of wounded pride. Indeed, catching the infamous Shadowcat during his crime spree had required some cleverness on her part.

Dari barked. Itzil emitted a chastened yelp. Her harness clanked as Dari herded her away from the ferry and the gathered people. Despite Lady Bathsheba's fate, the much larger bull hound remained a comical sight being harried by a dog a fraction of its size. Jhee read through her report again.

"Lady Bathsheba met with an unfortunate accident while wandering around the cloister. She ventured out too soon having thought the storm ended and took a wrong turn into the courtyard where Itzil was housed. The frightened creature on edge because of the weather mauled her to death. Ms. Anshula, I will, of course, have to fine you for improper housing of and failure to secure Itzil, a dangerous animal, properly. If the family and friends of Lady Bathsheba wish for further redress, they can take up the matter with the courts. She likely had to renounce any outside family to retire here, and with the Sanctuary statutes in effect standing will be difficult to establish. A solid case can be made that only the Drakist Order and the abbess has standing to do so."

With Jhee's conch charged and no longer low on space, she transferred over Mr. Akesheem's testimony. The two critical pieces of evidence she had, namely Pyrmo's confession and his witness account had no explicit mention of the vizier. She had to classify Leigh's death under accident and negligence. A tricky descent, at night, in a hurry, weak frame of mind, during a storm. Yet, he would not have been out on such a miserable night if the vizier were not after him.

The litter was brought aboard the ferry. Jhee waited on the dock until all her retinue had boarded.

Jhee turned to Shep. "What did Ms. Anshula give you?"

"Some of Itzil's bioplasm."

She glanced down at her conch and all the messages that had flooded in once she had proper access to off-isle communication. Among them, the confirmation of their reservation at the resort run by an old schoolmate of hers. "Are you sure you don't want to come with us?"

"I want to stay here a little longer and get my head right. I'm not fit company for festivals, right now. I'll go on ahead to the capital and get the house set up while you and the denyes bond."

Jhee paused. People surrounded them, least of all the younger spouses. Her hands itched to pull Shep close. A gesture utterly inappropriate in such a public venue. She knew Kanto, in particular, to be sensitive how much affection she showed Shep.

When Jhee turned back to the ferry, Mirrei and Kanto watched her with eager expressions. They both nodded. Propriety be drenched, Jhee and Shep indulged in a public display of affection by touching escae. Mirrei and Kanto grinned.

"You are wind and waves, my lady of the Isles," Shep said.

"Beloved cohort are we ready to cast off?"

"Your timetable is our timetable," Kanto said.

"As you lead, we follow," Mirrei said.

Jhee smiled. She stood near the prow of the yacht as they pushed off. She took a last look at the abbey with its many spires and congruous frogman's antenna. The hothouse and the fields of sun panels. She stared at the statues adorning the edifice of the abbey. This was one way to prevent them from becoming mist wights, wisps, or part of the region's fog. She shuddered. After her experience in the crypts, she could not help it. She studied one after another to see if she could pick out which of the gruesome figures were honored or fettered dead or mere imaginative fancies. She waved at the couples until they had passed from sight. She smiled. All in a day's work.

Kanto and Mirrei held her arms. Jhee would not break her promise to Miramar nor Kanto's grand dame. *I will fulfill the promise I made to their dames to see them safely to the capital where they can decide for themselves what it is they want.*

"Kanto, you mentioned not liking our robes. Would you be opposed to designing us new ones?"

"I would love nothing more. I've been waiting for you to ask."

Vast waters of enormous change lay ahead. Who knew where they might land? What Jhee knew is her household must stay vigilant in the trying times to come at court. They set sail for the trials and intrigues of the capital.

The End

Please, consider leaving an honest review on the bookseller's website, Goodreads, or BookBub so others can discover Justicar Jhee—and tell all your friends to download a copy as well.

Leave a review!

WANT MORE JUSTICAR JHEE?

Thank you for reading JUSTICAR JHEE AND THE CURSED ABBEY! Please check out these other Justicar Jhee mysteries and read about Jhee and her cohort's other adventures.

JOIN THE SWIFTNESSE COMMUNITY to get a free copy of **Justicar Jhee and the Spectral Armada**, receive special offers, and hear about future books!

http://swiftnesse.com/spectral/

Other Books in this series:

Justicar Jhee and the Hole in the World: https://books2read.com/hauntedmine

(Continue on to read an excerpt.)

Justicar Jhee and the House of Sorrows: https://books2read.com/sorrows

EXCERPT: THE HOLE IN THE WORLD

Please enjoy this excerpt from Justicar Jhee Book 2…

Galleon City is a central point in the Empire; the place where the Storm Shield protects the Blessed Isles from the wrath that surrounds them. But it is also a city that is being ripped apart by restless factions and swamped with refugees, the destitute and the unwanted.

Justicar Jhee arrives in the city in amid this chaos, but it isn't long before intrigue strikes once more, when a murder occurs.

Chapter 1

Jhee pointed the viewer at the stately villa where they would holiday for the next long-tides as artisans finished the last bit of construction on their new home on the capital island. She brought the viewer down so Shep, her senior husband, could see her face. "Our ferry arrived without incident, and we are safely at the resort. I wish you were here with us," she said.

Shep frowned. "Non-stop social engagements? I'll pass. You're in Kanto's world now. Allow him to show you around. This will give you more time with him in his element. It'll do you and him good to spend more time together especially in an environment that showcases his talents."

"It won't stop me from missing you anyway."

"Ether crest life never suited me, but it's cut to fit for Kanto. You three

287

need time together without me. Besides, someone needs to oversee the final work on our new home, so it's ready for your arrival. You'll be so busy with balls and parties you won't even notice."

"Don't remind me."

"Jhee, it'll be fine. Between them, I'm confident they'll see you don't make a fool of yourself."

Jhee spun to capture the rest of the private island off the cape's view of Straya, the largest island in the Blessed Isles, even larger than the capital isle. A few buildings from Galleon City towered in the distance. She ended on the magnificence of the ocean and the harbor, a combination of both Makers' and mortal achievements.

Kanto and Mirrei approached. "Is that our absent, boring, old *denme* who'd rather babysit a house than ride the high crests with us?"

"Correction: who'd rather babysit a house than babysit you."

Kanto made the childish gesture of pressing his nose. "Fine. Then every stick of furniture must be precisely where I specified and every possession as I outlined or else I'll blame you."

"A fair turn," Shep said.

This was the first time Jhee recalled Shep not being there to act as a buffer or point of friction.

Kanto had spent days laboring and poring over manuals and catalogs and images of furniture. He would see their new home brightly and gaily and fabulously and opulently appointed.

Jhee had the utmost confidence in his design skills. He would know what every stick of furniture and window treatment would convey about their situation. They had spent their night together going over it extensively. He quizzed her on what impression she wanted their home to communicate to visitors. Jhee did not much care herself, but it made him happy. She wanted him to feel fulfilled and tasks like this delighted him. He vowed to make their new home convey the tone and image she wanted while also remaining stylish and opulent as befitted her rank.

"I've seen images of places like this. In my grandmere's day, this was all the rave. A stay at a posh resort, then you motor up to the capital and stay at your own place or rent a townhouse during festival season."

Jhee tried not to think too hard about what that said about her taste or her age.

Lady Delphine, their host, awaited them atop the sandstone and seashell steps to the entryway. Jhee held out her hands. "Oh, Lady Delphine, thank you again for hosting me and my cohort."

Delphine clasped her forearms, then pressed each temple against Jhee's. "Oh, you old fool. Come here. Come here. Shame on you for thinking to slip through our waters without a visit. So good to see you. It's the least I can do for the help you gave me when we were in the academy together. I couldn't believe it when you told me you had expanded your household. When do I get to meet the rest of your welcome entourage?"

"Momentarily. Shep sends his regards. He's overseeing the final transport of our belongings from the barges to our new home."

"How regretful. He will join us later, I hope."

"He'll do his best. Shep isn't much for the festival scene."

"Ah. I won't press." Lady Delphine linked her arm with Jhee's. "About those other matters we discussed, have you mulled them over?"

"While the situation has been a little hectic, I gave your proposal some thought. Let's see how the stay goes before making any final decisions."

Lady Delphine cleared her throat and glanced from side to side. "And the last matter? The death of the mining supervisor?"

"I had no immediate conclusions to draw from what you told me. I might have a better idea once I've examined the work sites."

"You will be discrete?"

"As much as I can be."

Liveried barbarian porters bustled by them and picked up their trunks and suitcases. Mirrei held Kanto's arm as they ascended the broad stairs of the front of the island resort. Mirrei had a figure slenderer and daintier than her mother at that age. Her gossamer champagne traveling robe hid her delicate steps. She appeared to glide up to meet them. The pale complexion to her fuzzy skin along with her light gown gave her ascent an ethereal quality. It reminded Jhee of the stories of the Maid of the Mists. Right near the top, Mirrei's steps faltered. She coughed and turned red. Kanto held her steady.

Jhee offered her arm and helped Mirrei up the mansion's broad steps. "You should have let me secure a mobility chair or litter for you."

"Nonsense, *denbe*," Kanto said. "Poor Mirrei didn't want all that fuss."

Mirrei cut Kanto a brief look. "My fellow spouse is right, denbe. What would your friend think of me if I can't manage the simple task of walking up the stairs?"

And any situation Jhee might later wish for them. "As you wish, my... dear," Jhee said, trying a less formal term.

Both Kanto and Mirrei pulled a face. Mirrei smiled wanly and gave a slight shake of her head. Jhee agreed. Too much. Jhee had only said it to please. Her affection for her had not become even that deep yet. It was an insult to Mirrei to pretend otherwise. She rushed to amend herself. "As you wish, my wife."

"Thank you, denbe."

"Yes, thank you, denbe," Kanto repeated. He smirked. Those two and their teasing.

"Will I have to separate you two?"

"No," Mirrei said.

The three of them finished their graceful ascent to the landing. Misty rain had replaced the torrential downpour which plagued most of their journey. The island resort rested far enough away from the storm curtain to experience lessened effects from its significant weather disturbances. Once the storm curtain stabilized, even the drizzle might stop.

Hopefully, the drier weather would ease some symptoms from Mirrei's Fresh Lung Sickness. The less saline waters of the inner islands did not agree with many. Mirrei, like Kanto and Jhee, was used to the saltier waters of the Far Reaches. Though, their Fresh Lung Sickness had come and gone rapidly. The damp also did not help. Much like the storms, hopefully, the younger woman's condition would stabilize.

Jhee checked her pockets to see if she had any saline tablets on her. Even if they did not have to manage her saline levels and ensure her diet heavy in rock salt, Mirrei never had the hardiest constitution to begin with, according to her mother.

Miramar, Mirrei's mother, had had a difficult pregnancy. Mirrei had been Miramar's only child. A miracle child, much like Kanto. That may have been why the two spouses had bonded so quickly. Still, it was one more child than she and Shep had managed. Perhaps that would change. Or perhaps that was indicative of what difficulties Jhee might have if their plans for Kanto proceeded.

"Lady Delphine, may I present you Bright Harmony, my second husband."

"A pleasure, Lady Delphine," Kanto said. He gave the most formal of bows before planting a kiss on the back of Lady Delphine's hand.

"Likewise, Bright Harmony," said the Lady Delphine.

"This is Star Mirror, my youngest spouse," Jhee said. Jhee used their outside name because neither had been formally introduced to the Lady Delphine. Once they had stayed under her roof, they would be less formal.

Mirrei curtsied. "Lady Delphine."

"Delighted, Star Mirror."

"Are we the only guests?" Mirrei asked.

"I dare say we have quite the full house. There's a rather crude business-man, a travel writer, an organizer for fishing combines, a free-spirited advo-cate, and a mining director. We're also hosting an ambassador to the barbarian lands. He is also a man of waves."

"More clergy. My, we'll have to be on our best behavior."

"I don't know about all that now. He seemed a perfectly reasonable sort. Some others though are quite the characters."

"Speaking of waves and devotion," Jhee said. "I'd like to pay my respects to your Makers' Shrine."

"I'll have you brought to it once I've shown you to your rooms and given you a chance to refresh yourselves."

"Much appreciated." Jhee lowered her voice, "A mining director? I see, now, why you wanted my assistance."

"I'd like to put the issue to rest before Styrling sends any more help," Lady Delphine whispered.

Lady Delphine wrapped her arm in Jhee's and bundled them up the stairs to the solar where drinks with ice melon balls in them awaited them. Warm sunny drinks for these overcast times, but Lady Delphine loved them so even when they were first-years together. Lady Delphine had also been assigned to the intelligence pool just as Jhee had. The compulsory military service every citizen had to undergo had better positions than others. The intelli-gence pool is where the wealthier could get themselves or their offspring stationed and kept off the front lines. Not so much for Jhee and Shep, though. The Path Maker had had different plans.

Jhee shuddered and tried to shake off thoughts of her and Shep's military service.

"We have much to catch up on," Lady Delphine said. "I've put you up in the Observatory suite: one master bedroom with adjoining suites. If that doesn't suit, we can rearrange. I'll have the last bed put away until you need it."

At their rooms, Jhee turned to Kanto and nosed him on his cheek. Kanto pressed his *esca*, the star-shaped Makers' mark that adorned Water Folk's forehead, against hers. "See, here in time for festival season. Just as I promised," Jhee said.

"I had no doubt you would see your promise fulfilled. If anyone could, it would be you, dear wife."

"Thank you for your vote of confidence. You'll be happy to know, Mirrei, besides following Pascoe food protocols, they operate as Blue Waters certi-fied for environmental protection and sustainability."

"Excellent." Mirrei plopped down on the master bed. "Our own beds, again."

The yacht and the detour to the Tranquility Bridge Abbey had them sleeping double and sometimes triple. As denbe, the anchor spouse, Jhee was the only one who ever had the luxury of a bedroom to herself at any point since they left their home in the Far Isles. Though, if propriety would have permitted it, she would have allowed Shep to share it on her nights to herself.

Jhee looked over the invoice from their abbey stay. Now she understood more and more why so many rural Justicars were corrupt. The sum had almost matched the cost of booking the resort stay, due in no small part to purchasing Tranquility Gold at market price.

"Now if you'll excuse me," Kanto said, "I need to ready our outfits. I claim this space right over here for a sewing area and to do design sketches. From now on, it's off-limits to anyone but me."

"Far be it from us to interrupt the Maker at Making."

"Laugh all you wish, but I intend for us to make a splash and be the envy of even the most fashionable houses."

"Live your Make, *denye*, always."

Kanto and Mirrei waggled fingers at each other. "Pure truth."

Kanto pulled out various robes and laid them on the bed. He touched his chin as he pored over them, ever the fashion-conscious one. Jhee had better uses for her mind share. Let him and Mirrei tend to such matters, likely why the Makers had put them in her path.

Jhee cleaned herself up and went looking for the Makers' shrine to perform her devotions and thank the Makers for their safe arrival, as was her duty as the head of household. The shrine occupied a shell grotto off the central atrium. She gave of the elements of air, earth, fire, and water to the First Makers; the sweat of her brow to the water feature; incense shavings for the ever-burning candle; breath and warmth for the plants; a respectful touch of her esca to the ground for the Unknown Maker, so that one would not turn her way. Next, she paid devotion to the Lesser Makers. For Kanto, she jangled Maker geld coins and bounced a few off Futou's drum-like belly. She burned a scented prayer letter and gave an extra measure of laughter to Pascoe and Lashae for Mirrei.

Though now that Kanto had mentioned the subject, the suite provided them much more room than the yacht. Since they had space, setting up a workshop for her and Mirrei while they were here did not sound like such a bad idea. Although constructing a chemistry lab in your hotel room was a far cry from designating a makeshift sewing room. Jhee would have to ask Delphine if she had an area where they could practice.

With a few moments of quiet to contemplate, Jhee thought through the scant details Delphine had given her about the mining supervisor's death and minor acts of vandalism, theft, and a poisoning incident. Most disturbing was the mining supervisor's death. Her fall down the mineshaft had been called an accident, but with all the other happenings Lady Delphine suspected otherwise. She wanted to get ahead of the matter before Styrling Mining stepped in and made matters worse.

Jhee leaned against the balcony railing to catch a bit of spray and morning suns before Kanto arrived for their walk. Gentle rain patter and crashing surf eased the tension in her shoulders. Two figures yelling and gesturing at each other caught her notice. The strong winds and surf cut off most of their conversation. She had been refining her eavesdropping cypher. A small wind drawing might produce more than a clipped word. She synced herself to the winds. Such a strong presence of the winds here was hard to control. While this might make excellent practice, it made for poor ethics. Jhee allowed the winds to slip through her mental grasp. Unaided, Jhee still caught a word or two.

"You need to leave."

"Why you?"

"I have no answers. Just leave."

One turned to leave. The other grabbed his arm. The first man pushed the second to the ground. "Nowhere near us again."

The first man ran full on down the beach. The second got to his knees. He punched at the ground then clasped his hands into the traditional angle of the Makers where he meditated for some moments. He must have been Delphine's aforementioned ambassador and man of the coif. Jhee stepped back inside. She heard the door of the residence open and slam.

The encounter on the beach stayed with Jhee as she and her spouses went on an excursion. Jhee hung back while Kanto and Mirrei rushed along the Avenue from store to store. She was content to let them have their fun though she wished Shep were here to help her keep herself occupied.

Kanto came to a stop in front of a luxury clothier. "Oh! Let's go in this one."

They dashed inside and wandered the aisles handling bolts and realms of vibrant, high-end cloth.

"Denye, look at this fabric. Have you ever seen anything like it?"

"No, it's got an excellent hand, practically slips through my fingers." Kanto threw the fabric about Mirrei. "It drapes wonderfully."

"This pattern reminds me of our house watermark."

Kanto and Mirrei emerged from the shop sometime later with several bolts of expensive fabric. They walked further along the Avenue. Kanto came to a dead stop. "You want to be bad?"

"Let's be bad," Mirrei said.

"Iced fruit and cream. Let's get iced fruit and cream."

"Yes!"

Kanto and Mirrei ran inside giggling. Jhee smiled and trailed after them. The three of them found a lovely little table overlooking the deep blue water. Jhee kept her gaze focused beyond the immediate drop and further out to the crafts in the water. The two younger spouses gabbed about the latest doings and goings-on at the capital.

"The famous Hake Hill row. I've always dreamed of being able to shop here," Kanto said. "You'll love the capital city with all the finest foods, fashions, and entertainment."

"No, she'll be too busy with courses. The capital boasts some of the finest schools and academies in the inhabited worlds."

Mirrei raised an eyebrow, then shook her head and smiled. "Who needs to plan the rest of their life when I have you to do it for me?"

"My lady Justicar," a voice called. "Look, sibs, aren't those our guests?"

Jhee turned at the greeting. Two young women and a young man, all quite fetching, approached them with a few shopping bags in their hands. The young woman in the lead waved her arm then hurried to greet them.

"What a pleasant surprise. I'm Erma. This is Semele and Vash. We're Lady Delphine's children. How wonderful to meet you."

"Ah," Jhee said. She clasped forearms with each of them. "A pleasure to put faces to the names."

"For us, as well," the young man, Vash, said. Vash was one of those she saw arguing from her window. She now wished she had used that eavesdropping charm. He ended his forearm clasp with a rather forward extra squeeze before his attention immediately turned to Jhee's spouses.

"Allow me to introduce my consorts, Bright Harmony and Star Mirror."

"Pleasure to meet you," Kanto said

Vash's greeting lasted that extra fraction with them too, so she assumed him to be too affectionate. "Such evocative outside name choices."

"We picked them ourselves," said Mirrei. Her gaze lingered on the young man's.

"We didn't give you our outside names. You must think us terribly improper. It's just mumsy told us so much about you. We felt as if we already knew you. Given how close you and mumsy used to be, we didn't feel the need to stand on ceremony."

"Now, correct me if I'm wrong. You were mumsy's society fellow in the Academy days?" Semele asked.

"That is indeed correct."

"Come with us and let us give you the grand tour of the city."

Jhee checked for her junior spouses' reactions. Both bore eager expressions. "Very well then."

The Delphines escorted them to the heart of the city after they finished their treats. Jhee and her spouses stopped dead in their tracks near the monumental Cetus Fountains in the square. A group of Doombringers preached openly and proudly about the Unmaking, and no one, including their escorts, broke their stride. Young Folk protesting drowned out their proselytizing.

"Philosophy Making in the public square, a proud inland tradition," Semele said.

Each fountain hosted a different preacher.

Dusty folk in work aprons fought to out-yell the Doombringers, "The Empire thought nothing of them when it built the wall and submerged their isles. If the Empire didn't want to house or do right by them, it should have thought of that before it destroyed their homes."

"Yeah, put them to work in the mines," yelled someone from the crowd.

"Them and the barbarians," chimed in someone from another.

A group of young folk with crimson and ocher scarves countered, "Where they can get not one lung disease but two? We don't need another drain on Imperial resources. We need to improve the working conditions in the mines."

"A drain on the empire's resources? The empire's the one who destroyed our homes, our livelihood."

A group with a banner depicting the ocean with a giant numeral one on it spoke up next, "But that's the game, isn't it? Keep refugees and the Fire Folk at each other, so the Empire can do as it wills."

"The only true unity is that of the Final Sword and the glorious forces of remaking," the Doombringers said.

"Blast this trenched drizzle," Erma said. "At least it's better than storms.

When those rolled through regularly, it was a treat. However, everything is still moist and sodden. It's sinking into the food and draining the flavor. Meals need seasoning with twice as many sea peppers as before."

"I wonder what they are eating at the capital," Semele asked.

"I doubt the capital has all this rain," Jhee answered. She continued to marvel at the manic street preaching. "They are too far from the storm zone."

"Too true."

"What about you, gentlefolk?" Erma asked. "Looks like we had the same idea. I figure as part of your stay here we should get you started on joining the social scene at the capital as soon as possible. That way, you can learn who the players are."

Semele clasped her hands. "If you have time, stop by the street fair this weekend. It involves lots of local businesses. Mumsy, along with Styrling Mining, is one of the co-sponsors. It's to help raise awareness of Miners' Lung Disease."

"That and Fresh Lung Syndrome are causes of mine," Vash said. "I'm a fellow of the Breath of the Deep, a foundation close to my heart."

"Nice to know," Mirrei said. She fluttered her eye color. Vash grinned.

"If you're heading back, we'd be glad to accompany you," Vash said.

Mirrei glanced back at Jhee and Kanto. "No, we still have errands. Hope to see you at the villa later."

"I look forward to it."

Read More of JUSTICAR JHEE AND THE HOLE IN THE WORLD!

Thank you for reading this JUSTICAR JHEE AND THE HOLE IN THE WORLD excerpt! If you would like to read more, you can pick up your copy today!

ACKNOWLEDGMENTS

Adam C., Anne K., Molly K., Val A.

ABOUT THE AUTHOR

TREVOL SWIFT is a sometimes-sassy author of fantasy who grew up in Connecticut. She graduated from WIT with a BS in Computer Engineering Technology and now lives in Eastern Massachusetts. In her spare time Trevol enjoys gaming of all styles, cosplay, reading, writing and dancing. She also likes to relax by getting creative, with drawing and storytelling among her favorite pastimes.

Follow her on BookBub to get notifications of new book releases and sales:
    bookbub.com/authors/trevol-swift

You can also contact Trevol Swift at:

Website: swiftnesse.com

facebook.com/swiftnesse

pinterest.com/swiftnesse

twitter.com/Swiftnesse

instagram.com/swiftnesseauthor

www.ingramcontent.com/pod-product-compliance
Lightning Source LLC
Chambersburg PA
CBHW021132110726

47900CB00002B/315